Dark Mirror

Book IV of The Quietus of Fate

By Brian C. Kershner

ISBN: 1-942082-10-X
ISBN-13: 978-1-942082-10-1

Acknowledgements

When I started writing the Quietus of Fate series and got more invested in the world and the characters, it became clear that the characters and the stories were moving in directions that I couldn't always understand and couldn't always predict. Which is why two books eventually became four, which became six, and so on and so forth. The books also became much more personal and much more difficult for me to see a future for.

Once upon a time I did send sample chapters to publishers thinking there might be a future for what I was writing. Most of the companies sent nice responses stating that they did not accept unsolicited manuscripts, or that they were not interested in planned serials, so I just continued to write more for me than for any other purpose. I didn't really have the money to hire a literary agent, and later in life my clashes with professional editors made me wary of relinquishing the control I had on the at times uncertain and willful future of my creation.

So I just continued to write and to create, and by the time I got to book twelve in the series, I started to feel as though I needed to let go and be less protective. Fortunately, the climate had changed and the ability for authors to put their art out into the world had increased thanks to the wonderful Kindle Direct Publishing program through Amazon, and the awesome people at CreateSpace.

So, still nervous and still unsure I will continue to put my work out there, and will continue to create. I hope you will continue to enjoy.

B.K.

Table of Contents

Chapter 28

Chapter 29

Chapter 30

Chapter 31

Epilogue

Appendicies

As the Dragon falls a Ram shall sprout its Horns,
Where Legends walk Light shall become Shadow,
The Might of Kingdoms shall be silenced by a single word,
Circles broken shall be complete once more.

The path of kings will be written in Flowing Waters,
Salvation will be found in the heart of the Innocent,
Angels and Demons will fracture the world,
In the Dark Mirror will be written the Fate of all.

The future is not yet written,
The past never truly dead,
The present favors the driven,
Time is how legends are bred.

-   Aralias Imstra
Prophecies of the Coromor

Prologue

Legend and Legacy

The aftermath of the war between the forces of the Dragon and the forces of the Shadow was more devastating than any other war in recent memory, including the War of the Lion. The war between the Lion and Shau-ling had only claimed a few kingdoms, and though the death toll was large, damage to the cities themselves had been minimal. The only city that wasn't easily salvageable was Lakestone which remained half-submerged in Exeter Lake. This latest conflict in the war between Light and Shadow however had been much more costly. The sterling kingdom of Marcwell that had stood through so many battles, and had been the center of the strength of the forces of Light had been smashed by a devastating attack. The palace in the center of the city was broken in two, its high towers ground down under the force of the massive Stone warriors that assailed them. This was by far the greatest loss of the War of the Dragon, and its impact on the world could not be easily quantified. For a thousand years, the gleaming white walls of the royal palace of Marcwell stood as the pillar of peace and stability. No army had ever been able to topple those walls, and it had taken a deception from within to strike the final blow. On top of the losses to the palace itself was the sudden and unexplained disappearance of the hero that had sat upon Marcwell's throne. Marcwell's twin, the historically female-led kingdom of Trelon was also devastated, and the royal palace was nothing more than a pile of ash. While the fires had been contained to just the palace and some of the smaller surrounding buildings, the loss of Trelon's queen had greater ramifications than that of a palace.

These kingdoms were almost expected to have some kind of damage in a war of that magnitude, but some of the smaller kingdoms of the world suffered much greater losses. Scalla, the kingdom that had been under the control of one lord for centuries lost the most in the war. Their lord and master that was loved everywhere in Scalla, Basille Mystic, was gone, and the palace and town that he had built was almost beyond repair. Illimar too had seen losses in a bloody civil war, one that had pitted brother against brother and neighbor against neighbor. In the end, the queen of the kingdom, Queen Saris, really the phase Caris in disguise, had been overthrown plunging the whole kingdom into chaos. Though the Army of the Dragon swept in swiftly and turned the kingdom into a ward of the budding savior, there was much resentment created in the now military state. Brea too lost a great deal, its long-ruling king and queen executed for crimes against the Light, and the whole of the capitol city plunged into fear of reprisal by the malicious and malevolent Light Keepers whose authority was granted by the charlatan known as the Proclaimer. All over the world the blows from each of the war's battles were felt, and some of the wounds were so deep that they would never be healed. But, as is the human way, the survivors would go on. They would rebuild the towns and the palaces, and in some cases the new would dwarf the memory of the old. New kings and queens would mingle with the old as they retook their thrones, and they would do everything in their power to make sure that life would go on very much as it had before the war. For all the bad things that came out of the war, there was one positive.

The forces of the Light had won this act of the war against the Shadow. This brought a feeling of hope to the people of the world as they fought to reclaim their lives from the smoldering ashes. Very ordinary people had gathered from simple towns and fought against the forces of the Shadow and had survived. Even before these heroes returned from the palace of the evil Shau-ling, their names had reached legendary status, and the world once again had heroes. Lord Cedric Binosear, the Lion and the hero of the first battle with the Shadows, had given the world the name of his successor, Logan Ranthall, the Dragon. Logan had taken his force into the den of the evil Shau-ling and vanquished him. Upon Logan's return, the world celebrated in the name of the Dragon and waited in breathless anticipation for him to ascend to the throne of Marcwell and chair the rebuilding of life under the rule of the Light. That day never came. Logan had returned from his quest into Shadow a changed man. The weight of the world had made him weary of fighting everyone else's battles, and he refused the charge of leading the world again. What no one knew was that Logan's reclusiveness was due to the weight of a title that he never should have had, and the regret of the losses that no one but those who had walked into the waiting jaws of evil could understand. If the world were to be rebuilt, it would have to be done with another man seated on the throne of Marcwell. The last anyone knew of Logan Ranthall was that he retired to his home village of Aradon with his wife Elwyne and awaited the arrival of their first child.

Logan's decision was seen in some circles as the abandonment of responsibility, but those that held that opinion never dared to speak it aloud. Even if some people had wanted to criticize Logan's actions, they could not look past the fact that without him, the evil lord of the Shadows, Shau-ling, would have decimated the forces of the Light and ground the world under his boot. Logan's pass into anonymity was the path for other heroes from the War of the Dragon to step into the spotlight. Pike Rhuiden was the greatest of the heroes to make good on the expectations that Logan was unwilling to fill. To all the world, Pike was known as the hero of the battles of Illimar, Sarmeel, Brea, and the final battles inside of Shau-ling's palace. However, his war record was not what was sung by most of the bards in the world. The tale that resounded through the inns and taverns was the loss of his love Eldar, and his hunt of the mad phase Taron that eventually led to Pike avenging her death. This story spread quickly through the world, and within a few months' time, it was the best known and most often told story in the world. Not long after the final battle, Pike added his own final verse to the story when he returned to the city of Taren to pay his respects at the grave of his wife, Eldar Merin. His second night in Taren, he woke the master stone crafter from his sleep just past midnight and commissioned him to erect a statue of Eldar on the spot where she was murdered. The stone crafter accepted the charge, and with weeks, the statue was in place. Pike had stayed in Taren during the creation of the statue, and it was rumored that he was an integral part of its construction. On the morning that the statue was unveiled, the acting lord of the kingdom of Kandor, the nearest major kingdom, a young lord named Evan Sinn, was so overwhelmed by the gesture of love and the greatness of the man behind it that he bent his knee to Pike and relinquished control of his kingdom. From that day on, things changed very rapidly for Pike Rhuiden. His prominence as a ruler eventually drew him to the kingdom of Trelon, the very kingdom that had overseen his home of Aradon as long as most people could remember. Out of all the other noteworthy deeds of Pike Rhuiden's life, his first audience with the Queen of Trelon would be one that no one would ever forget.

* * * * * * * * * * * *

It was a hazy midsummer morning when the delegation from Kandor arrived at the newly rebuilt palace of Trelon. It had taken the better part of two years to remake the functional portion of the palace, but the improvements and final touches seemed as if they would never be finished. Cairyn Binosear now actually had a throne to sit upon in her third year as the queen, and she had already proven many times that she inherited the grace and elegance of her mother when it came to ruling a kingdom. Anabel Binosear was one of the most respected rulers when she sat on the throne of Trelon, and her name carried far-reaching respect as well as responsibility. As Anabel's daughter, Cairyn inherited the responsibility not only as the successor of her mother but also as a Binosear. That was a name that carried fear and respect everywhere in the world, even to places that no one in her family had ever been. That was the consequence of being the relation of the great Cedric Binosear. Her uncle had left a large legacy of his own, and as the only remaining Binosear, Cairyn shouldered the burden as best she could. One of the responsibilities of both the Binosear name and the position of queen was that Cairyn had to receive powerful figures on a regular basis. She had met with many dignitaries over the course of her life, both as a princess and as a queen. Some had been powerful military leaders, while others were polished diplomats, flatterers, panders, or suitors. There were those that wished to become an ally of the kingdom of Trelon, but most were out to change the conditions of existing treaties. Some of the lords in the area thought that Cairyn would be softer and easier to bully into more favorable trade policies. However, they usually left with less than they had before, and with an unexpected blow to their pride. The meeting scheduled for that morning however was going to be different. This was not a political negotiation or a nuisance of trade or economy. No, a war hero was coming to her kingdom to pay his respects to an ally from the war. This was the first time that she was meeting face to face, one on one with a legend in her new capacity as a queen. Legendary people were not new to Cairyn. Her uncle Cedric was one of the most legendary heroes in the history of the world, but this time it was different. Cedric had never been a legend in Cairyn's mind, he was always just Cedric, her mother's sometime distant brother. There was never anything to be intimidated about when Cedric came to visit. This man Pike Rhuiden was a man of many legends, not the least of which was that he had personally faced seven members of the phasia and lived. Most people who dared to face, or found themselves facing a member of the phasia never lived to tell about it. Even her sainted uncle, the Lion himself, Cedric Binosear, had only had to face two members of the phasia before he challenged Shau-ling. This Pike Rhuiden was unlike any hero that the world had ever known, and unlike the other surviving members of the People of the Dragon, Pike had chosen to embrace his role as a hero. He was fierce and unforgiving in battle, but he was passionate enough to forsake all else to avenge the death of a woman that he loved.

It was this avenging of his lover that plagued Cairyn's mind the most. She had heard many versions of the story from the bards that circulated through the area. There were conflicting stories about his relationship to the woman named Eldar. Some bards told that she was merely his lover, while some of the more reputable bards and storytellers said that she was actually his wife. This story plagued her mind so much that she did some research into the marriage customs of the people of Aradon, and upon discovering the ritual of the old church, she guessed the truth. Pike and Eldar had taken the vows of marriage, but they had never announced it to anyone. In the eyes of everyone in Aradon, Pike and Eldar were married. Avenging the death of a lover was one thing, but for him to forsake his place as a member of the *Erieal* and place the fate of the world on hold to challenge the phase Taron was an almost unbelievable feat. Cairyn inwardly wanted to meet this passionate man, and yet she almost feared him at the same time.

Through the night before Cairyn tossed and turned, the stories and anticipation clouding her mind. As the night crept by, the speeches that she had prepared seemed more and more inadequate as she tried to picture the man that was Lord Pike Rhuiden. She tried to picture what he would look like and how he would act, but the picture in her mind never seemed like it encompassed all of his characteristics. It almost seemed like no man she had ever met could measure up to her expectations. The first models that she envisioned were like her uncle Cedric. However none of those seemed right. Though her uncle was a very powerful and influential man throughout the world, he was never the incredible man that the world thought he was. The loss of his love Erika Belnosian had forced him into a reckless quest to find and destroy every force of evil in the world. Though he shared this revenge-fueled vengeance with Pike Rhuiden, Cedric was never as focused as Pike was. Cedric wanted to destroy every visage of evil wherever it reared its head, and when that wasn't enough, his need for vengeance turned into a deep self-loathing and a deep depression. This gave Cedric a dark edge that no one was able to lift from his shoulders. Moreover, Cedric never truly embraced his role as a hero. He did his part when it was thrust upon him, but he wore it like a man who wore clothes two sizes too large because he could afford nothing else. From the stories that Cairyn had heard about Pike Rhuiden, she could never see him with a dark cloud around him. Pike was renowned for his nights of carousing in bars, and for making the ladies swoon with both his voice and his well-built body. This was not a man that would be melancholy and morose like her dead uncle. Quickly those models were scrapped and she moved on to the next in a series of models.

Logan Ranthall, the Dragon. Surely he was a powerful and ample enough model to base her visions of Pike Rhuiden upon. Logan was handsome and rather well built. He was probably not as large as Pike Rhuiden, but that was not as important as the person inside the skin and muscle. When Cairyn had met Logan, he was very proper and had a good courtly manner for a farm boy, and she would expect almost the same for Lord Rhuiden. True, he might still have some of the same backward farm boy ways as Logan, but the fact that he was the lord and ruler of a major court in the world meant that he knew how to handle himself while sitting on a throne. Logan had seemed very in love and very devoted to Elwyne Tamerlane, and even when Cairyn made a pass a Logan, it failed regardless of the fact that she was seated beside him. Cairyn had decided later that his answer would have been the same had she been thousands of miles away.

However, Logan had also been very docile in that love and devotion. True he had the potential to be stirred up to act upon his emotions, but he did not seem the kind to let his emotions move him to reckless abandon. Elwyne was truly the fiery one of that relationship, and though the two women had started on rocky terms, it was soon enough that Cairyn began to admire and truly value Elwyne Tamerlane. The type of devotion and love that Pike Rhuiden displayed was one that Cairyn could not find an equal to in any of the men that she had ever met, and though it was probably a small portion of the overall character of Lord Rhuiden, it was the portion that she could not help but be fixated upon. His passions were to be admired, and she imagined that this passion would translate into everything he did.

As these thoughts whirled through her mind, she found that these thoughts translated to desires that her heart and body responded vigorously to. Had she not been a queen, and had been blessed with the freedom of any member of the court under her, she could have satisfied these urges, but that was not a luxury she was afforded. Many times she had heard her chambermaids speak of the wild nights they had enjoyed with members of her guard, or men from the entourages of the visiting dignitaries. Being able to have freedom of her body was something that she could never have. As a queen she was bound to her reputation and to the requirements of her station. If she were ever to allow that to be compromised by foolish whims or lust, she and her kingdom would be ruined. Her dreams and evening fantasies would be all that she would have until she married. She did not realize how strong her mother Anabel must have been to rule all those years without a husband or a lover. However, she had a husband for a time, and had known satiation for her passions. Cairyn had never had that. All she had were her fantasies.

Those fantasies now were dominated by a man she had never laid eyes upon. Most nights she was able to push the dreams away and sleep peacefully. On the night before Pike Rhuiden's arrival however, the dreams were not the only thing that she had to contend with. She also had anticipation, expectation, and nervous energy clouding her thoughts, and that was enough to make her lie awake all night. As the hours crawled by, the anticipation swelled, the nervousness mounted, and the expectations became even more unbelievable then they were originally. When her servants came to wake her the next morning, they found her bed in shambles, and Cairyn standing in her private little garden outside her bedroom window.

When life became too confusing or unbearable, Cairyn found solace in the peace and tranquility of her garden. It had been built to the specifications left by her mother, and it was even more beautiful than she had ever envisioned during the garden's construction. Cairyn had made the core of stone smiths that rebuilt the palace change their plans to accommodate her garden, and after many arguments, the smiths made the necessary changes. The reason that Cairyn had been so adamant about the garden was because of her mother. She remembered growing up and walking in the city's main flower garden, and her mother wanting to have one of her own. However, the palace had no room for such a thing, and the huge chamber that served as the queen's bedchamber had no windows. When the palace of Trelon was built all those years ago, the world's turbulence caused the stone smiths to think of security over comfort. There would be no assassins coming through the window in the middle of the night, and for a long time, function was a more important aspect than form. Now that the world had changed slightly, and the Binosear name was powerful enough to demand respect and fear, Cairyn believed that she was safe enough in Trelon and could have her garden built. But, no matter the safety that she thought she had, she was smart enough to know that there were times that she should not be alone in her garden, and the early hours of the morning were perfect examples of those times. However, even as her chambermaids scolded her for her foolishness, her thoughts were elsewhere. This preoccupation continued throughout her bathing and dressing, and as she took leave of her servants and walked slowly through the still dim passages to her throne room.

As Cairyn walked, she noticed the last minute preparations as they continued everywhere in the palace. These preparations had been going on for a week, and it seemed like nothing would ever be good enough for the legend that would pay them a visit. Visitors were common in Trelon, and the inns of the town were usually full. Inn keepers were constantly making more money than they knew what to do with, and the inns of Trelon had the best reputation in the world for food and service. However, while the inn keepers were making enough money to improve upon their inns, they could not afford to have many off nights. Regardless of this, the inn keeper at the *Lion's Head Inn* turned away all comers to keep the rooms open for Pike and his men. The *Lion's Head* was the largest inn in the kingdom, and it was known far and wide for its wonderful food and almost flawless service to its customers. If there was a place that Pike and his entourage would be most comfortable in, it would be the *Lion's Head*. To make sure that everything was perfect, exotic foods and flowers were brought in the day of Pike's expected arrival for the banquet in his honor.

Finally the day for his arrival came. All over the town, everything stopped as people left their homes and their work to line the main street. Everyone waited anxiously on the very sides of the road to catch a glimpse of the man they had all heralded as a hero. The bustle and anxiety was not limited only to the people of the town, but it was also to be found in the royal palace. The guards were hurriedly shining their dress armor and making the last minute changes to their royal salute, making the weapon substitute for an axe. The detachment of the Lion's Mane that was stationed in Trelon traded their engraved swords for large war axes on this occasion to honor Pike. Down in the kitchens, the same scene was to be found. Servants scurried about, making sure that all of the food was just right.

Cairyn was in a haze as she ascended the last few steps to the throne room. The memorized speech that she droned to all of the other visiting dignitaries was now long forgotten, and if she didn't know any better she would have thought that she was forgetting her own name. As she gracefully walked up the steps of the dais, the haze was broken as the crowd outside erupted into a powerful, enveloping cheer. Cairyn hurried to the window of the throne room and looked out onto the most impressive sight that she had ever seen.

The processional that followed Pike was immense. First in line was a unit of mounted troops with large ornate axes. In the center of each of these ranks was a standard bearer that held the crest of each of the kingdoms that bowed a knee to Lord Rhuiden. The next ranks were also mounted, but all of these riders were unarmed, but they did carry a variety of musical instruments, and their combined voice was enough to carry over the cacophony of the crowd and sang the praises of their lord and master to everyone within a mile. Next in line were the impressive foot soldiers. Their ranks were perfectly straight, and as the sunlight caught their armor, each gleamed with fury. They each marched with a heavy war axe in one hand and a large shield in other. The crest on the shield was a red dragon, extending out of a ball and spreading its wings across a blue background that appeared to have streaks of silver rain mixed into it. The next group were the bowmen. Pike's army had always been dependent on the infantry until Midarin Rice suggested that he add a few regiments of archers to 'break up the monotony.' Pike did it at first to humor her, but later realized the true strategic importance of huge ranks of bowmen. Unlike normal bowmen, whose only purpose was to strike from a distance and stay out of the true fighting, Pike's bowmen were in light armor with a sword on their hips and bow in hand. The most impressive part of the processional was the final group that marched through the streets. Full plate mail clattered rhythmically to the pounding of dozens of hoofs. The proud, large-chested war horses stepped heavily to make their power felt by all around, and in a charge, their pounding could make the ground shake. Each of the knights held their heads up proudly and kept their eyes trained on the man in the center of their ranks, the same man that everyone had come to see.

In the years since his coronation, Pike had grown to be a favorite among the kings and lords with beautiful and unwed daughters. Most of the time though, it was merely unwed. These kings saw a large kingdom and a way to marry into protection, money, and hereditary title. Many fine princesses had been paraded in front of Pike, and to a one they had all left his kingdom disappointed. Several times, these refusals turned into conflict, but these battles were usually isolated and never became a full scale war. Never once did Pike's army lose the day, and the king not only had a blow to his pride, but also to his pocket when he had to find troops to replace the ones that he lost in a petty attempt to avenge his daughter's honor. It was not difficult to see why a woman would desire a man like Pike. After taking into account the money and the power, Pike was also a physically attractive man. Early in life he had been an apprentice blacksmith in his village. After two years at the forge, his shoulders had widened, laden with muscle, and his arms were equally powerful. Normally his face showed the start of a beard, but on this occasion, he had shaved closely to make a better impression on perhaps his most powerful potential ally. As always, he rode his silver stallion with the black mane and tail that he had named

Spirit. His prized axe *Fury* hung from a loop on his belt, and a long bow, a gift from the Queen of Brea, was strapped to the side of his saddle. While it was obvious to everyone that looked at Pike that he was able to take care of himself in a fight, he was still inclined to travel with bodyguards everywhere he went. Unlike most kings that had a flock of trained bodyguards at their disposal, Pike only found it necessary to travel with two. To continue this unusual trend, the two bodyguards were women.

The two bodyguards always flanked Pike wherever he went, and that day was no different. The woman at Pike's left had a look of danger about her. She rode a white stallion with a white mane and tail, but she rode without saddle or bridle. Strangely, the horse stayed in step with the rest of the group and never faltered once. The clothes she wore were little more than common garments, a man's breeches and a red shirt. What the shirt hid was a light vest of close-fitting chain mail that she wore for protection. Her curly red hair was pulled back into a tail and held by a simple piece of red cloth. Most men would find this woman very attractive with her high cheekbones, flawless complexion, and shimmering green eyes. There was a fire in those eyes though, and coupled with the rough clothes and armor, she was more dangerous than she was beautiful. Adding to the dangerous edge was the fact that she was heavily armed. A long sword in a plain black sheath was strapped to her back, and another was on her hip.

The other woman that rode with Pike equaled the redhead in beauty, but she did not have the lethal appearance of her companion. Where the redhead was common in her dress, this woman was extravagant. The dress that she wore was the kind that was usually reserved for princesses or queens. Her long auburn hair was also pulled back into a tail, and carefully sculpted bangs framed her face, and along with big brown eyes, gave her an innocent appearance. Her saddle and tan horse were both flawless in their appearance, and it seemed that she needn't even pull on the bridle to keep control of the animal. She did not appear to be armed, and had only a bow and a staff tied to her saddle. Pike and his two guards formed an interesting trio, and in the presence of his entourage, he was more regal, powerful and intimidating.

The processional continued through the streets of Trelon until it reached the huge open courtyard in front of the newly built royal palace.

Each section leader gave their commands, and the infantry fell out to one side while the archers fell out to the other. The ranks of cavalry split, and Pike and his bodyguards dismounted and walked down the newly created aisle. When Pike approached the entryway of the royal palace, the two guards nervously fell in in front of Pike and led him through the winding passages of the palace, through the massive receiving hall, and right up to the large wooden doors of the throne room. After hesitating for just a moment, the guards opened the doors and motioned for Pike to enter. After a quick sideways glance at each of his bodyguards, Pike strode into the throne room.

When Cairyn saw the doors of the throne room opening, the strange nervousness hit her even harder. Her ladies in waiting stood close, and the royal guards all tensed and stood at attention as the man they had been waiting for finally came into sight. As soon as Cairyn caught sight of him, her heart fluttered. None of her dreams from the previous nights had even come close to the visage that stood before her. His dark brown hair was cut short, and his brown eyes were beautiful and strong. While his features were rough, and his body stocky, they proved to frame a picture of strength and power. Cairyn's eyes then shifted to the two female bodyguards that accompanied Pike. The women were also very intimidating, but this intimidation was not from an appearance of physical power, but more from a posture that spoke of the ability for quick and decisive action. Pike only stood in the doorway of the throne room for a quick moment, and then he strode proudly down the carpeted aisle that led to the dais. When he reached the foot of the small set of steps, he and his bodyguards bowed, and when he straightened, he spoke in a proud clear voice.

"Queen Binosear, thank you for receiving my entourage and I into your kingdom. The welcome that we received was heart-warming and well needed. As a token of my thanks, a detachment of my army will be made available to you for the training purposes of your army. They are some of my finest men, and I'm sure that our two armies can learn from one another. And, as long as I stay here in your kingdom, my forces and I are at your disposal."

Cairyn kept her features impassive.

"Lord Rhuiden," Cairyn said after a moment, "we are honored at the opportunity to host a man of your fame. I graciously accept the privilege of melding my army with yours, even for a few days. I am sure that the outcome will be truly remarkable. My ladies in waiting have prepared a room for you and your guards, and arrangements have been made for the rest of your group to stay in a local inn. A feast has been prepared in your honor, and I hope you would do me the personal honor of sitting by me at the royal table this evening."

Pike smiled and bowed again.

"Thank you Queen Binosear, I humbly accept your offer, on one condition."

"Which is?"

"That you will allow me to favor you with a song this evening."

Cairyn giggled to herself for a moment. Pike's eyes had this boyish, playful glow and his smile filled her with a warm feeling.

"I accept you condition Lord Rhuiden. Shall we retire to my study where we may speak less formally?"

"I would like that very much Queen Binosear, but first I wish to present you with a gift of thanks for all of your kindness."

Pike motioned to the red-haired woman, and she unslung the sheath that was strapped to her back. Pike regarded the sword for a moment before drawing it from the scabbard. As soon as Cairyn's eyes locked on it, her heart began to soar.

"Queen Binosear, I present you with your uncle's sword, the sword that is the birthright of your noble name. I present you with the Lion Sword."

Pike slowly ascended the dais, and as Cairyn stood, he placed the sword gently in her hands. She hesitated for a moment and then smiled.

"This is the most precious gift that anyone could have ever given me, Lord Rhuiden. This was thought lost forever when Lord Cedric disappeared after the siege of Marcwell. I don't know how you came upon this treasure, but my family and I are forever in you debt. Please, let us adjourn where we may speak at length about the purpose of your visit."

Pike bowed in ascent and he and his bodyguards followed Cairyn and two of her ladies in waiting out of the throne room and into a nearby study. Cairyn sat in a gilded chair near a window and motioned for Pike to sit across from her. He removed *Fury* from his belt and handed it to the red-haired woman before sitting.

"Here we may speak more freely, Lord Rhuiden," Cairyn said after a moment. "I would like to know what occasion has brought you to my kingdom."

Pike leaned back in his chair, almost too informally.

"First I think a few introductions are in order. Sometimes I forget to introduce my shadows here, and I have people worrying longer than they need to. The lovely redhead is Rachel, and the brunette here is Elizabeth. They are the founding members of an elite force of soldiers that I developed known as the Enforcers. And Cairyn, if I may call you that, the Enforcers are at the very heart of the matter that draws me here."

Pike's face was suddenly serious and powerful.

"Please," Cairyn said after a moment of hesitation, "go on."

"As you know, I was a member of the People of the Dragon, the force that followed Logan Ranthall into the palace of Shau-ling. Unfortunately, we were not able to win the battle against the Shadow permanently. So, the phasia and their evil master will rise again in this coming generation. Only this time, we are going to be ready for them. I have rounded up the best soldiers in the world and set them up in the kingdom of Sarmeel. They are all young and powerful, but I intend to make them better. With the knowledge that I have acquired about the phasia, I should be able to give them enough of an upper hand to last more than two minutes one on one with a member of the Brotherhood. Jerrard Mystic of Scalla and Midarin Rice of Brea have been contributing some funds and supplies to the cause, but I need more before I can fully begin to prepare. The third *Coromor* of the prophecies has been born, and soon will be old enough to begin training for the task ahead, so our time is growing short. I have a very unusual request to make of you Cairyn, but I don't know how you will react to it."

Cairyn leaned forward, her fingers steepled under her chin.

"Ask me, and then you'll know."

Pike took a deep breath and exhaled slowly. He had rehearsed this speech a hundred times, but now it sounded weak as he put his own voice to it.

"For as long as I can remember, Marcwell has been the center of the world. Power seemed to come just from its name. Cedric sat on the throne and everyone knew that they were safer just because he was there. Now Cedric is gone, the Binosear mystique is fading, and Marcwell is only a shell of what it once was. Its resources are being squandered, and the once proud Lion's Mane is becoming lax and nearly worthless in a fight. The world needs another hero sitting on that throne in Marcwell, and I need Marcwell's money and power to get my Enforcers ready for the third act of the war between the Light and the Shadow. If I were to try and seize the reins of power in Marcwell, I would lose favor with the people, and lose all that I have fought so hard to build. Cairyn, that throne belongs to your family. A Binosear has been seated on that throne from the very beginning. I'm offering you a chance to save your hereditary claim to Marcwell, and to Trelon through marriage. By law, no man may sit on the throne of Marcwell who does not have some link to the Binosear line, and by law, no woman may sit on the throne of Trelon who also does not have some link to Binosear blood. If you accept my proposal, I will only sit on the throne of Marcwell until our son is old enough to replace me."

Pike said something else after that, but Cairyn never heard it. Her mind whirled with the words 'marriage' and 'son.' Suddenly, she began to feel light-headed and before she knew what was happening, she fainted.

* * * * * * * * * * * *

The city of the gods was quiet as Emries walked down the long wide white path that served as the main street. The Creator had called the gods away and left the men and women of the world to their own devices. Yet, Emries lingered. There was still work for him to do, and there was still a battle that had to be fought. For hundreds of years he and he alone had guided the fates of some of the greatest heroes in the world. He manipulated bloodlines, reinterpreted prophecies, and even made up a few new ones just to stay one step ahead of his brother and sworn enemy, Shau-ling. And now the cycle was about to start all over again. Emries prepared himself to travel back to the mortal plane, but suddenly a flash of light engulfed him. Everything around him was light, and then the light spoke. It was the voice of his master, the voice of the Creator.

"EMRIES MY CREATION, YOUR WORLD IS DYING AND YOU AND YOUR BROTHER ARE THE CAUSE."

Emries felt the shock pouring through his body.

"YOU AND YOUR BROTHER HAVE FORGOTTEN WHY YOU STARTED THIS WAR AND YOU HAVE LET YOUR ARMIES FIGHT ON UNCHECKED. THE PHASE NAMED BASILLE HAS CREATED A RIP IN TIME BECAUSE OF YOUR CARELESSNESS. BEFORE HIS ESSENCE WAS ERASED FROM THE PLACE YOU CALL THE OTHER SIDE BY SHAU-LING, BASILLE USED HIS POWERS AND TRAVELED INTO THE PAST. IN THIS PAST HE RELINQUISHED CONTROL OF HIS STRING OF POWER AND GAVE IT TO A MORTAL. THIS MORTAL WAS DESIGNATED TO HAVE POWER, BUT FOR THE SAFETY OF THE WORLD, HIS POWER WAS GIVEN TO ANOTHER. THIS ALONE WAS HARMLESS, HOWEVER, ITS IMPACT ON THE FATES AND THE LAWS OR CHANCE WERE NOT."

The light pulsed brighter with the next words.

"BASILLE'S INTERFERANCE WITH MY LAWS OF TIME AND FATE HAVE CAUSED THE CREATION OF ANOTHER REALITY. IN THIS PARALLEL REALITY, THE FORCES OF THE SHADOW ENJOY THE ADVANTAGE SO BITTERLY WON BY THE LIGHT IN THE REALITY YOU MANIPULATED INTO BEING. FOR NOW A BALANCE BETWEEN LIGHT AND DARKNESS HAS BEEN ACHIEVED. EMRIES, THIS GRAVE SITUATION HAS CAUSED THIS DECREE. SHOULD THE FORCES OF THE LIGHT PREVAIL IN BOTH REALITIES, THE REALITY IN WHICH THEY HAVE AN

ADVANTAGE SHALL CONTINUE. SHOULD THE FORCES OF THE SHADOW PREVAIL IN BOTH REALITIES, THE DARK REALITY SHALL CONTINUE. IF NEITHER ARE ABLE TO PREVAIL IN BOTH, THEN BOTH REALITIES SHALL BE DESTROYED. FURTHERMORE, AS THAT THE GODS HAVE GONE TO OTHER RESPONSIBILITIES, AND BOTH YOU AND HALICON HAVE ALLOWED YOURSELVES TO BE CORRUPTED BY YOUR PERSONAL HATRED FOR ONE ANOTHER, A *REDAAR* SHALL BE DISPATCHED TO MONITOR THE PROGRESS OF BOTH REALITIES. IF YOU TRY TO INTERFERE IN THE SHADOW REALITY, YOUR LIFE WILL BE FORFEIT AND SHAU-LING AND HIS MINIONS SHALL RULE THE WORLD FOR ETERNITY. IF HALICON INTERFERES IN THE LIGHT REALITY, HIS LIFE WILL BE FORFEIT, AND THE *COROMOR* AND THE *ERIEAL* WILL LEAD AS LIGHT REIGNS FOR ETERNITY. THIS IS LAW, EMRIES. HEED IT WELL."

With that the light around Emries dissipated, and for the first time in a long time, he was afraid.

Chapter XXIV

Raven

Creator's Calendar Year 1205; Light Reality

Twenty-five years had passed since the end of the War of the Dragon and the victory delivered by the Lord Dragon, Logan Ranthall, and his People of the Dragon. For those twenty-five years, the city of Aradon had enjoyed a peaceful existence under the watchful yet respectfully distant gaze of the Queen of Trelon, Cairyn Binosear. For as long as Aradon had been a city, it had fallen within the borders of the Kingdom of Trelon. However, more often than not, Aradon was seen as a small fringe community out in the middle of nowhere. It was a simple farming community filled with simple people who kept largely to themselves and found it unnecessary to travel outside the boundaries of their community except during harvest season when trade was needed to replenish the city's stores. Even in those days, Trelon did not demand tribute or taxes from Aradon as the small community's town council had consistently refused military protection or any of the other perks offered by official membership within the kingdom. However, the prophecies of the *Coromor* had changed everything. In the first generation of the prophecies, Arin Ranthall and his soon-to-be wife Victoria Rhuiden had answered the call of war and joined the Lion's Mane in the march against Shau-ling's forces in Lakestone. But they had not returned with fanfare and heraldry. They returned very much as they left, two young people who were at the very start of a life not much different than the life that had been lived by their parents and grandparents. It was the second generation of the prophecies though that would change Aradon and much of the rest of the world forever.

Children of farmers, blacksmiths, carpenters, and merchants were supposed to follow in their parents' footsteps in Aradon. Profession changes were nearly unheard of, let alone anyone leaving to become something of any note. So when a group of the youth of Aradon set out following in the footsteps of one of the most famous and infamous members of the Lord Lion's inner circle, Aryx Terian, chasing the prophecies of the *Coromor*, it sent shockwaves through the community that were only rivaled by the destructive blazes set by a group of Shadowwalkers. But when the second generation of the prophecies of the *Coromor* came to an end, Aradon had not only a group of heroes it could call its own, but also the savior of the world.

The first of these heroes was the man named Pike Rhuiden. When he lived in Aradon he was little more than an accomplished troublemaker who at one time served as the apprentice to the blacksmith Torris Sandar. Little did anyone know that this aspiring singer, carouser, and drunk would be a member of the mystical *Erieal* and that he would one day be the lord who sat on the throne of Marcwell. Pike was at the heart of Aradon's new-found attention. As that Pike was married to Queen Cairyn of Trelon, he had asked her to keep an eye on his people. However, this was all that it would ever be. Queen Cairyn would not dare to interfere with the people of Aradon because of the other hero who was born inside her fences. His name was Logan Ranthall, and his name was known throughout the world as the Dragon; the second coming of the *Coromor*. But that was long since over. Logan did not live long after the final battle with Shau-ling, and seven short years following his return to Aradon Logan was gone and his legacy was fading away as well. Yes, the Ranthall name was still known throughout the world, but the fact that he would not allow himself to take a prominent role as Cedric Binosear had was one of the reasons that his legacy would never be as great. But there was still a legacy, and Logan's wife and widow Elwyne Tamerlane-Ranthall had made sure that the legacy was passed on to their only child, Wolf.

Wolf grew into a fine man and he, very much like his father had at his age, longed for adventure. But unlike Logan, Wolf's direction was fixed.

The battle with the Shadow would soon be entering its third act, and the Ranthall name would once against be called upon to stand with the forces of the Light to defend the people and to take the fight to those who would bring darkness in their wake. Elwyne had taught Wolf well that there was a time to temper desire with reality, and at the core of every decision was the emotion of the moment. She had taught him that within every act there was a force of will, and if one could learn to control that force then there would be nothing that could stand in his way. She had always taught that anger was the easiest to harness, but pain and anguish were the emotions that could make you powerful. These were the little lessons that came out of her stories about his father, and Wolf always wondered what it would have been like to know that man that his mother had loved. Logan Ranthall must have been a hero in every sense of the word, and that was what Wolf longed to be. However, this longing and this great boyhood desire was nearly dashed when his mother, the beautiful Elwyne Ranthall died suddenly at the end of his twenty-first year of life. She had been his only link to the past, and without her, he would never truly understand why his father had been fighting, why he nearly lost his life in the service of the forces of the Light, and why his uncle had also been part of the fray. More than that, there were the cryptic warnings left in Logan's last days, and the calculated distance from the rest of the world. But, there was a legacy to be filled, that much he knew, so Wolf decided that he would do the only thing that was left open to him. He would leave the town of Aradon, very much as his father had, and go out to search the countryside for the answers to the questions in his mind and the desires in his heart.

Unlike his father before him, Wolf had a direction for his ambition and a goal for his wandering. For every story that his mother had ever told Wolf about his father, Elwyne made sure that she had mentioned that Logan had a brother by the name of Korrd. When Wolf asked what had happened to Korrd, she had always told him that he had been killed in the war. As with all of the other conversations about the war, when Wolf tried to delve into the reasons that the war was being fought, Elwyne would brush off the question and say that 'you will find out when you are old enough. If I told you now, you would want to run off and fight like your father and I did, but you won't be ready, and you'll die before you have a chance to really live.' Those answers had always left him cold and wanting more, but his mother would never surrender any details about the war. He had tried to find out everything he could about why the war was fought, but all the bards would sing were the praises of his father and of a man named Pike Rhuiden who was apparently a friend of his father's. Elwyne had always said that Pike was a man that she had trusted with her life, but that he was no longer the man that he once was. He had become obsessed with fighting a war that was not his and that he would end up getting himself and everyone around him killed.

Still, Wolf had thought as he tried to decide where his travels should start, *he is a hero, and he did know my father. If he is as unstable as mother said he is, maybe my presence would cause him to fly further down the path than he already is. The first thing my mother taught me was that my name was both a birthright and a curse. For some people it would make me a king, but for others it would bring up enough painful memories to make them want to kill me. But the thing that always worried mother the most was me being used. She said that I wasn't supposed to trust anyone but family, and that I was supposed to trust family no matter what anyone else said.*

Pike may have been close to the family, but he was definitely not family. He would also probably use Wolf for whatever war he was still fighting. So, Wolf had to look in another direction, and that direction kept leading back to his uncle. Wolf's mother had a brother David, but he had died in the same war as Logan's brother. David had no children, but Korrd had one child. Elwyne wouldn't talk about Korrd's son very much, but what she did reveal was that he was much older than Wolf and that he had inherited his own problems due to his role in the last war. At the time Wolf didn't realize what that meant, but he saw that there was another war coming, and if there was anyone in the world that he could trust, then it was the man named Gwillim Sandar, his cousin. On her death bed, Elwyne had told Wolf that she didn't know where Gwillim was, but if there was someone who did know, it would be his adopted mother, Midarin Rice of Brea. The name really didn't mean anything to Wolf at the time, but when he finally started looking, he realized that she was the Queen of Brea. Yet there was still another option. The kingdom of Trelon was the closest major kingdom to Aradon. The queen of Trelon, Cairyn Binosear was apparently a friend of the family, and especially a friend of his mother's. The only problem with going to Trelon was the fact that Cairyn was married to Pike Rhuiden, the very man that Wolf wanted nothing to do with. It was a razor's edge that Wolf had no intention of walking, and yet there was something that told him it was the right place to go. He felt as if he were being drawn there by a force that he could not explain. In the end, it was this force that caused him to make his way to Trelon, and it was that decision that he could point to as the one that changed his life.

* * * * * * * * * * *

Even in times of war, the road from Aradon to Trelon held few perils other than those of time and boredom. Few but traders would bother to make the journey at all during the summer months, but as harvest approached there were always travelers to ensure that all business was concluded before the beginning of the almost always harsh winters. Spring was just bowing to the heat of summer when Wolf began his travels from Aradon to Trelon. Part of him felt guilty that he would not be there for the burial ceremony of his mother, but he had been able to say his goodbyes long before her final day had come. Elwyne wanted no ceremony and simply wanted to pass into the anonymity of time. It wasn't until the hours following her death that the town council of Aradon decided that more of a spectacle was needed. After all, she was the wife of the second *Coromor* of the prophecies, and had been instrumental in the victory over Shau-ling. The next morning, Wolf was on the road well before first light, not wanting anyone to try to talk him out of his decision. His mother was gone, and he wanted to hold on to her quiet dignity, even if the rest of the world would not understand.

The first day of travel was hot and tiring, and Wolf was happy to see the sun go down. He could have continued later into the evening, but as he was not as accustomed to traveling as many of the men his age, he was glad to set up camp for the night. He had been on travels before with his mother, but never to any major towns, and never over major distances. She had always said that she and Logan had decided that they did not want to be in the spotlight anymore and that it was better for them to just disappear. Both Logan and Elwyne had been popular figures after the war, and the world had always wanted Logan to do more than simply fade away into legend. Logan declined and told the world that he and Elwyne were going to retire to Aradon and live out the rest of their lives in peace. While many would never understand or accept this choice, the world would never have been able to change Logan and Elwyne's famously stubborn minds.

They took solace in the fact that they knew where Logan was should they really need him, but it was clear that Logan had earned enough respect that even the most ardent detractor would honor his wishes. It was a truly staggering situation when Wolf stopped to think about it, but Elwyne had always said that it was just another one of those strange situations that seemed to crop up when your last name happened to be Ranthall.

Wolf tied his horse to the nearest tree and placed its feed bag over the horse's mouth. As the horse ate quietly, Wolf gathered some firewood and made a small fire near a stream that ran through the forest by the road. The clearing that he had picked was a beautiful one, and the tops of the trees made an exquisite frame for the stars. There were no clouds in the sky on that night, and Wolf looked up at the tiny fires in the Creator's heaven and wondered if his father had looked up and seen the same stars on his adventures. Suddenly there was a rustle in the trees off to his right. His horse froze, but it did not spook. Then, after a moment, a person walked through the trees and came to a halt about four feet from Wolf. The man was not ordinary by any means, and his appearance could be termed unusual and almost intimidating. His body was built tall and lean, and his limbs looked as if they were no larger around than reeds. But as Wolf got a better look at one of the exposed arms that hung from the end of the short-sleeved black shirt that he wore, he saw that though the limbs were lean, they were coated with muscle. Wolf was sure that the story was same for the man's legs, and as the man in black approached, Wolf began to get nervous. The man looked around, and as he did, Wolf got a look at the long black hair that hung down to the middle of the man's back. About a foot away from Wolf, the man stopped and drew the sword that was slung to his hip. There was no gleam from the blade as it caught the moonlight, and the black blade was menacing enough to give a new edge to the man who wielded it. Wolf knew that the man before him had a lethal ability that would greatly outmatch him, and the fact that Wolf's sword was seven feet away strapped to his saddle wasn't much help. The man stuck the sword into the ground and then sat down in front of Wolf.

"You must be Wolf Ranthall," the man said as he sat and regarded his youthful companion, "my name is Basille Mystic, and I've been waiting a long time for you to leave Aradon."

Wolf tensed and then forced his body to relax. If there was one thing he had learned from all those years of practicing with the sword, it was that a tense fighter was a dead fighter. If you could not count on your body to react in every way possible in a second's notice, then you were never going to be able to block the attacks of a fighter who was. Wolf had no sword, but if the man tried to attack, Wolf would be ready.

"Don't worry Wolf," the man said as if reading his mind, "if I had wanted to kill you, you never would have heard me coming through the forest. I allowed myself to be heard because I wanted to see how you would react. You have a good natural instinct when it comes to fighting, but you are untrained like your father was, and the fact that you are alone makes your faults more pronounced. If you do not have allies to cover your mistakes, they can be exploited easily."

"So, Basille," Wolf said easing a little, "why have you been waiting for me to leave Aradon, why couldn't you have just come and see me at my house?"

"Your mother would not have approved of that Wolf. She and I were not close friends, but we knew each other well enough to know that I was not going to interfere in your life until you were ready for me. You showed that you were ready when you decided to walk in the footsteps of your father."

"Did you know my father?" Wolf asked.

"He and I fought on the same side for a while, even though he was not aware that I was an ally and not an enemy. How much do you know about the war that your father fought in?"

"Not much," Wolf said after a moment. "Mother always told me that there was a great war that she, both of my uncles, my father, and several of their friends fought in, but as to why the war was being fought, she would never tell me. She always said that when the time was right I would find the answers for myself. Perhaps she knew that you would come to fill in the blanks."

"Perhaps," Basille said distantly. "But I would not think so. I will fill in a few of the blanks for you though. Your father and his friends were very powerful and very heroic warriors, and they took it upon themselves to go up against a being that is purely evil. This being, a creature named Shau-ling, has dedicated his life to the destruction of all life on the planet that does not bend its knee to Shau-ling. A set of prophecies written lifetimes ago spoke of the coming of a being called the *Coromor*, and this being would be the only force strong enough to defeat Shau-ling. For a time, it was believed that your father, Logan was the *Coromor*, the second of the prophecies, the successor to Lord Cedric Binosear. However, it soon turned out that Logan's brother, your uncle, Korrd, was this *Coromor*. Logan was a being known as the *Chosen One*, a being that was almost as powerful as the *Coromor*. Logan and his friends, Pike, Talon, and Gideon were the pivotal force in the army that fought Shau-ling and his vicious children, the phasia. The phasia were the force that most concerned the world, because they were the most noticeable portion of Shau-ling's army. They had been known to take over kingdoms and rule them in Shau-ling's name. This was a very dangerous circumstance, and it was one of the factors that led to several deaths within your father's group. Before I continue, I want you to know that I was a member of the phasia."

Wolf looked at Basille for a long moment before he said anything else. The phasia were Shau-ling's children, and the very force that Wolf's father fought against with all of his power and passion. They had caused death and served evil, and yet this man Basille who had been one of their number was also an ally. Wolf's mind threatened to spin out of control. Though his mother had gone to great lengths to protect Wolf from the ugly truth of the war, she had not been able to prevent him from listening to the tales of the bards and storytellers who would make their way through Aradon during festival time. Granted, none of them would be so bold as to perform tales that would irritate Elwyne or the memory of Logan Ranthall, but there were enough snatches of truth that Wolf had been able to start to stitch together parts of the tapestry of history. He knew the name Cedric Binosear, the Lion. Elwyne had not been shy about her opinion of the great hero. Yes he had done great things for the world, but Elwyne had chosen to remember him not as a revered champion of the Light, but rather as a man who was consumed by his demons, and deserved pity not praise. Cedric had been known as the Lion, and Wolf's father had been known as the Dragon. As Basille filled in the pieces of the puzzle, Wolf was swift enough to connect these given titles with the so-called prophecies of the *Coromor*.

"If you were one of Shau-ling's children, how could you escape his power to serve good?" Wolf asked.

Basille nodded as though he already knew the question was coming.

"The answer is that I didn't," Basille responded. "Shau-ling found out that I was giving information to the forces of the light, and he wanted to make sure that my knowledge of the phasia and the battle between the light and the shadow would never be put in the hands of the Light, so he had me killed."

Wolf started to speak, but Basille waved him off and continued. Basille was annoyed that Elwyne had not prepared the boy for what was to come. But did she really have a need to? The war had cost her so much, and her stubbornness and defiance in the face of Shau-ling had earned something for her son that her husband had never been given; a choice. Elwyne had been held captive and tortured by Shau-ling, and no matter what the master of evil had tried, the woman would not break, would not relent. It forced Emries hand, forced him to make a deal, and so the mantle that would have rightly been Wolf's as the third generation's *Coromor* was passed to another. Wolf had no true role in the war to come. He was an outsider. Free. Though it seemed that his nature and name compelled him to be what fate had attempted to deny him.

"You see, the phasia are not like humans. We are moderately eternal. As long as Shau-ling lives, the phasia are reborn in each and every generation. No matter how we are killed, we are reborn just as we were in the previous lifetime. However, as you would expect, there is a way that you can kill and phase so that he will not be reborn into the next generation. This is called banishment. It requires the use of certain strings of power. When Shau-ling took it upon himself to kill me in the previous generation, he banished me to keep me quiet for the rest of eternity, but I fooled him. Every member of the phasia has a special talent that is different from lifetime to lifetime, and only one phase has it. My power in the last generation was my ability to travel from place to place at will, and to create phantom tunnels so that my travels could not be followed by the other members of the phasia. This talent served me well during the whole lifetime, but it served me even better when I was killed. After a person dies, if they served the Light or the Shadow, an echo of their being is transferred to a place called the Other Side, a limbo that was created after the first *Chosen One*, Aerith Seth, was killed by the forces of Shau-ling. When I was killed, my echo that served the Shadows was banished with the rest of my body, but my echo that served the Light was overlooked for a short period of time. Since one of my echoes still existed, my powers still existed. So, I decided to use my powers to travel backwards in time, to a point before I was killed. In doing so I created a rift in time, but I will explain that later. I traveled back to a time in which your mother was held captive by Shau-ling, a time when you were still only newly started inside your mother's womb. To make sure that my knowledge would be available to you and to this generation's *Coromor*, I gave my string of power, the thing that makes me able to channel the power that I was given by Shau-ling, to you. This string does not make you evil, but it does give you certain abilities that I will help you to learn. The reason that you can see me, is because in a way, you and I are the same person. However, you are the only person who can see or hear me."

Despite the seeming absurdity of Basille's explanation, to the young man's credit, Wolf did not balk and continued with a level-headed tone.

"What happened to the echo that traveled back in time?" Wolf asked after a moment.

Basille suppressed a smile of pride.

"Shau-ling discovered that part of me still lived and he tried to mold it into a new phase and failed when he realized that the essential string of power was gone. He wants the string back, but I'll make you powerful enough to defend yourself and those who choose to follow you. However my good intentions has sparked a series of events that could lead to catastrophe. You see, tampering with time is against the covenant of the Creator, and I have created an imbalance between good and evil by giving you my powers. To remedy this, the cosmos has created another reality in which evil has the upper hand, and good is at a disadvantage. In this other reality you do not exist, and in your place is the phase that Shau-ling had intended to make from my remains, a truly evil creature by the name of

Draven Batoe. It is mine to know that the Creator has made this a contest between the two realities to see which is truly stronger, Light or Shadow. If they are truly equal, then he has decreed that he will start over and sentence our world to fire. If the forces of Light are victorious in both realities, the world in which you exist will continue. If the forces of the Shadow conquer both realities, then the world in which Draven exists will continue. If neither reality wins both, then both will be destroyed."

Wolf waited a long time before he spoke. There was a lot riding on what he would do next, but now he had something he had never had in life, a guidance that would not coddle him and give him answers that would leave him wanting more. He never faulted his mother for anything that she did, and now that he knew the truth, he admired her. She was right when she said that he would have rushed off to follow the path of his father. Now that he knew the importance, he was willing to give his life for the quest that lie ahead. The look on Basille's face changed. He knew the thoughts in Wolf's mind, and he saw a lot of Logan in the boy that sat before him. However, there was much of the woman Elwyne there as well, and the touch of her raising of Wolf would be straining on the boy. He was not bred to be a warrior, he was bred to be a statesman and a diplomat, Basille could see it in his mind. Wolf had been taught the sword, but there had not been a sword master around to give him the ability that he needed to survive against the members of the phasia. Basille's powers would only serve Wolf if he knew how to use them in their most lethal capacity, and if the boy did not have a taste for blood, then the powers would flee from him when he needed them the most, and he would die because he did not have the vicious edge that once roamed proudly in his family. But, as Basille poked the edges of the boy's mind, he found memories of dreams and stories. He saw the retellings of the battles of Logan, Korrd, and Pike. He heard the reverberation of the words telling of death and victory soaked in blood. He saw the revelry of the boy who substituted the image of himself for the image of his father as he perched over the broken bodies of his enemy. The boy had the streak of power inside of him, and in the first battle that was thrust upon him, Basille would know if the boy would live or die.

"Why me Basille?" Wolf asked. "Why did you give me your powers? My father may have been an ally of yours, but I don't think that would have been enough to risk the lives of the entire world upon."

"You would be surprised," Basille replied. "Logan was a great man, and a great friend to my son. However, the reason that I risked the fate of this world was not because of your father, it was because of you. You see, the mantle of the *Coromor* is passed down by blood, and the prophecies say that the first born son of the *Chosen One* shall inherit the mantle of the *Coromor*. Unfortunately, a small group within phasia learned that they could manipulate this bloodline and spite the prophecies. They were nearly able to do just that with your uncle Korrd, the *Coromor* of the second generation of the prophecies. Your grandmother on your father's side, Korrd's mother, is a member of the phasia, a woman named Ellis Chandara."

Wolf's jaw dropped, and as he fought the shock of Basille's last statement, the former member of the phasia continued speaking.

"Ellis discovered, nearly purely by accident, that your grandfather, Arin Ranthall, was the first generation's *Chosen One*. Upon learning this, she devised a plan that would allow her to control the fate of the *Coromor*. Ellis took possession of the body of Arin's wife Victoria and together Ellis and Arin had a child, your uncle Korrd. Korrd by benefit of the prophecy inherited the mantle of the *Coromor*. Ellis had every intention of killing Korrd, but she could not bring herself to do it. She left the child and returned control of Victoria's body. However, this merging permanently weakened Victoria, and when the couple tried to have a second child, your father Logan, she died while giving birth. This infusion of power caused Logan to be born as the *Chosen One*, and according to prophecy, you were supposed to be the *Coromor*. However, when Elwyne was captured by the forces of Shau-ling, Emries was forced to interfere and bestowed his protection upon the girl and her unborn child, you. When he did this, Emries was forced to give his mantle to someone else, and so he gave it to the unborn child of the Queen of Brea, Midarin Rice, who was the lover of a very powerful friend of your father's, Gwydeon Sandar. You were cheated out of your birthright by my kind, and so I decided to give it back to you. It was not my intention to create the imbalance between good and evil, but I would do it again if I thought that it would help to defeat my former master Shau-ling."

Wolf just sat there floundering for a moment. This was a lot to take on his shoulders, and there was no way that he could process all of the information in that short of a time. It would take a good few hours of thought to get all of it right in his mind, and when he did, Wolf was sure that there would be many more question for the man who had once been Basille. However, all of that thought would have to wait for a time as there were more important and pressing matters that had to be addressed. The fate of the world was resting squarely on his shoulders for now. When he found the *Coromor*, the load would lift a little, but he would still have a great responsibility. He was truly going to follow in his father's footsteps, and the path he was about to follow led to the throne room of the creature known as Shau-ling.

"So, Basille," Wolf said smiling, "where do we start?"

"Trelon is as good a place as any. Queen Cairyn is a powerful woman, and her two children will be of great help to you on the quest. I know that you feel very uneasy about making yourself known to Pike and his people, so for now you should be Wolf. Don't tell people that you are part of the Ranthall family and certainly don't tell them that you are going after Shau-ling. Believe if they heard that, they would be very suspicious and start asking more questions then you are in a position to answer. Only a handful of beings know of the existence of this contest between Light and Shadow, and as that information becomes more prevalent, so too will the danger. Do what you have to, but get in to see the queen. After that, I'll be able to help you. You are one of the few heroes in this world that have the power to shift the tide to either the Light or the Shadow. With my help you'll be able to create a force strong enough to defeat Shau-ling, and hopefully your counterparts in the other reality will be able to rally enough of a force to prevent the ultimate destruction of everything we hold dear. Perhaps in time we will not only be able to win for the force of the Light here, but also be able to assist those who toil in the long Shadow. Now get some sleep, you have a long trip ahead of you tomorrow."

Wolf nodded and relaxed back against the tree he had been leaning on throughout the entire conversation. His mind was filled with wondrous fantasies, most of which were about to come true in one form or another. Finally, his excitement and confusion gave way to exhaustion and sleep took him. When the sun came up the next morning, dawn found a traveler saddling his horse and turning his sights toward the magnificent city which rose off in the distance. The city that was known throughout the world as the Court of the Lioness, Trelon.

Desolation

Creator's Calendar Year 1205; Dark Mirror

A harsh rain fell on the plains just outside of the burning rubble that had once been the city of Aradon. The burning and the destruction had only stopped an hour previous, and the final embers of the desolate remains were snuffed out by the downpour. Yet another town had fallen to the scourge of the phasia, and hundreds more broken bodies were added to the ever increasing death toll. This was a war that was destroying more and more innocent lives, and the cost to the world would not be fully felt until the war was many years over. The phasia had been utterly merciless in their systematic campaign of destruction, and their War for Power had either claimed or destroyed the majority of the major kingdoms as the years rolled past. Marcwell, Illimar, Falke, Sador, Scalla, and now Aradon had fallen under the boot of the phasia and their hordes of beasts. As always, the forces of the phasia were thorough in their devastation, and anyone who would not bow to their rule would quickly fall to the sharpened edge of their swords, or the brutal result of the use of the Blaze. More and more kingdoms were falling to the rule of the phasia, and very few still held out in the war against an enemy that seemed too powerful to fight. The forces of the Light no longer had any heroes to lead them in the battles against the forces of the Shadows, and when one did surface, he was only able to pull together enough of an army for the phasia to notice, not one large enough to be a danger. This was no truer than in the case of the army that Gwillim

Sandar led against the army of Lord Draven Batoe in Sador. Draven was the newest member of Shau-ling's children, but he was still powerful enough to command a kingdom, and he did so with the ruthlessness of even the oldest phasia. So, when Draven took control of the Kingdom of Sador, Gwillim took it upon himself to try to rescue the inhabitants who languished under the yoke of Draven's oppressive rule. Gwillim was known as the adopted son of the King and Queen of Brea, Gwydeon and Midarin Sandar. Gwillim was a strong man, and he chose to go against the will and advice of his adoptive father and lead his valiant army against Draven and his legion of monstrous aberrations. They met on the very same field that Gwydeon had fought on twenty-five years prior when he faced the army of the phase Zarsi. As was true with his father, Gwillim's army lost the battle, but Draven was not content to just take Gwillim prisoner. The duel between the two men lasted only a few minutes, and when Gwillim's head fell to the ground, it was a shock that radiated throughout the world. Gwillim was one of the heroes that the world needed to stand up to the will of the phasia, but now that he was gone, hope dwindled, and the world was thrown into a deep despair.

The people of the world would suffer another blow to the dwindling light of hope when the powerful kingdom of Marcwell lay under siege by the army of the first-born member of the phasia, Jeroch. Without a powerful lord to take the reins of the army of Marcwell, the siege only last three days before the walls fell, and the sterling palace was overrun by hideous monsters. Jeroch himself ascended to the throne and claimed the kingdom of Marcwell as his own. As a show of his power, he sent a message to the world that would never be forgotten. All of the commoners who would not yield to Jeroch's will and bow swearing fealty had their heads taken from their shoulders and mounted on a pole in the town square. After the last of the "rebellious" commoners were dealt with, Jeroch mounted the last head in the very center of the square. Gwillim's severed head was the final stroke that broke the will of most of the people of the world. However, not all of light had been extinguished from the world. Though their presence was not what it could have been, there were still a few heroes left in the world. Though they dedicated many resources and a great deal of blood to the effort, the phasia had not yet able to rid the world of them. It was these stubborn individuals, and the pockets of resistance that sprang up around them that kept the fires of hope burning among the oppressed masses.

Logan Ranthall, still known throughout the world as the Dragon, had suffered terrible losses in the war against the Shadow. His lover and the woman he had planned to marry, Elwyne Tamerlane, was killed by the forces of the Shadow with their unborn child still in her womb, during the final battle of the second generation of the Prophecies of the *Coromor*. He left the battle with Shau-ling with a heavy heart and an even heavier burden of responsibility. When he returned to the grateful world from the final battle, he was expected to take the responsibility for leading the people out of the darkness upon his shoulders. Having lost the love of his life to a war that would continue regardless of his personal victory, he became disenchanted with the plight of the world and isolated himself for a time in his home village of Aradon. But whether or not the Lord Dragon chose to fight, the war would come once more, and when they phasia and their hordes of killers re-emerged, they were not content with a slow and methodical takeover of the kingdoms of the world as they had been in previous generations. The new tactics were direct, brutal and bloody. Hundreds fell every day, crushed under the boots of the maniacal monstrosities. The brutal tactics were both a warning and a lure, baiting those few survivors of the first two generations as well as the fated heroes of the third generation in to the open. As more and more innocents fell, the growing cacophony of sorrow stretched across the land and found its way even to the largely isolated Aradon.

Logan could no longer sit idly by and let others die in his stead, and he reinserted himself in the lives of every person in the world. After the fall of Marcwell, Logan traveled to the palace of the long-time ally of the Ranthall family, the royal court of Trelon. Much to Logan's surprise, Cairyn Binosear was not the same woman that he had left all those years ago. The affairs of state and the tax of the war had strained her to the point where she was weary of her responsibility to the world. Her nineteen year old daughter was helping to ease the load of being a queen, but there was still too much for Cairyn to handle. Logan became her personal advisor, captain of her armies, and eventually her lover. Before long, the Army of the Dragon had been revived in Trelon, and it was seen as the only force in the world that would have been able to stand up to the phasia. However, the Army of the Dragon was never loosed on any targets. Logan thought it best to protect first and then worry about attacking. In many kingdoms, the rulers had order strikes on the armies of the phasia, and while the army was away, another member of the phasia would launch a crippling and most often fatal attack against the kingdom. Many kingdoms were lost this way, and even more were ready to fall because their armies were gathered quickly and trained poorly. Logan saw that every one of the soldiers under his charge were blade masters, and this enterprise sped training for his new recruits. Still, as it was, the Army of the Dragon was an almost insignificant pocket of resistance.

There was another hero that had built enough of an army to keep the forces of Shau-ling at bay. Gwydeon Sandar had pooled his resources and his vast knowledge of fighting with the skill and diplomatic power of his wife Midarin to build the force called the Order of the Blade. This army, unlike the Army of the Dragon in Trelon had been tested in battle and had survived. Brea was one of the favorite targets of the phasia because Gwydeon had been a sword in the side of the phasia for twenty long years. Zarsi, Jeroch, Rael, Trece, and Aldridge had all tried to take the palace of Brea, but all of their armies found themselves defeated at the end of the day and their siege ultimately futile. There were at least two sieges every month, and it was becoming a regular yet sobering routine for the Order of the Blade. But the order of the sword had a sister group that made them even more of a danger in battle. In a war of the type where loss means death for everyone who resists the will of the phasia, the women of Brea wanted to become involved with the army, but only a select few were strong and skilled enough to handle a sword. So, Midarin took it upon herself to train a crack regiment of archers made up almost exclusively of the women of the kingdom. Before long, their lethal hail of arrows were claiming as many lives in battle as the swords of the Order. Although they were also basically only a defense force, the Order of the Sword had won some battles outside the walls of Brea, and they were able to save some inhabitants of neighboring towns. However, every battle was more costly than the last. With so few recruits left to replace downed soldiers, every single death was a major loss. As the months rolled on, Gwydeon began to worry if they would be able to hold out much longer, well trained or not.

Gideon Viruci was not lucky enough to have a kingdom or an army to defend it. The man named Draven had ended all of those possibilities early into the war. As Shau-ling's vicious replacement for the phase Basille, Scalla was the first target for Draven's rampage. Gideon and his new wife Erika Mystic had just started to get the kingdom back on its feet after the heavy losses suffered during the previous war, and they were no match for the organized and brutal forces at Draven's command. Gideon didn't have much of a chance to rule. Erika's former husband, Jerrard Mystic had lost his life in the battle with Shau-ling, and Gideon's connection to the Mystic family was enough to get him the throne and Erika's hand in marriage. This marriage was popular with the people, as that most of the survivors knew who Gideon was. However, Gideon's rule over the people who knew him was very short-lived. Draven's army was too powerful for the poor undermanned and untrained peasants who were the largest portion of Scalla's standing army. Luckily, the royal guards and Gideon were smart and strong enough to get Gideon out before Draven made it to the throne room. Since that day, Gideon was nothing more than a wanderer, gathering troops when he could and making small scale strikes against the forces of the Shadow. For the most part, his targets were of no importance in the grand scheme of things, but little by little, the attacks were becoming more of an irritation, and the time for escaping notice was just about over.

These heroes were few and far between, but they were still a light of hope for those people that still believed there was a chance to defeat the forces of Shau-ling. However, as the days rolled by and there were no decisive victories by the forces of the Light, the hope in the world died a little more. The world would soon fall totally under the veil of the Shadow, and even if there was a chance, the people of the world would be too far gone to pull from the clutches of evil. Every day they were beaten just a little more, and that was taking its toll. Perhaps there was another *Coromor* out there to save the world, and perhaps the members of the *Erieal* were also out there, just waiting for the chance they needed to strike at Shau-ling and his perverse children. If they waited too much longer though, there would be no one left to save.

The war on the outside may have been between the Light and the Shadow, but there was another war that raged on. Inside the forces of the Shadow, battles of ideology and for supremacy among the elite continued to rage as they had through previous generations. The phasia may have been formidable foes when they were slaughtering innocents who did not have the power to defend themselves, and they may have been some of the most powerful creatures on the face of Onea, but when they were battling one another, it came down to who was trickier, sneakier, and often who got the first shot at his adversary. All of these battles got their start somehow, but most often they started with harsh words, and those words were usually spoken in the Council.

All of the phasia knew the Council as both a womb and as a possible grave. This was the very place that all of the phasia were created, and when their life energies were merged into them by their lord and creator Shau-ling, they also knew that he had the ability to strip it away and sentence them to death. But the Council had more power than just the forming and destroying of the phasia. The Council, which only Shau-ling knew the true location of, also acted as a sustaining force of the lives and powers of the Brotherhood of Phasia. Shau-ling's powers were derived from a mysterious force of pure energy called the Blaze. Most of the phasia believed that the Blaze was the very life-force of the being that they served, but no one knew for sure. Shau-ling claimed the Blaze as his, and he forbid the members of the phasia to draw upon it unless their lives were in the gravest danger. Some of the phasia believed that when you drew upon the Blaze that you were weakening Shau-ling, but that was only a few of the more foolish phasia. Those members of the Brotherhood that had touched the Blaze and drew deeply from it realized that it was effectively a bottomless source of energy, and even all of the phasia drawing all the power they could stand, and holding it would be like taking a drop of water from the great ocean. The insignificance of the power the phasia held was truly evident when contemplating the sheer power of the Blaze. Ultimately, while the phasia were not the masters of the Blaze, they could use its power to make the whole of the world shake, and to crush all who dared to stand against them, even if those obstacles were other members of the Brotherhood of Phasia.

In the universe, there were six primal forces of nature. As with all things, the Creator decreed that there must be balance in all of the facets. Opposing forces must have the strength and the number to completely negate one another on the primal level. The six forces were Earth, Air, Water, Fire, Order, and Chaos. Order was a construct that consisted of the four natural forces, Earth, Air, Fire, and Water, while Chaos was a construct that consisted of none of the four natural forces. Each of the four natural forces were able to negate another, and they were like polar opposites on a compass. In every generation there was a balance between the strings on the side of the Light and on the side of the Shadow. Because the phasia were not as powerful as the *Erieal*, the more phasia Shau-ling spawned, the more diluted the powers over the primal forces became. The *Coromor* was the embodiment of Order, the *Chosen One* was the embodiment of Chaos, and the members of the *Erieal* were embodiments of the natural forces. With the phasia, the strings of power for Fire, Water, Air, Earth, Order, and Chaos were tied into the Blaze and assigned to each individual member of the phasia. When a member of the phasia was banished, that string was taken from them and given to the replacement. However, there always had to be balance in the number of forces that were represented, and any imbalance would cause the Creator to spin out an equalizing force. Or, in truly dire situations, the Creator would find other remedies. The council over the centuries had seen many different configurations, and because of that Shau-ling was constantly having to become creative in the way in which balance was maintained. There were secrets that Shau-ling held that the phasia would only ever be able to guess at, and though at times the powers that made up the Council appeared out of balance, Shau-ling was meticulous in his adherence to the Creator's decrees.

Though the string of primal power was a part of every member of the phasia, they still had to return to the Council to feel close to that power. To be in the Council refreshed the link between the primal forces and the phasia. The more dilute the power of the primal force, the more often a member of the phasia had to return to the Council. If one ignored the call to return to the Council and refresh the link, the powers of that phase would begin to grow unstable and fight against the phase. Eventually, the raw power that had been mixed with the Blaze would begin to eat at the phase and send him spiraling down into the depths of madness and eventually to a very painful death. Though the phasia despised each other and hated their master, they would never risk a battle in the Council. The risk of a stray use of power damaging something vital to the Council would be too great of a cost for a petty little argument. No matter the fear of damage or the respect shown to the Council, the rule against fighting in the Council had almost been broken in previous generations. However, even at the height of conflict in the Wars for Power gone by, no incidents had ever occurred. Shau-ling hoped as he sent out the calls for his phasia that this meeting would not be the first time that a petty argument carried over into the Council chambers.

As the phasia began appearing one by one, Shau-ling became increasingly aware that his Council had grown greatly over the years. Perhaps he had created too many of his phasia, but then again, the need for them at the time had been enough to chance the imbalance and the displeasure of the Creator. The first Council had been a very powerful group. Jeroch Yetre was the first born member of the phasia, and he was given the distinction of being the First of the Shadows. Unlike the other members of the phasia, his birthright was the fact that he was given two of the primal strings, and that he was a truly neutral being because he possessed both Order and Chaos. This gave him powers that no other phase could ever have. The second member of the phasia was the irascible Grawn Aplee. His powers had always centered on the Water, and in each generation he found new and deadly ways of killing an adversary. Third was the first daughter of the Brotherhood. Bryn Aplee was a fiery red head that used her powers over the string of Fire to either ensnare her prey in a web of seduction or in a burst of flame. The fourth-born, the white-haired Ellis Chandara, did not use her powers as offensively as the rest of the phasia, and she used her inherent intelligence and her string of Air to get most of what she wanted. Warron was the sixth member of the phasia, and his connection with the Earth was not limited to his diminutive stature. His ability to control the very ground his enemies stood upon had won Warron Ysamaran countless wars, and in battle he was the most dangerous of the phasia. The next brother was the unstable wielder of Fire known as Saurn Macco. He always had his own agenda, and never did he let anyone know until the bitter end when he was usually gloating over them in defeat. Gloating was not the next phase's strong point, but Caris Vale could have gloated about plenty. While not physically powerful or a good war leader, Caris' ability at seduction and deceit couple with her powers over the Earth made her cunning and dangerous. Aldridge Farran was a manipulator at best, and a bad manipulator at worst. His power over the Air gave him strengths that no other phase had, but no one knew what they were because he never used them. The most annoying member of the phasia was Farax Soar. His high pitched voice and his tendency to talk too much made the other phasia wish they could wield his Air abilities to shut him up. The last born of the original phasia was Erdric Yarrow. His attitude and arrogance made him a delight, and his powers over the Water were very effective when dispatching his enemies. This Council had lasted for thousands of years until Grawn, Bryn, and Ellis betrayed their master and were expelled from the Council.

This expulsion left a hole in the Council that Shau-ling filled with three new phasia. The first of the new generation was Zarsi Aeron. Zarsi was given the power of Order, and he turned it to creating huge armies that conquered everything in sight. This led to his stupid challenge of Shau-ling in which he received the scar on his face that is a constant reminder of who was in charge. The second new recruit was Taron Steen. His size dwarfed the rest of the phasia, and his Fire powers were turned into a protective aura that he used to strike down his opponents in hand to hand combat. The newest last-born was Basille Mystic. Given the power of Chaos, he bent the will of nature and gave himself unbelievable reflexes and agility. His movements should have been impossible, but somehow he always seemed to land on his feet while his enemy lay dead on the ground. Then the War for Power started anew, and many of the phasia lost their lives. Also during this period, Logan Ranthall and his allies were knocking at the door of Shau-ling's palace. Shau-ling was forced to create two new phasia, and give powers to a third. This special addition was Aryx Terian, and Shau-ling used the powers of the Blaze to transform him into a creature known only as Nightwing. As Aryx was originally a member of the *Erieal*, Nightwing was imbued with all of the natural powers. The next creation was supposed to be just one more phase. However, due to a cosmic imbalance between Light and Shadow, two were created. These were the twins, Rael and Trece. The dark-haired male, Rael Starlin, had the power of Chaos at his fingertips, and he used it with the vengeance of an angry god. Trece Starlin, his red-haired female sibling, countered his powers with the string of Order. Together they were as formidable as Jeroch in battle, and apart they were also very difficult opponents. However, as there must be unity for there to be victory, Shau-ling forgave his rebellious children and allowed Grawn, Bryn, and Ellis to reclaim their seats at the Council. This mercy was not extended to Basille when his treachery was revealed. Basille was banished, and Shau-ling created his newest and most impressive phase Draven Batoe out of Basille's remains.

Draven was the last of the phasia to appear in the Council, and when he began to speak, most of the other phasia rolled their eyes in disgust.

"To what do we owe the honor of this little family meeting," the dark-haired newcomer to the phasia said briskly. "Perhaps you have all seen the futility of any type of war against me and wish to surrender your kingdoms. Very well, I accept."

"Quiet Draven," Grawn growled as his gray hair swept across his face. "Master has called us here for a reason, not to listen to your useless banter."

"It is obvious why you are called the Crow, Draven," the starkly pale Ellis continued, "all you do is caw and expect us to stop and take notice. Your abilities have proven to be pathetic and meager compared with the rest of us."

Draven laughed and sat down on a beam of black energy that extended from the floor beneath him.

"Pathetic and meager?" Draven chuckled. "Surely with your vaunted intellect you can think of more stinging insults than that my dear sister. After all, you and Bryn have had lifetimes to discuss inadequacy. Bryn must be an expert on it after all this time."

"What's that supposed to mean, Draven?" Bryn said taking a step forward.

"It means simply that after having a sexual relationship with Grawn, inadequacy would take on a whole new meaning."

Grawn didn't hesitate and charged head long at the youngest member of the phasia. Draven did not rise from his seat or make any motion to defend himself from the attack that was charging at him. Halfway across the chamber, a field of glowing space appeared directly in front of Grawn. With no time to stop or avoid the anomaly, Grawn entered the field. At that exact moment, another field of glowing space appeared in front of where Bryn and Ellis stood. Grawn emerged a second later and collided with his two sisters. Draven laughed loudly as the three phasia picked themselves off the Council floor.

"Poor old Grawn. I'm sorry you weren't yet aware of my special little power. See, any attack that is directed at me get turned in a different direction, and more often than not it backfires against the person who attacked me. Pretty good, huh?"

"That's enough, Draven," Jeroch chided.

The first-born member of the phasia always acted as the enforcer of Shau-ling's will in the Council. Most of the time, the other phasia listened to what he had to say. Draven, on the other hand, had no respect for Jeroch and he continued his assault on his brothers and sisters.

"Don't start with me, Jeroch," Draven shot back abusively. "You are the one that I really want to get my hands on. Everyone in the Council knows that I was the one that defeated Gwillim Sandar and spited the prophecies. Yet you took credit for the kill and used Gwillim's head to take control of Marcwell. That kingdom is mine Jeroch, and you will yield it to me."

"I doubt that, whelp," Jeroch commented with venom. "It is true that you struck the fatal blow on the third generation's *Coromor*, but only after his forces were weakened by my army. As for Marcwell, as the first born member of the phasia, that kingdom is my birthright, and until one of you has won the war of ascension and taken my place at the head of the Council, Marcwell will remain in my hands. As it has always been, you take what you can every way you can."

"Including the slaughter of other phasia," Warron added ominously.

The threat was there, and everyone knew that when Warron spoke you listened. His words often held the kind of truth that was both uncomfortable and frightening. The phasia were never the kind of group who depended on each other for anything, and when it came right down to it, they all hated each other. Backstabbing and deceit were common practices of the Brotherhood, and it would remain that way until they were all dead.

"Ah, the pig speaks!" Draven prodded.

"I am called the Boar, last-born, you would do well not to forget it. The next time, I'll kill you for it."

Draven brushed away the threat with a flip of his hand.

"Draven may not have the wisdom to temper his words, but his sentiments ring out true enough," the green clad Caris said stepping out from her place on the Council floor. "Since the forces of the Light have suffered great loses in the past few months, the War for Power and the Battle of Ascension must begin again. Only in the Council will a member of the phasia be safe, and outside of your own kingdom, the hunter will become the hunted."

"Caris read my mind," Draven said as he stood and the energy stool disappeared. "All of you know that though I am the last born, I have the power to lead this Council, and I will issue my challenge now to Jeroch. I will strike at the rungs of the ladder one by one starting with Trece. Prepare yourself big sister, you are my first target."

With that Rael and Trece both laughed. Though they were very different in appearance, they were alike in mind and thought. Each one knew what the other was thinking at all times.

"You should pick an easier target, Draven," Rael taunted, "but come anyway. Trece and I will be glad to end your path to the throne."

Before Draven could retort, Shau-ling began speaking.

"You impetuous fools. The war with the forces of the Light is not yet over. Yes, the *Coromor* is dead, but the *Chosen One,* and the *Erieal,* are still very much alive. Not only that, but Logan Ranthall, Gwydeon Sandar, Midarin Rice, and Gideon Viruci still live. You all remember what they did to you in the last lifetime. Kill them, then go on with this petty war."

"Father," Draven said coldly, "if I may. I was not the one who failed to protect you in the previous generation, but I will do so now. I will prove to you that I mean what I say, because I intend to do what no other member of the phasia was able to do. I will kill Logan Ranthall and bring his dead and broken body back to you as a gift. I will set aside the War for Power until then."

"There will be no need for you to worry about the War for Power if you face Logan Ranthall one on one," Aldridge commented. "He'll kill you for us."

Draven laughed.

"You pathetic blind fool. Logan Ranthall only beat you because you were weak. Besides, when you faced him, you didn't have this."

With that, Draven drew the sword that was strapped to his back. The blade was mirror perfect, and as the light caught the metal, the glow was nearly blinding. The hilt took the shape of Ram's horns that intertwined and spiraled up to the blade. Carved into the flat of the blade in golden etching was a ram. This was the sword that was the birthright of the third *Coromor*. Draven had taken possession of the sword when he took possession of Scalla. The sword was a symbol of power that even Jeroch could not dispute.

"This is the sword that will seal the fate of Logan Ranthall my brothers and sisters, and after I have dispatched your collective failure, this is the same sword that will be used to kill the rest of you."

After the last words were spoken, Draven disappeared.

New Beginnings

The recently reconstructed palace of Trelon was truly a stupendous thing to behold. Its walls gleamed white from the months of sanding, polishing, and painting of the already smooth stone. The stone, which could only be found in one place on the whole of Onea, was mined out of the infamous mines of Quea and brought to Trelon by master stone smiths who were paid quite handsomely for their work. This stone was not indestructible like the somewhat mythical berionite, but it did have special properties of its own that made it desirable and expensive to obtain. Though the stone had only been discovered in the mines of Quea, it was rare even within those dark and twisting tunnels. The stone was typically only found in small veins, and because it was typically found nestled within veins of berionite, it could only be mined by the strongest miners. The stone was incredibly strong, and resisted most attempts to damage it, but that was not the only characteristic that made it desirable. This stone, named Mirror Stone, had the smoothness of glass and shine of a mirror. However, the natural reflectivity of the stone was so intense that it could be blinding, which is why the stone had to be sanded, polished, and painted before it could be used in any construction. Even painted, when the sunlight hit the exterior of the stone, the palace shone with the grandeur of the sun itself. Assassins would think twice when trying to scale a wall made out of Mirror Stone, as the smooth surface would prevent even the most sure-footed assassin from finding a proper grip. That was why the exterior walls of the new palace of Trelon was built almost exclusively out of Mirror Stone. The expense of this was nearly untenable, but thanks to the nearly overflowing coffers of the Kingdom of Marcwell, almost anything seemed possible. Though the last assassination had taken place because of infiltration from the inside, there was still an assassination. It was not made common knowledge that a member of the phasia had disguised himself as the prince of Trelon and then used this position to assassinate the queen. There was already too much distrust and worry in the world with the phasia running around and the rumors of Shau-ling's return to the world of the living growing more and more every day. Cairyn thought long and hard about how she wanted her mother remembered, and it was much safer from Queen Anabel of Trelon to have been killed in a suicide raid on the palace instead of the truth in which she was killed by one of her own.

The birth of Prince Allan had been heralded throughout the kingdoms of Marcwell and Trelon. He was the first born of the next generation of noble Binosears, and he was the next in line to sit on the throne of Marcwell. The rejoicing would end when Prince Allan was kidnapped from his mother on a trip through the unfriendly countryside of a neighboring kingdom. For almost a year, nothing was heard from the prince or from the kidnappers. People began to lose faith, and the chances that the prince was still alive grew less with every day that passed. However, Sir Aryx Terian would not give up the search. The famous knight of the Kingdom of Trelon had been dispatched by Lord Cedric to find his missing nephew. For a solid year he searched, and Aryx was able to uncover the location of the missing prince. The kidnappers were petty thieves that used the boy as leverage to get the food that they so desperately needed. The infant had grown frail and weak from malnutrition, and the boy was only a few steps away from death's door. When Aryx found the kidnappers, his justice was quick but very painful. Blood coated the walls of the little shack that the five men lived in, but in the end Aryx carried the young prince back to his home alive and on the road to recovery. Unfortunately for many of the most powerful people in the world, things were not as simple as they seemed.

The trap that the phasia had concocted was one of their most devious ever. When Aldridge was reborn into the second generation, he made the conscious choice to come into life as an infant. This plan had been hatched near the end of the first generation, when it looked as though the war was on its way to being lost. Though he would be helpless for many years, Aldridge felt that the opportunity warranted the risk. Erdric was the part of the puzzle that Aldridge didn't count on. For as long as Erdric could remember, he had hated the Binosear family, especially Cedric. This hatred sometimes translated into carelessness, but whenever there was a chance to hurt the Binosear family, Erdric was there. So naturally, Erdric was falling all over himself to help Aldridge infiltrate the palace of Trelon. Erdric kidnapped the prince and killed him, and then laid the clues to his whereabouts for all of the search parties to follow. When Aryx stuck his nose into the search, he saw through all of the phasia tricks and started looking in the right places. Erdric had to distance himself for a while, for fear of being discovered for his role in the entire ordeal. Eventually, the searches died down but Aryx kept looking, and there was nothing that would dissuade him from his task. After a suitable time for the people to lose faith, Aryx was led to the little shack where the petty thieves lived. They only knew enough to be believable. No matter the training of fear put into agents, they could still break under the strain of watching one another and then themselves being ripped apart by a madman. Those who knew nothing about the plan however would cry in pain and die as miserable screaming cowards without divulging any information in the process. The trap had been laid perfectly, and Aryx took the infant phase Aldridge back to the palace of Trelon to be raised in the lap of luxury.

As Aldridge grew, he began to work his "magic" on the court of Trelon. His status as the Prince gave him access to everything in the palace, and he was constantly making trouble. His acts of misinformation and brewing of hatred caused the Army of Trelon to fall into such disarray that they were barely able to defend the country, let alone fight the coming forces of Shau-ling. Also, Aldridge tried to destroy the reputation of his "sister" Cairyn, and the reputation of his "mother" Anabel. But the two women were so revered for their benevolence and sterling characters that all of Aldridge's attempts failed. No matter what his position may have been, it seemed that it was impossible to soil the Binosear name with the people. However, the chance for Aldridge to strike a blow against the forces of the Light came when Logan Ranthall and his band of rebels came through the Kingdom of Trelon. It was easy for Aldridge to forge a letter from Cedric to Anabel, he had seen them hundreds of times before, and so he was able to lead Logan to the city of Castleer right into a trap. Unfortunately, this trap was not as well laid as the trap for Aryx. Logan and his friends were too powerful for the stoneworkers that Aldridge had hired, and they also were too loose-tongued. One of the pitiful men revealed to Logan Aldridge's plan to kill Anabel, and Logan raced back to Trelon to try and prevent the murder. He was too late of course, Aldridge had been preparing to strike for far too long, and the palace was already on fire and the queen was dead. Logan was able to save Cairyn from the blaze however, an oversight that Aldridge had not been prepared for. Logan's thief companion had also been able to track down Aldridge, which gave Logan the opportunity to avenge the death of Anabel Binosear and remove the first member of the phasia from the second generation of the prophecies.

Cairyn Binosear, emerging from the shadow of the false identity crafted for her by her mother to protect her, ruled the kingdom of Trelon in the Binosear name. Despite her marriage to the powerful Lord Pike Rhuiden, she was still addressed as Queen Binosear in the Kingdom of Trelon. As was her morning ritual, Cairyn strolled through the little garden outside her bedroom window and looked up at the blazing sun, feeling the fresh morning air sweep over her. Her garden was the only thing that she could take comfort in any more. As days and weeks passed, Cairyn found more and more events spinning out of her control. She found herself in this same position with growing frequency, trying to relieve the stress inside her by losing herself in the natural wonder of her beautiful garden. Every day there were more requests for protection of for trade agreements. Now that her daughter Sabrina was old enough, there were requests from old kings with young sons that wanted to cement a treaty with an arranged marriage to the daughter of the most powerful and prestigious family in the world. The suitors were few, now, but soon the numbers would grow, and it would become a terrible burden. Matters of the court were troubling enough, but often she wished they the only matters that plagued her mind.

For the past year, Cairyn's son Duncan had been off adventuring with a select group from the Army of the Lion. He was in any kind of danger, but it was further illustration of how distant and disconnected from the family he was growing as he got older. His distaste for the matters of the court was obvious from the beginning, and as the years passed, this loathing of court matters intensified. Duncan strayed farther from home, seeking to create his own identity outside of the power and fame granted by the Binosear heritage, and it seemed that he was successful in carving out his own place in the world. Before too long, Cairyn surmised that he would make a bid for his promised place as the ruler of Marcwell per the arrangement made before Cairyn's marriage to Pike. Pike agreed that he would give up the throne to his son when he was old enough to rule responsibly, but Cairyn was not sure that Pike could live up to his promise. Unconsciously, Cairyn sighed when her mind wandered to her husband. Pike Rhuiden had been everything she had ever imagined him to be and more. He was passionate, dedicated, committed, and totally involved. Unfortunately, that total involvement and passion rarely included his wife.

When Pike had proposed to her, it had been a simple and powerful moment. He made no veiled statements about his intentions, and was very open and up front about why he wanted to marry her. Pike knew that Shau-ling and the phasia, specifically Taron, were going to be reborn into the third generation of the prophecies, and Pike needed a kingdom powerful enough to draw the kind of soldiers and warriors that he needed to build his perfect army, the Enforcers. At the time, Cairyn was so infatuated with the aura of Pike Rhuiden that she said yes immediately. She rationalized it to herself that he would fall in love with her eventually, and that they would be happy together. But that never happened. After consummating their marriage, Cairyn was pregnant, and Duncan was born nine months later. She and Pike had a few passionate evenings in-between the wedding and the birth of Duncan, but they were disturbingly infrequent. Most of Pike's time was spent in Marcwell, gathering his army and attending to matters like military alliances and other demands fitting the man who would lead the fight against the coming darkness. He was rarely seen in Trelon, and the only times that he ever really made an appearance was when there was a military matter or an important dinner with an emissary from another kingdom. After Duncan was born, the sexual relationship between Cairyn and Pike became nearly non-existent, and since Pike had his heir, he had no real need for Cairyn anymore. Their daughter Sabrina had been one of those happy little accidents. One night, Midarin Rice had come from the Kingdom of Brea with her new son Nathaniel and her adopted son Gwillim. While the two children were tended by the ladies in waiting, Pike, Cairyn, Midarin, and Gwillim sat and talked over dinner.

The stories eventually turned to the war and then the laughter grew as the wine and ale mixed with humorous stories and fond memories. Cairyn felt left out of most of the conversations, having been an outsider from the forces of Logan Ranthall, and only laughed politely when the others roared. When the night was over, Pike led her to the bedroom and made love to her as he never had before. He gave everything that he had and when it was over he rolled over and fell asleep. Cairyn lay there that night, feeling like she was finally beginning to creep into his heart until she heard him mumble the name Eldar in his sleep. From that night on, the relationship has been one of business and court, not of love and passion.

But the death of one facet of their relationship did not change the way that Cairyn felt about her husband. As much as she hated the fact, her infatuation had turned into love, and she could not stand to be without him. There were times when she hated him for being alive, and she hated him for being so honest with her about the type of marriage it would be, but she could not stop loving him. This love soon turned to jealousy, and Cairyn began to look longingly at the women who held most of Pike's attention.

From the time that Cairyn had met Pike, his "shadows" had been with him. The women were named Rachel and Elizabeth. No last names were ever given, and it was understood not to ask. They were both beautiful to say the least, and they were as dangerous. Pike had only spoken of them a few times, and none of those conversations were able to reveal much about their identities. It was almost as if he didn't know much about them either. The most Cairyn ever got out of him was one night after he had been drinking heavily. He finally said after many questions and pokes and promises of love-making, that he had met them on a journey that he was taking to the Kingdom of Sador to pay his respects at Eldar's grave. The two women were kneeling before the bronze statue of Eldar when he arrived, and as he approached they rose, bowed, and offered their condolences for his loss. What he said next made little sense, and at the time she shrugged it off as the drink talking. He said that he felt at ease when he was with them, and that part of him that had been dead for a long time started to stir when they were with him. He would say no more, other than the fact that since they had been with him, no one had ever gotten close to harming him. Cairyn often found herself jealous of the two gorgeous women because of the time that they spent with her husband, but she could never allow herself to believe that Pike would take one of the two as a lover. She laughed to herself when she heard part of her mind say that he was just crazy enough to try and take them both, but then laughed it off as a joke of very poor taste. Of course, everywhere she went, she would hear gossip about her wayward husband, and the stories nearly always revolved around the two mysterious women that followed him wherever he went. These rumors never bothered Cairyn much, and she was able to laugh them off without so much as a second though. When the stories started about Pike and Midarin Rice, then Cairyn started to take more notice.

Pike and Midarin had known each other for a long time, and they had been in situations together that were so powerful that it would forge a friendship in steel. Being in situations like that, Pike had often said, were the most troubling back then. You were forced to put your life in the hands of a person that you knew only in passing, and when they were there in the time that you needed them most, you knew in that moment that they would be in your heart forever. However, there was more to the relationship between Pike and Midarin than that. Like Pike, Midarin had lost her love to the forces of the Shadow, but she also had to live with the fact that she had his child to look after. The bond between Pike and Midarin was difficult to explain, but there was no denying that it was a powerful one. They had been through heaven and hell together, and they had survived by trusting and caring about one another. As much as Cairyn hated to admit it to herself, Midarin probably would have made a better wife for Pike.

Then the rational side of Cairyn's brain kicked in again. Pike did not marry for love. If he had any choice in the matter, he would not have married at all, but at the time there was no other way that he could get what he wanted. Cairyn remembered the nights early in their marriage when he had pulled away from her in the night trying to hide the fact that he was crying. To all the world, a dark cloud never touched the man Pike Rhuiden, but when he was alone, the weight of his life crashed down around him, and there were moments when he ceased being human. In those moments he was ruthless and cold like the creatures he devoted his life to ending. There were times when his temper and anger that he tried too hard to master slipped out of control and turned him into a monster. No one wanted to make Pike angry because of who he was, not because of his temper. Cairyn did not fear her husband, but she did fear the man that he became when his heart began to pain him and the mood of the night had turned to sorrow. He had never struck her in all the time that they were married, but he came close once.

Sabrina had just turned fifteen, and she was beginning to take some serious, non-childlike interest in the matters of the court. Pike had always encouraged her in everything that she did, and she was by far his favorite of the two children. Cairyn was not yet comfortable with Sabrina being pushed to the forefront of the courtly side of life, but her protests relented under Pike's rather unforgettable persuasion. There was an envoy from a nearby country that wished an alliance, and Pike had agreed to receive him in a sitting room rather than in open court. This was a great courtesy and showed great trust. Sabrina was invited to join the meeting, and at one point felt that she had something useful to contribute to the conversation. Cairyn was caught off guard by her daughter's actions and immediately tried to silence her, embarrassing her in front of the envoy. She left the room fighting back tears, and Pike concluded the meeting quickly. What followed was a warning from Pike and then a rather heated argument. The insults flew from both of their mouths without thought, and at one point, without really thinking, Cairyn let slip an old grudge about his undying love for Eldar. He pulled his hand up as if to strike her and then stopped himself. He just stood there looking first over at his raised hand and then back at her. He then turned away and sat down in a chair across from her. There were no words, and there was no apology from either side. But in that moment, something between them changed. The respect that had held the marriage together had begun to slip away, and for the first time they were saying what was truly on their minds. There was fear in Cairyn, and a new respect for her husband's temper, but there was also an understanding that was reached in that minute of silence. Some wounds never heal.

But there was more for Cairyn to worry about than Pike. Sabrina was now at the forefront of her thoughts. Sabrina had been growing so fast, and now she was almost ready to get married, and it was very trying on the burdened mind of her mother. But, then again, everything she did was trying on the mind of her mother. From the time of her birth, it was obvious she was daddy's girl, and Cairyn was a little jealous of her own daughter for the attention that she received from Pike. For almost half of each year, Sabrina would stay with her father and do Light knows what. But whenever Sabrina would come back, she would not say anything more than that everything was fine and that Pike sent his love. Also when she would return, she would have new expensive gowns and other little presents from her loving father. Sabrina loved her father very much, and she looked after him almost as much as he looked after her. Pike had sat Sabrina down early in life and explained how his marriage to her mother was supposed to work, and Sabrina knew right away that it wasn't working. They shared secrets together, and she knew what Cairyn could only guess at, that Pike had indeed taken a lover, but even Sabrina couldn't find out who it was. However, this was not the only secret that Sabrina kept from her mother. There were many things inside the Rhuiden house that were not as they should have been, and they all started with Sabrina's playmate and the unofficial third child of the Rhuiden family.

Shortly after Sabrina was born, Pike and Cairyn received a visit from Diana Terian, the former wife of Aryx Terian. With her was her only child, a three year-old girl named Lissa. Lissa's birth had been kept very quiet, as Aryx had many enemies that would like to get a hold of at least one member of that family. In the course of the visit, Diana confided in Cairyn that things in Marcwell were not as they were when Cedric was in control, and many of the old guard did not feel right keeping high positions with the new king. As much as Pike tried to convince her that there would always be a place for them in the palace of Marcwell, Diana held firm and announced her decision to leave Marcwell and head out into the frontier with Lord Arathorn and Mailock. The three of them had been together for so long, and they decided that they might as well stay together as long as they could, their role in the war long since fulfilled and the aches of age pulling at them. Diana was not old by any means, she had been barely sixteen when the war of the first generation and the love of a man almost twenty years her senior called. Aryx's timelessness must have been infectious, because Diana looked barely old enough to have a child, let alone to have had a role in two generation's worth of fighting. Pike tried to convince her to stay, but no matter what he tried, she waved him off and said that she was tired of fighting, and that it was time for her to put up her sword and gauntlet and let the rest of the world pick up where she and the others of the first generation left off. Those words struck Pike like a blow, but he tried not to let it show. Before she left, she asked Cairyn to take care of Lissa and see that she was raised well. She joked that it would be fitting to have another Terian looking over a female Binosear. Then, as she fought back the tears, she said goodbye to her daughter, and left, never to be seen again. As the years passed, Sabrina and Lissa grew to be the best of friends and a terror for Cairyn. Pike simply loved the both of them and he often called Lissa his daughter as well. But, the show was put on for the masses that were always in the palace, in the private back rooms of the palace, Lissa and Pike had a truly different relationship.

As Lissa was a Terian, and she had the blood of two *Erieal* in her, Pike was sure that Lissa would have the power to control one of the primal forces of the elements. Pike did not have many of his powers left, but he had his *Debuisa,* and he had the *Debuisa* that had belonged to Arin, Gideon, and Talon. He was not about to let them fall with Shau-ling's palace, and he was also not going to let the third generation go into the fray with the forces of Shau-ling without a little protection. By no means did Pike just start grilling the poor girl from day one, forcing her to try to do things that she might not be able to do. First he took his time and tried to think of a way to coax the powers out of her if she had them. However, this came to no avail. Then, one night, he made the discovery that would change Lissa's life forever.

* * * * * * * * * * * *

It was one of the many visits of the Queen of Brea to the Kingdom of Marcwell for diplomatic talks that were in truth thinly veiled excuses for old friends to meet and discuss the upcoming war. They were all sitting at the dinner table: Midarin, Pike, Lissa, Sabrina, Gwillim, and Nathaniel. Midarin and Pike were telling some old war stories to the kids to try and keep them amused. During one of the stories, Nathaniel tugged on Pike's shirt and pointed to the scar on his arm that denoted he was a member of the *Erieal.*

"Is that a war wound?" Nathaniel asked with his eyes open wide and with the interest of a child.

"No Nathaniel," Pike answered, the smile wide on his lips. "That is a very special mark. It means that I am part of a very special group of people with powers to control the elements."

"Which one did you control, daddy?" Sabrina asked.

All of the facts of the war had not been told to Sabrina, at the behest of her mother. Some of the war stories were alright, as long as they were not too bloody and as long as they did not touch on what the war was about in detail. The children had accepted war, but they had no idea the depth of the conflict that their parents were involved in. However, at the time, Cairyn was not around, and it was high time in Pike's mind that some of the more ridiculous rules were broken. Sabrina was old enough to understand, and there was no point in letting her go into the coming conflict as blind as Pike had been when his role in the story began.

"Water, little one," Pike replied patting her head softly. "I had control over water."

"That he did," Midarin said after taking another drink from her glass and relaxing back in her chair. "He used his powers very well, and he saved my life at least twice. You should be very thankful for this man right here Nathaniel, he saved your daddy and I many times over and he is one of the main reasons that you are alive today."

The bantering about past greatness went on for a few more moments before Sabrina spoke up again.

"Is this one of those special marks daddy?"

Pike looked up from his glass and saw that Sabrina was pointing to a jagged scar on the underside of Gwillim's left forearm.

"Gwillim," Midarin said after a moment, "I don't remember that scar."

"Neither do I," Pike added.

"Well," Gwillim replied, "I don't remember how I got it, but I woke up one morning, and it was there. Funny thing was, it didn't hurt, and it has never really healed, it's just a scar."

"Wait here," Pike said as he moved quickly away from the table and into another room.

It was a longshot, but it was worth the attempt. After a moment or two, Pike returned carrying two boxes. One was quite a bit smaller than the other, but it had jewels all over it and it sparkled when the light hit it just right. The other box had a little ornamentation, but not near as much.

"What have you got there, Pike?" Midarin asked after a moment.

"Souvenirs."

With that he opened the smaller of the two boxes and pulled out what looked like a plain silver gauntlet. He looked at it for a moment and then put it on his right hand. He closed his eyes and concentrated. The lines in his face began to grow, but finally a reaction came from the gauntlet. In a matter of seconds, the color of the gauntlet shifted from a plain silver to a light blue. As more moments passed, the blue color grew in intensity, and the temperature in the room began to decrease. After nearly a full minute, Pike opened his eyes and the color drained away from the gauntlet. Pike exhaled deeply and then sat back in his chair, visibly exhausted.

"It takes a lot of effort to use my powers now, but I still have a little left. Here Gwillim," Pike said handing him the *Debuisa*, "see if you can feel anything."

Gwillim took the *Debuisa* and regarded it a moment. The fact that the young man had been able to even pick up the artifact was an encouraging sign, and Pike tried to temper the thrill that was growing inside of him. Gwillim slipped the cool metal onto his right hand, and then sat back in his chair and closed his eyes.

"Just concentrate Gwillim," Pike said softly, "push past the blackness and see if you can feel any power. Trust me, you'll know what I'm talking about if it's there."

Gwillim concentrated for a moment and then opened his eyes. There was a different look in his eyes, one of a man who had stumbled on a revelation so profound that it would change his very existence.

"I did feel something, but it was very faint."

"Well, these *Debuisa* are design for a specific power, and this was the one for Water. I guess you aren't Water."

"Too bad you don't have any of the other ones," Gwillim said sighing and leaning back in the chair.

"Ah," Pike said with a smile, "but you didn't ask what was in the other box."

Without thinking, Pike put the Water *Debuisa* back on his hand and started to open the second box. In the next moment, he laid three similar gauntlets onto the table. All of them were a slightly different shade of silver, but they were almost identical.

"Where did you get those?" Midarin asked sitting up quickly.

"I didn't like getting them, but I wasn't about to leave them behind. As we were leaving the palace, I took Gideon's and Talon's, and I learned a few years later that Jerrard had kept Arin's. So, we signed a peace treaty, and his gift to me was Arin's *Debuisa*."

"And what did you give him?" Midarin asked.

"Marcwell's stone smiths built him a new castle."

"And here I thought you were a shrewd negotiator," Gwillim commented, his eyes locked on the *Debuisa*.

Just at that moment Sabrina tugged on Pike's shirt.

"What is it little one?"

"Are you sick daddy?"

"Why?"

"Your face is all blue."

Pike chuckled a little, and then answered his little daughter.

"No, it's not little one."

"Yes it is daddy, Nathaniel sees it to, don't you Nathaniel."

Nathaniel balked at first, his face filling with the crimson of embarrassment, but finally the boy nodded in response. Pike started to laugh, and so did Gwillim, but Midarin didn't join in.

"What's wrong, Midarin?"

"Your gauntlet Pike, its blue and you're not concentrating."

Pike looked down, and sure enough, his gauntlet was a brilliant blue, the same color that it would get when either Korrd or Logan were close to him during a battle. He could never get it that color on his own in the old days, and after the death of Shau-ling, he didn't even get close any more. Suddenly it hit Pike.

"Little one," he said softly to his daughter, "does anybody else in here have a strange colored face?"

Nathaniel and Sabrina both looked at everyone seated at the table, and Sabrina shook her head. Nathaniel on the other hand nodded.

"You see something, Nathaniel?" Midarin asked.

"Yes mommy," he answered politely. "Gwillim's face is dark, almost green, and Lissy's face is all red like her hair."

Pike just stared at the little boy for a moment. He could not believe what he was hearing. It took Logan a long time before he learned what to look for when he was trying to spot the *Erieal*. Without a word Pike handed the gauntlet that used to be Gideon's to Gwillim, and then handed Arin's *Debuisa* to Lissa. Gwillim was quick to put his on, but Lissa hesitated before she snaked her little hand into the cold metal. Almost immediately, Gwillim's gauntlet began to glow a faint green. After a second, Sabrina began to giggle.

"What's so funny sweetheart?" Pike asked.

"Now Gwillim's face is all green."

Pike was struck. His little girl had the power to see the *Erieal* too. It wasn't as advanced as Nathaniel's ability, but she did have it. By this time, Lissa had slid her little hand fully into the gauntlet and was concentrating as Pike had told Gwillim to do. In a matter of moments, the gauntlet became a faint red.

"Well, doesn't that just figure? That remind you of anything Midarin?" Pike asked softly, looking at the red gauntlet on the little girl's hand.

"Another Terian with powers over fire. Just don't start shooting lightning at people okay sweetie?"

Lissa just looked up at Midarin, the comment lost on her. Pike and Midarin both laughed, and the night became a celebration of things to come. Like the four special men that came out of Aradon, four very special people came out of that room that night forever changed. All of these revelations were hidden from Cairyn, and she was never told that Lissa and Sabrina had both been training with Pike in the use of their powers over the elements, and she had no idea that three members of her family were about to take a big step into the war against the Shadows.

CHAPTER 24

Chapter XXV

Glimmer of Hope

Creator's Calendar Year 1205; Dark Mirror

The former capitol of the Kingdom of Brea, the city of Brea was once an awesome sight to behold. No matter what was thought of the politics of the land, or the way that the kings and queens ruled, it had to be admitted that Brea had the most beautiful court in all the world. The palace of Marcwell may have had more power, and the city of Illimar may have been the City of Lights, but the sheer magnificence of the city of Brea was beyond all of them. But that was in an age past. Where once stood large opulent towers of glass and wood, guard towers now rose. Where once the massive city gate stood open for all to enter as they saw fit, the gate was now closed and reinforced with a secondary one. The walls too were heavily reinforced, and a single look at the outer wall would show the necessity of such work. Many sieges had worn down the once seemingly impregnable white walls and turned them black with stains from fire and blood. However, for all the hardship that the people of Brea had gone through, there was still a glimmer of hope. The city had seen daily sieges for the majority of the previous month, but this latest flurry of activity had fallen into a lull that was stretching on for nearly a week, and the people were being given a rest from the constant fight for their lives. Brea was one of the few pockets of resistance left in the world, and the phasia were bound and determined to squash the rebellion under their collective boots. There was one man though who was not about to let that happen.

Where the gleaming towers and beautiful palace should have been stood a burnt out shell of a castle and a stone fortification. The whole of the city had tasted the ravages of the seemingly endless fighting, and it was seen no more clearly than in the heart of the resistance. This was the center of the rebellion, and in that very fortification sat the mind and will of the fight against the forces of the Shadow, the reluctant leader and even more reluctant king, Gwydeon Sandar. While the old Gwydeon, the Gwydeon that fought against the forces of Shau-ling with the Ranthall brothers, was a man that could get through any situation with that trademark dry sense of humor, this Gwydeon Sandar was aged and far less naïve. The many battles had left him with scars that wrenched deeper into him than just his flesh, and they were the kind that never would fully heal. For the past fifteen years, he had seen the forces of the Shadow kill most of his friends and destroy the place where he was born. More than that, he had watched as the newest and most intolerable member of the phasia, Draven, had killed his adopted son Gwillim in a duel that Gwydeon had begged Gwillim not to fight. The forces of the Light suffered a bitter defeat that day, and the sting still lived on in the hearts of the survivors of the destruction of Aradon. There had not been a major victory for the Light in many years, and while once every raid that was repelled was seen as a victory, survival was now looked upon as a chore rather than a reward. People were beginning to lose faith in the Light and hope that one day the *Coromor* would rise up and smite Shau-ling, bringing humanity back from the brink of extinction. Until that day, Gwydeon would have to serve as the beacon of hope, a weight that grew with every life that was lost.

Gwydeon looked over the battle plans that his lieutenant, a former lord named Evan Sinn, had drawn up. At one time, Evan was an aspiring lord and a suitor for the hand of Cairyn Binosear, but that was before the war. Rana and Rama were two of the first to be leveled by the march of Shau-ling's children. Evan was lucky to make it out alive, but in the struggle, his right arm was severed at the shoulder, and he lost most of the vision in his right eye. It took months for him to learn how to fight again, but he had earned his rank in the Order of the Sword, and he was now one of the more cunning war leaders in the army. Gwydeon liked the way that the man thought, and he had the same edge to him that Pike Rhuiden had always seemed to carry. Gwydeon shook away thoughts of the past and tried to focus on the task at hand.

At Gwydeon's right was the woman that he loved more than anyone else in the entire world. Midarin Rice was a woman of great beauty and even greater character. Once banished from the same kingdom that she now ruled, she fought and scraped until she ascended back to her rightful place on the throne of Brea. Along the way she had stumbled across a rag tag group of farmer's children from Aradon and found herself caught up in the war with Shau-ling. She was smart and tenacious enough to stay alive, but she wasn't ready to fall in love. Gwydeon was the surprise of her life, and when they settled down together in Brea and had a child, she thought that life would finally get easier. She was wrong. No more than five years after the final battle with Shau-ling, the phasia reemerged and started carving up the countryside. Kingdoms fell one after the other, and before long only a few of the strongest were left. Midarin and Gwydeon had barely been able to hold the phasia off long enough to gather a sizable army for defense. But as the months rolled on, more and more refugees from the other fallen kingdoms began to stagger in. All were welcome in Brea, and if any of the refugees could fight, so much the better. But defense wasn't enough. Before long the phasia would put aside their petty squabbling and descend upon Brea in a force large enough to collapse the kingdom under its sheer weight. Midarin knew that Gwydeon was getting restless, and it was time to put it all on the line and start taking back some of the land that the phasia had plundered.

"And so my lord," Evan continued pointing at the strategic map that lay on the war room table, "with this information from our scouts, the other generals and I were able to plot a safe passage to the old palace of Sador. These back routes used by the assassins of Sador were an obvious choice for our movement, and no one would ever expect us to . . ."

Gwydeon cut him off with a raised hand. The plan was thorough, but it lacked the one thing that would make the difference in a raid like this, experience.

"They would expect us, Evan," Gwydeon said in a tone that was more of acceptance than disappointment. "I fought a battle on that same field twenty-five years ago against an army led by a member of the phasia, Zarsi. He used those paths to defeat me. Of course, at the time we were outnumbered about a hundred to one, but we still should have won the day."

Gwydeon looked down at the map for a moment, disgusted, and then suddenly looked up at Evan, tapping a place on the tactical map behind the palace of Sador.

"What's this?"

Evan looked down at the map for a moment and then ran his finger along the small brown line that Gwydeon had pointed out.

"The scouts found this trail on their way back from the forest paths. Our minister of intelligence thinks that it's an old escape path for the King of Sador, but that it's been out of repair for so long that it would be too narrow and treacherous for us to even consider using."

"That sounds like Tol," Midarin said after a moment. "If he had his way, he would be here planning all of the raids and not letting those of us who have actually seen combat have any say in the matter at all."

Midarin looked over at her husband for a moment, and saw that he was still engrossed in the map. She had seen that look before. Gwydeon had a plan. It was almost as if she could see his mind working, and when that happened, it was clear that it was a moment that would change everything. The only problem was, there were times when this inspiration struck that were extremely inconvenient. Several times when they were making love, he would stop, get out of bed, and then begin pouring over tactical maps laying plans for a raid that had been mentioned in passing over dinner. That was the problem being married to a brilliant strategist, he was constantly trying to find ways to be brilliant.

"What is it, Gwydeon?" Midarin said putting her hand on his shoulder.

He didn't respond for a moment, but he did run his finger several times back and forth between the forest paths and the escape route.

"How wide would you say that little escape route is Evan?"

"Oh," Evan started, scratching his beard, "about wide enough for five people to stand side by side, if they were thin and crowded."

"Cover?"

"A little. There is enough brush around to provide a little cover, but it wouldn't hold a sustained assault."

"Canopy?"

"Full tree cover. Nothing could see you from the air."

"How close are the trees packed?"

"Tight," Evan said after a moment. "The forest extends along both side of the path, but much denser than the old hidden forest routes. This escape route is designed not to be penetrated by anything, and the forest was very obliging. A person would have a hard time moving through the forest at full speed. Hell, it would probably be tough moving at half speed."

"Good."

That was all Gwydeon said for a moment. He just kept looking at the map, muttering to himself about angles, times, and movement schemes. Finally, Midarin spoke up.

"Well, am I the only stupid one here, or does anyone else but the genius here know what's going on?"

It was an understood rule that no one interrupted Gwydeon while he was working on a plan. Midarin was the exception to the rule. She was his wife, and she could say pretty much what she wanted when she wanted.

"Midarin darling," Gwydeon said sighing, "what is the perfect shot for an archer?"

"Clear field of view, no wind, short range, full cover."

"Right. If your opponent can't see where the arrows came from, how is he supposed to fight back?"

"What's your point, Gwydeon?"

One corner of Gwydeon's mouth curved into a smile and his eyes lit up with a coy look. Midarin returned the look with a smile, and then watched as Gwydeon laid out his plan. He reached for the models of both his army and the representations of the opponent's army. He placed the brunt of his army on the old forest paths, but he held the units of archers aside.

"Now, as we had planned earlier, our forces will move up the forest paths and exit the forest on the west side of the castle. That gate is the easiest to get through and it would be the best point of penetration for our forces."

"What about my archers, Gwydeon?" Midarin questioned pointing at the models that were held aside.

"I'll come to those in a minute. Now, with all due respect to our intelligence minister, the army of Sador will not be guarding the south entrance, but they will in fact be at the west gate and at the exit of the forest paths. Moreover, there will be a few of their ranks in the paths themselves waiting on us. Now, the archers will not be coming with us this trip, but they will be involved in the battle."

Gwydeon moved the models for the archers to the point of the escape route and looked around the table at the faces of his war generals.

"This is where our archers will deploy."

"Are you sure that is a wise decision my lord?" General Ebios asked. "Wouldn't it be more to our advantage to keep the archers at close proximity and use their extended range to pick off those that are coming at us?"

"That's good in theory Ebios," General Sol retorted, "but the archers would be cut to ribbons in a battle like this. The size of the paths and the cover make them in effective in taking out long range targets, and once our troops charge, they would merely get in the way."

"What about a rear charge Sol?" Rachel, the leader of one of the archer regiments chimed in, "if what Gwydeon says about these paths is true, there's got to be a way for the army of Sador to get behind us. While you are busy watching our front, the archers could be protecting our back."

"That's what the scouts are for," Evan remarked, "the scouts should be able to get a feel on where the enemy is once we get into the paths, and they'll be better able to deal with a rear threat than the archers. As far as I'm concerned . . ."

That was when the bickering started. Unfortunately, this was a normal occurrence at battle meetings. Gwydeon looked back and forth between the men and women around the table, listening to their opinions and their plans. It was not that his generals had bad ideas, it was just that most of them were old and set in their ways. Both Ebios and Sol were career soldiers who got their start in the army of Rama. They were then indoctrinated into the Army of the Dragon. Both of those armies were heavily cavalry and infantry dependent and had very little use of archers. Usually their plans were to crush the enemy in the first charge using superior numbers as their biggest advantage. Evan was a man that primarily relied on stealth and information to defeat his enemy. He believed that a battle plan was a thing that changed up until the victor stood upon his opponent's dead body. Scouts were an important piece, but only a piece. Rachel on the other hand understood the importance of a diverse army. She had been born and raised in Brea, and had been an archer almost all of her life. However, she put too much faith in the skills of archers, and held them in higher regard than any other unit. After a moment of the useless banter, Gwydeon rapped on the table twice with his sword and waited as the bickering stopped and everyone turned their attention back to their leader.

Gwydeon didn't reply in words, but rather looked down at the table and pointed to the escape route. He then reached for a metal right-angle, a tool used for laying out exact maps and measuring angles, and laid it on the map. He moved the angle so that the point was at the exit of the escape path, and the open ninety degree angle pointed back toward the exit of the forest paths. Evan whistled softly to himself. Over forty-five degrees of the angle touched the exit of the forest paths.

"Anybody else see what I see?" Gwydeon asked, no emotion in his voice.

"A clear kill zone," Rachel replied looking closed at the map. "The archers will have a clean view from the western gate all the way the exit of the forest path. There are no obstructions in the field of view."

"Clear field of view," Midarin muttered to herself, and Gwydeon smiled.

"The castle and the trees will cut down most of the wind," Rachel continued, "and from the looks of this map, it would be an incredible easy shot."

"No wind, short range," Midarin muttered again.

"And from the report of the terrain from the scouts," Evan added, "the archers wouldn't be seen by the enemy, and there is no way that they could be touched because of the tight conditions."

"And full cover," Midarin finished looking over at a smiling Gwydeon.

"A perfect shot, huh?"

Everyone was silent for a moment as Gwydeon and Midarin shared a bit of a romantic moment. Gwydeon looked back at the table again and then up at his generals.

"They're planning to try and trap us. Fine, we'll walk into it, but we are going to lay a bit of a trap for them. As soon as their main force comes out of the western gate into full view, the archers open fire. Knowing our archers, they'll take over fifty percent casualties before our infantry even gets there. Then, after we get into hand-to-hand, the archers can pick off the stragglers. We'll regroup here," Gwydeon said pointing to a spot just outside the western gate, "and then make our march into the castle. Once inside, there is no way to tell how much resistance there is going to be. Our intelligence section has been unable to determine whether or not a member of the phasia still makes this place his residence. Regardless of that fact, our course of action is clear. We will take Sador."

There was a cheer all around and then the men were dismissed by Midarin. After the last of them had exited the war room, Gwydeon sat back down in a large wooden chair and softly rubbed his left knee. Midarin had followed Rachel out of the room, and when she returned, she frowned at her husband.

"Your knee bothering you again?"

Gwydeon nodded.

"Been on my feet too long. It only hurts when I stand in one place for too long and don't keep moving around. How's your side?"

Midarin put her hand on her left side and rubbed lightly.

"It still hurts a little, but it's nothing that I can't handle. Besides, it was only a flesh wound, and it wasn't that deep really."

Gwydeon laughed and motioned for her to come over to him. She hesitated for a moment and then sauntered over to where he sat.

"Wasn't that deep? Darling, I hate to disagree with you, but he had his sword buried into your side and then he twisted it. I'd say that was a little more than a flesh wound."

Midarin stopped where she was and glared at Gwydeon. Then, after a moment she laughed, took off her shirt, and turned her left side to face him.

"Well, whatever it was, its healing pretty well."

Gwydeon didn't pay much attention to her scar, but had his eyes fixed on her half naked body. Midarin never wore anything under her shirt or breeches, and she was never shy about her body.

"Gwydeon?"

He didn't respond, but he did reach up and pull her onto his lap. After a passionate kiss, she laid her head on his shoulder and held him tightly.

"So, is your knee well enough for our pre-battle ritual?"

Midarin laughed slightly after her comment and hugged Gwydeon even tighter before kissing him again. He broke the kiss this time and looked deeply into her eyes.

"How are you holding up Midarin?"

She sighed and then shook her head.

"I'm getting tired a lot easier now, but the morning sickness is starting to lighten up a bit. All in all, I'd say I'm in pretty good shape."

"Are you up to this raid?"

Midarin looked at him with a puzzled look on her face.

"Why would you ask that Gwydeon? I've been by your side on every raid that this army has ever gone on. Besides, with the archers split off on this one, you're going to need me there."

"Rachel can handle the archers."

"Rachel can't handle the archers, not without me. She's a good young warrior Gwydeon, but she doesn't know the way that you think. What if something goes wrong and you have to alter the plan and take another route through the forest? Rachel is the kind that would sit there all day and wait for you to come out of the path you said you would come out of before she would shoot. By the time she realized what had happened, you would all be dead, and the battle would be over. No, there is no way that I would let Rachel lead the archers into this battle. Not with so much riding on their role."

Gwydeon laughed as he stroked Midarin's hair.

"I thought you would say something like that darling. You are taking the lead of the archers, and Rachel is going to stay here and make sure the point defense stays sharp while we're gone. One of the phasia is bound to get wind of our little attack and descend like a pack of vultures. If we're not careful, we won't have a home to come back to."

After that, Gwydeon went silent and just kept stroking his wife's hair. This was the kind of silence that Midarin could not stand. She knew what he was thinking, and she knew that it was tearing him apart. He had been there when Gwillim's army took the field in Aradon to battle the Army of the Crow. It was a doomed battle to begin with, but Gwillim wanted to fight anyway. Gwydeon did too. It was his home that was about to be destroyed. Draven had too many creatures behind him, and there was no way that the rag tag group of rebels would ever stand up to a full assault by Jeresei and Shadowwalkers. Then when the challenge came in from Draven, Gwydeon begged his adopted son to decline and order the retreat, but Gwillim would not listen. He had the Ranthall streak of stubbornness in him, and he had learned the Sandar will. There was no way that anyone short of a god could make Gwillim leave the field that day, and when Gwydeon watched his son walk out to face Draven, he knew it would be the last time that he would ever see his son alive. The battle was quick, and when Gwillim fell, the army that had been gathered to protect Aradon fled. Gwydeon fled too, taking those he could with him back to Brea. It was a great loss for the forces of the light, and an even greater victory for Shauling's minions.

"Still broken up about Gwillim?"

Gwydeon sat silent for a moment and then shook his head. Midarin was a bit surprised, but she waited for Gwydeon to open up rather than to try and pry it out of him.

"Gwillim made his own decisions Midarin, I realize that, but I wish he would have listened to me. I mean, I know that I wasn't his real father, but I thought that he would listen to me."

Gwydeon fell silent for a moment, but before Midarin could comfort him, he started speaking again.

"The thing that bothers me the most about that whole ordeal was the fact that Logan wasn't there. There was no way that he couldn't know that Aradon was going to be hit. At the very least I would have thought that he would have sent part of his army to help us. It was his home too after all."

Midarin rubbed Gwydeon's chest for a moment and then responded.

"Trelon has been under about as many attacks as we have, maybe more. Besides, you know how much the phasia want the Ranthall boys dead. They would do anything in their power to get in there and get him. Not only that, Trelon would be a considerable prize for the phasia. With its ties to the Binosear family and now to the Ranthall family, it is ripe for the picking. The rumor also has it that Cairyn is expecting again, and that this one is Logan's."

Gwydeon looked up at his wife a little shocked. He knew Logan Ranthall, and he could not believe that Logan would have taken a lover. At that moment the events of the final battle sprang into Gwydeon's mind.

* * * * * * * * * * * *

They had all made it to the Hall of Terrors, and that's when everything descended into madness. Arin was the first to fall, and then Talon was cut down by Jeroch's blade from behind. Korrd and Logan were powerless to stop Jeroch, but Gwydeon was able to cut him down. Then, in the throne room, the biggest surprises of all were waiting for them. Cedric had been corrupted by the Blaze and stood at Shau-ling's side. Aryx had been turned into the thing called Nightwing, and he was also ready to kill every single one of them. Then, Shau-ling played his trump card. Nightwing brought out Elwyne and laid her on the stone steps before the throne of power and had Cedric kill her. Emries may have protected Elwyne from Shau-ling and the phasia, but Cedric still had some of his free will, and he was a champion of the Light, so he was not bound by the rules that Emries had laid down. After that, Logan just snapped. The first shot of power took Cedric full in the chest and killed him on impact. Korrd and Pike lashed out next, taking Nightwing full in the chest, knocking him down. Little did the remaining forces of the Light know that the stubborn old warrior was not dead. As a show of strength, Shau-ling killed Jerrard and then started taking his shots at Logan and Korrd. Logan took a shot to the chest, but it only served to make him madder. The full release of his power slammed Shau-ling against the back wall of the throne room, and then Korrd hit Shau-ling with a blast from the Jeweled Dragon's Flame. Shau-ling was staggered, but far from beaten. Nightwing by this time had made it back to his feet and was about to reinsert himself into the fray when Shau-ling opened himself up to the Blaze and took the form of a huge black dragon. Logan kept using his powers to keep Shau-ling off balance, and Pike was going to close the channel of Blaze energy, but Nightwing had other ideas. His charge sent both he and Pike spiraling down the column of Blaze energy and set off a massive explosion under the palace. Shau-ling was rocked by the explosion, and it only took another combined shot from Logan, Gideon, and Korrd to finish him off. But Shau-ling would not just die. As he fell, he launched a last gasp attack against Korrd. There was no way that Korrd could have dodged the pure beam of Blaze fire, and when the flames receded, there was nothing left. After that battle, Logan was severely jaded. He went back to Aradon for a time and hid from the world, his only company his pain and misery. He vowed that he would never take another lover, and that he would never marry or have a child.

* * * * * * * * * * * *

Gwydeon's thoughts drifted away from the past and back to the present.

"Where did you hear that Midarin?"

"When the traders were here from Trelon a few days ago, I heard one of them say that Cairyn was a round as a balloon and that she would be having the child at any time. Also, he said that Logan was never far from her side and that he had moved into her chambers."

Gwydeon was dumfounded. The fact that Logan had taken a lover was not the important part. The fact that he had taken the queen of the largest non-phasia run kingdom was. This was his way to get the power he needed to take on the phasia all by himself. If Logan had not recovered his wits in the last twenty-five years, there was no way that Trelon would make it with him leading the army.

"We have to go to Trelon, Midarin. I need to see Logan."

Midarin hesitated for a moment and then nodded.

"What about the raid?"

Gwydeon suddenly remembered the raid and cursed under his breath.

"If we live through tomorrow, then we'll go to Trelon."

"Well then," Midarin said snuggling closer to Gwydeon, "let's start thinking about tonight."

It started with another long deep kiss, and would have turned into more had it not been for the insistent knock at the war room door. Both

Gwydeon and Midarin groaned, and after Midarin finished putting her shirt back on, Gwydeon barked for the person to enter. The unwanted intruder was Evan Sinn.

"Sorry to interrupt you my lord," Evan said bowing, "but there is someone here to see you."

"Does this someone have a name?" Midarin asked shortly.

"He wouldn't give his name sire, but he is clean. There are no markings on him, and our sniffers say that he is not a member of the phasia. Besides, he says he's a friend of yours."

"Well then," Gwydeon said after a moment, "show him in."

Evan disappeared for a moment and then returned with the mysterious visitor in tow. When Gwydeon and Midarin saw him, they were both frozen by shock. No one else could copy that look or that attitude in stance. From the shoulders pulled back hard, to the start of a beard that begged for attention, there was no mistaking the man who stood in the doorway. The only thing that was missing was the ax in a loop on his belt, but otherwise, Pike Rhuiden had not change a bit from the last time he was seen alive, twenty-five years ago, in the throne room of Shau-ling's palace, plummeting to his death in a column of pure green flame.

Too Many Secrets

Creator's Calendar Year 1205; Light Reality

The castle of Marcwell has always been a place where anything could happen, and despite the infusion of new blood into an old ruling bloodline, that fact still rang true, for better and for worse. It had all started with the surprise marriage of Pike Rhuiden to Cairyn Binosear, then continued with the birth of their two children nearly four years apart, Duncan and Sabrina. Pike's announcement that he would abdicate his throne to Duncan when he reached the age of twenty-five was another shock, and it was also a surprise when it was learned that the girl Sabrina had not taken her father's name, but had remained a Binosear. Those were the good surprises. The bad surprises started with Pike's announcement that the phasia would soon return and that the people of the world should prepare themselves for the upcoming war. Then, when the rumors started about Pike's infidelity to his wife, Pike's popularity began to slip. Pike had begun to spend more and more time away from Marcwell, and the times that he was there, it seemed that his mind and heart were not.

Pike slept soundly in his bed on the morning that would change his life forever. He was in Trelon for a small meeting that his wife had scheduled, and he had not heard her come to bed that night. He knew that the rumors had reached her ears, but she had yet to give any of them voice. However, Pike was not a fool. He could see the uncertainty in her eyes, and he could tell that she was trying hard not to give in to the pain in her heart. She was trying hard to have faith in her husband, and it seemed like there were times when faith was almost enough. When he awoke, he rolled over and opened his eyes, immediately closing them again as the bright sunlight flooded through the open windows right onto the bed. Grumbling to himself, he sat up, rubbed his eyes, and pulled on his breeches. It was not a difficult deduction to know that Cairyn was out in her garden. She always walked there in the morning when she had something on her mind. This morning was no different. As Pike approached her and put his arms around her waist, she shivered a little and then turned to face him.

"Good morning my darling," he said as cheerfully as he could manage. "I'm sorry that I wasn't better company last night, but you know how I am after I travel."

Cairyn smiled and nodded. Pike was notorious for drinking while traveling to keep the pain in his body from becoming too intense. As much as he hated to make it known, Pike suffered many deep scars during his war with Shau-ling, and many of them had never healed fully. Many times, being drunk was the only wholly effective way of dealing with the pain. However, Cairyn had begun to suspect that the physical pain paled in comparison to the emotional pain who's only sedative came in the form of several bottle of wine and ale.

"I know dearest," Cairyn replied kissing the larger man on the lips softly. "I just wish that you would let the healers look at your wounds to see if there was any way to keep them from reopening as often as they do."

Pike laughed and looked down at his wife with a warm soft glow in his eyes.

"Cairyn, this old body is too rough and tough for those healers, and besides, they would probably tell me that I would have to sit around for the better part of a year and not fight, ride, hunt, or . . . "

Then he kissed her hard on the lips, pulling her body closer to him. Cairyn melted into his arms and held the embrace as long as she could before he pulled away. There were times when Pike could be affectionate, and when he was, it was the most wonderful of sensations, but those times were growing farther and farther apart as the years crept by.

"So," Pike said after a moment, clearly changing the subject, "what matters of diplomacy was I too drunk to remember?"

Cairyn laughed softly to herself and sat down on a little marble bench that stood in the center of the garden. She knew it was pointless to probe the physical issues any further. She had had years to try to get Pike to admit his problems ran deeper than the scars that he could see, and he would never see anything more that the necessity of moving forward. Pain fueled the man, and he needed it for the tasks ahead. Pike relaxed against the doorway, folding his arms over his chest.

"The emissary was from the city of Aradon. He came to offer the year's tribute and thanks for our protection. Also, he brought some bad news. At the time you were on your way to our chambers, and the emissary almost did not want to tell me, but he went on to say that Elwyne Tamerlane had passed away. He rode here with all haste, and the news is barely two days old."

Pike's look did not change for a moment, as if the news did not register. Then, slowly, the light and passion that was in his eyes disappeared, and a shadow fell over his features. Cairyn had seen that look on her husband's face before. It was the same look that he had when he was told that Logan Ranthall had been murdered. Elwyne had been his friend for many years, and her passing was hitting him hard.

"Was there any news from the emissary about their son?"

Cairyn just shook her head and walked over to Pike, taking him in her arms and holding him tightly. There was no return of the embrace this time, and he just stood there, hard and cold as the marble she had just been seated upon until he finally pulled away. Cairyn waited in the garden for several long minutes, giving her husband the privacy of his mourning. When she finally returned to the bedroom, she found him fully dressed with his ax on his belt and his saddlebags packed for travel.

"Where are you going Pike? I expected you to be here for the rest of the week at least. Sabrina and Lissa were looking forward to seeing you, and Duncan should be back sometime this week."

Pike frowned to himself and sighed hard. This was a tough decision for him, but with the death of Elwyne, things were changing. He had to follow Logan's last request of him, and he had to make sure that all of the preparations were finished in Sarmeel.

"I have a promise to keep, Cairyn, and I have to make sure that Turok and the rest of the Enforcers are ready. I haven't told you, but there have been sightings of Shadowwalkers and Jeresei around the borders of some of the fringe kingdoms. Shau-ling's back, and the raids will start any time. I also believe that the forces of the Shadow have been around a lot longer than just a few months. I don't think that anyone but a member of the phasia is responsible for Logan's murder."

Cairyn was struck for a moment, but then slowly began to regain her wits. She had known that this time was coming, and really, she had thought it would come long before now.

"So," Cairyn said after a moment, sitting down on the edge of the bed, "what should I do in your absence?"

"The same as usual my dear," Pike said laughing. "After all, you are a far better ruler than I am. One thing you should consider is declaring a holiday in honor of Elwyne Tamerlane Ranthall, much as we did for Logan after his death. She was a great hero in the war too, and it would be a shame to see that honor forgotten. You and Sabrina should go to Aradon, make a proclamation, visit the grave, and pay your respects for the people of Marcwell and Trelon. Also, convey my apologies to the citizens of Aradon for my absence. Oh, and look up my father and see how he is."

Cairyn smiled and nodded.

"Thank you my dearest. Also, apologize to the children for me. I don't mean to be such a chore to keep track of, but . . ."

"You don't need to explain it to me, or to our children. They understand, and so do I. Remember that my uncle was once the one gallivanting throughout the countryside. We Binosears have been at the hero game much longer than the Rhuidens. Now, get out of here. Oh, make sure you take a bottle or two of ale for the trip."

Pike smiled and bent down to kiss her. The kiss was one not of passion, but of true heartfelt love, at least on Cairyn's end. Pike then stood, smiled, and left. After a moment or two, Cairyn left the bedroom and traveled down the long hallway to the other end of the east wing of the palace to where her daughter slept. Cairyn knocked on the door once, and then entered.

Most mornings, Sabrina and Lissa got up early to practice with swords and bows, while other mornings they merely got up and talked about events of the night before or gossip with the ladies in waiting. This was a gossip morning. When the door opened, Cairyn saw her daughter, Lissa, and several of her ladies in waiting sitting around the room, many of them laughing. When they saw Cairyn, they all stood quickly and the noise in the room fell to a quick hush.

"You are all dismissed. Go and prepare our things and our horses for travel later this morning. Have a courier ride ahead to Aradon to tell them of our impending arrival."

With a curt "yes my queen," all of them filed out of the room, the last closing the door behind her. Cairyn looked at Sabrina and then Lissa and then sat down in a chair across from them.

"So," Cairyn said breaking the silence, "what is the morning gossip? Surely there is more this morning than your father's drunken condition at last night's dinner, so you may skip that."

"Well," Lissa said, her fire red hair catching the light for a moment as she tilted her head to look directly at her queen and adopted mother, "rumor has it that Pike has mobilized the Enforcers, and they will be marching into Lakestone on the morrow to investigate reports of monsters."

"And how did you come by this information?" Cairyn asked, wondering why she didn't have this information herself.

"One of your ladies in waiting is the lover of the captain of Pike's personal guard. Whenever he is here in Trelon, he pays her a visit, and she, um, pumps him for information," Sabrina responded blushing.

Cairyn laughed a little to herself and then spoke again.

"Your father apologizes, but he had to leave this morning, apparently for this same advance of the Enforcers. He wanted us to go to Aradon in his stead to pay our respects at the grave of Elwyne Ranthall, the wife of your father's best friend Logan."

Sabrina look down at her feet, and then up at her mother.

"Was she murdered like Logan?" Lissa asked before Sabrina could.

"No dear," Cairyn answered, "she died of natural causes in her sleep. It wasn't that she was old or anything, but your father and I have spoken about Elwyne over the years, and we both thought that it was only a matter of time before her loneliness got the better of her."

"Loneliness?" Sabrina asked.

"Yes dear," Cairyn said settling back into the chair. "You see, Elwyne and Logan were very much in love, and they did everything they could to make one another happy. Then, after Logan died, part of Elwyne died too. It was only a matter of time with her cooped up in that house all alone with all that heartache before it got the better of her. Pike and I tried to get her to come and stay with one of us, but she would not hear of it. She said that she wanted to stay in Aradon to raise her son."

Sabrina looked at her mother pensively for a moment and then opened her mouth as if to speak. Then, as if she had thought the better of her words, she closed her mouth and looked back down at her feet again. Cairyn waited for her daughter to say something else, but when no such words came, Cairyn prodded.

"What is it Sabrina?"

"Are you and father . . . What I mean is . . . Do you still . . ."

"Are we in love like Logan and Elwyne were?"

Sabrina silently nodded. She knew more than she let on, and Cairyn knew it. Sabrina had always been a very perceptive girl, and there were very few lies that she could not see through. Plus, with her sources of information both in Trelon and in Marcwell, there was no way that she could not have known about the rumors of Pike and his mistresses.

"I love your father very much, Sabrina," Cairyn commented after a moment, "and I know that he cares for me. But in answer to your question my daughter, no. Your father and I have never loved each other that powerfully."

Sabrina just nodded as if she knew it all along and sat silently. She would have continued to do so had not Cairyn prodded her daughter again.

"Why do you ask child? Is there something that is bothering you?"

"Yes, there is," Lissa interjected.

"Lissa!"

Sabrina's face wore a look of shock. She had not expected to get into this conversation with anyone, let alone her mother, but her best friend and protector was about to push her to the point that she had no choice but to say the words that were in her heart. The silent tense exchange that can only be had by siblings raged on for several more seconds before Lissa's voice broke the stalemate.

"No Sabrina," Lissa said coldly, "you need to tell her."

Cairyn looked at her daughter puzzled.

"Well Sabrina?"

Sabrina scowled at Lissa and then looked back at her mother, those brown eyes masking whatever she was thinking.

"You know that it's not true don't you, mother?" Sabrina blurted out. Her face was flushed, and she seemed to be thinking so many things at once, that that statement was the only statement that escaped her lips.

"What isn't true darling?"

"That father is being untrue in his marriage to you. He does not have a mistress mother, and neither Rachel nor Elizabeth share his bed. Mother, you must believe me, with the information that Lissa and I have available to us, we would know."

Sabrina almost started crying. Cairyn had never realized how much these rumors had upset her daughter.

"It's alright Sabrina," Cairyn said trying her best to console her daughter as well as herself, "I know your father is true to me. Is this what upsets you so much my dear? Are you worried that your father and I will dissolve our marriage because of some petty rumors? Then let me tell you that your father and I have agreed to stay together as long as we both live, and we intend to do so. Sometimes our relationship is strained a bit by matters of the court either here or in Marcwell, but we have enough together that no problems could pull us asunder."

Sabrina smiled at that and breathed a sigh of relief.

"Now," Cairyn continued after a moment, "gather your things and meet me at the stables. We have a long trip ahead of us, and we need to get started."

Cairyn stood and after a loving glance at both of the young women, turned and left. After Cairyn closed the door behind her, Lissa turned to Sabrina with a serious look on her face.

"Well done, Sabrina," Lissa said putting her hand on her friends shoulder. "I think she actually bought the caring daughter routine."

Sabrina smiled and stood.

"That should get us through the next few days with the bitch, after that we're going to have to be a little more careful covering father's tracks. If she ever found out about Liette, she would have all of our heads before the day was out. As it is now, we've done well to hide her while mother is in Marcwell, but that's not going to last once the war starts."

"You know your mother," Lissa retorted. "When the war does start, she'll stay here in the palace and play the good little queen while Pike takes the Enforcers out to fight Shau-ling. Once we join up with the Enforcers, we won't have any more covering up to do. Until that happens, we have to play the young, innocent, doting daughters."

"Agreed," Sabrina said calmly, "just remember, we have to be careful what we say and do around mother. She can't know about father's plans, and she can't know about our powers. So, that means no practicing and no fighting until we get to Marcwell where it's safe. Also, don't forget to send word to Brea that we will be coming for Nathaniel when we get through with this little chore in Aradon. I'm sure he's ready to be back with us instead of with his mother."

"I don't know," Lissa said as if deep in thought, "out of our three mothers, I think he got the better of the deal. My mother was a war hero, so was his. Your mother didn't do anything but sit here when the palace fell in around her ears. The only difference between my mother and his mother is that she still wants him."

Lissa was silent after that.

"Do you still think about your father?" Sabrina asked after a moment.

Lissa looked up quickly with an angry look in her eyes.

"My father is dead, and Pike is my new father. I thought we agreed never to talk about him."

"Sorry," Sabrina said reaching for her bag, "I didn't mean to upset you. I just forgot, that's all. Come on, let's get ready and get down to the stables."

Lissa nodded and started to gather her things, but her friend's comment had stoked a long-raging fire that burned within her. First her father had abandoned her and her mother when they needed him the most. Then, her mother had dumped her on an old ally's doorstep abandoning her too. Lissa could understand her mother not wanting to raise a child, and the circumstances of her departure had been explained to Lissa many times over the years. However, the constant irritant of the situation was her wayward father, the legendary Aryx Terian. Lissa had no memory of her father, except for the stories she had read and those she had been told by her mother. No matter what he had done to further the cause of the Light, she still resented him for not being there for her. As far as Lissa was concerned, the only part of her that was connected to the Terian family was her last name. Her heart, soul, and mind were fully part of the Rhuiden family, and Pike was her father, and Sabrina was her sister. That was her family now, and she wouldn't have it any other way.

* * * * * * * * * * * *

To the dismay of the captain of the Lion's Mane, Cairyn refused to have any escort on her journey to Aradon. She said there was no reason to go in force to a town that had been their ally for as many years as the Kingdom of Trelon had existed. The captain of the guard had argued that it was not a matter of a show of strength or anything of the kind, it was just a precaution and a matter of protection for the queen and her heir. Cairyn slammed the door on any argument when she replied that the citizens of Aradon would consider it an insult if any army other than the Army of the Dragon entered its borders due to the influence of Logan Ranthall on their community. Also, due to Logan Ranthall, there was no danger in the woods that surrounded Aradon, because no one would be stupid enough to use Logan's Wood as a place to launch an attack. Bad things always seemed to happen to bandits who based themselves in that wood. Most of them either ended up dead, or disfigured in ways the defied description. The captain of the guard relented after Cairyn's vehement opposition, and then bowed, turned on his heel and marched away. When Lissa and Sabrina arrived at the stables, their horses had already been prepared and Cairyn was mounted and waiting. Lissa and Sabrina exchanged looks and then got on their horses. After a word or two to her ladies in waiting, Cairyn rode away with her two daughters in tow.

About an hour into the journey, the silence began to lift between Cairyn and the girls. It had not been a total silence, but the conversation had not been free. When the subject finally turned to Aradon, the three of them began to speak more freely.

"When was the last time that you went to Aradon, mother?" Sabrina asked.

"When Lord Logan was found dead. It was a day of great sorrow for the world. He was a hero in every sense of the word girls, and he deserved the honors that he was given. However, this would have never showed in his funeral. As is the Aradon way, there were very few people at the funeral, and only family members, or longtime friends were allowed at the actual ceremony. The only people at the actual burial were your father and I, Elwyne Ranthall, Midarin Rice, Jerrard Mystic, Gwillim Sandar, and a man that everyone called Emries."

The name sparked in Sabrina and Lissa's mind, but they both tried hard to contain their reactions. They knew of their father's stories about the man called Emries, and they also knew the role that he would play in the upcoming war.

"He was laid to rest in a small glade that was down from the old church that is the center of Aradon's religious ceremonies. He was laid to rest beside his father and his mother. There was also a plot there that was marked with the name of his brother Korrd. Pike did not stay long after the actual ceremony, but he did take the time to pay his respects to Elwyne in person and he also visited the graves of some of his fallen friends, Lane, Talon, and Gwydeon. While none of them were actually buried in Aradon, out of respect for their families and for their accomplishments, they were given a plot of land in their honor."

The night was growing close, and by this time, the travel had turned to camping. However, the conversation continued undaunted by the approaching night.

"What about Eldar?" Lissa asked.

"What?!?"

Cairyn's unexpected reaction to that name nearly made Lissa lose her nerve and not ask her question, but she swallowed roughly and spoke.

"What about Eldar Merin? Was she given a grave too?"

"Why yes," Cairyn choked out, "yes she was. As I recall, your father visited her grave too."

"It's alright mother," Sabrina said softly. "We already know about her. Father told us a long time ago how they were supposed to be married but she was killed in battle."

Cairyn inwardly breathed a sigh of relief and nodded. She was glad that Pike had not told them the whole story about the fate of Eldar Merin. It was not that Eldar was a fact that Cairyn wanted hidden from her children, but it was more of a situation where Cairyn wanted to keep it hidden from herself. Suddenly their conversation was interrupted as a hideous laughter filled the woods.

"Looky what we have here," the voice called out. "Three little girls lost in the woods."

"Now isn't that terrible," another voice replied. "Terrible things could happen to them alone in the woods."

"Yeah," came a reply from yet another voice, "they could be hurt, or killed..."

"Or worse," another voice said.

Five men leapt from the thick brush and surround the three travelers. All of them were large and well-armed with either a sword or an ax. The one who must have been their leader, spoke. Cairyn recognized the voice as the first voice she heard from the woods.

"Sweet little collection we have here lads. All of them look good enough to eat."

The largest of the men, well over six and a half feet in height, bellowed in a proud voice. His voice was they last that they had heard from the brush.

"I want the red-haired girl. You guys can have the other two. Then, when I'm finished with her, you can have your turn. That is, if there's anything left."

Lissa cursed herself for having her sword tied in her pack and not on her hip, and cursed Sabrina for making her promise not to use her powers while Cairyn was with them. The big one was on her the next second. With one hand he ripped her shirt while with the other he pinned her hands to the ground. Lissa was a strong girl, but not strong enough. Sabrina and Cairyn were both too frozen with fear to help their friend, and could only watch as he greedily clutched her breasts and forced his tongue into her mouth. Then, out of nowhere, an arrow slammed into the side of the large man's neck. The momentum of his shock pulled him off of Lissa, and she spat a mixture of blood and saliva on the dying man's face. Another shot leapt from the brush and claimed another of the robbers. Two of them started to flee, but Lissa had already made it to her saddle and had her sword in hand. The two robbers hesitated for a moment when she blocked their path, but then charged wildly at the girl. Her sidestep was enough to trip one off balance, and to get her out of the way of the arrow that claimed the other through one of his eye sockets. Lissa's sidestep also cause her problems. The leader of the rogues grabbed her from behind and held his dagger to her throat.

"Come out!" he screamed to the forest. "If you care about this girl you'll come out."

There was no answer from the forest except for an arrow that imbedded itself in the back of the neck of the robber that Lissa had tripped, killing him instantly. The leader of the robbers staggered back away from his fallen comrades and screamed into the forest again.

"Come out now, or I kill her!"

"I could kill you where you stand," a voice from the forest answered. "You've seen my skill with arrows, and I'm sure you know that I could take you down here and now. Let the girl go, and I'll let you live. You have three seconds to decide."

The robber looked up into the forest trying to figure out where the voice was coming from.

"One."

Beads of sweat rolled down his face as his grip on the dagger at Lissa's throat tightened.

"Two."

The robber knew he was dead.

"Three!"

The robber dropped his dagger and ran for the bushes as fast as he could screaming at the top of his lungs. Lissa fell to the ground, partially in pain and partially in relief. A second or two later a young man emerged from the forest with a bow in his hand and a sword strapped to his hip. His dark hair was slightly mussed, and his clothes were common by any standard. However, his blue eyes shone brightly in the advancing moonlight.

"Are you three alright?"

Remembering her partial nudity, Lissa covered herself quickly and returned to the others.

"We are fine now stranger. Thank you for saving us," Cairyn responded. "You have done an incredible service and you will be rewarded."

The man smiled and shook his head.

"No reward is necessary. I just heard a little commotion, my camp is a few yards from here, and I thought I'd check it out. Sorry it took me so long to get here though."

"Well," Cairyn said shortly, "we are glad you came at all good sir. You have just saved the lives of the Queen of Trelon and her daughters, and we are forever in your debt."

The man looked at Cairyn in shock for a moment and then quickly fell to one knee.

"Stand good sir," Cairyn said softly. She looked over her shoulder and saw that Lissa was pulling a fresh shirt from her pack, and keeping her back to their savior. "Please, join us for the night. It is obvious that this forest is dangerous and we are in need of protection."

"I will my Queen," the man replied and started to gather wood for a fire.

"You were really going to take that shot?" Lissa asked as she finished pulling on the shirt and turned back to the young man.

"Actually, I was hoping he would run," the young man said, rubbing the back of his head and smiling.

"What," Sabrina countered. "no confidence in your eye?"

"No," the man said as he slung his quiver off his back and held it in clear view of everyone seated there, "I was out of arrows."

He then dropped the quiver, laughed, and then began to gather more firewood.

"Who are you?" Lissa asked joining in his laughter.

The young man straightened slightly, looked Lissa in the eye and then gave his best serious tone.

"Your savior," he said confidently.

Lissa rolled her eyes and then refocused on the man with an insistent look.

"But you," he said looking directly at her, "can call me Wolf."

To Be A Martyr

Creator's Calendar Year 1205; Dark Mirror

There are times when you find yourself in situations that you know there is no way out of. There are also times when you can do nothing but watch as the situation whirls around you, and you wait for an opportunity to come when you can regain control. Logan Ranthall found himself in this situation when he looked out the window of the royal palace and saw the hordes of beasts approaching the already battered walls of the royal palace of Trelon. It was not a sight that was unfamiliar to Logan, it was just unsettling. He turned away from the window just as the rallying cry rang out again. His troops, the Army of the Dragon, were already beginning to mobilize, and it would only be a few more minutes before they would engage the enemy fully. As he walked out of the throne room, Logan buckled his armor and headed to his bedroom to retrieve his sword. When he entered the room, his lover, Cairyn Binosear looked up at him and tried her best to smile. This pregnancy was hard on her, and her sickness had left her confined to her bed. She didn't say a word, the urgency of the battle cries becoming more and more apparent, and just watched as he came over to the bed, took his sword off the table, kissed her lightly on the forehead and went back out the door and to the battle that had begun to rage down below. Several soldiers met Logan in the hall and fell in behind him as he quickly strode out of the palace to the courtyard which stretched out below. At this point he drew his sword from the scabbard and held it aloft.

As the sun glinted off the polished metal, all of the guards behind Logan sent up the cry, "Long Live the Dragon!" The Dragon Sword had not been meant for Logan in the last generation, but now that Korrd was dead, and Logan was the last of the Ranthall line, at least for the time being, the sword was his to carry into battle. While carrying the sword, Logan felt a power in him that he had been severely lacking over the past few years. After the battle with Shau-ling, the powers granted to him as the *Chosen One* had diminished almost to nothing. However, while he had the Dragon Sword in hand, it seemed almost as if he had all of his powers back. Yet, even with the invigoration that the Dragon Sword brought, Logan was not the force of nature that he once was. There were no *Erieal* at his side, and all that he had to depend upon was his own courage to win the day. The monsters that pounded at the walls did not fear the powers of the diminished hero, but they would have to fear his steel on the battlefield.

The cry went up again, and then there was a loud explosion as part of the wall that surrounded Trelon suddenly gave way under the assault of two dozen impossibly large Stone warriors. The massive gray hulks clamored into the town with waves of red-skinned warrior clans of Jeresei and the mindless green skinned Kalbraks dancing around their feet ready to cut down whatever came in their direction. Had this not been a regular occurrence for the Army of the Dragon, they may have broken at the sight of the monstrous Stone, but they stood firm and waited for the orders from their leader.

"Fire!"

Logan's booming voice resounded through the courtyard, and was then followed by a volley of boulders hurled towards the Stone by catapults. Several of the boulders did not connect with the Stone, but did manage to crush many of the smaller Jeresei and Kalbraks under their weight. Those that did connect, toppled the walking mountains and sent them backwards, flailing for balance, before they crashed to the ground, shattering on impact, killing whatever they landed on before shattering. Almost half of the enemy's advance troops fell in the first two volleys, and by the time the catapults fired for the third time, all of the Stone had been taken down, and

Logan had ordered the charge of his troops. That was when the true bloodshed began.

For all their training and discipline, the Army of the Dragon not a match for the savagery of the forces of the Shadow. The men were weary, morale was low, and most had some form of wound or another that diminished their effectiveness on the battlefield. However, every man that was capable of bearing arms flooded out into the courtyard, their only goal to defend their home and the honor that their patron had bestowed on them by letting them fight under his sacred banner. Symbols still had power, and though Logan did not feel like the man he once was, his men would never see him as anything other than the personification of the manifest destiny that had defeated the Shadows in the previous generation.

Steel gleamed in the sun as it struck the bone-like nails of the Kalbraks, and the sound of tearing metal and muscle filled the air mixed with the all too human screams of death. The Army of the Dragon was losing the day, and their forces were being beaten back by the superior numbers and brutal savagery of the Jeresei. More and more of the beasts fell, but not enough to make a dent in the waves of enemies that continued to flood through the breech in Trelon's defenses. The battle was all but lost when Logan took one long last look over the battlefield and then charged the nearest Jeresei.

The blood-stained creature looked up in time to see the Dragon Sword arc down out of the sunlight and sever its head from its body. Logan recovered the blade quickly and plunged forward into the sea of death. Left and right enemies fell to his immortal metal, and Logan could feel the power inside of him surge with each and every kill. He was a god on that battlefield and there was nothing that could stand in his way. More and more of the enemy fell, and Logan was leading the next charge into the receding enemy line. Those that had survived the initial surge were energized by their leader's power and tenacity, and as he screamed a feral battle cry, his soldiers forgot their training and their discipline and just became the very things that they were fighting against, cold-blooded killing machines. The tide had turned, and the forces of Shau-ling were retreating. After the last of the rallying calls went up, the Army of the Dragon reformed and found themselves severely diminished by the engagement. Over ten thousand had lost their lives, and as Logan looked at the dead and broken bodies around him, he breathed hard and wiped some of the blood off of his brow.

That was only a small force, and there were no Shadowwalkers. Either Shau-ling is toying with us, or he doesn't consider us a threat any more. My bet is on toying. Still, we didn't do nearly as well as I thought we would. If that had been a full raid, the Shadowwalkers would have picked us apart, and the Jeresei would have run over us. As it is we've lost more troops than I can easily replace, and if they rush us again soon, before we have the wall repaired, I'm not sure any of us will be left standing when the dust clears.

Just then clouds began to fill the sky, and thunder rolled over the plain and echoed through the air. The black storm clouds formed out of nowhere and blocked out the sun so completely that an early night fell over Trelon. Lightning flashed everywhere, an eerie red lightning that had an ominous feeling to it that chilled everyone who saw it to the bone. Then, another crash of thunder and a huge gust of wind went up. When the wind receded, Logan looked up and saw a familiar man sitting on the top of the protective wall with his arms wrapped around his knees, pressing them to his chest. His long black hair fell around his face in the soft wind, and his black cape and cowl flapped behind him as though it were simply an extension of his body. The cape seemed like a shadow that hung around him that could hide him at any moment. Then, just as suddenly as the wind had started, it stopped completely, and the thunder and lightning ebbed down to nothing.

"Too much?" the man in black said with a truly arrogant tone.

"You always did have a way with entrances, Draven," Logan replied turning to face the phase fully. "But then again, it wouldn't be you if you didn't find new ways to impress yourself."

Draven laughed and leapt down from the top of the wall, making sure to do a full flip and a twist before landing perfectly in front of Logan. He bowed facetiously, and then stood straight again, smiling as widely as ever.

"Too true my dear Logan," Draven said shortly, full of pride and vigor. "Sometimes even I impress myself. For you to be impressed though I know is a low bar. After all, you choose to share your bed with someone as common as Cairyn Binosear. Though, is that her name any more? Aren't you one of those do-gooders who should have thought to marry your woman before making her bear your child?"

Logan tried not to let his growing irritation show on his face, and kept his jaw set firmly.

"What do you want Draven?"

The statement was short to say the least. Of all the phasia that Logan had ever dealt with, Draven was the one that Logan hated the most. Of course, there were other phasia that were as cocky and proud. There were other phasia that boasted about being powerful and destructive. And there were many other phasia that were evil and diabolical enough to put that arrogance to lethal use. However, the most disturbing thing about Draven was the fact that for every boast, there was a subtle truth. For every threat, there was the certainty that he could back up every word. After all, Draven had been the one that crushed Aradon under his boot and killed Gwillim Sandar in the process. He had also been the phase responsible for the destruction of Scalla, and for the execution of Erika Mystic. Wherever Draven was, death and destruction were sure to follow, and this occasion was no different. The phase in recent months had become fixated on Trelon, and it had been proven over the past few years that being the target of Draven's single-minded devotion was the way to a premature end.

"I am hurt that I don't get a warmer welcome old friend," Draven replied mocking pain, "I was hoping for an invitation inside for dinner, perhaps a drink with you and your lover. Perhaps we could toast your new child, and then perhaps you and I would have a long talk about young Sabrina's future, and her need for a strong man in her life."

"Stop Draven," Logan responded angrily. "No phase is welcome in the Kingdom of Trelon by order of the Queen herself, Cairyn Binosear. As her high commander . . ."

"And evening distraction," Draven poked.

" . . . I am authorized to kill you. But, as magnanimous as you seem to think I am, I could just let you leave here in peace. Now, which will it be?"

"My dear deluded friend," Draven said laughing and leaning back against the wall behind him, "you and I both know that the battle between the Light and the Shadow is over. Your child is dead and Gwillim Sandar is dead. Before too long, the city of Brea will fall, and your petty rebellion will be over. The only pieces left in the way are you old men who think that you still have some use in this war. Well, I have news for you my friend. Your act of this little play is over. Curl up and die and get out of the way. In case you haven't heard, the bad guys win this one."

Logan just scowled at the phase and tightened his grip on the hilt of the Dragon Sword.

"Gideon Viruci is a hunted man, a man without a kingdom. Before too long, he and his daughter will be found and killed. Gwydeon Sandar is too crippled to be much of a challenge, and the only reason I would keep Midarin Rice alive is just to see what all the fuss is about. You aren't banished from a kingdom and labeled a whore without being at least somewhat interesting. But then, you know all about that don't you Logan. It must not be easy making a queen into a whore. Perhaps you can give me some pointers before I take Midarin to my bed."

"Watch for hidden daggers under the pillow, and don't let her within a step or two of any type of weapon," Logan replied trying best not to lose his temper.

"See," Draven said taking the sword and scabbard off of his belt and bringing them within sight of Logan, "we can get along when we want to. You and I could be allies Logan. All you have to do is come over and start working with us instead of against us. Just bow a knee to Shau-ling and give your powers to our side."

Draven put on his best diplomatic tone and for a moment Logan thought that the phase actually believed what he was saying.

"Elwyne's dead, Logan. I'm sorry to be so blunt about it, but it's a fact. It's also a fact that we weren't responsible for that as much as you would like to blame us. We couldn't have been. Emries put his damn law down that said we couldn't touch her. Well, we didn't. Cedric was so jealous of you and Elwyne that he killed her."

Logan shook his head and beamed at Draven.

"No Draven," Logan said coldly, "that's not the way it happened. Cedric touched the Blaze and became Shau-ling's servant. Shau-ling ordered Cedric to kill Elwyne."

Draven's wicked, almost predatory grin widened.

"Did you hear an order?" Draven countered. "Besides, if Cedric had been one of master's servants, he would have broken Emries' law by killing Elwyne. Now, just admit that I'm right, and we can move on to more important things. You have just as much of a grudge against Emries as we do. Drop your sword, walk out of here with me, and we can go kill him together. You know it would feel good."

Logan shook his head again and scowled.

"I can't believe I'm actually standing here listening to this. Get out of here Draven, or fight for your life, it makes no difference to me. You and I both know you couldn't take me on your best day, and I'm ready to start making the phasia pay for all the carnage they've caused and all of my friends they've killed."

Draven laughed and drew his sword. As soon as Logan saw the sword, he recognized it. Draven had somehow come into possession of the Sword of the Ram, the birthright of the third *Coromor*.

"Oh," Draven said with a look of mock surprise on his face, "did I forget to mention the new toy that I just happened to take off the very dead body of Gwillim Sandar? See, it does a lot of neat things. People just seemed to die really easily when I hit them with this sharp end, and when I use my powers with this little thing, whew, it makes me ten or twelve times more powerful. It just makes killing my enemies so much easier, I think I'm getting spoiled."

Where Logan would normally have had some kind of retort for Draven's insults and sharp commentary, this time he had none. Logan knew that he was about to enter the most important and the most difficult battle of his life, but this time, the odds weren't stacked in his favor. He no longer had a team of friends and powerful men and women behind him, and he no longer had the protection of a god to depend upon. As he raised his sword in front of him and waited for the first blow to be struck, he inwardly hoped that Aerith Seth or Emries was somewhere looking on.

"Oh Logan," Draven said raising the sword, readying for his first strike, "you know you can't possibly win."

Logan didn't respond and just dug in further.

"Very well," Draven sighed, "goodbye Logan."

The phase leapt into the air the next second, diving at his ill-prepared enemy. Had it not been for the increased reactions that the Dragon Sword gave him, Logan would have surely fallen to Draven's strike. As it was, Logan was pushed backwards to the ground. Draven recovered quickly and watched as Logan pulled himself back to his feet. When he finally regained his footing, Logan dusted himself off and then sank back into an all too familiar defensive stance. He had not fought a duel in a long time, and the last member of the phasia that he fought one on one was Aldridge, and that was over twenty five years ago. Logan was the next to strike, and his charge on Draven should have connected. The biggest problem with the phasia was the fact that they could use the Blaze to enhance their physical prowess and make them almost god-like in their abilities. Some, like Warron and Taron, turned this power into physical strength and size. The Blaze flowed through them and allowed them to crush mountains with their hands. Others, like Caris and Bryn turned their attentions from power and size to beauty. Caris and Bryn were both incredibly beautiful women, and they used this attractiveness to seduce any man that they wanted in order to get what they wanted without fighting. Draven and his predecessor Basille were a little more imaginative with their powers. They chose to turn the Blaze into a kind of defense mechanism, making themselves faster and more agile so that they could avoid most of the attacks that came their way. This made them very dangerous in battle because at any moment, they could turn a defensive maneuver into an attack.

Draven took two steps back from Logan, respecting the man's skill despite his taunts and jibes, and watched his opponent get up.

"You're getting old, Logan," Draven prodded. "Twenty years ago you were able to stand up to Aldridge and defeat him. But remember that without the intervention of Aryx Terian, you would have been a dead man. There is no way that you could have defeated me then, and there is no way that you can even hope to offer me a challenge now. So, I give you one more chance to surrender to the will of Shau-ling and save yourself an eternity of suffering on the Other Side."

Logan lowered his sword and looked up at Draven coldly. Then, the idea hit him.

Draven is no different from Taron or any of the others. He is driven by his ego and by his arrogance. If I can lure him in, maybe he'll lower his guard long enough for me to get one clean shot at him.

After a moment or two of what looked like contemplative thought, Logan lowered his sword and eyed his evil counterpart.

"What are your terms?"

Draven's expression never changed. His smile was still wide and his eyes were still full of hate and disgust.

"Simple. You lay down your sword and bend your knee and swear everlasting allegiance to me. Then, after you prove yourself worthy, I'll take you to Shau-ling and let him bond you into service. I thought that you would come to your senses eventually Logan, and I am glad that I don't have to kill you, yet."

Logan lowered his sword to his side but did not release the hilt and then approached Draven. He knew he would only have one shot, and he would have to make it count.

"There has to be more than that that you want Draven. I know you and more than that, I know your kind. You didn't come here just to get me, there is something else."

Draven laughed loudly.

"I wish that you were right Logan, but as usual you are dead wrong. You are the exact reason that I came here. Shau-ling and the rest of the phasia doubt that I will be their next ruler, so they wanted to test me. I told them that I would present them with your head."

Logan kept approaching Draven, edging slowly closer to the phase.

"You see Logan," Draven said lowering his sword and leaning again on the wall, "you were a major embarrassment for the phasia in the last generation. They were able to kill just about everybody else, but still you persisted. And believe me, there is nothing that the phasia hate more than persistence. It is not enough that they wanted you dead, it was the fact that your death now would mean so little to them. You have beaten them once, and they don't want to take the chance of losing again."

"So they sent you," Logan commented smiling.

"Right. If I kill you, they can claim that you have no powers and you were not what you once were. If you kill me, then I am out of the way and the War of Ascension has one less step to worry about. If you join me though, we can crush the rest of the phasia, and then Shau-ling. Sabrina is the *Chosen One* of this generation, I have known that ever since I raided Scalla."

Logan's face suddenly went blank.

"Basille was very meticulous with his notes and with his studies of the prophecies. He was able to put many of the pieces together and then plot out the lines that would give the world the *Coromor*, the *Chosen One*, and the *Erieal*. I don't know how he did it, but he was usually right. I was just lucky enough to stumble onto a little known secret basement under the rubble of his palace, and in this alcove was all of his notes and secrets. Now that I think about it, it is logical that the old Binosear line still held some power, but who would have thought that it would be fragile little Sabrina."

"That's why you want her."

It was not a question, it was a statement of fact. Logan knew that the phasia were bent on thwarting the prophecies, and that they would and had gone to any lengths necessary to accomplish that end. It had started with Bryn, who had tried to bring the first *Coromor* into the world by seducing Aerith Seth. However, she was too late, and the soon to be Lady Binosear was carrying his children, Cedric and Anabel. The next target was Arin Ranthall, Logan's father. This time, Ellis was the phase who tried, and unlike Bryn, she succeeded. No one for sure, except for Ellis, knows what her true intentions were when she had Korrd, but after he was born, she left Arin and returned to the phasia. In the last generation, Caris had tried to seduce Logan, but Elwyne was already pregnant with his child, and Emries had figured out that the phasia were onto the succession of power, so he changed it. Logan knew that Nathaniel Sandar was the third *Coromor* of the prophecies, but the phasia still thought it was Gwillim. They were starting the War for Ascension thinking that the battle with the forces of the Light was already over. Now Draven wanted to put the final nail in the coffin, either by killing the *Chosen One*, or by having a child with her. Either way this would give Draven incredible power.

"That's right Logan," Draven said smiling, knowing that his opponent had pieced together the greater picture, "I want Sabrina to be my little toy. She will pleasure me as long as I want her to, and then I will give her a child. A very special child, mind you. He will have Emries' mantle of power, and he will also have a little bit of my power running through his veins as well. After the child is born, I will kill Sabrina, canceling out the prophecies entirely, and then I will begin to train my son in the use of the Blaze. Without any of you meddlers around, he will grow to become a truly powerful and truly evil tool for me to use in hunting down my brothers and sisters. Finally, when all is said and done, and the phasia are all dead, I will take my boy to the throne room of my master, and watch as he tears Shau-ling to pieces. After it is over, I will destroy my son and sit on the Throne of Power."

"You phasia are all alike," Logan said finally, no longer able to control the anger that was welling up inside of him. "No matter what is going on in the world around you, all you can think about is how you are going to get your hands on Shau-ling's throne. Don't you think that he knows what you are all after? I know that to me it sometimes seems that he doesn't know what the hell he's doing, but Emries and Shau-ling are brothers after all, and while Emries can be cryptic at time, he always knows what is going on.

Shau-ling is sending you all out to hunt us down, and then when the prophecies no longer bind him, he will kill you all one at a time until he is the supreme power and there is no one left to challenge him. More than that, do you honestly believe that he will allow you to bend the *Coromor* to your will? As soon as he found out, he would have you killed, then he would turn the child into his tool until he thought it was time to dispose of the tool. You phasia are the same way. You are all expendable for his greater purpose."

Draven's laughter rolled from his chest as he braced himself against the wall.

"You are truly amazing in your naiveté, Logan. Shau-ling does not care what the phasia do so long as they bend their will to his call when it is required. He is too busy with his own matters to worry about the phasia. Trust me when I say that there is no reason that Shau-ling will know what I am doing until such time as I wish to make the information known."

Logan stopped in his tracks and looked dead into the eyes of the phase. It was clear from the look on his face that Draven believed every word of his tyrannical ravings, and that his intentions were as clear as he had laid them out to be. The phasia were never more dangerous than when they were sure there was no danger in their actions. They did not have to worry about holding back any of their powers or any or their army when they thought that there was no way they could be hurt. Draven had thought this plan through and was ready to carry it out, with or without Logan.

Well Logan old boy, you are really in a fix now. If you challenge Draven now, you'll probably lose, and he will have a clean shot at Sabrina and Cairyn. There is a small chance that you could take him, but there are no guarantees. Maybe if I had some of my powers left, I could be more of a match for him, but with that sword in his hand, even that's a stretch. Also, I've heard that Draven has some sort of power that lets him deflect any power or attack that is thrown directly at him. Wait a minute, that's it.

Logan raised his sword and backed away from Draven slowly.

"No deal, Crow," Logan said coldly, his eyes locked on his adversary, "you will have to kill me before you get at my family. I've lost one; I'll be damned if I'm going to lose another."

In response, Draven laughed and leapt at Logan. The two crossed swords, and for a moment, the duel seemed to be even. Then, as a show of strength, Logan dug in and pushed with all his might, sending Draven tumbling backward. To his credit, Draven recovered quickly and popped up to one knee. The tip of the Sword of the Ram glowed slightly for a moment before a beam of green energy erupted from it and sped toward Logan. This was the moment that he had been waiting for. With a quick downward slash, the beam of energy struck the flat of Logan's blade and ricocheted back toward Draven. The phase had no time to react, and the shot struck him in the shoulder and sent him backwards. The wound in Draven's arm smoked for a moment, and then the phase growled angrily before leaping back to his feet. The time for play was over, and as the two combatants rounded each other, Logan began to feel more and more that the battle was out of his control. Draven's first slash was a little wild, but it was close enough to the mark to cause Logan to have to block. Steel met steel again and again as the two pushed each other to the limits of their endurance and skill. Logan's parry flowed into a strike that barely grazed the burnt shoulder of the phase. Draven howled in pain and leaped away from Logan, landing on the top of the wall.

"I hate to say it Logan," Draven called wincing, "but in single combat, you might be able to beat me. However, I cannot afford to lose my life this early into the game. But, I am also not willing to simply withdraw to fight another day on this same field. You have lost Logan, and I am the new champion."

With that, Draven raised his sword and eyes to the heavens, and Logan could only watch as the storm clouds began to circle. Lightning danced between the thunderheads, and the thunder rolled through the courtyard and echoed in Logan's ears. Then, a bolt of pure blue light pulsed down from the heavens and struck at the former champion of Aerith Seth. Logan was able to get the Dragon Sword up in time to block the brunt of the blow, but Draven's power and Logan's weakened condition proved to be too much for Logan's will as he fell under Draven's onslaught. As the smoke rolled from the burnt patch of land where Logan Ranthall once stood, Draven laughed to himself and leapt down from the wall and stood where the once savior of the world had been only a moment before. Draven would not normally have been moved to mock an opponent, but spitting on the ground where Logan's remains should have been was enough recognition of his accomplishment. Perhaps later he would go to the trouble of creating a grave for the fallen hero, just so he could have the honor of dancing on it. The though brought yet another evil grin to the phase's face as he began a slow walk to the palace of Trelon and his prize.

Chapter XXVI

Bonds of Love

Creator's Calendar Year 1205; Light Reality

Despite the power and the prestige the rank brings, to be a queen, many sacrifices have to be made. The first of those is any hope of having a personal life. Once in the eye of your public, you stay there, morning, noon, and night. There is no peace from the prying eyes of the public, and this was no truer than for Queen Midarin Rice of Brea. She had been in the spotlight since her birth, and as the princess and only heir to the throne of Brea, things would not get any easier for her. Through her entire life, everything that she did was put under constant scrutiny; every success lauded and every failure met with disapproving scorn. She was poked and prodded by her parents as they constantly pushed her to excel in everything that she did so that they could brag at diplomatic meetings about their brilliant daughter. That was all it seemed at times they wanted a daughter for, just to keep up with the exploits of the other rulers' children. There is usually no problem with a little competition between children, except when it becomes the whole life of the child. Midarin found that this competition became the only subject that her parents ever wanted to speak to her about. Everything she did from writing to speaking was compared with one of a hundred other princesses, and there was nothing that Midarin could do that would not be considered beneath the talents of one of her "rivals." There was one exception to this however, one that thrilled Midarin and horrified her parents.

For as long as Midarin could remember, she had learned the art of the bow, and the feel of the supple wood and taut dangerous twine in her hand was akin to that a master painter feels of the perfect brush. She was taught by the captain of the royal guard from the time that she was able to pick up a bow. Every day she took instruction on how to measure up shots, time them perfectly, and also correct her aim with whatever conditions happened to crop up unexpectedly. She was taught to control her breathing so that her aim did not wobble, and to slow the beat of her heart the second before the arrow flew from her hand. For every lesson she proved to be a perfect student, unsurpassed in all categories by any of the other archers in Brea. However, this excellence was not seen in the best light by the other rulers and princesses in the other kingdoms. Most said that it was not the place of a true lady to be a warrior, and her time would be better used if she devoted it to matters of the court rather than to the silly dream of being a fighter. For the most part, these comments were ignored by Midarin and the people of Brea, however, her parents were unable to just let it go. Before too long, the jibes and mockery of their warrior daughter began to play on the minds of the king and queen, and before long they hatched a plan to settle her down and quell the rebellious spirit within her.

Secretly, Midarin's parents arranged a marriage for her. The kingdom of Alimidar had always been a good ally, and the king wanted to make that alliance a permanent one by having his first born son marry into the Rice family. To the king and queen it seemed like a wonderful opportunity, and they agreed after very little time to consider other opportunities. The alliance would have given them access to Alimidar's vast trading network, as well as an opportunity to lay claim to the Sacred Swords. When Midarin found out about the arranged marriage, she was devastated. She had always seen herself falling in love with some handsome noble, and then living out her life in the court of Brea with her husband that she loved with all of her heart. She never intended to let her life be dictated to her by her parents or to the ugly man that they had matched her with. Up until this time, Midarin had done everything in her power to please her parents, but to give the rest of her life to their whims was not something she could let herself do. And so she set about to do the unthinkable.

When the royal retinue from Alimidar that contained her future husband arrived, Midarin watched from a secret vantage point, looking for her quarry. It didn't take long for her to pick out a member of the prince's guard who would suit her purpose, and that night Midarin set out to seduce him. Her wiles proved too much for the poor guard, and he was easily drawn to her bed. Before anything could happen, Arin Domae, a member of the royal guard, burst into the bedroom after he heard the commotion. The resulting trial for treason sent the guard to his death, and banished Midarin from the kingdom forever. While for most, this would surely mean passage into anonymity, such was not the case for the incredibly resourceful Midarin Rice. Of course, at first things did not come easy to her. She had never had to use any of her own abilities for anything, and once that safety net of privilege and power was gone, it did take her a while to adjust. The easy part was getting what she needed to survive. While she was traveling, it was simple enough for her to use her attractiveness and desirability to get her jobs as a barmaid or a waitress. She treaded on these qualities, though often to her chagrin, and they kept her alive for a long time. However, more than once there was a scuffle over her, but more often than not, she was able to escape from harm, and the next day, after collecting her money, she would move on to the next town. Few people who saw her ever recognized her, and even if they did, they usually passed it off as some kind of strange coincidence. Her luck with these scuffles ran out when she found herself in the middle of a bloody bar brawl in the town of Illimar. It was in this very fight that she would cast her lot in with the forces of the Light and join their battle against Shau-ling. Also in their journey together, she would fall in love with Gwydeon Sandar, a man that no woman could ever truly have.

He was the kind of man that made a person feel special with the amount of personal attention that he paid. Whenever she was around him, he always made sure that she was alright, and that there was nothing more that he could do to make her feel good. He attended to every one of her needs to the best of his abilities, but in the long run, they both knew that there was one need he could not fill. He had been destined from birth to be a great man, and a champion of the Light, but unlike most of his companions, Gwydeon was very much a mortal. Regardless of that, he placed his life on the line, fighting against gods and powers that no mortal should ever see, let alone fight. He survived combat with three members of the phasia, and was responsible for the deaths of two. But, the prophecies about him did not allow him a life after the quest. And, he died there in the Hall of Terrors, right beside Jeroch, his last victim. At the time, Midarin had made her way back to the kingdom of Brea, with her newly adopted son Gwillim and her still unborn child Nathaniel. Days later, Logan Ranthall and his wife Elwyne Tamerlane came to the kingdom to pay their respects to the new queen and also to deliver the bad news that Midarin already knew in her heart. She had known the moment that he died, because there was a pain inside her that she could never explain. When Logan came and spoke Gwydeon's final words to her, she understood the pain that she had felt.

Love was not lost to her though. While part of her would mourn for the rest of her life, there was still her children that took up much of her heart. She loved Gwillim as though she bore him herself, and her love for Nathaniel was even greater. She made sure that they both knew the great deeds that their father had done, and they both followed in his footsteps, preparing for the next coming of Shau-ling. Pike was eager to help Midarin through some of the rough times, and with his help, Midarin was able to make the Order of the Sword possible.

Pike had his own scars and losses from the war with the Shadows, and most of those revolved around his lost wife, Eldar Merin. After his return from the final battle, Pike had a statue erected on the spot where she had fallen as a tribute to the woman that he loved. Midarin also wanted to create a memorial to her fallen love Gwydeon in order to ensure that he was remembered for the great man and warrior that he was, but a statue was not in keeping with who Gwydeon was in life, so it could not have been what represented him in death. Gwydeon never cared about glory or titles, he just wanted to fight and win, and to protect those who could not protect themselves. So, Midarin pooled the money and resources of her kingdom and began to create one of the most elite armies in the history of warfare. Blade masters were contacted from all around the world and invited to join or to help train the Order of the Sword, and many left their armies for a chance at being the best of the best. It took only a matter of months before the Order of the Sword supplanted the vaunted Lion's Mane as the most imposing army in the whole of the world. The crowning jewel in the army came two months into the life of the Order when Sir Aryx

Terian, long thought dead by many in the world, arrived to lend his skill and power to the effort. Midarin accepted him willingly into the Order, but he would not relent that easily. He had a few conditions to his membership, and the first was that no one outside of Brea know that he was alive. As much as she resisted, he remained firm on that point, and so eventually she conceded, and the secret of Aryx Terian was kept inside the walls of Brea. This was not an easy secret to keep by any means. White Lightning was a name that was feared throughout the world, and the mention of the name Aryx was usually enough to set a person off. However, very few people outside of Marcwell had ever seen the face that went with the legend. So, when Aryx appeared, he used only the name Lan and kept very much to himself. So, it was easy to keep this Lan a secret when Pike or the Enforcers were in Brea.

Aryx, though a bother to keep track of, was more than worth the trouble when it came to the Order of the Sword. He accelerated their training by an unbelievable amount, and sword apprentices under his training were besting sword masters by the end of their first month under his steady teachings. Soon, he was made the headmaster of the training of the Order of the Sword. Also, he became a favorite of many of the ladies in town. Midarin had to admit to herself that Aryx Terian was a very handsome man, but she would never consider him to be a visually appealing as Gwydeon or even Pike. Though he was rapidly approaching the age of seventy, he looked barely thirty. His body was hard and his blond hair and blue eyes tended to make women a little weak in the knees. He never lacked for company in a bar, and when the night of carousing turned to a night of passion, Aryx never found his bed empty. One night, after having a little too much to drink, Midarin and Aryx found themselves sharing the same bed, a mistake that she regretted later, and one that she would never repeat. Upon returning to her chambers, Midarin found that her bed was not empty, and another suitor waited for her. Though the second coupling was more calculated, it was no less a mistake. She had never been so reckless, and the recklessness would have unintended consequences.

One of the two unions had produced a child, and it took an incredible amount of lying and deceit on the part of the royal court to keep the pregnancy a secret. All of this turned out to be effective, and Midarin was able to take a "holiday" from the matters of court to a secret location. In a little cabin in the woods, Midarin was waited on by a friend of the family, Emily Forer. Emily attended to all of Midarin's needs, and when the time came, Emily delivered the baby. Midarin's daughter was named Liette, and given to Emily to raise as her own to keep suspicion at bay. When both women returned to Brea, the matter of the secret holiday was revealed, only the roles were reversed. Midarin said that she had gone to help an old friend, and that she had helped to deliver Emily's new daughter. Only a few people knew the truth. Gwillim knew because he had arranged everything for his adopted mother. Aryx knew because he was in charge of all of Midarin's military and security concerns, and lastly, Midarin's lover knew.

Though Liette was not recognized as a member of the Rice family, she was treated as one. She had everything that Nathaniel had, and she was shown the same courtesy. Liette and Nathaniel were only five years apart, and so they were together most of the time. Just like Nathaniel, Liette was put through sword practice and she always sat in on Pike's training of Lissa, Sabrina, Gwillim, and Nathaniel. Whenever they would do something impressive, she would clap and giggle. Much to Midarin's chagrin, Liette showed no interest in the bow, and she tried to put as much of her time as she could into learning how to use a sword. In many respects, Liette began to remind all who knew her of Eldar Merin. As Liette grew older, she began to grow into full womanly splendor much before all the other girls her age. By the age of thirteen, she looked to be much older, and was much more mature because of her upbringing and the proper manner taught to her at court. Quickly she became the fancy of many of the soldiers, and taking sword practice with them often became too distracting.

Unlike most would expect, Liette was not left out of the loop when it came to her parentage. Though she was not told who her father was, she was very well aware that her mother was Midarin. In private she would call Midarin mother, and there would be stolen embraces and other such sentiments. Emily was always around the court with Liette, and she was treated as if she were Midarin's sister. After a time, they were both invited to live at the palace full time. Given Liette's age, Emily agreed, and the two of them began to live at the palace, becoming full members of the family, much as Gwillim had years before.

Midarin sat and reflected on her family the moment that the courier arrived with the letter from Aradon. The letter hit Midarin hard when she read the words that told of her friend's passing. Things between Elwyne Tamerlane Ranthall and Midarin had never been the most pleasant. Both women were strong willed and opinionated. Elwyne didn't trust Midarin because she was too bold and arrogant in her abilities some of the time, and there was little room left for friendship. Later, when Gwydeon and Midarin began to get closer, Elwyne extended the olive branch, and the two women began to get along a little more. However, this friendship was cut short when Elwyne was kidnapped by Taron and the forces of the Shadow. Midarin did not see Elwyne again until she and Logan came to Brea to offer their condolences on Gwydeon's death. After that, there was no real friendship, as no one really saw Logan or Elwyne again until Logan's death. At the time Midarin tried to convince Elwyne to come to Brea, but she would not hear anything of it, and she would only say that her son needed her to stay in Aradon. The argument continued for only another moment until Elwyne put the final stamp on the issue saying that Logan would have wanted her to stay in Aradon. Midarin gave up at that, knowing there was nothing that could change her mind. The Tamerlane stubborn streak was long, and with a little bit of Ranthall thrown in for good measure, it would take a miracle to make her do anything she did not want to do. They would exchange letters over the years that followed, Midarin attempting to keep Elwyne updated on matters of the war, but Elwyne's responses were usually curt yet never rude. She would talk about the goings on in Aradon, the spring festivals, the flowers on the hill, anything but the coming conflict. At times Midarin felt that Elwyne had been the right-thinking one out of the survivors of the second generation. Now and then Midarin would read the letters from her erstwhile friend, taking some solace in the quiet life that she chose to build for herself.

Midarin only slightly felt the first of the tears roll down her cheek, and it wasn't until the first of many hit the parchment before she stopped reading and just let herself cry. There were not many times when she was alone and allowed herself to be weak. It was not a luxury that a queen could afford. As her tears began to slow, she heard a familiar rap on the throne room doors. She rolled the parchment quickly and pawed at her face trying to wash away the streaks of her tears. The doors opened a moment later to admit the captain of Midarin's personal guard, Aryx Terian.

Aryx over his term of service with the Order of the Sword had let his blond hair grow out, often pulling it back into a tail held by an ornate piece of jewelry. The tail fell about to the middle of his shoulders. His armor had been crafted to look more like clothing than armor, and its weight was obviously low. The crest of the armor arched over his shoulders and looked more like ruffles of a cloak. For once, Aryx was not wearing the black cloak that seemed to be part of him, and the plates of the armor were clearly visible on his shoulders. They were stained red, and crested with gold. The front of the armor was not bulky, or overly covered with thick metal plates. It looked as though the front of the armor was all chain, but the chain was tightly packed and almost solid in appearance. From the appearance of the symbol on the front of the armor, the sword and sunburst which was the symbol of the Order of the Sword, there were no breaks in the armor, as with normal chain mail, and unless you were right up on the mail, you wouldn't know it wasn't full plate. As always, there was a sword on each of Aryx's hips, and Midarin could tell from the strap that went across his chest that there was another short sword on his back. Usually this would have been concealed by the cloak, but in the palace there was no need for deception. Like his armor, Aryx's face looked as though it had never been through any battle. There were no lines or scars on his face, and his blue eyes shone brightly. Before he reached the throne, he stopped and fell to one knee. He stayed down, with his head bowed for a moment before speaking.

"My Queen," Aryx said proudly and formally, "I have heard that there was news from Aradon. How fare matters?"

Midarin looked down for a moment and then commanded her friend to rise. He quickly rose and locked his gaze back on his queen.

"I'm afraid there is bad news Aryx," Midarin said with a hint of sadness in her normally powerful voice. "Elwyne Tamerlane died in her sleep five nights ago, and the Rhuiden and Binosear families have both declared that there will be a holiday in her honor. This command is also to be followed in Brea. There will be a holiday in her honor in every town and kingdom that owes its allegiance or alliance to the Brea. Also, I must travel to Aradon to pay my respects to our fallen comrade. I would ask that you accompany me, but I know the situation is still tenuous."

Aryx nodded, looked up as if to speak, and then remained strangely quiet. Aryx was not the kind of man that guarded his words or took a second of refrain before saying what was on his mind. For a man such as this to stay silent was both disturbing and unexpected.

"Perhaps the time for my reemergence has been pushed forward your majesty. Things are about to change in this world, and the war against Shau-ling is going to begin again. Pike also knows that this is true, and I imagine that he will not attend Elwyne's funeral, but instead he will head to the south to rally his Enforcers."

Midarin nodded and sighed. She knew that what Aryx said was exactly right. There were secret marching orders for the Order of the Sword as well, and Pike had entrusted them to her years ago when Logan left his final requests with Pike. There was something that Logan knew about the war that was to come, and he wanted to make sure that if anything happened to him, the battle would not go badly for the forces of Light in his absence. Midarin's hesitation prompted Aryx to clear his throat loudly, and the sound shocked Midarin out of her thoughts and back to the situation at hand.

"I'm sorry Aryx, this news about Elwyne hits me harder than I expected. She was a very strong woman, and a valiant warrior for the forces of the Light, it is a shame that she could not be here with us to see the next part of the battle."

"Perhaps it is better for her that she is not going to see the war Midarin," Aryx countered, some of the formality ebbing from his tone. "Unlike Pike, I am not looking forward to this war. I fight because it is my duty to do so, not because I want to. Elwyne did what she did because she was in love with Logan. No matter what anyone else said, that was the only reason that she stayed with the group. Then, when he died, things were too difficult for her alone. She did not want help, and she would not allow anyone to help her because of that damn stubborn streak."

Midarin laughed and then smiled. Aryx was right, and she knew it. Slowly she rose from the throne and walked toward her chambers. Aryx hesitated for a moment, and then after a quick look back from Midarin, he strode forward and then matched her stride.

"So," Midarin said as she started to open the door to her chambers, "are you going to be traveling with us this time, or should I make arrangements for another escort?"

"I will be going with you my Queen," Aryx replied quickly, "but right now I am more interested in what you know about the plans that Pike has for the Enforcers and what you intend for the Order of the Sword to do in preparation for the coming war."

Midarin could not suppress the heavy sigh.

"We will get to that momentarily my good friend," Midarin replied, "but right now I need to make plans for our travel. Pike has most likely sent Cairyn and the girls in his stead to Aradon. With Cairyn there, it complicates the situation immensely. Liette will have to go on to Sador to meet up with Pike, and so I will put her with a company of guards and members of the Order as I have promised Pike."

Aryx gave Midarin a long sideways look and then stopped waiting for a response to his silent question. Midarin had begun gathering her things from her chamber and did not realize for a moment that Aryx was just watching her. When she looked up and saw those eyes glaring down at her, she sighed, straightened, and then withdrew a parchment from drawer that stood open before her.

"I know that look Aryx, and you know that I don't like it one bit. This deal was made long before you ever showed up, and at the time, it did not seem important enough information to let you know what was happening."

"Not important information?" Aryx fumed. "You were going to give part of my army away and you didn't think that it was important enough to tell me?"

Midarin waited for a moment until Aryx had started to calm down and then she started speaking in a calm even voice.

"Aryx, listen to me. There are a lot of things going on that very few people realize. The Order of the Sword is not an army that was intended to battle the forces of the Shadow on its own. Brea was the perfect training grounds and had the finances necessary to pull off what we did. Pike contributed to the effort, as did Logan. With the help of a few other sources, like Jerrard, we were able to put together your army. However, to get this kind of backing, I had to promise pieces of the army to our benefactors. Really though, most of it should be split up. Pike and his Enforcers will get a small portion, while most of the rest will be split between the Lion's Mane in Marcwell, and the detachments of the Army of the Dragon that seem to be scattered just about everywhere. There will be a small force kept here as a home guard, but once Pike's plan goes into effect, there won't be much of a reason to defend."

"What do you mean?" Aryx did not like the sound of that statement, and he was afraid that Pike was further over the deep end than he had originally believed.

"Pike has heard rumors from his spies in the fringe kingdoms that the forces of the Shadow have been seen lurking around, building their forces. He has determined that Lakestone would be the most logical place for them to strike. That was their first striking point in each of the last two generations, and if they are coming back, and they are on the fringe, Lakestone would be an easy target. Besides, that would put them in good striking distance from Marcwell and from Scalla. Those are two kingdoms that the phasia would love to get a hold of. The Enforcers are going to check out Lakestone, and then they will engage if they find any trace of the phasia or the beasts of the Shadows."

Aryx shook his head.

"That is a suicide mission Midarin," Aryx said as he paced back and forth across the floor of her private chambers.

Normally Aryx was much more reserved than this, but this time was an exception to the rule. Aryx was very much animated in the way that he moved, and his voice had a very passionate quality to it.

"In the last generation, the monsters of the Shadow only struck Lakestone to warn Cedric that the time was drawing close. They were baiting him, mocking him with their obvious repetition of the first generation's war. When Arathorn came back from Lakestone, he found that very little of the town was damaged, and there was no sign that anything but a pack of bandits had been there. However, as they turned and started back toward Marcwell, a large group jumped them and there was an incredible fight. Only Arathorn and a few members of the group made it out alive, and all of them were wounded. Taron knows that Pike is looking for him, and it is a very safe bet that the forces of the Shadow and the Brotherhood have been around for quite a while. I still find it hard to believe that Logan Ranthall just died. I know that there was no wound and that there was no indication that anything happened, but a man like that, with or without his powers, doesn't just die. A member of the phasia killed him, and they have been watching everything that we have been doing since their rebirth. Somewhere, Shau-ling is just sitting back laughing at us."

Midarin looked at him, watching the fire in his eyes as he pleaded his case. The fact of Logan's death had been haunting all of them, and no one yet had been able to reconcile for themselves that what had happened to Logan was a natural thing.

"There is no way to stop Pike from what he's intending," Midarin said as she sat down on the edge of her bed. "You know that Pike Rhuiden is the most stubborn man on the face of the planet when it comes to what he wants, and I have found that revenge makes him even more unbearable. If there is even a chance that Taron is in Lakestone, he would walk there naked through a desert with his arms tied behind his back just for a chance to spit in Taron's face. So, whatever you propose we do Aryx, you had better not count on Pike going along with it."

Aryx nodded finally. He knew that Midarin's portrait of Pike's passions and stubbornness were accurate if not understated.

"Then it is just as well that he would send Lissa and Sabrina with Cairyn. Nathaniel and Gwillim can travel with us, and then we can look for Wolf while we are in Aradon," Aryx offered finally.

"Wolf?" Midarin asked.

"I know that Emries said that Logan and Elwyne's son would not have the powers of the *Coromor* in this generation, but that does not mean that he will not have some kind of power. It could be just our luck that we might stumble onto another member of the *Erieal*. Besides, Logan and Elwyne might have given the boy some knowledge that could be useful to us. I don't know what that could be, but you never overlook any possibility when you are dealing with a member of the Ranthall family. They always tend to surprise you."

Midarin considered for a moment, and had no choice but to accept Aryx's logic.

"Point well taken. Well, after what you have said, I don't think that I will be sending Liette to Pike's side. I will have to chance her coming with us. You get Nathanial and Gwillim together, and we will ride for Aradon this afternoon."

"As you wish my Queen."

Aryx bowed and then turned sharply on his heels to leave.

"Are you sure that Pike is walking into a trap?"

Aryx stopped, looked back over his shoulder and just looked at her.

"I'll take that as a yes," Midarin said shortly.

Midarin turned to gather some more of her things.

"I hope you said all of your good-byes."

Midarin stopped and looked back at Aryx who had turned around and was starting back toward the throne room.

"I also hope you didn't expect him to be anything other than what he is."

With that he was gone and the door was closed behind him. She knew that the tears would start again any moment. She would be faced with the situation again. She would again have to live with the child of a father lost to the ravages of war. And while she did not know for sure that Liette was Pike's daughter, it felt right in her heart.

Past Becomes Future

Creator's Calendar Year 1205; Dark Mirror

Gwydeon and Midarin just sat there for a moment in shocked silence looking at the man who could not have been Pike Rhuiden, but who could have been no one else. The man standing before them looked no different than he had when the quest was begun all those years ago in the little town of Aradon. He had been a charter member of the group Logan Ranthall gathered, and many times he proved that he was the true power and leadership of the group. Many times his powers and his tenacity had saved the lives of all of them, and it seemed as though luck was on his side. That luck however had run out in the throne room of the mad god Shau-ling. He was trying desperately to stop Nightwing from doing any more damage, and he paid for the attempt with his life. At least he took Nightwing down with him. Pike waited in the doorway and didn't say anything. The look on his face was one of determination, not joy or sorrow. It was as if he was just waiting for the shock to die and for his friends to come back to their senses. Soon enough, Gwydeon pushed back the confusion and helped Midarin off of his lap as he stood. With a wave of his hand, Evan bowed and closed the door behind him as he left. Both Gwydeon and Midarin approached Pike slowly, trying hard to believe that the man who stood before them was Pike. Pike said nothing and just waited. Suddenly, a smile leapt onto Gwydeon's face, and he wrapped the larger man in an embrace that lasted for only a matter of moments before he stepped back with the smile still very apparent.

"If you're not Pike," Gwydeon said scratching the back of his head lightly, "than you've got the best disguise that I have ever seen."

"It's me alright Gwydeon," Pike replied, "but for a minute I wasn't sure that you were you. Besides, you've gotten a lot older since the last time that I've seen you, and those gray streaks were not in your hair when we fought together before."

Gwydeon laughed and went back to sit down in his chair behind the war room table. Midarin joined him after a moment, and Pike sat in a chair across from them after a motion from Gwydeon.

"Yes Pike," Gwydeon commented, "I suppose that I do look older, but you don't seem to have changed a bit. You've still got that awful beard, and you look like you've worn the same clothes for a week."

"Well, it was either keep the beard or shave with my axe. I have a lot of faith in my skill, but my neck is just a little too valuable to me right now. As for the clothes, well, lack of money tends to make a person do what they have to for survival."

Gwydeon nodded and rubbed Midarin's back softly.

"Yes, survival makes you do some strange things. Midarin and I have been surviving out here for a few years now, trying our best to hold off the phasia and their raids. Sometimes it seems like they're going to get through our defenses, but then the tides turn, and they go scrambling for the hills with their tails, or whatever, between their legs."

Pike nodded and looked down at the ground. Midarin nudged Gwydeon in the ribs and pointed insistently at Pike. She wanted to ask Pike about where he had been for the past twenty-five years, and Gwydeon seemed to be avoiding the subject entirely. The silent argument went on for a moment, and then when Pike looked up, it was silenced completely. Pike smiled and let out a small laugh.

"The world sure has gone to hell without me hasn't it?"

Gwydeon just shook his head and locked his eyes on his long lost friend.

"Where have you been Pike?" Gwydeon questioned, his eyes never leaving Pike's. "When we all saw you and Nightwing fall down that column of Blaze, we had pretty much written you off. There was no way that you should have lived through that. We had hoped that the explosion we heard also destroyed Nightwing."

Pike sat there silent for a moment, as if going over things in his mind. He knew there were a lot of questions for him to answer, and they would not stop with Gwydeon and Midarin. Everyone who knew him that was still alive would want to know what had happened, and he wished that he had more answers.

"I still don't remember exactly what happened," Pike began, his voice betraying the confusion of his mind trying to piece together events. "We were all there in the throne room, and things were pretty much falling our way. Logan and Korrd were keeping Shau-ling off balance, and it looked like it was just about over. While we were jabbering with Shau-ling about Cedric, I saw that there was a huge piece of metal just standing behind the throne. Then later, when that huge column of Blaze opened up, my mind went back to that metal slab, and I thought I could use it to try and block the flow. I know it probably wouldn't have lasted more than a minute, but that would be one minute that Shau-ling would be distracted and not trying to kill us with every breath. But, I forgot about Nightwing. I think we all did. That shot that Korrd and I gave Nightwing should have been enough to destroy him, but for some reason, he lived. I guess Aryx was just too stubborn to die. As I was trying to use my powers to make that piece of metal tumble over, Nightwing had gotten up and started flying at me full speed. He hit me from the side, knocking the wind out of me and making me lose my grip on my powers. The next thing I know, I look over my shoulder and see us hurtling toward the Blaze. By the time I regained enough of my wits to try and fight him, it was too late. We hit the fires of the Blaze at full speed, and I felt the burning run through me."

Here Pike paused, a grimace of phantom pain coming to his features. The following words were filled with a visceral gut-wrenching clarity.

"My lungs and brain were on fire, but my grip on my powers seemed to intensify. I struck Nightwing as hard as I could, and manage to dislodge his grip. At the time he was in no position to do anything about me, so he tried to extend his wings to get out of the fall. A quick shot of my powers froze his wings, and he kept falling down the column. There was not much left for me to do, so I just kept a hold of my powers and tried to create a sphere of ice around me to absorb some of the fire. At first, I couldn't keep enough of a hold of my powers, but then after focusing as much as I could, the shell started to take form. The battle between the flames and the ice kept growing more vicious as one would seem to have the upper hand, and then the other would battle back with more intensity. Then the explosion went off below me. Suddenly this wave of power hit me and I lost consciousness. When I woke up, I found myself lying on a slab of rock just outside the mountain cave where we had entered the palace on the Island of Mist."

"To be honest, I didn't recognize the place at first," Pike continued after a long sigh, "but when I saw Blood Lake, I knew that I was still on the island. I'll tell you, the thing that threw me the most was the fact that the mist was no long above the island, and there were actual living creatures other than Jeresei and Shadowwalkers that were roaming around. Unfortunately, I didn't have any food, so some of the little creatures found themselves being roasted on a spit for my dinner. When I saw that the boat was gone, I figured that you guys thought I was dead and left the island. So, over the next few days, I started to fashion a raft and store up enough food to make it back to land. I almost didn't make it. The day I ran out of food, I made it to shore, but it wasn't the shore that I remembered."

Pike shifted in his seat and sat back. He did not seem to be very comfortable, but when he started scratching his beard, he looked as if he was trying hard to remember exact detail.

"Scalla was just as we had left it, burned to the ground and there were still pyres burning everywhere. I started toward what looked like a camp, but I caught a familiar motion out of the corner of my eye and managed to get out of sight before a band of Jeresei came walking by. I was going to attack them, but I looked and saw that the camp I was heading for was made up of all Jeresei, Kalbraks, and a few Stone. I waited until dark, and then made my way through the forests. By day I hid and slept, and by night I traveled. When I made it to Marcwell, I stopped short when I saw Gwillim's head on a pole, and the fortifications being manned by members of the Army of the Shadow. I tried to think of someplace to go that I would be safe and that I would find allies. I almost went to Trelon before coming here, but I decided that I would take the chance on finding a still alive Gwydeon, and a very much alive Midarin. When I saw that Gwillim was dead I feared the worst, but apparently my fears were not reality."

Gwydeon nodded and waited for a moment to see if there was anything more to the story. Right now that was all it was, a story. In his mind he hated the fact that he could not take Pike's word for his whereabouts, but the tale was just a little too convenient, and Gwydeon could tell by a look from Midarin that she was thinking the same thing. Pike looked up at them and then spoke again.

"I know it sounds a little hard to believe, and if I were in your position, I probably wouldn't trust me either. But I tell you this, but if I wasn't me, would I have gotten past your 'sniffers'? Where did they come from anyway?"

"He's right Gwydeon," Midarin said after a moment, ignoring Pike's question. "The sniffers can feel any member of the phasia, or anyone that has been touched by the Blaze. Remember how crazy they went when Gideon was here. Even though he was a member of the *Erieal* in our generation, they were still able to pick up on his phasia blood. Maybe we should give our old friend the benefit of the doubt."

"Well," Gwydeon said trying to suppress a smile, "as I recall, I owe Pike for saving my life once, so, I suppose."

"As I recall," Pike countered, "I saved your life twice."

Gwydeon and Pike both laughed, and Midarin joined in after a moment. Laughter was rare in a world ruled by the forces of evil, and moments like these were ones to be treasured. It was this fact that prompted Pike's next series of questions.

"What the hell happened, and how long have I been out of it?"

"Twenty-five years," Midarin said trying hard to cushion the blow, "almost twenty-six now."

Pike just stared at the two of them for a moment, trying to form the concept in his mind. Gwydeon nodded when his eyes caught Pike's and after a long few moments of adjustment, Pike swallowed hard and continued questioning.

"So I take it your son has been born?"

"Oh yes," Midarin replied cheerfully. "Nathanial just turned twenty-five. He continues to practice with his powers, but he doesn't even have the kind of mastery that Logan had. It is kind of tough for him, as neither Gwydeon nor I can help him, but if we can hold off the advances of the phasia for just a few more years, we think we may have a shot."

"What happened to this world?" Pike asked shaking his head. "I thought that things would be easy with us still around."

"That's just it Pike," Gwydeon replied, "we weren't around for long. You were in the column of Blaze when things really started to turn in Shau-ling's favor. We killed him, but not before he killed Korrd. After the fight we were all a little broken and bruised. Midarin and I decided to come back here to take over for her parents. Gideon made up his mind that he was going to rebuild Scalla. Logan changed a lot after we left the palace. I always thought that he was self-absorbed before the quest, but after he watched Elwyne die, he became more distant and started hiding from everyone and everything that threw responsibility his way. He went back to Aradon and shut everything out. It was a long time before we heard from him again, and it was not until years after the reemergence of Shau-ling and his followers that he started to take a role in the war."

"How long have they been back?"

"The first raids started almost twenty years ago, and the phasia were seen not too long after that. But what surprised us was that none of the phasia that we knew were the first to appear. This new member of the Brotherhood called himself Draven. To tell you the truth Pike, if I had my choice, I would have rather dealt with any of the others. Draven is so evil that he exudes it. There has never been a battle that when he took the field, he was defeated. Everywhere he went, another kingdom fell, and he claimed more power. The first major piece fell when he destroyed Scalla."

"Gideon had gone back to Scalla to rebuild, and he started that by claiming Erika Mystic's hand in marriage," Midarin continued. "Erika agreed, and the two of them were able to create a steady kingdom after a few years. It was going to be very solid after the birth of their first child Taya, but things would go downhill from then on. The raids were starting, and it was obvious that Draven wanted Scalla for his own. He claimed that he was the rightful heir to the throne that Basille once sat upon, and he would not let a tainted ruler sit on his throne any longer than was absolutely necessary. It only took a few years of constant battering before there was no more of Scalla left to defend. Gideon was able to get away with his infant daughter, but Erika was not that lucky. She was executed in front of her remaining subjects as a show of force. Most of them were quick to fall in line under Draven's rule."

"But that wasn't enough for him," Gwydeon countered. "Draven wanted to prove himself to the other members of the phasia and to Shauling. The target that he wanted was Logan, which was obvious to everyone. However, a few years into the raids, Logan got fed up with the killing, and he cast his lot into the war. He gathered his things and walked all the way to Trelon and asked to see Queen Cairyn. Cairyn had suffered from the effects of the war, and she was not much of a ruler. As compared to her mother, Cairyn was just a little girl when it came to matters of the court. She had married the son of a weak lord in order to cement a military alliance. He was only around long enough to get Cairyn pregnant, and then in the first raid on Trelon, he got himself killed by getting too close to a Jeresei. When Logan showed up, she eagerly accepted him into her court, and from what we have recently heard, she also accepted him into her bed. Cairyn's daughter is growing up quickly, and with Logan in Trelon, the Army of the Dragon is bound to rise again. Draven knew that he would be taking a risk if he hit Trelon, so as is the way of the phasia, he decided to be a little sneakier. He set his sights on Aradon as the target of his next raid."

There was a look of shock on Pike's face for a moment, and as Midarin continued the story, the look turned from shock to a kind of sorrow.

"The raid would have been a complete slaughter had it not been for the fact that we found out about it. Neither Gwydeon nor I thought that we would be able to repel Draven's army, but for Aradon, we had to try our best. Both of our armies took the field, and it looked as if we might have a better chance than we initially thought. The first day of the battle, we turned away most of the invaders, but as the sun began to set, it seemed that the enemy grew more powerful, and their advances were pushing deeper into our defense. Before long, they broke through our line, and we were just fighting desperately for our lives. Up until this time, Draven had not done much but oversee the battle, but when the fighting began to get hot and heavy, he interjected himself. One by one he cut down all of the soldiers that he faced, and after a moment, he was deep into our lines. By this time we were incredibly outnumbered, except in the category of dead and wounded, and we were about to retreat. Draven had gotten close enough that he could see us, and he called Gwillim out for a duel. As much as Gwydeon tried to stop him, Gwillim would not listen and he was drawn out to battle the phase. The battle was over quickly, and Draven stood over the headless body of our son. With a laugh, he stole the Sword of the Ram from Gwillim's dead hand, and then claimed Aradon for his own. We had too many dead and wounded to stop him, so we retreated and let Aradon fall."

The expression of pain on Pike's face was obvious, and as much as he wanted to admonish his friends for not fighting harder, he knew that they had done everything there was to be done.

"Since then," Gwydeon said with a very soft and pained tone, "we've been stuck here in Brea trying to stay alive. Our allies have all fallen, and between us and Trelon, we are the only kingdoms still standing who oppose the rule of the phasia."

"What about Marcwell?" Pike asked shortly.

"Jeroch wanted Marcwell so bad that he could taste it," Midarin replied. "He sieged that castled for weeks until it finally fell under the sheer power and number of his forces. He claimed it as his birthright as the first born member of the Brotherhood of phasia. As a show of his new found power, he had every single peasant in the kingdom brought to him. They were ordered to swear their undying devotion to him, or they were killed. Each peasant that lost his life because of his stubborn devotion to the way of the Light was hung on a pole outside of the city. That was why you saw Gwillim's head. Jeroch considered it his trophy, not Draven's. Slowly, the population of Marcwell is disappearing, and they are being replaced with Jeresei, Kalbraks, and Shadowwalkers. However, as far as we know, these peasants are dying of natural causes. Jeroch has put them all to work building what he calls the 'Black Tower'. The tower stands where the old palace of Marcwell used to be, and it glows with a power that you can see for miles. Our spies have never even gotten close enough to tell us how many entrances there are. Marcwell is even more well-guarded than it was when Cedric was in control of it. What we've been able to uncover is that this tower is where the monsters are coming from. People go in and creatures come out."

A look of horror came to Pike's face, but Gwydeon continued.

"You asked about our 'sniffers'. It seems that not all of the people who go into the Black Tower come out as creatures. Those changed humans that come out are used by the phasia and the armies of the Shadow to sniff out those with power so they can be quickly and easily eliminated. That is how they hope to hunt down the *Chosen One* and the remaining members of the *Erieal* of this generation. We were able to smuggle a few out of Marcwell for our own protection, but it was at a cost I don't like to think about."

Pike nodded, understanding the need for secrecy. If people knew the truth about the Black Tower or the fate of the people of Marcwell, it would either paralyze them with fear or cause them to do something reckless like attempt a siege. Either choice played into the hands of the enemy, and Pike didn't envy the kinds of decisions that Gwydeon and Midarin had been forced to make just to survive this long. When they were together they had only been forced to fight a war for a little over a year. Now Gwydeon and the others had found themselves embattled for almost two decades in a war that looked very much like it was unwinnable.

"So we are the last ones," Pike commented.

It could have been taken as Pike giving up, but Gwydeon and Midarin both knew better. Pike saw a challenge.

"Not exactly."

At Gwydeon's response, Pike perked up a little.

"For the last few years, I've been rounding up stragglers who are sympathetic to the cause of the Light. These men and women have become a rather formidable fighting force, and in the end I think they are the biggest reason that we are still alive. Some of them I'm sure you will remember from the army of Rama. Sol and Ebios were two of the generals that followed us in the war against Rana. Also, Rachel Core, an archer from the Army of Brea joined us. Evan Sinn, from the kingdom of Sarmeel is also on our side. Slowly we have put together an army that I think can not only launch an attack against the forces of the Shadow, but I also think we can win and hold our ground."

"Not only that," Midarin added, "I wouldn't count out Gideon Viruci. He may have lost a kingdom, but he was always a thief, and I know that he can survive out on his own. Before too long, I know that we will hear from him. Then there is always Logan."

"I'm afraid not Midarin," a voice said from the entryway.

During the conversation, none of the three friends had heard the door open. Evan Sinn had stood there for a few moments waiting for an opportunity to bring in the news that he knew no one wanted to hear.

"Evan," Gwydeon said looking up at his one-armed ally, "what are you talking about?"

"We've just received word that the forces of Trelon have taken an assault from a member of the phasia. From the descriptions of the army and the events that followed, there is no doubt that it was the Army of the Crow."

"What was the result of the battle?" Gwydeon asked, already knowing what the answer was going to be.

"Trelon has fallen my lord," Evan said despairingly, "Lord Logan is counted among the dead. Draven challenged him to a duel, and Logan was enveloped in a bolt of lightning that Draven called down upon him. No one saw Logan walk away, and there was a burn mark were the body used to be."

Despair filled the room, but it did not touch the still youthful Pike Rhuiden.

"What about the sword?" Pike asked after a moment.

"What?" Gwydeon asked.

"If Korrd didn't make it out of Shau-ling's palace, I would figure that Logan would have taken the Dragon Sword. I mean, I know Logan. The sword was given to him first, and he is not the kind of person to just leave something like that behind."

"Yes," Gwydeon replied thinking back, "Logan did pick up the sword. What's your point Pike?"

"Evan, you said there was nothing left of Logan, only a burn mark."

"That's correct sir," Evan replied puzzled, "there was not even his armor remaining. It was concluded that anything he was in possession of at the time, including his sword was utterly destroyed."

"Ah," Pike said smiling, "but that's where you're wrong. If you knew anything about the powers of that sword you and your spies would have never made that determination. Gwydeon, you and I both saw Korrd block an attack from Shau-ling with that sword, and I don't think that a single blow from this Draven character would be enough to vaporize the Dragon Sword."

"You're right as usual Pike," Gwydeon replied. "Evan, post a watch and make sure that all refugees are searched by the sniffers tonight. Chances are that Logan will make his way here if he can."

Evan bowed and turned to leave the room. Gwydeon stood after a moment and then motioned Pike over to the table where the model for the raid still stood.

"Do you recognize this old friend?"

Pike looked down at the map for a moment and then regarded the tree lined path that led to a palace at the heart of the city.

"Sador."

"Right. My army is going to hit Sador and take possession of it. Our spies were able to get perfect maps of the paths through the woods, and we have a plan that cannot miss."

Pike looked down at the map and looked at the placement of the different regiments and then frowned.

"It is a good plan Gwydeon, but I only see one thing that you have forgotten about."

Gwydeon looked at his friend insistently for a moment and then looked back down at the map.

"What?"

Pike pointed to the southern gate and then to a place in the northern wall.

"If you position your archers where you are planning, you will be able to cover the western gate and the southern gate. That cuts off reinforcements from there. But, if you remember, when we were in Sador, there was also a northern gate that had a full barracks. I notice that it is not here on the map, but I remember it as if it were yesterday."

Gwydeon's blood ran cold.

"By the Light, Pike," Gwydeon said looking at the map hard again, "you're right. That little holding army there was not enough to stand up to a forward assault, but it never needed to be. With the western and southern gates hidden by the forest, the real forces of Sador were able to flank their opponents and they would never knew what hit them until it was all over."

"And," Pike said pointing at the route that Gwydeon had plotted through the forest, "if you go through on this route, you will be able to counteract the southern and western gates, but the garrison and whatever other troops are there will be able to get behind you and rip you to shreds.

It would only be a matter of time until they got to the archers once your rear flanks were occupied."

"But the scouts gave no indication . . ." Midarin started.

"Is there a member of the phasia in that castle?" Pike asked.

Gwydeon nodded.

"We think so."

"It is not outside one of their abilities to make a gate disappear for one of your scouts. Besides, you know as well as I do, that there is no way that a member of the phasia would not know that you are scouting out his territory. He may not think anything of it, but that doesn't mean that he won't make sure he has the upper hand if anything does come of it."

Gwydeon nodded again.

"We have to rework the plan."

Just then the door to the war room burst open, and Evan Sinn followed by several men in black robes flooded into the room. Each of the men were armed, and they all looked nervous.

"Evan," Midarin chided, "what is the meaning of this?"

"My apologies my lady, but the sniffers have detected a portal forming here in the war room."

Gwydeon grabbed his sword off of the war room table and readied himself for a fight.

"I never thought that the phasia would stoop to attacking like this. They were always more inclined to attack with incredible numbers rather than sneaking in. They like for everyone to know that they beat you at your own game."

Suddenly, a whirling blue portal appear in the roof of the room, and out shot a form. The body slumped to the floor and was instantly surrounded by black robed men with swords pointed directly at it. The form stirred slowly, and as soon as Pike got a good look at the man, he parted the group and grabbed the man by his arm and rolled him over. Logan Ranthall had looked worse, but not by much. Logan roused after a moment, and when he looked up into the face of the man who held him he smiled meekly.

"Hi Pike," his voice was weak and raspy, "you weren't the first face I expected to see when I got here. Where's Elwyne?"

With that he passed out.

Chapter XXVII

First Blood

Creator's Calendar Year 1205; Light Reality

Wolf sat by the fire, gazing silently between the three women seated across from him. Their introductions had been brief, and there had not been much conversation between the four of them since. As it was, Wolf felt discomfort knowing that he was only a few feet away from the Queen of Trelon, the very person that he so desperately wanted to see. However, now that he was here, he had no idea what he was going to do. It was as if part of him never expected to get this far, and now that he had, he was out of his element. Part of him fully expected to hear Basille's voice ringing though his mind, but that voice never came. As Wolf looked back across the faces of the women, he caught a glimmer of light from the girl named Lissa's eyes. She had been the one that he saved from the bandit. To say that she was beautiful would probably be an understatement, but it was her strength that caught him the most. From the stories that his mother had told him over the years, he found a respect for women who could protect themselves, and really in his eyes, there was no other way that a woman should live. On the battlefield, there were no genders, and if you died, it was because you were not strong enough. As Wolf cautiously eyed Lissa, making sure that she did not notice him looking at her, he concluded that Lissa was a very fine warrior. She seemed to have an edge to her that Wolf found very comforting. In some ways, Lissa reminded him of his mother, but there were stark contrasts between the two. Besides the obvious, Lissa's hair being red and her eyes being green where Elwyne had brown hair and blue eyes, Wolf had always thought that his mother exuded a quiet kind of power that she could soften with her voice and with certain looks. Everything about Lissa spoke of authority and strength. Even when she was obeying the wishes of the queen, it looked as if she did it for her own purposes, not merely because it was an order.

The night progressed on without further incident, and when the others decided to try and sleep, Wolf sat silently on the other side of the dying fire and pondered the situation that he had just stumbled across. He was only supposed to get here, there was nothing in Basille's words that ever prepared him to go the rest of this alone. Maybe the whole scene with Basille had been a dream. Perhaps though, there was a blessing in the confusion. From what Wolf had been able to piece together, his father never had a choice in his future, it had been written for him before he was even born. Wolf had been spared that inescapable fate. Had he wished it, he could have stayed in Aradon the rest of his life and known nothing of the war between Light and Shadow. The uncertainty could have been seen as a comfort. Wolf shook the thoughts away as he focused his gaze back on Lissa. She was snuggled up tightly in a blanket trying to keep warm in the advancing autumn coolness. Wolf had grown accustomed to the temperature though his many years working the fields for his mother, and the cold didn't touch him regardless of the light shirt and pants that he wore. Inwardly deciding that the fire needed some more wood to keep his new companions a comfortable temperature, Wolf silently quit the fire and moved off into the woods to gather some more firewood. After collecting a bundle, he turned back toward the makeshift camp and found that he had an audience. The fiery-haired beauty that he had been so intently watching for the last few minutes had turned the tables on him and now had her eyes locked on him without his knowledge.

"Kind of disturbing," she remarked quietly moving closer to him, "not knowing that someone is looking at you, isn't it?"

Wolf did his best to hide the embarrassment, but the red creeping into his cheeks betrayed his attempt at a calm appearance. As the two stood there looking at one another, the silent questions kept floating back and forth between them. Wolf smiled and tried to laugh a little. The nervous laughter hit Lissa's ears and she smiled in response.

"I'm sorry for staring," Wolf responded the next moment. "I just found you very beautiful and . . ."

Wolf closed his mouth and silently cursed himself for speaking what his mind was repeating. He had never been able to hold his tongue when it came to the emotion tainted thoughts, and at this point in his life everything with him was emotion. As he thought about it, he was surprised that he was able to hold his tongue when he was finally introduced to the Queen. Part of his openness could be credited or blamed to his mother who constantly spoke of harnessing emotions rather than repressing them, and the more one was in touch with emotion, the more powerful one would eventually become. Aradon was also an extremely close-knit community, and it was rare to not know everything about someone, and so hiding anything was often out of the question. Whichever was the main culprit however mattered little. He would have to learn to temper his words, or he would never be able to claim a tactical advantage over any opponent.

"You are rather handsome yourself Wolf," Lissa responded with that same smile on her face.

It was the kind of smile that tried hard to hide the true emotion in the eyes. If Wolf had only known her better, a fact that he would try hard to remedy, he would have been able to see the uncertainty and the unfamiliar uneasiness that permeated Lissa. The two of them stood there for a moment and just took turns looking at one another and then to either the forest or to the ground. It was Lissa that was the first to break the tense silence.

"I can understand you being a little hesitant to talk around the Queen, but now that she is asleep I would hope that you would open up a little more and tell me who you are. If I didn't know any better I would say that you were the leader of those bandits and you killed them off just so you could get close to us. If that were so, you could easily kill the queen or the princess without much of a thought."

"Why would I have to get that close," Wolf countered without thinking, "you have seen my skill with the bow. I would have had enough clear shots that I could have taken out both the Queen and the Princess and yourself before any of you knew what was happening."

Wolf found himself shocked at the words that had just tripped from his tongue. It was as if a part of him he had not known was there suddenly took control of his mouth and spit venom at the pretty girl that stood before him in an effort to wound her with pure spite. But as Wolf stood there he was not sure what shocked him more, the words from his lips, or the wide smile that hung from Lissa's. After a moment the smile became a quiet laugh.

"I knew that I could trust you Wolf," Lissa said after a moment. "You are far too honest to be an assassin or a thief. Why don't we sit and talk for a while, unless you're tired."

"No, I'm not tired," Wolf said motioning to a spot deeper in the forest. *Besides, I have the rest of my life to sleep and only a few chances to be alone with a beautiful woman like you*, his mind added.

Lissa smiled in response and followed his lead to where a fallen tree had splintered into several pieces. Wolf and Lissa sat across from one another and waited in silence for a moment before Wolf finally spoke.

"You and your sister don't look very much alike," Wolf commented. "And you don't look much like the queen either."

Lissa laughed to herself, and then spoke.

"Well, that is an interesting way to start a conversation. But in answer to your question, I was adopted by the queen and her husband when my parents abandoned me."

"Oh," Wolf said his eyes dropping to the ground.

"Do you have any family?"

"No," Wolf said after a moment, trying to hide the hurt of his mother's recent death. "Both my mother and my father died a long time ago, when I was just a baby. My uncle has been raising me here in the forest, but he passed away not too long ago."

"Does that mean you are from Aradon?"

"No," Wolf responded trying not to sound too defensive, "my parents were from Kandor, and my Uncle used to live in Illimar, but he thought it was too busy and noisy so he moved out here to Logan's Wood. He thought he would be able to live a peaceful life, but he never counted on having to raise a son."

"I see," Lissa said looking dead into Wolf's eyes.

He tried not to flinch or to give any indication that anything was wrong. But it was no use, he felt his grip on his will slipping and if she kept looking at him with those soft green eyes he would never be able to keep up the charade. For a moment he wasn't sure why he lied, especially a lie that he would not have been able to continue under any kind of scrutiny. He should have kept his lie closer to the truth. He could have said that he was from Aradon, and simply substituted himself for one of the other young men his age. Lying, like controlling his emotions was certainly not his forte. Suddenly there was the sound of several snapping twigs coming from deeper in the forest. Lissa reflexively whirled toward the sound and reached for where her sword would have been had she been wearing it. Silently cursing herself for not having her sword, she turned back to Wolf.

"We should go back to camp," she said shortly, "there's no telling how many more bandits are out here."

"Funny," Wolf said after a moment, "you didn't strike me as the paranoid type. We're perfectly safe out here. After all it is Logan's Wood."

"Paranoia and preparedness are close cousins," she countered. "I like to be prepared."

Lissa did not take any reassurance at Wolf's words and looked back toward the direction the sound came from with an uneasy stare. Wolf could feel the tension radiate from Lissa as she sat staring into the dense forest. She kept rubbing her left hip like a part of her was missing, and Wolf could only imagine that she wanted her sword and that she did not feel safe without it. After a moment of hesitation, Wolf stood and started to walk in the direction that the sound came from. Lissa saw Wolf as he passed, and clutched his arm as he started to stride past.

"Where are you going?"

"It was probably nothing," Wolf said calmly, "but that doesn't mean we shouldn't check it out."

Lissa rose from the log that she was seated on and followed Wolf as he walked toward the source of the sound.

"Is there something about you that I should know Wolf," Lissa said as lightly as she could manage. "Do you have a hero complex or something?"

Wolf just looked back in her direction and smiled.

"Or a death wish," Lissa mumbled after the fact.

The pair walked cautiously through the woods trying to look at everything at once, and not miss anything. In the darkness of the wood, Lissa felt alone and isolated as if there were going to be attackers jumping at her from every angle all at once. Wolf was a little calmer than his fiery-haired companion. He knew this place like the back of his hand, and he had been running through these woods since he was a boy. From the markings on the trees and the condition of the path, he knew that they were coming closer to Mirror Lake, a lake in the very center of Logan's Wood. Unlike most of the lakes in the area, Mirror Lake had no wildlife living beneath its surface, and very few animals came there to drink. It was not that the there was something wrong with the water, but it was as if something was special about it. Wolf motioned for Lissa to follow close as he ducked under a tightly packed group of branches and made his way down an unmarked path which was a more direct route to Mirror Lake. It may not have been the source of the sound, but it was a more private place for he and Lissa to continue their "talk".

For another few minutes, Lissa and Wolf walked cautiously through the thick underbrush and tightly packed trees. Soon they came to the edge of the clearing that housed Mirror Lake. Both Lissa and Wolf stood for a moment, silent, looking at the beautiful undisturbed waters of Mirror Lake. Not even the evening breeze seemed to stir the waters, and it was a truly beautiful sight. Lissa may have been absorbed in the beauty of the lake, but Wolf's eyes were focused on a different wonder. Standing on the very edge of the water was a woman dressed all in green. She was beautiful to look at to say the least, but even at distance, Wolf could feel the danger radiating off of her. Her brown hair flowed to the top of her mostly bare shoulders. The green dress that she wore sparkled in the moonlight, and the shimmering of the material was reflected in the waters of Mirror Lake. The dress clung tightly to the curves of her body, and the moonlight seemed to accentuate every curve and feature. Her bare arms were folded under her impressive bosom. Her eyes, though not clearly visible from where Wolf was standing, were obviously searching around for something. Finally Lissa tugged on Wolf's sleeve and brought Wolf's attention back to her. From the look in her eyes, it was obvious that Lissa was angry about something. After a silent inquiry, Lissa pointed to the woman in green and then pointed toward Wolf's sword. Wolf hesitated for a moment and then handed his sword to her. For some reason, Basille's voice had not yet come to him and he wondered why. But there was something in him that told him that Lissa was right in her actions. As she was about to burst through the forest and charge the woman in green, Wolf spotted a flash of motion out of the corner of his eye. Wolf turned his head to see a human size, red skinned thing duck into the forest near where the woman in green was standing. Wolf grabbed Lissa by the arm and held her back. Wolf pointed to the forest in answer to Lissa's angry question, and was greeted by the downward slash of sharp red claws.

The force of the red-skinned creature's strike was enough to send both Wolf and Lissa reeling. The claws did not strike either of them directly, but the threat was enough to send them to the forest floor. Lissa recovered after only a few seconds and was able to get her sword up for a strike against the enemy that hovered over them. Her short thrust was enough to send the beast jumping backward, but it did not surprise it enough to draw blood. As she struggled back to her feet, Lissa took another slash at the beast but missed wildly. The years of training had led Lissa to this moment, her first live combat against forces of the Shadow. As the monster dodged each and every attack that Lissa launched at it, it appeared as if it was laughing at her. Its face was very much human in appearance, but the features of the face were so impossibly sharp that it appeared to be much more demon than human. This was furthered by the two small round horns that protruded from the top of the thing's head. It wore a large smile on its face, and the bright white teeth shone in the moonlight and gave it a much more evil visage. Wolf had just dragged himself to his feet as Lissa charged the beast again. Her strike was easily parried by the razor-sharp claws of the red-skinned thing and the beast answered with a strike of its own that sent warm red blood flowing from Lissa's right shoulder.

The plume of blood surprised both Lissa and Wolf, and as Lissa toppled to the ground in pain, she screamed in a mixture of both agony and anger. The scream rang out through the forest and everything seemed to stop for a moment. The woman in green that Wolf had been watching out of the corner of his eye stopped looking for whatever it was she was searching for and started walking toward him. From the purposeful way that she was walking, Wolf could have sworn that she knew exactly where he was. As Wolf turned to try and help Lissa, he saw the thing hovering over her laughing. Lissa was down on her knees holding her right arm close to her as if trying to take away some of the pain by cradling the wounded appendage. The haughty laughter of the beast could be heard clearly, and before Wolf could jump the larger creature, he saw more flashes of movement all around him. More of the red-skinned creatures had appeared and closed in on the source of the scream. If Wolf moved now, he would surely be cut down by one of the others. As he scanned the forest, he could not get an accurate count of the number of adversaries. All he knew was that there were more of them than he could handle. The red-skinned beasts formed a circle around the three of them and appeared to be waiting for something. Lissa had not moved an inch and sat there trembling under the watchful eye of her attacker.

"What have we here?" said a melodious voice from behind Wolf.

Wolf didn't even have to turn around to know that the woman in green was standing right behind him. He could feel her moving closer to him and could almost smell the sweetness of her skin. The hairs on the back of his neck stood up as her hand brushed across his back and came to rest on his right shoulder. She looked at him steadily for a moment but his eyes never turned to meet hers. It was as if she was not looking at him, but rather she was looking through him. Her hand left his shoulder and then he saw her cross in front of him and walk over to where Lissa lay. Her walk was purposeful, and she did not even acknowledge that the red-skinned beasts were even there. She knelt down beside Lissa and put her hand on the bloody wound on her exposed shoulder. The fabric had been ripped away by the strike of the beast, and the remaining material had become soaked and matted with her blood. The woman ran two fingers lightly down the length of the wound and pulled her fingers away covered with hot blood. She looked at her soaked fingers and scrutinized the red liquid that dripped from her nails. After a moment of seeming reflection, she slowly slid the fingers into her mouth and closed her eyes, obviously savoring the taste. After a moment of sitting there with her eyes closed, the woman stood and motioned for the Jeresei standing over the fallen young woman to back off.

"So, the two of you thought you would be safe in Logan's Wood? Fools. When the Lord of the Shadows returns to this world, all parts of the world will belong to him and unless you are one of his chosen, you will be doomed for eternity. The blood of mortals will wash the world clean of all remnants of the *Coromor's* stench, and the rule of the kingdoms of this pathetic world will fall to their proper rulers, the phasia. Now, the two of you are intruding in my wood, and I want to know why."

Wolf did not look at her and continued staring at Lissa who had stopped shivering and appeared to be inching her hand toward her belt, and the dagger that she had concealed there. Just as Lissa began to draw the dagger from the hidden sheath, the woman dug her claws into the open wounds in Lissa's shoulder causing her to scream in agony and drop the dagger onto the ground. The woman did not remove her claws, but bent down to retrieve the lost dagger.

"I'll give you one more chance before I start carving you two up. You have no idea how aroused the feel of blood against my skin makes me. I cannot stand the feel of water against my skin, so I have to bathe in blood. You have no idea how many people I have to kill before I can fill my bath with enough blood to make it worth the trouble. And the trouble with blood is that it only stays warm for a short time. So the kills must be done near the time that I want to take a bath."

The woman dug her nails deeper into Lissa's flesh and twisted them as she turned back to face Wolf. Lissa's scream faded to a whimper as the pain rocketed through her and threatened to make her slip into unconsciousness.

"I like to lie in a bath as the bodies hang above me and drip their lives onto my naked body. It is a feeling that I cannot describe and it is the one of the most intense pleasures that I have ever felt in my life."

She ripped the nails from Lissa's wound a second later and instantly plunged the fingers into her mouth. Her eyes closed again as the taste seeped into her mouth. After a moment there was an audible swallow, and then a large smile crept onto the woman's face and her green eyes sparkled in the moonlight as the pleasure of the taste filled her. The display through, she regarded the dagger in her hand and walked over to Wolf, stopping just in front of him and looking directly into his eyes. It was a battle of wills. Wolf stood trying hard not to look directly into her eyes but rather just stare through them. His will stayed firm, and her eyes bored into his soul but could not delve as deep as she wanted. Her gaze then traveled from his face down his body. One of her long nails traced the lines of his muscles through his shirt and seemed to find every nerve. He could feel the nail digging into his flesh through the light material of his shirt, and he knew that if she were to press any harder that she would draw blood. The finger slowly traveled down the length of his chest and then stopped at his stomach, right above his belt line. His breathing grew erratic as the woman's finger was replaced by the tip of the dagger. The sharp point repeated the motions of her nail as it worked its way down to his stomach.

"But there are times," she said softly, "when one of those that I mark as my blood donors excite me in another way. These lucky men and women get a very special honor."

Her voice was soft now rather than piercing and evil. The point of the dagger no longer touched his body at all, and he waited, still tense for what was about to happen next. He was in no position to take any action at all, and something told him that there was something far more dangerous about this woman that her exotic taste for blood. Her references to the Lord of the Shadows could only mean Shau-ling. That meant that she was either a member of the phasia as Basille was, or one of their children. Wolf had yet to see any evidence of power, but that did not mean that she didn't have any. The fact that she was with these beasts was almost enough to secure the fact that she was a member of the phasia.

"These men and women are hand-picked by me to help me with my bath and to make sure I am in a constant state of pleasure. They get to touch me and make love to me in any way that they think will keep me at the pinnacle of pleasure. Then, just as I am reaching the very heights of arousal, I have my pleasure slaves ripped open and their blood poured all over me."

Wolf could feel his stomach churn as her description filled his ears. His mind filled with disgusting images, and he shut his eyes trying hard to shut away the thoughts. Again the dagger pressed to his flesh. He could feel the cold steel blade press through the fabric of his shirt and threaten to cut him.

"Perhaps you could be one of my pleasure slaves my little boy."

Wolf's eyes snapped open and found that the woman was no longer standing in front of him, but had sunk to her knees and was eyeing the dagger as it slid back and forth across his abdomen.

"That got your attention . . ." she said softly looking up at him.

" . . . and you got mine," Lissa screamed as she rose to her feet and clutched Wolf's sword hard in her left hand.

"Ah," the woman said as she stood again and turned to face Lissa, "so you do have some will after all. Maybe you have what it takes to be one of my slaves as well."

"I would rather die than fuel your sick and twisted desires. If you want my blood you bitch, you better take it yourself."

The dagger dropped to the ground a second later, and a bolt of power erupted from the woman's hands and claimed Lissa in the chest sending her sprawling to the ground. The front part of her shirt was charred black, and small wisps of smoke rolled from the burnt patch. The woman laughed softly to herself and turned back to Wolf with an evil grin on her face.

"Is that the best you can do?" a voice groaned from past Wolf's field of view.

"You poor deluded girl," the woman said without turning around, "there is no way that you can hope to match your feeble pathetic skills against the powers of a member of the Brotherhood of Phasia. Rane Larion may be one of the youngest of the phasia, but I still have more than enough power to pound you into the ground without much of a thought. If you wish to throw your life away and not have the honor of serving me as a pleasure slave, it is your loss."

"That is all I needed to hear. . . "

That next second, a burst of light came from somewhere behind the woman. Rane screamed out in pain and toppled to the ground. The back of Rane's dress was burned to a cinder, and the skin underneath was a bright red. As Wolf looked back to where the blast of light and apparently fire came from, Wolf saw Lissa standing, leaning on her sword, with one hand extended. On the extend hand danced the remnants of the fire that had been launched into the member of the phasia. The red-skinned beasts faltered for a moment, and then began to advance on Lissa. Wolf ran to her side and tried to support her and defend her at the same time. He may not have been able to do much against the savage creatures, but it might have been enough to save her long enough to do some damage to the advancing ranks. Just as the first wave of attacks was about to hit, Rane screamed in the most terrible and horrific voice that Wolf had ever heard. The shrill scream echoed through the forest, and the beasts stopped in their tracks.

"You know the law Jeresei," Rane said as she pulled herself to her feet, "no one touches one of the *Erieal* but one of the phasia."

Rane walked toward Wolf and Lissa slowly, her eyes filled with a different look, one of anger, hatred, and power. She wanted to avenge herself against the upstart attack of the little red-haired girl, and she was ready to flay the skin off of her bones with her own fires if need be.

"You wish to use your petty power to challenge the might of a member of the phasia little girl? So be it. Prepare yourself for battle . . ."

Family Ties

Creator's Calendar Year 1205; Light Reality

The forest seemed to grow darker as the tense seconds ground past. Lissa and Rane were face to face and waiting for the other to make a move. Wolf could not tell if Lissa was frightened or if she was so consumed by anger that she could not think straight. It was clearly going to be a fast and frantic fight, but as to who would be the victor, Wolf could only guess. He knew from what Basille had told him that the phasia were very powerful. However, in Wolf's mind, Lissa had the advantage. She had been able to surprise the phase, and Rane had no idea the amount of power that Lissa did or didn't have. Basille had not told Wolf much about the group known as the Brotherhood of Phasia, but what Wolf did know was that they were all very evil, self-absorbed, arrogant, and powerful. The fact that Rane was here and looking for something meant that it was worth the time of one of Shau-ling's elite to come, on their own, to look for it. It was either a weapon to use against another member of the phasia, or it was something that was important enough that it would change the balance of power in the war between the Light and the Shadow.

"You don't really think that you can beat me do you little girl?" Rane taunted. "I will make you feel pain in places that you didn't even know that you had."

"Phasia flesh burns as easily as human flesh Rane," Lissa said in answer, "I just hope the smell isn't as putrid as your disposition."

Lissa's tone was one of mocking hatred. From the moment that Rane admitted that she was a member of the phasia, Lissa's whole posture changed. It was as if Rane's existence was an affront to Lissa's whole life. It was true that the phasia were an abomination to say the least, but it was almost as if Lissa were prepared to take on all of them at the same time just to prove a point.

"I will enjoy drinking your hot blood after this is over little girl." came Rane's venomous reply.

Just at that second, a bolt of red electricity arced from the extended hands of the phase and raced toward the injured mortal. Lissa raised her hand to her chest in the next instant, and a field of white lightning appeared around her and when the bolts of electricity struck the field, there was a bright flash of light, and Lissa stood where she had been in the moment previous without any other wounds upon her. A smile had crept onto her lips, and as Wolf looked back at Rane, he saw the look of disbelief painted there.

"That's impossible," Rane stammered as she looked first at her hands and then back to Lissa. "Only one person should be able to do that, but he's dead."

"Aryx Terian has a legacy Rane," Lissa said proudly, "and while he may not have been there to train me, I do have his powers and the knowledge to use them."

That second, a ball of fire jumped across the distance between the two combatants and enveloped Rane. The phase screamed in pain, but after a moment or two the fires were extinguished.

"Lightning is just not my style though." Lissa added.

Rane glared at Lissa and then straightened and let a truly evil laugh burst forth. She showed no obvious scars from Lissa's attack, but when she focused her eyes back on her prey, it was clear that the phase's attitude had changed. The playfulness that was in her eyes was gone, and there was this look of death blazing between the two of them.

"So, you do have some power after all, don't you little girl? I will enjoy watching you die, writhing in agony before me. Playtime is over child, I will show you the true essence of power."

With that a ball of black energy leapt from what seemed like the very heart of the female phase and flew across the distance with incredible speed. There was no way that Lissa had time to erect any kind of defense, and from Rane's words, it seemed as if there would be no defense strong enough to stop this latest assault. Just as the ball of darkness was upon Lissa, a bolt of white lightning erupted from the brush near Mirror Lake and the ball of darkness dissipated. Rane turned around in time for an arrow to zoom past her ear and claim one of the Jeresei in the throat. The Jeresei fell, and as the others tried to react, Rane waived them off again, and watched as the new players in her little game emerged from the thicket.

The new arrivals from their appearance were very experienced adventurers. All of them, save one. As each of the new players entered the scene, Lissa's face lit up, but when the last emerged, a black shroud fell over her features, and the hatred in her eyes magnified. The first through the wood was a woman. She was of average height, and her long brown hair trailed behind her in an exquisite braid. However, besides her figure and her face, nothing else of her spoke of femininity. She was dressed in a man's pants and shirt, and on her hip she wore a sword. There was a single strap of leather that cut diagonally across her chest which was attached to a quiver of arrows that was slung tightly to her back. The bow in her hand was simple-looking, but as the moonlight glinted off the gold which was flaked all over the length of the bow, it became obvious that it was a prized treasure. She quickly nocked another arrow after bursting onto the scene, and trained it directly on Rane.

Two men followed quickly behind the woman. The first was older than the woman and had a dark brown beard that was neatly trimmed and cleaned. His sword was held close to his body, and his eyes scanned everywhere, marking all of the directions that an attack could come from. His armor, while once most likely a bright red, had faded to a more dull crimson. Wolf noted that the change could have come from being bathed in the blood of ones enemies, but that seemed to him more like the activity of a member of the phasia rather than one who would work for the forces of the Light. The other man was more of a boy than a man. While his build looked developed enough for a man of Wolf's age, his face and eyes still held a boyish glow. At the most he looked fifteen, but it was clear from his eyes that he was much older. Though still he fell in beside the woman and held his sword pointed at a group of Jeresei near the border between the forest and the lake.

Next emerging from the wood was a young girl. At least, her face looked young. Her body was very developed, and her eyes burned with an intensity that Wolf had only seen in one other place in his life, Lissa. The girl's hair was light brown with some wisps of blond strewn in here and there. The sword that she wielded looked too large for her, but she hefted it like a sword master. Her body was developed for a woman in her late twenties, and her armor did well to show off her rather impressive endowments. Her armor consisted of a small plate of chain which hung like a loose jerkin from her shoulders all the way to her waist. However, the center had been cut open to the middle of her breasts, and she wore a light white shirt only half buttoned over the top of it. Wolf could not help but stare at her for a moment, because her exotic look was enough to be called beautiful.

The last one into the fray was a man who appeared to be about thirty. His blond hair was cut short, and his features were very smooth and flowing. Wolf immediately locked his gaze on the man's eyes. While Lissa and the young girl seemed to share an intensity in the eyes, they both pales in comparison to this new addition. Where the man in red armor's eyes obviously moved from opponent to opponent, it seemed as if this man already knew where all of his enemies were and as if he were prepared for any attack that would come from any angle. Wolf had to look twice to see that the man was wearing armor. There were no visible breaks in the chain mail that he wore, and from the distance Wolf was standing at, the armor itself looked like normal clothing. This was the man that caused Lissa to change her look. Her gaze no longer fell on Rane, and it looked as if she were ready to loose a volley of fire against this man. His sword was still in its sheath on his right hip, and his black cloak flowed behind him in the evening breeze. When he finally spoke, his voice carried a power that could be felt as deep as your own soul.

"You are not welcome here in Logan's Wood, Shadow-spawn. Take your Jeresei and return to your master wherever he is, or we will be forced to end you."

Rane stood there for a moment, looking in disbelief at the man. Finally she laughed an obviously uneasy laugh and spoke to the new arrivals.

"My name is Rane Larion, interloper, you would do well to mark it and remember it."

Rane took a moment to let her eyes scan across the new arrivals before letting another flurry of jibes hit the air.

"So, the old 'People of the Dragon' have come to intrude upon the business of the phasia again. I would have thought that you would all be dead by now like your sainted Ranthall brothers. Sad that this war has been relinquished to the inferiors. No matter, dead or alive, you have no power anymore to defeat us. This is no longer your fight, and if you knew what was best for you, you would walk away now and let me destroy these pathetic whelps."

Now the woman with the bow stepped forward and began to speak.

"I may not know your face phase, but I know enough about your kind to know that you do not stand a chance against us. Against the combined might of three members of the *Erieal*, and two expert swordsmen, you have zero chance of survival. Now, you can either withdraw, or we can cut you down where you stand. Go back to Shau-ling's throne room and tell him that the forces of the Light and the People of the Dragon are more than ready to stand and fight. If it has to start here in Logan's Wood, then so be it. I can think of no better place for it to start."

"The People of the Dragon," Rane mocked in a sickening-sweet voice, "it does ring very nicely to my ears. You were truly an interesting bunch back then weren't you? First there was your hero, Logan Ranthall, what a fine man he was. Delusions of Grandeur and of Power, nothing can be more crippling than thinking you are greater than you are. Then there was his loving wife, Elwyne Tamerlane. She was a weak little girl who could never own up to the fact that it was the need for revenge rather than her love for Logan that kept her there."

Wolf reflexively tensed as the words poured from Rane's mouth. He could feel a power rising inside of him that he had never felt before, and the thought crossed his mind that he could strike Rane down where she stood.

"Next were the *Erieal*," Rane continued. "Pike Rhuiden, he showed some potential, but after we killed his woman, he lost his mind. So much the pity to lose something you never had."

Now Lissa tightened the grip on Wolf's sword and pulled herself to a more stable standing position.

"Talon Aielin, dumb, arrogant, and dead. Gideon Viruci, he was one of us, but he decided to work for the People of the Dragon, and he got what he deserved. Now he's dead just like his *Erieal* counterpart Arin Domae. Then there was the true hero of the cause, the Dragon himself, Korrd Ranthall. He too was one of us, and for a time he served our brother Saurn in the race to eliminate Logan. But he betrayed us and added his voice to the war cry against my master. The most disappointing of all of these people was Gwydeon Sandar."

The woman with the bow drew the string back tighter and aimed carefully. The man in red armor and the boy also looked as if these words had struck them the wrong way.

"He had such potential for a mortal, but he chose to waste it fighting for the Light. He could have been a member of the phasia, but he was too weak of character. He cared. He fought to protect the innocent rather than subjugate them. Still, he did have a lot of potential. He had the fury in him that it took to stand toe to toe with a member of the phasia and survive. He took Rael and Jeroch both before it was over, and he showed almost perfect tactics against Zarsi's army outside of Sador. It is a pity that he tied his fate to Emries and a slut of a queen."

The arrow flew from the bow before the last word was out of the phase's mouth and struck Rane in the shoulder. Unlike Wolf had expected, that was not a signal for an all-out attack. No one moved but the woman who had fired the arrow, and she only calmly lowered the bow, reached into the quiver, removed another arrow, and nocked it into the bow and reset her aim. Rane only reacted slightly. She tensed in pain and then looked at the arrow shaft which emerged from a bloody spot on her left shoulder. Her gaze continued to fall on the arrow, but a second later, the wooden shaft burst into flames, and the wound was immediately sealed by the searing heat. The Jeresei had not moved from their positions and were obviously waiting for the command from their leader to attack.

"Ah, Midarin," Rane said not looking up, "you still have a temper when it comes to Gwydeon don't you? I'm not surprised. He was a very attractive man for a human, and he had a heat to his blood that was most assuredly rare. I'm sure that he was exceptional in every way. Unless of course that the production of your son was a vile and repulsive torture. Though if it was I'm sure it's because your stock is lacking."

Midarin didn't flinch, and the tip of her arrow remained steady and sure.

"You should watch your tone, Rane," Midarin answered. "My temper takes some time to ignite, but I can assure you that once it does, I will not be satisfied with warning shots. Believe me, I have more than enough skill to put this arrow through your heart, and I'm very sure that it will kill you."

Rane laughed, ignoring the threat and pointed toward the blond man.

"You are the one that I am the most disappointed in, Aryx Terian. You were one of us and yet you were willing to give your life for the forces of the Light. You gave away the gift that Master gave you so that you could live as one of these mortals. How pathetic."

"I don't know you child," Aryx replied with venom. "You were not yet alive when I did my time in that hell that you call service. My body was imprisoned, but my soul was still free. When my chance came to avenge the deaths that I had caused, I took it and never looked back. I was one of the reasons that the forces of the Light defeated Shau-ling in the last generation, and I would like to do it again before I die. I would feel my life had been complete if I could watch Shau-ling die in each of three generations."

Rane tensed, and it looked as if her playful disposition was fading slightly at Aryx's powerful comments.

"I'm just sorry I won't be alive to see Emries and Aerith Seth reborn, and watch them defeat Shau-ling once and for all."

"Enough!"

Rane's voice rang through the forest, and all of the Jeresei sank low to the ground as if they were about to pounce. The scene was quickly becoming ugly, and it looked as if there was going to be a fight after all. Wolf watched as all of the warriors for the Light prepared themselves for whatever onslaught Rane was about to release upon them.

"You have no idea what you are Aryx Terian. Your soul still lies mired in the power of the Blaze and there is nothing you can do to stop it. When Master calls, you will be drawn to his side and you will be forced to do his bidding. And you Midarin Rice, if you only knew what Master had in store for you, you would weep and curse the day that you were ever born. Make no mistake, People of the Dragon, this is not your war, but if you insist on trifling in the Lord of the Shadow's victory against the forces of the Light, then he will have no problem with dispatching you like the pathetic children that you are. Now, I have business to attend to elsewhere. I will leave this band of Jeresei to deal with you."

With that, a swirling blue portal appeared underneath Rane, and she sank through it, her eyes never leaving Aryx's face. As the portal began to close, the Jeresei sprang from their places and started their attack. The arrow that had been trained at Rane's heart now leapt from Midarin's bow and struck one of the Jeresei in the throat, sending it hard to the ground in a pool of its own blood. Aryx was the next to lash out against the red-skinned Jeresei. With his sword raised high, he cried out and charged a group that had leapt in his direction. All Wolf could hear in that next few seconds was the sizzle of lightning and the screams of death as each one of the five Jeresei fell to the ground in pieces. That was the only part of the ensuing battle that would come easy for the forces of the Light.

Lissa dropped Wolf's sword on the ground near him and sprinted across the distance to where Midarin stood. She drew the sword from Midarin's scabbard and held fast behind her waiting for the assaults to begin again. It appeared as if after the initial devastation caused by Aryx that the Jeresei were rethinking their strategy and looking for a different plan of attack. Wolf bent to recover his sword just as one of the Jeresei felt bold enough to strike. Wolf felt the attack coming before his saw the flash of red that was streaking down upon him. What happened next could only be described as a reflex. The Jeresei dove down from a great height, and a foot from connecting its claws with the back of Wolf's neck, a wave of darkness erupted from Wolf's back and collided with the Jeresei. The wave cut like an axe through the body of the Jeresei, and it fell to ground in half, blood spattering everywhere. There was a call from another one of the Jeresei, and several of them surrounded Wolf at once. Now with his sword in hand, Wolf could feel a new power coursing through him. His mind was open to a spheres of knowledge and thought. He could feel what the Jeresei were thinking, and the grunts and screams that emanated from the Jeresei now seemed to form a coherent language of instructions and battle plans. Their thoughts were their language, and all of them knew what the others were doing. Suddenly a pain shot through Wolf's body. It was like lightning had struck his heart and now pulsed down through every vein and artery. As the spasms flooded through his body, his wrist contracted, causing him to lose his grip on the hilt of his sword. It fell to the ground, and Wolf fell to his knees seconds later. As the pain racked his body, he felt as if his insides were on fire and that he was going to explode if it did not stop soon.

Suddenly, there was an explosion of energy around where Wolf cowered in pain. The explosion sent a shockwave of force and heat blasting in all directions with Wolf in the exact center. The shockwave was powerful enough to take the Jeresei off their feet and shake most of the newcomers. Only Aryx and the young woman seemed unaffected. That was when the fires inside of Wolf stopped, but that was also when the rush of power began. As Wolf stood, he felt as if he could move a mountain with his bare hands. As he looked down at where his sword lay, he watched as it floated off the ground and laid itself in his outstretched hand. For the next few moments, no one moved a muscle. Some of the newcomers looked almost as much to Wolf as they did to the Jeresei who were slowly picking themselves up off the ground.

"You will die today Valtamine," Wolf growled in the Jeresei's native tongue. *"You have trifled with the wrong man today."*

The Jeresei looked around puzzled, and as they prepared for a last desperate attack, that was when the battle truly began. From Aryx came the first signs of extraordinary power. The bolt of lightning that raced from his hands claimed a few of the Jeresei, and they fell to the ground as charred remnants of their former selves. Lissa lashed out too, with small globes of fire that jumped from beast to beast, forcing them to the ground as their flesh melted and dripped down their bodies. It was the man in the red armor that made the most devastating attack. He stood perfectly still and then plunged his sword into the ground beneath him. From the point of the sword, a crack appeared in the ground. It raced toward the Jeresei, and try as they might to avoid the growing crevice, it shifted and turned to follow them. Finally they ran out of places to run and fell into the crevice. After the Jeresei had been claimed, the man in the red armor withdrew his sword from the ground and the crevice sealed itself. After these attacks and a volley of arrows from Midarin, only one Jeresei remained standing. It waited near a tree by where Wolf had been standing, and its eyes were focused on Wolf the whole time.

"That must be the leader," Aryx said confidently, "they are always the last to enter a fight."

Wolf looked dead at the Jeresei and pointed the tip of his sword at the monster's face. The Jeresei didn't move for a moment and then began to tremble. The sounds that came from Wolf's throat were primitive at best, but the Jeresei looked at him and answered, his attention completely arrested by the young man.

"I want to know what you are doing here beast. Tell me what clan you represent and what you are doing out here."

The Jeresei hesitated for a moment and faltered. It looked as if it were uncertain as to why this human was able to speak to him in his own language and how he knew so much about the Jeresei. Inwardly, Wolf wondered the same things.

"I am the Elder of the Clan Eurawa. We were ordered to assist Lady Rane Larion in her search for a man here in Logan's Wood. We were not told who she was looking for, but the fact that almost an entire family of our clan was dispatched means that he was fairly powerful."

"And did you find this man?" Wolf asked.

"No," the Jeresei replied. *"We caught his scent when we first entered the forest, but it quickly disappeared. Whoever this man is, he has the phasia ability to hide himself from us completely. All humans give off a scent unless they have the power to disguise it, like a member of the phasia."*

"You have answered all of the questions that I have for you Elder of the Clan Eurawa. I would ask you to join us, but I know that your master's bonding would never permit it. As you are the Elder, you must return and face your failure."

The beast regarded Wolf for a moment, and then turned to leave. Aryx cried out and started toward the creature, but Wolf turned and held his sword pointed toward Aryx.

"I have allowed the Jeresei to leave. Believe me, his fate at the hands of his master will be much more agonizing than anything you could ever do to him."

Wolf could not believe the words that were coming out of his mouth. Somehow he had inherited the knowledge . . .of the Blaze. Basille. Not only had Basille given him the powers of a member of the phasia, but he had given him a link to the infinite knowledge of the Blaze. He could not recall all of the knowledge on command, but when the time demanded him to have certain information, he had it. Wolf inwardly wondered if the flow of information went both ways.

"What do you mean you allowed him to leave?" Aryx questioned, his voice filled with hostility. "He could have given us information as to why he was out here. And who are you to be speaking with the Jeresei in their own tongue and threatening those who have more information about the nature of this war than you do?"

Wolf opened his mouth to speak, but it was Lissa's voice that filled the momentary silence.

"He's no one to be trifled with Aryx," Lissa countered moving to Wolf's side. "I know the people that you travel with old man, and I would have never believed that they would allow a traitor and a scoundrel like you within their ranks."

"Lissa," Midarin chided, "calm down. Your so called friend there was just talking to a member of the Jeresei in their own language, and he is displaying powers very much like a member of the phasia."

"Not much like mother," the young man said, "exactly like. When we arrived I felt the power of Lissa and of the man there, but his power seemed dormant at the time. Now it is fully active, and he glows with Blaze tainted power."

"But so does Aryx," Wolf countered looking into the strings of power in his mind.

Basille's knowledge of the Blaze and of the powers of the champions of Emries was now flooding his mind, and he was trying to put all of it to use before it fled from him again. Lissa radiated with the power of Fire, the man in red armor held the string of Earth, the young man was bathed in the white strands of the *Coromor.* Aryx however had a different look to his string of power. Everything about him on that level seemed to be bathed in a black film. But as Wolf started to delve deeper, he felt a surge of power come from Aryx and Wolf had to break contact.

"I don't trust him," Aryx said coldly.

"And I don't trust you, Aryx." Lissa responded holding her sword up and ready for battle.

"Is that a challenge little girl?" Aryx asked as he drew his sword.

"I'll kill you where you stand if you make any move against him," Lissa responded.

"Then prepare yourself."

"Aryx!" Midarin shouted.

Aryx had begun to move toward Lissa but stopped short when he heard Midarin yell.

"You can't kill her."

Aryx held his ground, but did not lower his blade.

"She is siding with a member of the phasia, or worse, one of their children. I don't care if she has power or if she is a member of the *Erieal,* she can't be allowed to assist that scum."

"Aryx," Midarin said walking toward him, "she's your daughter."

Aryx just stared in disbelief.

"His daughter?" Wolf asked turning to face Lissa.

"I have a daughter?" Aryx finally said.

All Lissa could do was nod.

Chapter XXVIII

Retaliation

Hours had passed since the reunification of old friends in the war room of the Kingdom of Brea, and the Order of the Sword was beginning their preparations to march on the Kingdom of Sador. Ever since the scare of the portal, the generals of the army had been locked in a strategy session revising the plans of attack. What the rank and file members of the Order did not know was that two men had been added to the ranks of the Order, and that the complexity of the battle to come was about to be radically increased. Inside the stone building that served as the throne room of the kingdom, the war room buzzed with arguments and excitement. Gwydeon had called all of his generals to him only moments after Logan Ranthall's arrival, and the assault on Sador was quickly becoming a rescue mission to Trelon. Many of the generals were skeptical about their chances, knowing that they would be facing Draven and his army, but there was no way that they could let Trelon fall without some attempt at saving Queen Cairyn, Princess Sabrina and the rest of the survivors still willing to fight against the falling Shadow. Gwydeon was not about to let Trelon become another Aradon; a losing battle that ended up costing the world a huge amount of ground against the advance of the Shadow, and the loss of a powerful symbol like the last of the Binosear family.

"The front gates and the walls of the town were ripped open like so much paper by the Stone advance, and the Jeresei and the Kalbraks did their normal amount of damage," Logan said quietly, looking down at the map of the city that Evan Sinn had provided. "What bothered me the most then was the fact that there were no Shadowwalkers. But I think I know why that is now."

Pike and Logan had been wrapped in deep conversation ever since Logan woke up. Gwydeon and Midarin were too busy rousing the troops and the generals to get the over-hasty preparations underway to wonder much about what the two old friends had been talking about. Gwydeon had assumed that Logan was asking similar questions of Pike that he and Midarin had, but now, it seemed that there was much more to the conversation than simply "where have you been?" Logan and Pike both stood silent and stared intently at the map laid out on the table. Occasionally one would whisper something to the other, and that would begin a silent battle of ideas. Logan had changed a lot since Pike last knew him, but there was one thing that hadn't changed, the way Logan thought in battle.

"Logan and I have been talking," Pike said finally, "and we think that there is another piece of the puzzle that we have been missing. Most of the raids have been led by phasia, but some of the raids were done at night and caused so much damage that it must have been done by a massive army, but there wasn't one. Also, Logan has told me that there have been a few assassinations in some of the major kingdoms during the war. Now all of you know that the phasia have never been the kind to assassinate anyone and just let the death go. From what Logan has told me, these murders were of fairly powerful members of the resistance, and they just disappeared in the night. That does not sound to me like the act of a member of the phasia that I remember. Some of them would not know the meaning of subtlety if it fell on them. Now, all that I have described sounds familiar, but the thing wears a different name."

Gwydeon just thought for a second before he raised his eyes to Pike and frowned.

"Nightwing."

Pike nodded.

"Just think about it, Gwydeon. I survived my encounter with the Blaze only because I had my powers. Aryx may not have been that lucky, I can't say for sure. However, something like that, a creature like that. Shau-ling built it to be able to kill members of the phasia, built it to be the perfect assassin. Then he made it so that it could contain someone as power as Aryx Terian. That isn't the kind of thing that Shau-ling would just let go."

"It is reasonable to assume," Logan continued, "that if Aryx did not make it off of the Island of Mist alive, that Shau-ling would have recreated Nightwing, but with a different person inside the shell. With all the kingdoms that have fallen, one of the other members of the *Erieal* of this generation, or even the past generation might have fallen under his will. Who knows, as bad as we are being beaten, it could be Arathorn Geoffry under that armor. As Pike said, the phasia don't do subtle, except for maybe Saurn. They like big grandiose gestures, and now that the tide has turned in their favor, they are more interested in sniping at each other and gaining as much territory and power that they can. That can't be done quietly. They want each other to know who is the biggest and the toughest."

Gwydeon shook his head and sighed. He had been keeping some things to himself for a long time, and now it was time for the truth to finally come out.

"I had a feeling that this was going to come out into the open, and to tell you the truth, I am not too surprised that Nightwing lives, however, I don't think that he is alone anymore. I remember standing on the battlefield in Aradon after our forces had started to flee. I turned around to look one more time at where Gwillim fell, and I saw something in the sky. At the time, I just passed it off as nothing, a trick of my mind, but now that I think about it, I saw them."

"Them?" Logan asked. "Them who?"

Gwydeon stood silently for a moment and then began to speak. His voice had a low tone, and it seemed that he was straining to remember exactly what it was that he saw.

"Up on the hill where the old church stood was a group of people that I had not seen before, or noticed during the fighting. As I said, what caught my eye was something hovering in the air, but it was too massive to be Nightwing, and it did not gleam as if it were made of metal. The wings were like that of a bat, and it had what looked like the body of a bull, just five or six times bigger. As I looked at the hill, I saw a group of figures standing there as well. I can't tell you what they looked like, but I could make out four separate forms, and maybe a fifth, but I can't be sure."

"A phantom army?" Ebios said quietly. "That sounds like what struck Rama before the first days of the siege that leveled the Twin Towns. It blew in with such strength that nothing could stop it, and most of our army was decimated in only a few minutes. But they were killed in their sleep, and no one saw a thing until it was over."

"The carnage was incredible," Sol continued, "and most of the men lost the will to fight after they saw what had happened to their comrades. Before, the armies of the Shadow were frightening, but we saw that we could kill them with our swords, and take a few shots with our armor and our shields and still fight. Jeresei, Kalbraks, Shadowwalkers; we could fight them, we could kill them. Even the phasia despite their powers were still enemies that we could fight. They were mortal after a fashion. We knew that Gwydeon had stood up to their best and killed him in one on one combat, and that made us almost fearless, but this, this wind of death that blew though us like wheat before the scythe was different. This was an enemy that we couldn't see, let alone fight, and it killed whatever it came across. Most of our men were so scared that when the real siege came, they ran. When some of the members of the Army of the Dragon started to break and run, we knew the battle was over."

Logan hung his head for a moment, and then as if a fit of temper leapt through him, he pounded his fist on the table and drew the Dragon Sword from his scabbard.

"It doesn't matter what it is. Cairyn and Sabrina need our help, and we have to save them before Draven does something unthinkable. Knowing Draven, I can only expect that he has already killed Cairyn and has trapped Sabrina in her bedroom. It will only be a matter of time before he has taken her to bed forcefully and started his bid to become the father of the next generation's *Coromor*."

Gwydeon could feel Logan's anguish and pain radiating through his voice, but the man was distraught and not thinking clearly. Gwydeon needed to ensure that Logan's grudge didn't get them all killed.

"It does matter what it is Logan," Gwydeon countered. "If this phantom force does exist, and if we leave to go on a rescue mission to Trelon, we leave Brea open to an attack. My point-defense can handle an assault by the army of a member of the phasia, but I don't know if anything can handle the destructive power of what Sol or Ebios describe."

"I agree with Gwydeon," Pike commented. "As much as I would love to take a huge army into Trelon and watch as Gwydeon's army work their magic on a group of Jeresei, it's too much of a risk. Trelon is not that important."

"But Pike..." Logan interrupted.

"Wait 'till I'm finished," Pike chided. "However, we can't just let Cairyn, Sabrina, or the others just die. Anyone we save is another person who can fight. And, Draven can't be allowed to control Sabrina's fate. Back in the 'old days', a small group was able to do some pretty amazing things when they knew how each other thought and how they would react. I think that a small group could break into the palace of Trelon, steal the princess and the queen, and get out without too much trouble. Now, if no one has any objections, I think that the group should consist of: Logan, because he knows the palace better than anyone, and once we get Cairyn and Sabrina he can open a portal to get us out, Gwydeon, because he is the best swordsman here and if there is any fighting he can handle himself, Midarin, just in case we need some extended range, and myself, because of the powers that I still have left and my deep seated loathing of the phasia. Besides, I'm expendable and it was my idea."

"Sir," Evan Sinn spoke up after a beat, "I agree that this is probably the best plan to save the queen and princess . . ."

"Thank you," Pike interjected.

"But I have to question the personnel chosen," Evan continued. "To risk both you and Midarin is very unwise my lord, and if the mission were to go badly, then the resistance would be seriously crippled. No offense intended Lord Dragon, but the gain is not worth the risk."

Logan's fist tightened around the hilt of the Dragon Sword, but before he could speak, Gwydeon spoke up.

"I believe it is Evan," Gwydeon countered, "you have to look at the bigger picture. What is at risk here is the next generation's *Coromor*, and the *Chosen One* of this generation. We know, thanks to Gwillim's death, that we can't kill Shau-ling once and for all in this generation, so we need the *Coromor* in order to survive. Without Sabrina, our chances dwindle incredibly. Now, the phasia and Shau-ling still don't know that Nathaniel is the *Coromor*, and they think that they will break our backs and destroy the Light's chances if they kill Sabrina. Draven's agenda to overthrow Shau-ling may buy us the time we need to rescue her and her mother."

"But shouldn't at least one of you stay?" Evan persisted.

"I have to agree with Evan," Midarin said as she sighed.

"What?" Gwydeon asked turning to face his wife.

"Nathaniel has been training and fighting well with the Order, but when the battle changes and he needs to face down the phasia and stand against Shau-ling, he needs one of his parents to make sure that he continues down the right path, and that he has all of the knowledge that we have accumulated. Logan had Aryx, Nathaniel needs someone to guide his path. If he were to lose both of us, he would most likely be crippled emotionally and mentally and he won't be much good to the forces of the Light when the time comes for him to insert himself in the war. Or worse still, it might make him vulnerable to one of the phasia. If someone like Saurn could get his hooks into someone as strong-willed as Korrd, think of what he could do to a broken young man traumatized by this nightmare."

Gwydeon frowned, but Midarin put a reassuring hand on her husband's shoulder.

"This is our kingdom Gwydeon, and the people have gotten used to having us in control. I'm afraid to think what would happen to the morale of the army if they were to lose us both. So, I will stay behind and send Rachel in my place. She will be able to help you as much if not more than I will."

"I would be honored," Rachel said after a moment.

"I don't think it's a good idea to send a girl in your place Midarin," Pike replied strongly.

The red-haired Rachel shot a look of disgust at Pike.

"And why not?" she asked hotly.

"I know I've been away a while," Pike said moving toward the girl, "but I still know what it is like to fight the phasia where any wrong move could mean your death. I lived like that for a while and it is fresh in my mind. In situations like that, you have to know how your companions will act in a second's notice, even less. You have to think just like your companions, because if you don't, in that second when you are figuring it out, someone will rip your heart out and serve it to you. That's why I chose who I chose. Granted it has been twenty-five years, but I know Logan, Gwydeon, and Midarin. I know how they think in combat, and I know how they will react to certain things. We were a team for a long time, and we have been to hell and back again. Gwydeon may have fought with you Rachel, and he may know you that well, but I don't and neither does Logan. Not only does that unfamiliarity put you at risk, but it puts us at risk too."

Rachel smiled and leaned against the table looking dead at Pike.

"I know you Pike, probably better than anyone in this room. I know how you think, I know how you fight, and better still, I know what drives you to do what you do. There is nothing that you have ever done that I don't know about, and I am willing to bet that your recklessness and anger in battle would get us killed long before my reaction time would. Now, if you have a problem with me personally, I suggest that you put it aside and do what you said you could do, or stay behind and let the real warriors do the fighting."

Before Pike could retaliate, Gwydeon cut him off.

"What do you think Logan?"

All this time, Logan had been sitting rather quietly on the other side of the table just watching. He had a slight grin on his face, and as he looked back down at the Dragon Sword, he stood and extended his hand to the young fiery woman.

"Welcome to the people of the Dragon, Rachel, it is good to have you with us for this mission. Oh, and don't let Pike get to you, he is always like that."

Pike let a low growl slip past before he bit his tongue and turned away from the woman and focused his attention on the map which lay before him. Seemingly unbothered by Pike's reaction, Rachel took Logan's hand and shook it firmly once before withdrawing her hand and straightening.

"When will we be leaving my lord?" Rachel asked after turning to face Gwydeon.

"Whenever Logan has the strength to use a portal to get us close to the palace."

Logan looked at Gwydeon crossly for a moment and then sighed. Gwydeon knew that Logan did not like to use his powers except in extreme circumstances, and only if he was defending what he loved. Even then it pained him and made him feel uncomfortable. Logan blamed Elwyne's death on a lot of factors, and the fact that he was the *Chosen One* was one of the top two. He hated both Emries and Aerith Seth for what he had become, and he hated his own powers, and sometimes himself for the fact that Elwyne was dead. Every time that he used his powers, he was reminded that even with the power that he had, there was nothing that he could have done to save the woman that he loved more than life itself. Power had a price, a price Logan to that point had been unwilling to pay. He would have rather given up every ounce of power for just one life. Now, Logan had to once again depend on powers he did not trust to save the lives of people who could never survive without him.

"The longer we wait," Logan said slowly, "the more time it gives Draven to do what he wants to do. I don't know how long he will stay in Trelon, but if I know Draven, he will want to gloat a while before he goes back under whatever rock he crawled out from beneath. The more he can taunt Jeroch with his successes, the happier he is. We have to use that tendency to our advantage. Whenever my team is ready, I'm ready."

Rachel lifted her bow and quiver off the ground and slung them both over her shoulder.

"I'm ready, Lord Dragon," she replied proudly.

Logan tried his best to smile. He was still very uncomfortable with that title, and he knew deep in his heart that it really wasn't his. Korrd had been the Dragon of the prophecies, but the title was given to Logan first by Aryx Terian, and then by Cedric Binosear in a public declaration. No matter what the truth was, the whole world would remember him as the Dragon, and never remember the fate of the true *Coromor* of the second generation.

Gwydeon took a moment longer to respond to the question. He drew his sword, regarded it for a moment and then returned it to his scabbard. He kissed Midarin on the cheek and then strode over to a large wardrobe that held most of the maps and charts that Gwydeon had collected over the years. When he opened the doors, a few of the loose scrolls and maps tumbled onto the floor, but Gwydeon ignored them, and instead reached for an unseen latch in the far right wall of the wardrobe. He then dislodged the front half of the wardrobe revealing a secret compartment behind the mass of paper and parchment. There, in that hidden niche was a red suit of armor that everyone recognized as soon as the glint of the moon reflected off its fine polished exterior. The breastplate and shoulder plates were stained bright crimson, and had an eerie glow in the moonlight. Engraved in the breastplate of the armor was a dragon, etched and filled with gold. Gwydeon took only a moment to regard it before he slipped it on and buckled it down. Gwydeon now took on a much different appearance than he had a few moments earlier when he was standing at the war room table.

Gwydeon had always been a strong looking man. One could see the outlines of his muscles through his shirts, and he trained harder than any other man in his army to stay in top physical condition. It was said that his workout sessions were both inspiring and painful to watch. Gwydeon was notorious for working those around him to the point that they would collapse from exhaustion, and he would just keep going until he himself threatened to pass out. But now, in that armor that was made for the man who by all rights should have been his son, Gwydeon looked ominous and powerful. If the expression on his face would have been anything other than the sorrowful remembrance of his fallen child, he could have easily passed for a member of the phasia.

He turned to the wardrobe again and retrieved two more items from the hidden niche. The first was a sword. When he drew it from the scabbard, it glistened as though it had been well taken care of over the years, and from the figure on the blade, everyone knew that the sword was very old. The sword had the figure of a springing lion on the blade that was flaked with gold so that it shown above and beyond the polished silver of the blade. The hilt of the sword showed two lions sitting back to back, each with their two front paws extended to from the cross below the blade. He put the sword back into the scabbard and then strapped it to his hip. The next item brought a smile to Pike's face. The axe was no sooner out of the wardrobe before it was put back into its proud owner's hands. Pike's smile beamed as he held *Fury* in his hands once more. The ax had been a present from Lord Cedric on the occasion of their visit to Marcwell all those years ago. It was a double-headed, double-bladed war-axe that had a dragon etched into each side of the blades. Pike remembered that when Nightwing collided with him as they tumbled back toward the column of Blaze fire, that the axe became dislodged from his belt and clattered to the floor just as the two of them entered the flames. Pike had not felt whole all this time without the axe, and he had grown very attached to it during the time that he had it.

"I think Pike is ready," Gwydeon commented aside.

"Why did you save this?" Pike managed to ask.

Gwydeon sighed and then smiled.

"That ax saved my life many times in all of the battles we were in Pike, and I wasn't going to let it be destroyed as the palace caved in around itself. At the time I thought you were dead, so I took it and brought it back with me so that I could have a personal memorial to one of my best friends. That is the same reason that I kept Gwillim's armor. It reminds me of him, and it reminds me of why it was given to him. Korrd saved Gwillim from the Light Keepers here in Brea when they found that Gwillim was trying to sneak a sword into town. Gwillim was wanting to join up with the Dragon when he arrived because he felt drawn to the battle. He was fooled, like most of the people, into believing Saurn's prophecy that the Dragon would come to Brea and rule over the people. We didn't know it at the time, but Saurn was right and Korrd was ruling the people. Anyway, Korrd saw the guards taunting Gwillim and he started to get angry. Then the guards chained Gwillim to the city walls, and set him on fire for treachery. Korrd had had enough of the display and he extinguished the fires with his powers, startling the guards. Then he waded through the onlookers and rescued Gwillim from the Light Keepers and wrapped him up in the Dragon Banner. Gwillim didn't know what was happening at first, because people were falling to the ground all around him bowing and scraping at his feet, but he soon realized that it wasn't his feet they were groveling at, it was at Korrd's. So, when the wise men here in Brea got wind of Korrd's actions, they made this armor for Gwillim, denoting him as the Dragon's personal champion and his right hand. I keep it for both of them, and for remembrance of all the things that happened to us along the way when we followed the Dragon into battle after battle."

Logan winced.

"I know you hate that name Logan," Gwydeon continued, "but you were as much the Dragon as Korrd was. It didn't matter to us that you weren't the *Coromor*, it mattered that you believed in that what we were doing was right. And even after you learned the truth, you continued the war and you fought. We would have stood behind you even if you weren't the Dragon. And I think we proved that. The world may not know the truth Logan, but for those of us who do, it doesn't matter. If you wanted to lead another strike on the forces of Shau-ling, I would follow you. I would and have followed you into the bowels of hell and come back again, and for that I will always respect you."

Logan's eyes had not turned away from Gwydeon since he began speaking. The words of his old friend filled him and he felt a new confidence that had been lacking over the last few years.

"I know why you stayed out of the war this time," Gwydeon said as he walked over to Midarin and took her hand, "and to tell you the truth, I probably would have done the same had it been Midarin and not Elwyne who was killed there in Shau-ling's throne room. I didn't lose any respect or confidence in you when you did not fight, and I knew deep in my heart that when you were ready, that Ranthall pride inside of you would push you back into the fray. It took you longer than I expected to tell you the truth, but I am glad that you took up the sword rather than being slaughtered when Draven decimated Aradon."

Pike's eyes dropped to the floor and he winced. That was the part about the war that he had not yet been able to cope with, the fact that his home and his family no longer existed.

"Is there anything at all left?" Pike asked quietly.

"Most of the town burned to the ground, and those inhabitants who did not run when the first wave hit were killed," Midarin answered somberly. "Most of your families made it out, but only a few of them made it here. Your father is among their number, but he died defending Brea in one of the sieges by Jeroch's army."

Pike seemed unfazed by the news, except for the fact that his chest swelled with pride at the mention of his father's bravery.

"But one thing does still stand," Gwydeon said after a moment. "Though the church was burnt down by the forces of the Shadows, the old book still encased in its glass box on the stone pedestal is still right where it was. No matter what the phasia or the Jeresei or anything else tried to do to it, it remained just as it has been for as long as any of us can remember."

Everyone was silent then. The old book in Aradon was one of the man mysteries that still floated around in the world. The vault of Scalla, the Heart of the Dragon, and the Temple of the Light were myths that everyone talked about as signs of possible hope and salvation, but the rumors were becoming fewer and farther apart, and hope was slowly dying.

"We better get going."

Gwydeon took a deep breath and nodded at Logan's statement. Pike hefted his ax, and Rachel readied her bow.

"Here we go."

The next second a whirling blue portal appeared in the center of the room. Logan was the first one through followed quickly by Rachel and Pike. Gwydeon lingered for a moment looking deep into Midarin's eyes and then entered the portal. Midarin inwardly wondered as the portal faded away to nothing if this was the last time she would ever see her husband alive.

Infiltration

Creator's Calendar Year 1205; Dark Mirror

Pike found himself in what he would ordinarily called a bad dream yet again. From their position high on a hill overlooking the capitol city of Trelon, Pike could see the watch fires of the new military force that occupied the castle as well as the remnants of the city. The city walls had been broken down to their foundations, and those that still stood looked as if a stiff breeze could have turned them to powder. The castle, once white and proud in its purity, was now stained black by the filth of the Shadow, and appeared to be bending and twisting in agony to the will of Draven, the most contemptible of all the phasia. Detachments of ten Jeresei guards patrolled the winding streets and alleyways of the city looking for survivors of the siege. These patrols were also a way to discourage armies of other members of the phasia from attempting a quick invasion. It had been the tactic of some of the more cowardly or shrewd, depending upon the viewer's prospective, members of the phasia, to wait until another member of the Brotherhood took a target kingdom and then launch a full-scale assault on the depleted and ill-prepared occupying army. As one of the frequent perpetrators of that tactic, Draven was not about to let one of his fellow phasia beat him at his own game. As Pike surveyed the situation below, the axe in his hand seemed to pull him away from the crest of the hill just as a patrol of Shadowwalkers zoomed over the hill and circled back to the palace, their errand seemingly done. The presence of Shadowwalkers disturbed Pike. Logan had mentioned that there had been none during the initial assault of Trelon. Draven must have summoned them as soon as the battle had been concluded in an effort to quickly consolidate his position. Either that, or they had been there the entire time, and this creature Draven was so arrogant to feel that they were unnecessary. As Pike turned back toward where the encampment had been laid, his heart was heavy and his mind spun with nightmarish visions. How many of the other cities that he remembered being in just to him days earlier had been decimated in this same fashion? How could anyone have conjured the will to continue fighting in the face of such utter devastation?

Gwydeon met Pike at the edge of the encampment and upon sight of his old friend's face, he knew that the news was not good. They had expected the city to be guarded, but when they arrived, they were immediately surprised by a roving Jeresei patrol. The combined efforts of the group were able to take down the feral warriors before they were able to send up a cry for reinforcements. However, it was only a matter of time before the patrol was missed, and the search would be on for their bodies. Pike walked without a word past Gwydeon and towards the rest of the small strike force which consisted of just two other warriors. The young Rachel, while obviously confident in her abilities and wicked with a bow in hand, did not have the kind of experience she needed for a battle like this. Then there was Logan, and perhaps it was Logan concerned Pike more than Rachel's inexperience. He was not the same as Pike remembered him. He was brooding, old, and hard. He had been troubled in the old days, grasping to cope with the role that fate had destined for him, as well as the risk to those he knew and loved, but this was different. The fact that Elwyne was dead and his new lover and unborn child had been captured and were in serious jeopardy was not sitting well on him. His mind did not seem as sharp as it once was. In many respects, Pike was reminded of Lord Cedric in the way that he was tortured by the death of Lady Erika, but Logan was different in his suffering.

Logan's heart was not the only thing tortured it seemed. It was as if the plague in his heart had migrated to his mind to create a kind of scar there as well. His mind was slowed and labored in all thoughts, and there was the specter of Elwyne in every thought and every action, though most times he did not make it know with speech. Pike could see the anguish in his eyes, and perhaps it was because Pike knew a similar heartache that he could see, but it was not important. What was important was the fact that Logan could freeze at any moment, and his sense of revenge, while powerful especially in his hands, was unfocused, and it seemed as if he wished the world could share in his suffering. His pain radiated though him and would not stop merely at the blood of one member of the phasia. No, this lust for blood might not even be quenched at a hundred phasia deaths. Pike knew in his heart that Logan would kill himself long before his need for vengeance would be fulfilled. However, what was most disconcerting was the fact that Logan still had frightening power at his disposal. He could still create portals, still summon otherworldly forces, and could take a life with a thought. In the hands of a rational and sane person, that power could be frightening, but in the hands of someone holding on to the ragged edge of stability, the possibilities were potentially horrifying.

Pike heard the heavy footsteps behind him and felt his thoughts pulled to the man who followed him. Gwydeon had changed too in the years that Pike had been missing, and they were not good changes, at least to Pike's mind. He was older, graying at the temples, and very troubled. The years seemed to be tripled for Gwydeon, and he had troubles of his own weighing down his heart. The death of his adopted son, a son that should have been his in the first place many had said, still weighed heavy upon him, and that was in no more evidence than the red armor that he wore. That armor was given to Gwillim by the true Lord Dragon, Korrd Ranthall, and worn proudly for many years in the service of Gwydeon and the forces of the Light in defense of both Brea and Aradon. Pike had once thought that Gwydeon was a bit jealous of Gwillim in that while Gwydeon had always thought himself the right hand and protector of the Dragon, he was really serving a pretender. Logan had only thought that he was the man of prophecy, and while Gwydeon played his part of protector well, it was really Gwillim, Korrd's son by birth, that served in that capacity. Though Gwydeon would never truly admit it, this was a fact that bothered him. But the fact of Gwillim's murder set even fouler upon the conscience of Gwydeon Sandar. They were about to come face to face with Gwillim's killer, Draven, and while Gwydeon had not said a word about it yet, it was most assuredly a fact which rung out in his mind over and over again.

Pike was well acquainted with that type of singularly focused hate and the way that it burned in every fiber of one's being. He remembered watching Eldar die over and over again in his head as he dreamed of his chance to take revenge on the phase Taron. Fortunately for Pike, Taron's death had been bloody and agonizing enough for Pike's taste for revenge to be sated. In his mind, Pike could never see that happening for Gwydeon. But hate and the need for vengeance alone did not plague Gwydeon's mind. Unlike Logan and Pike, who in their respective ways could let everything go when they fought for vengeance, Gwydeon could not so easily let the need for retribution consume his soul. The desire was no less, but the cost for such reckless abandon would be much higher. Gwydeon had found the love of his life, Midarin, and together they had produced one child and had another on the way. His family needed him, and he knew it, and he would not allow his children to grow up on stories of their father's greatness. He wanted to be there to watch every day as they grew, and the pride in his heart for his family consumed him almost as much as his hatred for Shauling and the phasia. Pike worried more about Gwydeon's part in this than he did about Logan. Logan would be reckless and would fight with every inch of his being to save his lover and his child. Gwydeon would fight hard too, out of a sense of revenge for his son. However, Gwydeon had the potential to freeze at the wrong moment just like Logan. Pike had to be ready if both of his old allies were unable to do what needed to be done.

There is a point in battle, a moment which all true warriors are trained for, a moment when time becomes nothing more than a collection of seconds, and your life becomes nothing more than your next action. Where a warrior has committed himself to a battle so fully that he expects to both live and die in the same breath. Gwydeon once had that edge. When he dueled against the warrior in Illimar, he had no fear and nothing to lose. His life did not matter once he entered that duel, and whether he lived or died meant nothing so long as he fought with all of his heart and soul. He knew he would be victorious no matter if he walked away or not. And in that battle he almost did not walk away. And such was the case many times. The showdown with Zarsi, the duel with Rael, and then his duel with Jeroch. Each time he cheated death because he did not fear it. He embraced it and used it to make him powerful and nearly invincible. Not one moment in any of those battles did the consequences of death enter his mind. Never once did he walk into a battle worrying about who would miss him if he were to never walk away from the fight. The edge, the desire to live to fight on, the thing that drove him was now gone. His thoughts were now dominated by "what ifs" and "maybes". In a critical moment where life and death hung in the balance, Gwydeon could freeze because he valued his life and the lives of his wife and children more than he valued winning a battle. The edge lost, he was no longer invincible, and the quality that made him immortal in a group of powerful immortal adversaries, was now gone and his mortality shone as brightly as the sun at mid-day.

Pike hesitated for a moment and then started to realize exactly what they were up against. Not only did they have to overcome the forces that Draven had amassed in an attempt to stop any invasion, but they also had to overcome the relative inexperience of Rachel, the powerful, reckless vengeance of Logan, the tempered and almost debilitating vengeance and conscience of Gwydeon, and the uncertainty and doubt inside of Pike. Disheartened, Pike entered the small thicket where Rachel and Logan waited, ready to brief his companions on what might be their last battle.

Logan looked up immediately at a sound just outside the thicket, and upon seeing the faint metallic sparkle of red in the moonlight, he relaxed the grip on his sword, the Dragon Sword, and sat up in preparation for the briefing that Pike was about to give them. The woman Rachel who sat near him also tensed and then visibly relaxed. She had been very jumpy the whole time that Gwydeon and Pike were gone, and it was clear that being next to the great and powerful Dragon was not helping the situation any. Logan had no delusions left about being the Dragon of the prophecies, but the general public as a whole had no idea that it was Logan's brother Korrd who was really the *Coromor*. So, for all intents and purposes, to the public, Logan Ranthall was the Dragon. Logan had lived with that fact for a long time, and even the voice in his head had stopped saying, "remember, it's not true." So, when anyone called him the Dragon, while at times he still flinched, he had gotten used to it. Pike approached and then sat across from Logan with Gwydeon taking a crouched position on his right. He exhaled slowly and then laid his axe on the ground.

"It looks bad," Pike said in a hushed voice. "There are patrols every few minutes of at least ten Jeresei, and there is a Shadowwalker fly-by about every fifteen minutes. Most of the patrols are confined to the perimeter of the palace, but there are also a few roving gangs moving through the streets looking for survivors. There is a Stone or two at every gate, and the breeches in the walls are also heavily guarded. The one bright spot is the fact that I haven't seen any sign of any Kalbraks, or any of Gwydeon's mysterious 'other phasia.' But, out in the open the Kalbraks would be a little bit more of a liability, so they are probably confined to the halls of the palace."

Gwydeon nodded. Tactically speaking, Draven had set up defenses perfectly against a full assault. The roving patrols and the fly overs would also prevent the kind of infiltration that they were about to attempt. Pike looked over his shoulder back in the direction of Trelon, took a deep breath, and then continued.

"What I can tell you is this. There is a small unguarded hole in the back on one of the inns. If you remember back in our bar brawling days in Illimar, there was a tunnel leading out of the *Wandering Maiden*, which led not only into the courtyard, but also out under the wall. This passage isn't nearly as extensive as that one was, but it is still there. The bad news is that it looks like has been buried by the years, also if I can see it from the crest of the hill, that means that the Shadowwalker patrols can easily see it from the air. Our window to cross the distance to the wall, dislodge the grate, get into the passage, and then replace the grate is going to be very tight. One the bright side, it shouldn't take very much to pry the grate loose. Once inside the city, it will be pretty ugly trying to get though all the defenses and into the palace, but I'm sure that we can think of something."

Logan's expression was one of concern but quiet confidence.

"If we can get to the temple just on the other side of the main road," Logan answered, "there is a passageway under the altar that was used so that the royal family could pass to and from services without having to worry about the public. It was an old family trick used by the Binosears, and it was also an easy way for Lord Cedric to visit his family without the mobs of Lion fanatics swarming him."

"So, all we have to do," Rachel said in summation, "is get to the city wall, find the grate, open it, get into the bar, cross the street into the temple, find the passageway there, and then get into the palace?"

"It may sound that easy Rachel," Gwydeon responded as evenly as he could, "but I can assure you, that when the three of us are involved things are never that easy. Remind me sometime to teach you about the Ranthall luck, or Logan's Doom as we used to call it."

Logan shot Gwydeon a hard stare and then stood. Gwydeon still had his dry humor, but apparently it did not have the ability to lift spirits the way it used to. It was clear that this was not going to be a cheerful reunion, or the same old fight. The group was much older now, and they had a friction between them that was not there in the past.

"We should go," Logan said shortly, "the longer we wait, and the more time we waste, the more likely Draven is to harm Cairyn or Sabrina. We have to move now."

Pike was not sure if the urgency that Logan was feeling was reality or just the fears and doubts in his mind creating specters for him to jump at. Perhaps this was all Draven's doing. From what Logan and Gwydeon had been able to tell Pike, Draven was not only a master of war, but he was also a master of mind games. Like all of Shau-ling's children, Draven had a precluded arrogance, but with Draven it wasn't just part of him, it defined who he was. Draven was constantly trying to find new and better ways to impress himself, and more often than not, the vehicle of choice was the outsmarting and total humiliation of his opponents. Whether or not Draven actually intended on harming Cairyn or Sabrina was anybody's best guess, but the fact that Draven had Logan worrying about it was enough for Draven. It was the first blow in the combat, and the battle would rage until one of them was dead.

Without another word, the four member force set out though the thicket, the moon peering down on them from above. Silently they moved through the wooded areas, stopping short when patrols turned suddenly, or one of the long, dark, menacing forms of the Shadowwalkers streaked overhead. There was a sense of urgency now as they approached the wall of the city, and it was as if with every step they took, the chances of them being discovered increased. Pike lead the way through the forest with his axe drawn and his eyes in constant motion. Whenever he would see a patrol, he would stop and flash his hand to his companions signaling that they stop. Then, after the patrol passed, they would continue, slowly at first, and then at full speed. Within a matter of minutes, they reached the edge of the forest. Ninety feet away from them was the buried grate that led to the *Queen's Rest* tavern, the inn that had once served as the royal palace of Trelon shortly after the murder of Queen Anabel Binosear and the destruction of the original palace. After another fly-by of Shadowwalkers, Pike broke from the cover of the trees and sprinted across the distance stopping at the wall in the sparse cover of the long shadow of the wall in the moonlight. After a moment, Pike hefted his axe and buried it into the ground with a hard downward stroke. Again and again the axe fell until finally, Pike heard a faint metallic clang, and he stopped. After looking around once more to make sure there were no patrols, Pike bent down and moved away the broken earth. The old iron grate had been pitted and scarred though the years, and apparently being buried had not improved those conditions. The single stroke from Pike's axe had been enough to split the grate down the middle, and now the passage stood open, with the grate hanging from both sides by its two sets of hinges. Again, Pike checked the area and then ducked down the open hole into the dark passage.

From the look of the passage, it had not been used in some time. There were many dense tangles of intricate spider webs that had been overlapped many times over the years so that the once beautiful patterns overlaid and meshed looked like a convoluted disaster. After making sure the passage was clear, at least so far as he could see, he slowly raised himself back up and motioned for the rest of the group.

Gwydeon saw the signal first and looked to Logan. It was agreed that Gwydeon would be the next one to go. If there was trouble, Rachel could cover them with her bow, and Logan could use some of his powers in order to gain them a little time. With the Lion Sword clutched tightly in his hand, Gwydeon sprinted the distance and ducked down the hole. His breathing was a bit labored at first, unused to the weight of the armor and the sword, but he was still in better than top condition. Logan was the next to run the length to the open grate, and as he made it to the hole he tripped on an unseen root and tumbled into the passage. The root snapped at the impact sending a sound resonating through the still night air. Rachel glanced nervously around, looking for the patrols that were most assuredly just out of sight. In a matter of moments, one such patrol came up over a nearby hill and started down toward the exposed grate. Rachel, fearing that her companions would be discovered, tried to form a plan. Out of the corner of her eye, she suddenly saw a large black bird hovering near her. It was facing the Jeresei, and did not seem to notice her. As silently as she could, she pulled one of the black arrows from her quiver and nocked it onto her bowstring. As she drew back the string, the sound of the twine and wood being stretched sounded impossibly loud to her ears, but then came the hiss of air as the arrow was released, and the loud caw of the bird as the arrow struck just at its feet. With all the flapping and cawing of the bird, and the rustling of the leaves and branches, the Jeresei were distracted just long enough for Rachel to sprint the distance to the hole and dive in. She came bursting down into the hole, much to the surprise of Logan who just barely caught her before they both toppled over. Gwydeon quickly stepped over the toppled pair and with a piece of iron that lay discarded near the entrance was able to bar the fractured pieces of the grate back together in an effort to cover their tracks.

During the interim, Pike had begun to clear the path and scout ahead to make sure that the tunnel was indeed a safe passage. Aside from the spider webs and occasional insects, it seemed as if it was safe, so Pike waited for his companions to get themselves ready and then they started to walk the few feet to the next grate. As Pike crawled up under the grate, he saw that it was still very much intact, and the release from the inside appeared to be functional. Holding his breath and clutching his axe tightly, he released the lever and slowly slid the grate to the side. With the grate out of the way, he pulled himself up and started to move the wooden panel that served as the cover piece inside the bar. Pike pushed up on the panel only to find that it would not move easily. He strained, unable to push up but a few inches. He then started to slide it to the side. Suddenly, an arm fell down into the hole and dangled in front of Pike's face. The arm was almost impossibly white, the veins shriveled and dark blue, almost black. There was dried blood caked to the hair of the forearm, and it reeked of death. Pike moved the arm out of his way and slowly stuck his head through the hole into the darkness of the bar. The arm belonged to a fairly large man who met a rather unpleasant end at the hands of what looked like a Jeresei. The marks were short and fine like from very sharp nails, however, they were well placed and left the victim mostly intact. When a Kalbrak attacked a person, the victim was usually in five or six pieces by the time the Kalbrak was done. They were clumsy though deadly, and never cared what shape their opponent was in so long as they were dead. The Jeresei on the other hand like to inflict pain for the maximum amount of time before killing. It was some sort of weird sadistic instinct that was bred into them, probably by Shau-ling himself.

Pike pulled himself up through the hole and stood crouched behind the bar. He motioned for his companions to follow, but to stay within the passage until he signaled all clear. With axe in hand, Pike moved to the end of the bar and peered around slowly. There appeared to be nothing in the bar except for the dead bodies of the former patrons. Surprisingly, there was the carcass of a Jeresei lying on the floor among the patrons. Pike smiled to himself when he thought that even though the patrons knew they were going to die they were bound and determined to take at least one of the monstrosities with them. Aside from the shattered windows in the far wall and the overturned and broken furniture, there appeared to be nothing else in the bar. Satisfied that they were safe, Pike motioned for Gwydeon and the others to come up out of the hole.

"How does it look?" Logan whispered to Pike.

"All clear as far as I can see. Now, how do we get to the temple from here?"

"Out the front door, to the left, it's the first building on the right."

Pike nodded. He knew it would be risky getting across the way, but at least they still had the cover of night to work with.

"I'll take a look and be right back."

The others nodded, but before Pike could dart off, Rachel grabbed him by the arm.

"I'll cover you from here."

"Thanks," Pike said slowly.

This was unnerving for Pike. He had always been more comfortable with a straight forward assault, not all this sneaking around. He sighed to himself and then crawled quickly from shadow to shadow making his way to the mostly open front door of the tavern. Propping himself between the bank of windows and the door frame, Pike looked out the door down the road to the front of the temple. There were many Jeresei wandering around, and it seemed like there was no way that they could get from one place to the other without being discovered. So, Pike sighed to himself again, and then made the long crawl back to the safety of the bar.

As soon as Pike returned and Gwydeon saw the look on his face, Gwydeon knew something was wrong.

"No chance," Pike whispered shaking his head. "The Jeresei are all over that place. We wouldn't so much as make it out the front door before we were nailed. It's almost like they know that there is a way into the palace from the temple."

"We have to find another way," Gwydeon concluded.

"There is a side entrance to the temple," Logan answered. "There is a branch off the tunnel that leads out to the wall, and it should take us out to the docks. I'm sure that Draven isn't worried about a naval assault, so hopefully the patrols will be lighter. From the docks, we can double back and get into the temple that way."

"It's worth a shot," Pike said after a moment, "because we surely aren't getting there through the front door."

After a moment, Pike crawled back to the open hole and slid down into the smaller tunnel. It was clear almost immediately that the passage had not seen much use. In his mind Pike imagined that the passage was used more often to smuggle illegal goods into the bar rather than sneaking people out. Because of the darkness and the damp conditions, it was not a pleasant crawl, but after several minutes, Pike found himself looking out toward the docks. He lay in wait for a few moments, watching the rotation of the patrolling Jeresei. It seemed that Logan's theory about the docks not being as heavily guarded proved to be accurate, and only one or two patrols were on duty. Pike waited until he was sure he had enough time and then opened the grate slowly. The grate was moved easily away from the hole and Pike sat shadowed in the darkness. When the next break in the guard rotation came, Pike bolted from his hiding place into a nearby building. The door had been shattered off its hinges, and Pike was able to find a place where he could see the alley that led to the temple and the hole in which his friends were still hiding. Gwydeon waited at the mouth of the hole, watching Pike for a signal to advance. As the Jeresei passed out of sight again, Pike gave the signal and Gwydeon ran across the few yards of distance and slid in behind Pike in the safety of the building.

The building seemed to once have served as a storage shed of some kind. There were no windows, and there were many different tools adorning the walls. Pike waited a few moments before motioning both Logan and Rachel along. After the four of them were safely in the building, Pike set his sights on the alley that would lead them to the temple. It was narrow and well drenched in the nighttime shadow, but he wanted to make sure that everything was accounted for first.

"Do you know where we are Logan?" Pike whispered.

Logan chanced another look out the door of the warehouse and then down the alley before looking back at Pike.

"Yes, through that small alley is the temple. At the mouth of the alley is where the main through road narrows. The temple itself is round in shape, and its curve is at the greatest point where you will emerge from the alley. Just across from you when you get there will be the door. I don't know whether it will be open or not, but it is the best chance we have. If we have to break down the door, we'll only have a few seconds before the Jeresei guarding the front will come to investigate. The temple is defensible, but not indefinitely, and certainly not once the presence of intruders gets back to Draven. Quick, quiet, and careful is the only way we'll be able to get into the temple, uncover the passage under the altar, and then make it to the palace. If we have to fight, we've already lost."

"Ok," Pike sighed, "Rachel, you're with me. In that alley, I won't have much room to do anything, but maybe with your extended range I'll have a chance."

Rachel just nodded and looked on as Pike moved himself back to the door to check the position of the patrols. Satisfied with what he saw, he motioned for Rachel to follow, and he darted across the fifteen yards to the dark alley. Together they ducked into the alley, trying hard to control their breathing so that nothing further down the alley could hear them. The alley was narrow, so much so that Pike and Rachel could not stand side by side and could barely slide to facing each other with their backs pressed firmly to the walls. Pike inched forward, the whole time watching the open end of the alley for any movement. For his position, he could see the door that Logan was talking about, and he figured that if he had a couple seconds, he would be able to dart across without being seen. The door had been broken open, and still clung loosely to the door frame by one set of iron hinges. That at least was in their favor. Pike moved forward slowly and looked out toward the narrow pathway past the door to the temple. He watched for several moments and did not see any Jeresei. Then, he moved to the other wall and looked out. There were many of the red-skinned beasts roving around, just as he had seen earlier, but they did not appear to pay too much attention to the secondary door to the temple. Pike was about to inch away from the opening when Rachel grabbed him and pulled him down. Pike tried his best not to shout, and after an accusing glance at Rachel, she pointed to the open doorway of the temple. There was a faint hint of movement, and then one of the Jeresei came into clear view. Rachel drew herself up slowly, and fired an arrow first into the creature's windpipe, and then straight into the Jeresei's skull. It fell to the ground without emitting so much as a growl, and Pike waited for the screams from his brethren and the rush to find whoever killed it. But no cries came.

Pike breathed heavy, the nervousness of the situation starting to get to him. Rachel's act was reckless. She couldn't have known if there were more Jeresei in the temple. Pike inwardly cursed that he hadn't stopped her. He had been so worried about Logan or Gwydeon making mistakes that he quite possibly had allowed the fatal one to be made. Without the adrenaline rush of a full bloody battle, Pike was not emotionally strong enough to handle the pressure of this mission, but he was managing as best he could. He slipped past Rachel and waited for the Jeresei at the other end of the alley to move so he could bring Logan and Gwydeon into the alley. After a moment or two, the four companions were reunited, and they moved their way through the alley and waited for the perfect opportunity to enter the temple.

Rachel had been watching the activity outside the temple, waiting for any backlash to her rash killing of the Jeresei. She had been cautious in her shot selection to keep the Jeresei from crying out, but there was still the chance that it would be discovered. As Pike and the others approached, the nervousness hit her like a hammer, and she darted from the alley into the temple, her bow drawn and a lethal arrow waiting to fly.

Pike saw Rachel tense and then watched in horror as she leapt into the open. He wanted to call out, but he refrained from that stupid action and waited for any sign. After a moment, there was a signal from Rachel signaling all clear. Pike breathed a heavy sigh of relief and then thundered across the distance into the temple with Logan and Gwydeon in tow. Pike's nerves were ragged and his hands were shaking. He wanted to collapse. Luckily, the others were too busy assessing the condition of the temple to notice him.

The temple itself was in no better condition than the rest of the city it seemed. All of the symbols devoted to the old gods had been destroyed or horribly mutilated. Many of the statues were now disfigured into horrible and blasphemous representations of their former selves. Pike winced at the sight of the temple, but only paid it mind for a few seconds before locating the altar that contained the passage to the royal palace that Logan had described. Rachel looked over to Pike and sighed with a worried look on her face. She knew that Pike had probably disapproved of her actions, but she had no time for that now. She did what she had to do, and it was his problem if he didn't like it. Logan moved around the edge of the temple slowly, his eyes in constant motion, checking every door and window with every step that he took. They were so close now that discovery could mean the death of everyone that he still held dear. Within moments, he had circumnavigated the room and worked his way behind the burned and mutilated altar. The charred rugs crumbled away at his touch, and he found the hidden latch at the base of the altar to release the panel that would lead to the secret passage. As the others moved into positions where they could quickly get to the altar, Logan opened the panel, and descended into the passageway. Pike, Rachel, and Gwydeon followed quickly behind, and once below, Logan sealed the passage behind them.

"Well," Logan said slowly, "this will take us under the palace into the dungeons. We should be able to find some allies there, and if our luck holds, we should be able to get out of there without alerting Draven. Once inside the palace, there are many secret passageways to the throne room and to the Queen's bedroom. Depending on how many prisoners are still alive, we may be able to split up and increase our chances of saving Cairyn and Sabrina."

"We're with you, Logan," Gwydeon said calmly, "lead on."

As they walked through the dimly lit stone passageway, Gwydeon tapped Pike on the shoulder and smiled.

"Just like old times, huh Pike?"

"Yeah," Pike said groaning to himself, "I should have stayed under that damn island."

CHAPTER 28

Chapter XXIX

Power and Passion

Creator's Calendar Year 1205; Light Reality

Tension rippled through the forest with every second the crept by. There was no telling who would act next or what exactly would happen. There were only two people who were truly caught off-guard by the revelation of Lissa's parentage, and those two men were probably the most dangerous in that little clearing. The first, Aryx Terian, his face a patchwork of anger, puzzlement, and shame stared at the red-haired girl who had just been revealed as his daughter. Midarin tried hard to console him by staying right where he could see her, but it was clear that Aryx was far beyond any consolation. Whatever wars were raging in his heart and in his mind, he alone could call a truce of the warring factions. It was obvious it would take time, but the cold hard exterior of White Lightning would return. Wolf Ranthall on the other hand had no such wars of conscience raging inside of him, merely questions and puzzles. Since his mind had been opened up to the memories of the Blaze, he had been able to know things from lifetimes that were not his own. He knew Aryx Terian in many forms, including the one that Shau-ling had called Nightwing, and he also saw through the memory of the Blaze the death of Nightwing. As to what happened to Aryx Terian after Nightwing cast himself down into the funnel of Blaze energy was not known. But the fact that he stood before Wolf meant that it was an incredible story that was waiting to be told, and it would only be a matter of time before Wolf either pried it out of him, or he cracked and revealed it to all.

"How is this possible?" Aryx stammered.

"Just before you were commissioned to go on the quest with Logan and the others, Diana became pregnant," Midarin explained as calmly as she could, "when you disappeared, she thought you were dead, as we all did. The fact that you came back at all is a miracle. Diana, thinking that you were dead, could not bear the thought of raising a child by herself in a world that was doomed to see the scourge of Shau-ling again. She was tired of fighting, she had fought twice already, and didn't have the strength to do it anymore. So, she took Lissa to Marcwell and asked Pike and Cairyn to watch over Lissa and help her grow into a strong woman. Pike fell in love with the charming little girl very quickly, as did we all, and she became a member of the Rhuiden family. She kept the last name because she wanted to be known for who she was, not for who her family was. So, there is another Terian in the world, and as you have already seen, she is a member of the mystical *Erieal*, and there is another Terian who possesses the power over Fire. I'm sorry that we hid this from you Aryx, but it had to be done. For your safety, and for the safety of our kingdoms. Besides, Lissa was too young to take the blow of finding out that you were still alive. I didn't think it was worth the risk. Besides, you were the one who said that you didn't want to be revealed to anyone until you were ready. It was you who suggested the guise of Lan while you were in Brea."

"Yes," Lissa said after a moment, the sudden recollection hitting her, "I thought those stories of the great Lan sounded familiar. If Pike would have ever heard the stories, he would have been tipped off for sure."

"That begs the question Aryx," Wolf prodded, "where were you all that time? Why did you disappear?"

Wolf's tone showed that he knew the answer to the question, and Aryx picked up on it immediately. There was a look resembling horror in his eyes. For him to be revealed now, so close in proximity to the new *Coromor* could almost certainly mean his death. If not by Midarin and her children, then certainly by the young man and Lissa.

"He doesn't remember," the young girl said coldly, her sword poised and ready for a fight, "and even if he did, why would he tell a member of the phasia?"

"Little girl . . ." Wolf started.

"Liette."

"Liette," Wolf restarted, "my apologies. Liette, he knows exactly where he has been, and you can see it on his face. There is horror in his eyes. He has been under the taint and the thumb of evil for so long that it oozes from every one of his pores like an oil. It permeates his being, and he practically glows with the evil power that courses through his veins. Come old man, tell your friends how you betrayed your cause. Tell them your real name as Shau-ling called you."

Midarin took a shocked step back and almost instinctively reached for her bow again. Then, as if something inside her clicked, she stopped and rounded on the young man.

"And who are you?" she questioned harshly. "For someone with no name and with no background so far as we know, you know a lot about Aryx. How do you answer to the charges that you wield the powers of the phasia and that you are in fact one of them? How do you answer the questions of the knowledge that you possess? Come boy, use that wicked tongue to answer honest questions."

Wolf was about to speak when he heard a voice inside of him. It was a voice that he had been waiting to hear for some time. Basille was telling him that it was time to reveal his identity. Wolf regarded the words in his mind for a moment before speaking, and he lowered his sword, and the control of the powers of the Blaze for a moment before he spoke. Lissa seemed to listen most intently as she waited for the answer to the question she too had asked only a few minutes previous.

"Whether or not you believe this, I will never know, and I have to trust that you will ask whatever questions that you need in order to validate my story. I was born in a little town not too far from here to a lovely young couple who loved each other very much. My father tried to teach me everything he could, but his teaching days were short-lived when he was struck down by an unknown ailment in my fifth year of life. I don't remember much about him, as far as what he looked like or what he sounded like, but his words to me were always kind and soft, even when he was trying to fill me with more information than my young mind would ever be able to retain. My mother over the years told me almost everything about him. All of his adventures and all of his failings. She was very proud of him in every way, and she made that pride show though in all of her stories. She wanted me to revere him for what he tried to be, not necessarily what he was. It was the thoughts and the reasons behind the actions that had the most importance, not the actions themselves. My mother loved him very much, and she loved me too. She would have been forty-five in the fall, but she could not live alone anymore. They were to bury her tomorrow."

Midarin's eyes dropped to the ground. Her heart sank with every word, and it only took hearing the tone in his voice and the passion in his words to know who was standing before her. It was painful to see him tell the tale of his life, but she knew he was not doing it for their benefit, but for his own.

"After my mother's death," Wolf continued, "I came to the conclusion that I would cast my lot into the same fight they had believed so strongly in. But I found a surprise waiting for me. A birthright that I didn't know I had. The legacy of power that I display is not my own, but rather another who allied himself first with the Shadows, and then with the Light. He gave his power to me, and that is why it appears as if I were a member of the accursed phasia. I'm sure that my father Logan and my mother Elwyne would have been a little shocked to see the spirit of Basille walk up to their front door to tell them that their little boy had been given the power of a full member of the phasia, but that did not happen, and so here I am. So, for a formal introduction, may I introduce myself as Wolf Ranthall."

Midarin waited for a moment before she did anything. She knew that there would be some very strong reactions from the rest of the people in the clearing, and it was safe to assume that some of those reactions would not be pleasant ones. There was always a lot of uncertainty when it came to the Ranthall family, and you could never know when one was good or bad, or even a little bit crazy. One thing was certain. Like the Binosear family, the Ranthall family had been touched and was a force to be reckoned with in this every evolving war between Light and Shadow.

But then again, Midarin thought to herself, *I guess we all have to be a little crazy to be in this war anyway.*

Lissa stared at Wolf so hard that he could feel it. He knew that he had lied to her, but at the time he was trying to protect himself from basically this very situation. However, he had not revealed himself to the queen, and therefore he had not revealed himself to Pike. Wolf, through the cautions of his mother as well as Basille was worried about was being used by those people who were so invested in the war that they could not see past their own desires. Here he found himself between a rock and a hard place. On one side he had Lissa, a woman that he was genuinely interested in as more than just a companion, and she just found out that he was lying to her about himself. And then there was Aryx Terian, a traitor to the forces of the Light, even if no one knew it, and he could probably strike Wolf down where he stood if he wanted to bad enough. The far greater problem was the growing number of unknowns, and the increasing uncertainty about the aims and goals of the forces of the Light. There were too many wildcards in the mix for Wolf to be comfortable. The greatest advantage that the forces of the Light had enjoyed was a singular focus; the destruction of Shau-ling. Cedric had it, Logan had it, but now, the third generation seemed to have inherited too many distractions. Secrets and factions were what kept the phasia from being a force that would decimate the world. If the Light could not be unified in its purpose, then there was no hope.

The *Coromor* of the third generation stood right in front of Wolf, and one of the *Erieal* to his left, obviously his protector. Then there was Queen Midarin, a supposed friend of the Ranthall family, but she had been the one hiding Aryx all along. As Wolf scanned all of their faces, his gaze came to rest on the little girl with the very large sword. Her gaze had not left him since he revealed his identity, and there was an intensity in her eyes that struck chords of fear somewhere deep inside. Aryx was a known danger, however, what this little girl could do was still unknown, and that made her even more dangerous than Aryx. Here they all stood, weapons ready, willing to strike each other down, and for what?

"You are Wolf Ranthall?" the man in red armor choked out after a moment.

Wolf nodded silently. The man sheathed his sword and walked over to Wolf slowly with his hands at his sides. The two men stood face to face for a moment. Wolf and the older man were about eye level with one another, and Wolf could see some similarities in the face with the one that he saw in the mirror every morning. Without warning the man in armor embraced Wolf and then pulled back with a wide smile on his face.

"It is good to finally meet you, cousin," he said brightly, "though I wish the circumstances could have been better."

"Cousin?" Wolf thought for a moment. "That would make you Gwillim?"

"Very good cousin," Gwillim responded, his smile widening. "I see that Elwyne did tell you about me. That is good. Besides, you can never have enough family."

"Mother always said that you could only trust family," Wolf responded in an unconsciously cold tone.

Gwillim felt the intonation like a punch in the gut. However, he couldn't blame Wolf for the sentiment. Gwillim had been at the very center of the angst between brothers in the last generation, and he wanted nothing more than to forge as much unity as he could for himself and for his adopted family. Though like Wolf, Gwillim's blood was that of a Ranthall, and that was a tie that could not be denied.

"It would seem that is more and more true these days Wolf," Gwillim responded, "and so I would like you to trust my family. After all, in a way, they are your family too."

Gwillim walked back over to where the younger boy stood and put his hand on the boy's shoulder.

"This is my younger brother Nathaniel. As you have probably surmised, he is very special. Here," he said motioning toward the little girl, "is my sister Liette. Don't worry," he said looking into her eyes, "she gives that look to everyone she likes."

Then she must really like me, Wolf thought to himself.

"And of course you have already been introduced to our mother Midarin, though you may not remember her."

"I came to visit you when you were only just a few days old, Wolf," Midarin said stepping towards him. "You have grown up a lot since then, it's a pity that your mother and father will not be able to see what a fine man you will become."

Lissa took this opportunity to turn Wolf by both shoulders to face her. There was this look in her eyes that Wolf could not fathom. She was angry, that was certain, but Wolf was not sure whether it was because he lied, or because she was trying to control her urge to burn her father to a crisp. But there was something under the anger, and that was the part of the look that Wolf could not explain.

"You lied to me."

It was more of a statement than an accusation. Her voice was calm and even, with a very low tone. Had it not been for the close proximity of everyone in the clearing, it was doubtful that anyone else but Wolf could have heard it.

"You weren't so truthful yourself."

Wolf felt that surge of combativeness well up inside of him again, and could not help but let that comment slip. Lissa smiled, amused at his words, and then sighed heavily.

"If you ever lie to me again, I will kill you."

Maybe it was the way she said it, but Wolf would have sooner said that the Creator did not exist before he doubted the truth of her words. Suddenly, as if struck, Lissa turned to Midarin.

"Mother and Sabrina are a few yards away, near the road. Obviously we didn't expect to see you. How were you able to get here so fast?"

Gwillim smiled and patted Nathaniel on his shoulder.

"He's been practicing with portals," Gwillim said pride thick in his voice. "He finally got it right a few weeks ago. But it takes a lot out of him, so I'm not sure how much we'll be able to rely on that. But then again, with Wolf here now, we may not have to."

Lissa wanted to know more, and it annoyed her that her training had not advanced as far as Nathaniel's had. Nathaniel was two years her junior, and yet he had always grasped the concepts of power much quicker than she had.

"We had better go check on Cairyn and Sabrina," Lissa said finally. "You should all probably stay here until we get back. You know how mother is."

"Yes," Midarin said after a moment. "However, after you check on them, you had better come back. We have many things we need to discuss, not the least of which is the encounter here. We can also arrange to run into you in the morning."

"Should I wake Sabrina?" Lissa asked.

"No," came Midarin's reply. "She needs her sleep, as do we all, and trying to explain what just went on out here to her will be complicated. There is still too much we don't know about her powers and how vulnerable they make her."

Lissa frowned, but finally nodded. The *Chosen One's* mantle was a mantle of balance, and like the man whom it came from, Aerith Seth, it could be leveraged by both the Light and the Shadow. Logan Ranthall had been fortunate that he was never tempted as his brother had been, otherwise the outcome of the second generation could have been much different. That was why Lissa had been appointed Sabrina's protector. It was not only to ensure her physical safety, but also to ensure that the tempting darkness could never touch her.

"I can check on them Lissa," Wolf said after a moment. "The way is easier though the trees, and they have less chance of hearing me if I am alone."

"It's ok Wolf," Lissa said walking toward the path, "I'm supposed to be Sabrina's protector, I want to go check on her."

Wolf shrugged his shoulders and followed as the Lissa led the way through the forest back to the campsite. The fire was just beginning to die, and as Lissa looked over her adopted mother and sister, Wolf silently stoked the fire and checked the area for any animal tracks. It was not unheard of for strange creatures to be in Logan's Wood, but they were never heard to attack those with good intentions in their hearts. Satisfied with her family's safety, Lissa and Wolf made their way back to Mirror Lake. A few yards from the clearing where Midarin and the others waited for their return, Lissa stopped and pulled Wolf close to her. Without a word, she pressed her lips to his and held him tight. Wolf's senses swam from Lissa's enflaming contact, and he tried hard to keep a firm grasp on the situation in his mind. However, the strands of control on his emotions, while not strong to begin with, were being taxed to their furthest length. Finally, his resolve snapped, and he clutched her tightly to him, and increased the intensity of the kiss. After a moment of passion, Lissa pulled herself away from Wolf and looked him square in the eyes, steadying herself with her hands on his shoulders. Wolf knew that look now. It was one of passion, but passion that was being restrained.

"Later," she whispered pressing a finger to his lips and then kissing them softly.

He smiled to her and then they continued to the clearing beside Mirror Lake. When the two of them arrived, Gwillim and Nathaniel were just finishing setting up camp, and Liette had apparently been out gathering firewood with Aryx. Midarin had taken a seat on a nearby log and was restringing her bow. During the showdown with Rane, the twine of the bow had become frayed, and she wanted to make sure that she was able to fight effectively should the opportunity arise again. Gwillim waived to both of them as they approached, and Wolf decided that he should do a little investigating of his own. He started with Nathaniel.

Nathaniel seemed to tense a little when Wolf approached, but Wolf understood that. After all, Nathaniel was the *Coromor* of the prophecies, and Wolf now had the ability to wield the powers of one of the *Coromor's* greatest enemies. He had every right to be a little jumpy. However, after a moment, the tension started to ease, and a smile returned to the young man's face. Even though the two men were roughly the same age, Wolf could not help but feel that Nathaniel was his junior, looking more like a teenager than a man in his early twenties.

"I have a question for you Nathaniel," Wolf said smoothly, "and I think the answer could be beneficial to all of us."

Nathaniel smiled and nodded.

"I don't know that I can be of much help, but maybe between Gwillim and I, we can come up with something."

At that Gwillim sat down next to Nathaniel and began polishing his sword. He had already removed his armor, and it sat neatly next to him. Wolf knelt down beside the two men and looked out into the forest before looking back at Nathaniel.

"The Jeresei that I let go was the Elder of one of their oldest clans. He said that they were out here with Rane looking for someone, but they weren't able to find him. Now keep in mind, that this was after you all showed up and pretty much wiped the floor with them, so there has to be someone else here that has something that Shau-ling wants. And if Shau-ling wants it, we can't let him have it."

"Why should we trust what any of those creatures had to say, Wolf, Rane included?" Gwillim asked. "That Jeresei could have been lying to you. They don't strike me as the honest type."

"You're probably right Gwillim, the Jeresei serve their own needs first. But the fact that I was wielding the powers of the Blaze had something to do with his tongue loosening. If this were nothing, why would Shau-ling send a member of the phasia? Shau-ling has used Jeresei for scouting missions before, but not members of the phasia. I don't care how young this Rane character is, phasia don't just wander about looking for people. Also, this is Logan's Wood. It would take something pretty huge for a member of the phasia to put their neck on the line to come through here without a good reason."

"That's a good point Wolf," Nathaniel responded, "but what do you think that the phasia would look for here?"

"That's what I need your help on. You were able to pick up my powers, even when I didn't know I had them. Is it possible that someone else who has power is here in Logan's Wood?" Wolf asked.

"It's possible," Nathaniel answered. "Besides, in the last generation, four of the six of the prophecies were born in Aradon, so coincidence is heavy on the side of possibility around here."

"How long will it take?"

"Give me a few minutes. If I need your help or if I come up with anything, I'll let you know."

"Done," Wolf replied.

Wolf looked around and found that Lissa was sitting by Midarin and they were wrapped in a seemingly light conversation. Aryx and Liette on the other hand seemed to be having a very serious discussion on the other side of the fire. Liette must have sensed Wolf was looking at her, because she shot him a look that would have killed the tree behind him. The sheer power of the stare sent a shiver through Wolf, and he tried hard to shake his thoughts away from the little girl and back to the other young woman that currently held his fancy. As he started to walk over to interject himself into the conversation between Midarin and Lissa, Gwillim tapped him on the shoulder and motioned for him to sit down. The look on Nathaniel's face when he sat was one of concentration. His eyes were closed, but underneath the closed lids, his eyes moved with frantic intensity. His breathing was rapid and seemingly uncontrolled, but in all other facets, his body seemed to be at perfect peace.

"You have something already?" Wolf asked quietly.

"Nathaniel has always been able to pick up patterns of energy very quickly. When he was only a few years old, he sensed my power and Lissa's power while they were only newly forming. And, as you know with your experiences with him, he can find powers even when they are dormant."

"So, Nathaniel," Wolf said almost in a whisper, "what have you found?"

"There is a lot of power here."

The voice was otherworldly. While he spoke in a quiet tone, his voice seemed to come out in several different pitches at once, with a low rolling timbre that dominated the overall voice.

"From where exactly?"

"First off," the eerie voice continued, "it is in the wood itself. There is a power here that moves from tree to tree and surrounds the inhabitants. I can feel it move around through the leaves and the branches of the trees. It guards us. Then, there is the obvious powers from you, Gwillim, myself, Lissa, and Aryx. But there is another power here, one that I have never experienced before. Its ties are close to the phasia, but not of the phasia. But there are also strings of power much like that of the *Coromor* and the *Chosen One*. Were we not already sure of the identity of the *Chosen One* I would say that this person is that being. This person's powers are fully active, but he is not yet aware of my presence. He was able to keep the woman Rane from knowing where he was by shielding himself in the energy of the woods and turning off his connection to his powers. It would make him virtually undetectable here in Logan's Wood."

"Can you find where he is?" Wolf asked expectantly.

"No. The power here in the wood is clouding his location from me. It is as if the woods themselves are trying to protect this man."

Nathaniel's breathing started to even out, and then after a moment, his eyes opened slowly and he relaxed back against the fallen tree.

"Sorry I couldn't be of any more help, Wolf. Maybe this guy is the one who has been protecting Logan's Wood from the evil people and creatures. It wouldn't be that strange considering the fact that strange things happen when the name Ranthall comes up."

Nathaniel's smile dwindled after that, and there came a look on his face that seemed as if he thought he had made a terrible mistake.

"Sorry, Wolf," he said almost immediately, "I didn't mean anything by it."

"That's alright, kid," Wolf commented, laying his hand on the younger boy's shoulder. "Really strange things tend to happen when your last name is Ranthall. Just be glad that you aren't related to me the way that Gwillim is, or you would really see some strange things."

Gwillim laughed at that, and Wolf rose after a moment and found Lissa standing alone near the path that led to the Queen and Princess's camp site. Wolf walked over to her and smiled as he leaned against a nearby tree.

"What are you doing over here by yourself, beautiful?" Wolf asked smiling.

"Waiting for you to quit talking to the guys. Its late and we ought to be getting back."

"Alright."

Wolf motioned for Lissa to lead the way, and then follow as they made a slow pace back toward the other encampment. Lissa did not seem to be in too much of a hurry, and at one point while Wolf was looking around at the forest, he missed the fact that she had stopped right in front of him. He bumped into her, but it was not enough of a jolt to knock her down. He smiled, and started to apologize when she kissed him again.

This kiss was not gentle like the first one, but a passionate lingering kiss that sent waves of pleasure crashing through Wolf's body. Slowly they sank down to their knees on the soft dew covered grass, and the kiss was slowly broken. Lissa's smile warmed Wolf to the core, and as she slowly began to kiss his mouth and face, he felt the sweet rushes of passion flowing through him. She pulled back from him, smiling, and answered his silent question when she leaned in and whispered in his ear.

"It's later."

Then the chorus of kisses and sensation started again. As Wolf felt himself being pushed back onto the bed of grass, their bodies began to slowly mingle, and their hands began to explore. Their mouths rarely left each other's except for half stifled gasps of pleasure as they made love under the clear moonlit sky.

Savior

Creator's Calendar Year 1205; Dark Mirror

There was very little sound in the small dank passage except for the occasional drip of water that echoed against the old stone walls and floor. Many years of roots and weeds had broken their way through the ancient masonry and had created a tiny jungle far beneath the surface. Along the walls could be found starts of mushrooms and other fungus, and the humid dankness of the passage surely gave rise to other lower forms of life. As if aware of the newest trespassers into their domain, the life in the passage seemed to shrink away into the walls and the floor, not wanting to be trampled by a wayward foot. Without a torch, the passageway could have been considered hazardous, but there was a green glow that emanated from one of the moss-like plants that grew on the walls, and the glow was almost enough to light the way. Logan took point through the passage with Rachel almost on his heels. Next in line was Gwydeon, followed by the troubled footsteps of Pike. None of them could stand completely upright in the passageway, but Rachel had to slump the least. Gwydeon in his unfamiliar armor was having the most trouble navigating the twisting passage, but he would never complain about the situation. Logan desperately wanted to channel a small amount of power to add to the light in the passage, but this close to a full member of the phasia, any trickle of power would be noticed. Yet they trudged on in the murky light, breathing in humid still air, and a mixture of pollen, spores, and dread.

Despite the relatively difficult task of getting into Trelon, and then into this passageway, Pike still felt that it was too easy. If this phase Draven was as powerful as he was made out to be, surely he would have felt the presence of Logan and Pike this close to his new throne room. But perhaps he had not considered people like Logan and other warriors of the Light capable of sneaking around. It seemed like large offensives and epic scale battles were the norm in this new reality, but to Pike, the old ways were still the best. Pike only liked a battle when he could see all of his opponents in front of him and not have to worry about who was going to stab him in the back when he wasn't looking. Though truly in the past, he occasionally had to worry about members of his own party stabbing him in the back, but after those few incidents, Pike had learned that in battle, anyone in front of his axe was his enemy. Logan stopped ahead, and pulled on one of the torch mounts on the wall to his left. There was a barely audible click, and then a section of the wall opened ahead.

"Through here is the dungeon," Logan whispered. "If we're lucky, some of my army will be waiting for me. If there is any resistance from Jeresei or any other of the Shadow spawn, kill them quickly so they cannot raise an alarm. Rachel, it will be up to you to scan the stairway and make sure that none of the Jeresei get to the door. We do have a bit of an advantage though. The doors and the walls have been reinforced so that those in the dungeon could not be heard. This was done back in the days when prisoners were still tortured, of course that was long before the Binosear family. Surprisingly, even though the palace burned, the entire dungeon and the subfloor above it survived the blaze, and the new palace was built right above it."

He paused for a long moment, looking back at the open section of wall and the small dark passage that led to the dungeon. He felt his heart raging, and could hear the blood racing in his ears like thunder. If he hadn't been clutching hard to the hilt of his sword, his hand would have been shaking. Finally he turned back to his companions and exhaled slowly.

"Well, I guess this is it."

Logan took another deep breath and drew the Dragon Sword from the scabbard on his hip and lightly stepped through the dim passage into the wide expanse of the dungeon. The exit of the passageway came out under an outcropping of stone on the far wall of the dungeon. Across the wide dungeon stood the single staircase that led to the upper floors. Logan winced as he looked around the area. In a single night, Draven and his armies had captured nearly all of Logan's men, and many of them had been tortured to death already. Many of the torture devices, not a part of the dungeon that Logan remembered, had broken and bleeding bodies still strapped to them. There were anguished moans coming from the overfilled cages and cells, and there were quite a few roving Jeresei guards that lashed out with a thin whip that sparkled with green fire randomly to further humiliate and punish the survivors of the siege.

Without warning, two arrows flew with rapid succession from behind Logan. The first arrow claimed the Jeresei at the very top of the stairs near the door through the forehead, sending him toppling down from the height onto the floor, his bones cracking loudly as he landed. The second shot struck a Jeresei through the side, catching him off guard and sending him sprawling down the stairs, striking many of them hard before he landed in a heap at the feet of another member of his race. The remaining Jeresei seemed too shocked by the unexpected attack to climb up the stairs and open the door to call for help, but rather they moved across the floor of the dungeon slowly, searching for the source of the ambush, ready to engage in combat against the thing that killed two of their brethren. Logan exploded from the passageway as soon as one of the red-skinned beasts got close, and his first stroke with the Dragon Sword sent a fountain of blood streaming from the wounded chest of a Jeresei. The beast fell with only a primal cry of pain as the fury of the last of the Ranthall family danced through the throng of opposition like a man possessed. But the initial shock of Logan's entrance was not enough to keep the wild Jeresei off-balance for long. Already, they were starting to recover and mount an offensive of their own. Their whips, sparkling with Blaze energy cracked and popped as they struck again and again at the crazed human. Before long they would have cornered Logan and killed him, had it not been for the fact that his allies interjected themselves.

Rachel, still hidden under the outcropping of stone, fired arrow after arrow into the red-skinned mob that rushed toward their newly revealed opponents. Most of the shots claimed a beast in the head, neck, or chest, while others were lucky enough to be taken in the arm or the leg. While those were not fatal injuries, they were enough to slow the assault. Gwydeon, armed with the Lion Sword, and Pike, with his ax *Fury* joined the fray with the reckless abandon that had made them famous. The flashes of steel and the glow of Blaze green became a blur of color and motion in the mass of confusion that grew in the dungeon. Pike, sidestepping the lash of a Blaze whip, buried *Fury* into the scalp of a Jeresei and then spun him into one of his comrades giving Gwydeon enough time to sever the stunned beast's head. The shrieks and cries of the falling Jeresei mingled with the cheers of the surviving warriors and the battle cries of the Heroes of the Light. Logan's thirst for blood claimed Jeresei after Jeresei as he waded deep into the ranks forsaking safety and cutting down everything that got in his way. Blood splattered in his face and on his armor, but his blood boiled in his veins more and more with each and every kill. Jeresei continued to fall rapidly, until the floor was littered with bodies and body parts. Not a single beast that served the Shadows walked or crawled in that blood-covered dungeon, and as the brave warriors took in the sight of their saviors, they saw faces covered with blood, and weapons that were more red than silver. Bending down to examine one of the still whole Jeresei bodies, Pike took one of the Blaze whips from the fallen form and strapped it to his belt.

"Help me free my men," Logan said after a moment. "Hopefully enough of them will be able to fight. That's the only way we're going to be able to counter the occupying force above. In the palace's passages, we need numbers."

Gwydeon had already begun to move around the dungeon opening locks and chains where he could. The master set of keys were easily found, and before long, all of the bonds had been released. At least, all the chains and manacles had been removed. The physical scars however proved to be far more restraining than even the heaviest of chains. Many of the men had long burn marks on their backs and legs from when they were driven into the dungeon by their Jeresei tormentors. Some of the blows with the cruel Blaze whips had been enough to sever a leg or an arm completely. The unspeakable cruelty shown to the prisoners of the Shadow was truly evident, and this had only taken place over the span of one night. Had it been any longer, surely even the bravest of the men would have begged for death. Out of the three hundred imprisoned there, only twenty were still strong enough to fight. While the others may have had the will, their bodies did not have enough strength remaining. If they had been led into battle, it would be practically sentencing them to a painful and unnecessary death. However, those incapable of aiding the siege of the palace vowed that they would defend the escape tunnel with their lives, and they would gladly do anything that their Lord Dragon commanded. The grimace that usually followed the title did not show itself in the presence of these men, and Logan's lust for revenge and sheer respect for those who followed him had taken him over. The fire in his eyes betrayed whatever calm demeanor he tried to exude, and it was clear that Logan would not rest until his men and his love had been avenged. After the men able to fight had been gathered, Logan addressed them.

"I'm very proud of you all. You have fought the hardest battle of your lives, and now you twenty men still able to fight after the hardships you have been through will be able to strike a blow for your brothers in arms against those who imprisoned you. Make no mistake, our goal here is to protect the queen and her daughter at all costs. I will gladly lay down my life for them, so none of you will try to save me if it means putting the queen or the princess in danger. I am just a man now, like all of you. My days as the Dragon are over. Now, half of you men will come with Gwydeon and I. We will head to the armory on the north end of the palace and then try to retake the throne room. We will have the most difficult task ahead of us friends, as that we will most likely meet the most resistance. The other half of you will follow Pike and Rachel to the southern armory, and then you will proceed to Sabrina's quarters. If I know Draven, there will be many guards there. Take faith in those who command you, men. They are the best warriors in the world, and if anyone can get you out of this alive, then it is these people who can do it. Now, it is time."

With that, Logan gathered his men and headed through one of the two secret passages that he had opened in the northern wall of the dungeon. Pike watched him go, and then turned to Rachel.

"You take the men to the armory, and I'll meet you at Sabrina's room."

Rachel looked at him for a moment, prepared to argue, but then held her tongue. Pike had always had a reputation for being one of the most stubborn men in the world when it came to what he wanted, and in battle, his stubbornness was magnified. With a defeated nod, Rachel led her men through the passageway toward the southern armory. After they were gone, Pike found an old man in one of the cages that he had seen earlier while the able men were being rallied. The old man had gray hair and a gray beard, and had it not been for the severely burned back and the advanced age, he could have fought with the rest of the men.

"You look like you've been in the palace for a while old man," Pike said kneeling down by his side.

"I have been the advisor to the royal court for nearly sixty years now, my lord, and I have seen the world change many times over."

"Were you here for the construction of the new palace?"

"Why of course," the advisor answered.

"Are there any passages that lead directly to the Princess's bedroom?"

"As I recall, Sabrina was very inquisitive about the design of the new palace when she was ten or twelve. She spent almost a year charting out all the secret passages, and if I remember correctly, in the kitchen, which lies just down the hall, in the ceiling of the pantry is a passage that leads to the room across the hall from the princess's bedroom."

"What is in the room across the hall old man?" Pike asked.

"It was supposed to be the Princess's study, but she turned it into a gallery for art and sculpture."

"Thank you old man. You have been very helpful."

Pike then stood and lightly ascended the stairs to the door of the dungeon. He slowly pulled the bolt on the door back, and opened the door. The passage was clear, and as Pike pulled the door closed behind him, he turned the corner heading toward the kitchen. There was a grunt and a roar from somewhere ahead of him, and Pike ducked into an alcove in the hall, and waited. There were a few more shrieks, and as Pike waited, several Jeresei rushed passed him in the hall, not even seeing him, and moved quickly toward the strange and horrific sounds. Suddenly there were more shouts and screams. Pike moved down the hall, closer to the source of the confusion. As he reached the threshold of the kitchen, Pike stifled a laugh.

In the center of the kitchen, several Jeresei and Kalbraks scuffled amongst themselves over something which lay on the table. What it looked like to Pike was a plate of meat. The three Kalbraks slashed wildly at the much quicker Jeresei, and grunted each time the nails of the Jeresei connected to their reptilian flesh. Pike moved, unseen by the chaos claimed horde across the kitchen into the pantry. Without drawing attention to himself, Pike was able to close the pantry door behind him and began looking around for something to stand on to get to the secret passage in the ceiling. Suddenly, the sounds of battle in the kitchen stopped. Without warning, the door to the pantry was ripped from its hinges, and two Jeresei darted into the room. Pike was only able to spin around and swing wildly with his axe, but the prepared Jeresei easily darted out of the way and slashed downward at the slower human. Two sets of long claws raked against the steel of Pike's armor, and the screeching meant that there would be claw trails in his armor for as long as Pike wore it. Though with many more blows like that, there wouldn't be much armor left. Pike's next swing was much better than his first. He recovered from the blows that scarred his armor and then swung around completely with axe extended and claimed one of the Jeresei in the side of the head and propelled him, with the axe still very much imbedded, into the wooden support of one of the shelves. Before Pike could recover his axe, the downward slash of a Kalbrak that had entered the pantry caused Pike to jump backwards and relinquish his hold on *Fury*. Sensing that he was close to defeat, Pike pulled the Blaze whip from his belt and quickly lashed out toward the Kalbrak. The whip cracked with energy as it struck the large green beast, and the monster cried out in agony as a black mark was left where the whip had connected with its flesh. The remaining Jeresei seemed a little more leery now, as Pike wielded the whip with the grace of a master. The next lash wrapped around the leg of the Kalbrak. The green fires leapt from the leather of the whip and began to soar up the body of the Kalbrak as if it were devouring the beast. In a matter of seconds, the reptilian-skinned monster was reduced to ash. Pike withdrew the whip, a new sense of power filling him, and lashed out at the final Jeresei. The whip struck the Jeresei in the neck, wrapping itself around tightly. Pike then pulled hard on the whip, snapping the neck of the Jeresei like a twig. Its lifeless body crumbled to the ground, and then burned slowly in a dark green bonfire. Satisfied with his new weapon, Pike reattached it to his belt, and then pulled *Fury* away from the support and the former Jeresei. Using a chair from the kitchen to boost himself up, Pike found the passageway, and began the climb toward Sabrina's study.

* * * * * * * * * * * *

Logan winced as he climbed the narrow ladder which led up to the armory which lay a floor below the throne room. One of the Jeresei had managed to strike a blow to his right side during the battle in the dungeon, but at the time he had not felt it. He could now feel the blood as it oozed under his armor, but his clothing had been enough to stop a lot of the blood flow, and after a time it should have been enough to close the wound until he could find a healer to take a look at it. Logan knew that he had suffered worse injuries in the past, but at the time, this wound could seriously hurt his chances against an enemy like Draven who would exploit any weakness that he could find in his opponent. Logan knew that he was lucky the last time that he faced Draven, and once the phase learned he had not succeeded in killing Logan, he would make sure that when the next opportunity arose, nothing would stand between him and his ultimate goal of succeeding where all of the other phasia had failed. That meant that Draven would be more vicious, and more cunning in the next confrontation, and it would not end until one of them lay broken and bleeding on the floor in front of the other. Logan knew in his heart that if it came down to it, Draven would be the victor.

The ladder now came to its end, and Logan pushed the rectangular hatch up just slightly and then moved it to his right, sliding the floor tile above him out of the way. Slowly he poked his head out of the newly created hole and looked around. The armory stood empty of guards, and most of the stock of weapons remained untouched. Logan shook his head and thought how strange it was for there to be a passageway from the dungeon to the armory, but he thanked the Creator that someone was stupid enough to do it. After pulling himself quietly into the armory, Logan motioned for his companions to follow, and put a finger to his lips to denote the silence needed in case guards were outside the door to the armory. If they were discovered now, while they would have a fighting chance, it wouldn't take long for them to be overwhelmed by superior numbers. One by one, the men entered the armory and quietly began to don armor and take up weapons. Gwydeon was the last to come up the hatch, and after he was in the room, Logan helped him to close the passageway.

"Now," Logan whispered to Gwydeon, "we leave this room and head down the hall. There is an auxiliary staircase there that leads to the throne room. It will be a tough fight, but we should be able to get there. Cairyn's sleeping quarters are adjacent to the throne room. Once we get there, I'll go after her. Good luck old friend."

"And to you Logan," Gwydeon replied.

Logan nodded and readied his men. The fight for their lives and their way of life was about to be renewed, and it was the opening of the armory door that brought the spark back into Gwydeon. He saw the astonished faces of the Jeresei as Logan and his men sprang forward, chopping down everything that moved. There were screams and cries of terror as each and every member of the Jeresei fell to the blades of the newly freed Army of the Dragon. Gwydeon did not strike a blow, and lagged behind as the invigorated men charged forward behind their battle-crazed leader. Jeresei and other servants of the Shadow emerged from side passages only to find themselves cut down by either the Dragon Sword, or by the weapon of one Logan's followers. Not one of them had the time to even extend its claws before it found its life at an end. Gwydeon realized how far behind he had dropped from the rest of the pack, but he could not help but feel that there was something wrong; that the entry to the palace and the fact that they had gotten this far was just too easy. Gwydeon held the Lion Sword close to him and felt a rush of power that he did not recognize. The sword pulled toward a passageway in the opposite direction from Logan. There was something down that hall that the Lion Sword wanted Gwydeon to see, so Gwydeon turned and separated himself from the rest of the group and ran down the hall following the lead of the sword that belonged to a fallen hero.

There was no opposition between Gwydeon and whatever it was that the sword was leading him to, not even a wayward Jeresei. Suddenly, the

Lion Sword pulled itself from Gwydeon's hands. It hovered in front of Gwydeon with a strange blue glow emanating from its tip. The glow traveled down the length of the blade until the whole sword pulsed with the strange new energy. The blade then turned toward the nearest wall, and buried itself to the hilt. Before Gwydeon could do anything, the sword began to cut the stone of the wall. It inched itself through the mortar and the stone until it cut a small doorway. On the other side of the new passage, there appeared to be another armory. This one was much smaller, with very ornate weaponry lining the walls, and a large cauldron standing in the center of the room. Gwydeon stepped into the new armory. After Gwydeon was fully in the room, the sword floated past him, and upon turning around, Gwydeon found that the wall had sealed itself. Gwydeon began to worry for a moment, but then this feeling of peace and familiarity entered him.

"Welcome Gwydeon Sandar, hero of the old gods," a voice said in his mind. "You are welcome here in the home of the Elder. You have not met us before, but we know of you. Emries has spoken highly of you in the past, and he wanted us to make sure that you knew that we had not abandoned you."

"What are you?"

Gwydeon thought that he had spoken, but suddenly he realized that his lips had not moved and no sound came from his throat. He then realized that he was communicating with the Elder through his thoughts.

"We are a race of creature that live inside the molten core of the world. We were born and raised there, and our lives are tied to the life of the world. This world is dying because of Shau-ling's twisted children, and because the *Coromor* is not strong enough yet to oppose him. If something is not done soon, this world will fall into the hands of the Shadow, and the world will die. Shau-ling has forgotten what he once was, and in doing so, he will sentence this world to death. Our allegiance lies with the *Coromor* and his chosen servants, the *Erieal*. We are responsible for the *Debuisa*, which help to harness the raw power of the *Erieal* into something that the *Coromor* can more readily use."

"Are you going to make *Debuisa* for this generation?"

"Not yet; the time is not right. You must save this palace at all costs
Gwydeon Sandar. We are the last of our kind, and without our help, the
Coromor and the *Erieal* will be unprepared to fight the forces of Shau-ling.
Go now. Remember what we have said."

Just as suddenly as the strange incident had started, it ended, and
Gwydeon found himself standing outside the armory again, more confused
than he had ever been before. Hearing the sounds of battle further down
the hall, Gwydeon ran toward his comrades, hoping that he could do what
was demanded of him.

* * * * * * * * * * * *

Pike could not believe that the passage he was in was ever intended for
anyone larger than a child. His armor was pressed horrendously tight
against his body, and it made it hard for him to breathe as he dragged
himself toward the study of the Princess. His axe dragged behind him, a
concession of the tight space, and his arms stretched in front of him,
dragging him inches at a time closer to his goal. The sweating had started
just after entering the passage, and the humidity in the cramped space was
almost unbearable. Had it not been for the fact that his adrenaline was still
pumping like mad, he probably would have passed out long ago. But Pike
Rhuiden was not the kind of man to quit. Finally, the passageway widened
a bit, and a few feet later, the hatch that led down into the study was before
him. Relieved, he slowly opened the latch and slid the panel out of the way,
looking down into the study. Pike found an easy place to land, and a quietly
as he could manage, dropped from the ceiling onto his feet.

For a few moments Pike waited to make sure that no one had heard him
enter the room, and he pressed his ear to the door to see if he could hear
anything outside of the study. There were a few pieces of the guttural
communication between members of the Jeresei, but other than that, Pike
could not hear very much. Surprise was still very much on Pike's side, and
as he looked around the room, he found the perfect way to distract the
guards. A dark blue vase toppled from the shelf with a crash, and Pike
pressed himself flush against the wall behind where the door would swing
open and waited. After a moment, the door swung open, and one of the
Jeresei cautiously stepped into the room. As it turned the corner, out of the
doorway, but before it could look up, Pike cracked its skull with his axe and

pulled the body down to the floor without a sound. There were many puzzled sounds coming from the passageway, but Pike could only make out one set, where there had once been two. The second guard walked into the room, and was greeted by *Fury* in the chest, and a hand over its mouth. The Jeresei wailed as best it could, but only minimal sound came out. Pike then closed the door and waited a few more seconds before opening it again. With a quick look out in the hall, Pike could see that there were guards outside the door across the hall. They had not yet noticed the disappearance of their cohorts, but that wouldn't last too long. Concentrating his powers on one of the guards, Pike could see the faint tendrils of cold begin to weave around the Jeresei. While there was no outward appearance of a change, the blood inside the Jeresei had been frozen to a standstill, and the poor beast was only a helpless observer in its last moments alive. Within a matter of moments, the second guard had suffered the same fate, and Pike was able to walk quickly across the hall to the Princess's bedroom.

With a slow turn of the handle, Pike opened the door and entered the bedroom. There on the bed lay the Princess Sabrina, tied and gagged. Her clothing was terribly ripped, and her legs were splayed open in the most lewd and vulgar of positions. There were stains of tears on her face, and there was also some blood coming from her nose. Pike's stomach lurched when he saw the pool of blood in between her legs. Wincing to himself, Pike quickly unchained the poor girl and held her tightly as she sobbed on his shoulder. He knew that they could be discovered at any moment, but the important thing now was to make sure that the girl was alright. What had been done to here was anyone's best guess, but Pike had a pretty good idea. Now the hatred began to boil in him. This man Draven had to die. Pike had not felt hatred this strongly in him since he watched Eldar die at Taron's hand.

There was the sound of battle coming his way, and he hoped that Rachel and the men of the Army of the Dragon were winning. After a moment or two, the sounds subsided, and the door to the bedroom began to open. Rachel was lucky that Pike was not the nervous type, otherwise she would have been split in two as she bolted through the door. She stopped short when she saw that Pike had his axe raised for a fight. Pike relaxed a little when he saw Rachel, but without a word, he picked up Sabrina in one of his strong arms and held her lovingly to his chest after placing *Fury* in the loop in his belt. He carried her through the door without a word to Rachel and moved toward where the men had come from. Just then, there was a brilliant flash of light, and one of the soldiers fell to the floor screaming in pain. He was on fire, but the flames were not natural. Their peaks were black when they should have been white and orange. This could only be done by a member of the phasia, and Pike knew which one. Pike lay Sabrina down on the floor, still curled up in a ball, and strode forward, axe in hand, and waited.

Suddenly the passageway went dark, many of the men began to mumble or mill about with fear, but Pike stood firm. When the lights came up again, a man dressed in black with a flowing cloak stood before Pike with sword in hand. His face held a look of both anger and disbelief. Suddenly those conflicted looks disappeared and the man smiled.

"Who dares to enter my kingdom and steal my queen, seemingly out from under my nose?"

"She is a little girl Draven," Pike answered with a growl, "and this is not your kingdom. This kingdom is the property of the people inside its borders and it is ruled by Queen Cairyn Binosear. This is the Kingdom of the Lioness, and I am here to take it back for the people."

"Who is this fool who dares to speak to me in this way?" Draven said looking up at the ceiling. "Surely he knows that he will die by my hand if he does not yield."

"I have killed phasia stronger than you Draven, and it will not pain me in the slightest to cover my axe with your putrid blood."

"A warrior of the Light, here, in my palace? Surely not. You were all supposed to be extinct. Now," Draven asked playfully, "which one are you?"

"Ask your brother Taron."

Draven smiled even wider.

"It is good to finally meet you Pike Rhuiden."

Pike nodded mockingly, and Draven's head cocked to the side, the smile taking a more quizzical slant.

"Aren't you supposed to be dead?"

"People like me don't stay dead long."

"We shall have to correct that," Draven replied suddenly serious.

"Then I take it that this will be a fight?"

Draven nodded.

"To the death?"

Draven nodded again.

"Winner gets Trelon?"

Again a nod in response.

"Good."

"Goodbye Pike," Draven said raising his sword to a ready position.

"Stop!"

The shout came from down the hall, and everyone looked to see who it came from. A lone man was running toward them, sword in hand, a look of anger and determination etched on his face. Pike recognized Gwydeon as soon as he set eyes on the red armor. Draven smiled when he finally recognized Gwydeon.

"This is not your fight Sandar," Draven said finally, "Pike and I have an agreement and we are going to finish this here and now. The winner gets Trelon, and the loser dies."

"This is not his fight, Draven," Gwydeon replied pushing his way past Pike. "You and I have had a score to settle for the longest time now, and it is high time that I collected on the debt that you owe me. Pike has his own vendetta against the phasia, but he does not know you. You and I will settle this, where it all began. Portal us to Aradon, and let us make an end of this battle."

"Old man," Draven said nearly laughing, "are you really that eager to die? Don't you have a wife to go home to, and a pitiful rebellion to run?"

"My wife and the rebellion will go on without me Draven, and if there is a chance that I can kill you with my last breath, they will be better off for it. My life means nothing so long as you are still alive."

"Then I accept your challenge, Gwydeon Sandar. Follow me to your graveyard."

Draven turned, laughed to himself, and then opened a portal and stepped through. The portal hung there in the passageway, waiting for its second passenger. Gwydeon was about to step through when Pike grabbed him by the arm.

"Don't do this Gwydeon," Pike cautioned, "he'll kill you."

"Yes, but he won't rip up the palace or kill everyone in his sight if he kills me. We will be away from Trelon, and that gives you time to get Sabrina and Cairyn out of here. Also, tell Logan to follow the Dragon Sword and get the Elder out of here. Don't ask questions just do it. Now, get out of here, I have work to do."

With that Gwydeon pulled himself free and leapt through the portal leaving Pike wondering if he would ever see his friend alive again.

Betrayal of the Heart

Creator's Calendar Year 1205; Light Reality

The sun had just begun to crest over the hills to the east when Lissa and Wolf made their way into the makeshift camp of the queen and princess. Wolf and Lissa had slept longer than they had expected, and it was only Wolf's habit of awaking before sunrise that had saved them from possible discovery. After a brief kiss and caress, the two newly found lovers separated and began to break camp. The noise stirred the princess first and then the queen. Cairyn sat up slowly and gracefully, keeping the dignity of her station while Sabrina seemed to move much more causally, stretching and yawning as though she had just awoken in her chambers rather than on the forest floor. After taking in the surroundings Cairyn turned her attention the young man who was helping to pack Lissa's belongings into her saddlebags.

"Good morning Wolf," the queen said softly. "I trust that there were no problems during the night while we slept."

"None my queen," Wolf responded as graciously as he could manage, "Logan's Wood protected us."

"Very good," was her reply. "I do not know what your plans for travel are today Wolf, but we are continuing on to Aradon, and we would appreciate it very much if you joined us."

This caught Sabrina's attention and she stood, smoothed her dress and crossed her arms, frowning.

"Mother," Sabrina said not missing a beat, "surely Wolf has other places that he needs to be today. I doubt that he would want to accompany us on our chore."

"The funeral of a beloved friend is hardly what I would call a chore Princess Sabrina, in fact, were I a more unforgiving man, I would have taken that as a direct insult."

Lissa winced at Wolf's tone, and Sabrina easily noticed this. There was a dead silence for a moment, and then Sabrina rounded on the older man.

"I would not think that a man of your stature would be wounded by a mere mistake in wording, Wolf. Our errand is none of your concern and while we appreciate your bravery where those bandits are concerned, we are not beholden to you for anything more than our thanks. Anyone could have fired a few arrows into that rabble."

Sabrina's tone was harsh and pointed. She did not like being challenged or belittled in front of her mother, and she knew that if she was upstaged by a common boy in front of the queen that her chances of learning the ways of the court from her were greatly diminished. Cairyn had never been comfortable letting Sabrina have a hand in the matters of court, but she was starting to ease up on her position because of the way that Sabrina handled herself. However, that might all change if she allowed herself to be out maneuvered and out thought by a commoner. It would have been acceptable had it been a lord with more experience in courtly matters, but not a boy.

"Your lives were in danger," Wolf retorted. "I had to pick my shots for the most effective result, otherwise you all would have been dead. Surprise is only effective as long as it keeps your opponents off-balance and in your control. Once the advantage of surprise has been negated, the battle falls to numbers and arms. And in case you didn't count Princess, we were out-numbered."

"So it's 'we' now, is it? All they probably wanted was to scare us into giving them money. It would have been over after that. Besides, if you hadn't shown up, Lissa and I would have been able to take care of them."

Wolf laughed and he knew the moment he did that it was harsher than he intended it to be. When he looked back at Sabrina, her face has hardened and it appeared as if she were trying to hold back her emotions. Lissa's face was flushed, and she was trying not to react at all. The queen on the other hand had sat down on a log and was watching the whole scene with a wide if seemingly misplaced smile on her face.

"Princess," Wolf said in a very dignified and respectful voice, "with no offense intended to your abilities or the abilities of your companion, there is no way that you would have been able to defend yourselves from the attack. You were out-numbered, your opponents had the element of surprise, you were unarmed while they had weapons, and your fear had overpowered your ability to act. And, just to clarify matters, they were not looking for money. People of that ilk would not have attacked in that manner if their intentions were to simply rob you. Robbers do not linger, they would have taken your belongings quickly and cleanly. These men, these thugs, had only one intention. They would have raped all three of you and then left you for dead. Also, if you think your identities would have protected you, think again."

Here Wolf paused once more. He wanted to be sure that Sabrina understood his next statement, and that there would be no doubt.

"If they would have known who you were, they never would have attacked in that manner. They would have threatened only, never taken direct action, and would have moved to subdue you all. If you would have identified yourself and they didn't know who you were already, their fear would have likely caused them to simply kill you and make sure your bodies were never found. The last thing a petty criminal wants is to have the whole of the Army of Trelon hunting for them. No offense intended princess, but you were lucky that I came along. Otherwise, you would likely have been dead or worse."

Wolf's tone never wavered from a calm steady voice, and never grew louder than a normal speaking tone. He was not matter-of-fact in his presentation of his opinion, and was trying not to be on the offensive or start an argument, he was merely trying to put across the facts like his mother taught him to do.

"You seem to be an expert on these men, Wolf," Sabrina countered, "perhaps that is because you are one of them as Lissa and I originally thought."

The Queen smiled wider at this counter, but she waited and held her judgment. There was something very familiar about the way that the boy was arguing and the way that he kept his tone. She had heard that voice and seen that manner before, but she could not quite place where. There was a natural diplomacy and force of will in him that she had only seen one other time...

"If that were a statement that I felt deserved an answer princess, I would defend myself, but you are now merely trying to injure me so that I will lash out and make myself look guilty. So, I will simply say that you are mistaken and that I did what I did because that is my way. The simple fact that you are alive and unharmed should prove that I had no intentions other than those that I have already made known. Now, if there is nothing else that you wish to say princess, then we should start moving if you want to be to Aradon before mid-day."

Sabrina fumed for a moment, and was about to speak, but a hand rested lightly on her shoulder and somehow restrained her words. Cairyn had walked up behind her and intentionally interjected her presence into the argument. She had heard enough.

"You are right, Wolf," Cairyn said after a moment, "we had no right to doubt your intentions, and we would greatly accept your company on this trip."

Sabrina turned at stared her mother straight in the eyes. Cairyn saw the look of shock and dismay on her daughter's face, and smiled.

"Don't worry Sabrina," Cairyn responded to the silent question, "there are few alive who could have outmaneuvered Wolf from an inferior position. He is possessed of two of the most powerful forces in the world, Tamerlane stubbornness, and Ranthall pride. Together they make for a nearly unbeatable combination, and I doubt I could have fared much better than you against him. I have had the displeasure of encountering that side of a Tamerlane before, and let us just say that I hope I never fare that badly in any political arena."

Sabrina looked puzzled.

"My mother could be a bit difficult at times my queen," Wolf commented, "but she was always fair and honest in her opinions and her views. I doubt that she had the ability to lie."

"Not when it came to matters of the heart my dear boy," Cairyn added. "She was a fine woman. I count her as one of my greatest teachers, and one of my most treasured friends."

Now Sabrina turned and stared Wolf in the face.

"You are Wolf Ranthall?"

Wolf nodded. Sabrina turned back to her mother and silently questioned again.

"If you had ever had the pleasure of meeting Elwyne Tamerlane, Sabrina, it would have been easy to see her in Wolf. He looks a lot like his father, but he acts more like Elwyne. Tell me Wolf, whose temper would you say you had?"

"Probably my father's," Wolf responded.

"It is a good thing for the phasia that you do," Cairyn said laughing, "or they would never stand a chance."

Wolf chuckled to himself and continued to help break camp. Cairyn didn't say another word and gathered her things. Still bewildered by the turn of events, Sabrina walked over to Lissa and sighed.

"Please tell me that you didn't know."

"I didn't know," Lissa said flatly.

"Is that a lie?" Sabrina asked, already knowing the answer.

Lissa nodded.

"I just made a complete fool out of myself in front of him Lissa," Sabrina fretted as she helped Lissa put their things in to the saddlebags, "he probably thinks I'm a spoiled brat who doesn't know anything. I was trying to impress him by standing up for myself."

"You weren't standing long," Lissa said trying to be strong and yet not too cruel.

Sabrina winced and then turned Lissa to face her. After a cautious look around, Sabrina looked Lissa straight in the eyes.

"What do you think of him?"

Lissa looked to find where Wolf was, to find him chatting with the queen. They were probably talking about his mother and catching up on what had happened to his family over the years. When she looked back at Sabrina, she saw that her younger friend's eyes had taken on a glow that she had never seen before.

"He's nice," Lissa said trying not to be too obvious. "He is strong, confident, and arrogant as hell..."

"And handsome," Sabrina added.

Lissa sighed.

"What are you telling me Sabrina?"

"Well," Sabrina hedged, "I don't know. He . . . he just, I don't know. The way he looks at me with those eyes of his. It's like, he not looking at me, but he's looking through me."

Lissa shivered. She remembered his eyes staring down at her as they made love in the forest. Now, every time he looked at her, she shivered. She could still feel his arms around her, and his strength as he held her. Suddenly she realized that she had drifted from the conversation. After snapping herself back to reality, she realized that she had to tell Sabrina the truth.

"Ladies?"

Lissa and Sabrina both jolted when they heard Wolf's voice. He was only a few feet away, but he had apparently not heard any of their conversation. At least Lissa hoped that he hadn't heard anything. With his newly manifest abilities, anything was possible.

"What is it Wolf?" Lissa asked, trying to keep her tone even.

"The queen wanted me to tell you that we were going to ride ahead, and that when you two are ready, you should catch up with us. I have to go get my horse from my encampment, and the queen said that she would come along with me. We'll meet you in the clearing just outside the wood."

"We're almost done here," Lissa responded, "we'll meet you there."

Wolf nodded and then walked toward the queen who patiently waited by one of the many forest paths. Wolf said something to her, she nodded, and the two of them set out through the woods. After watching them go, Lissa turned back to Sabrina and sighed hard again.

"I have something that I have to tell you Sabrina, and I don't think that you're going to take it very well, so you would probably be better off if you sat down."

Sabrina looked puzzled at her friend, but she shrugged her shoulders and sat down.

"It's becoming clear to me that you are trying to tell me that you have feelings for Wolf. Is that true?"

"I don't know Lissa," Sabrina said, trying to be as honest with her friend as she could, "I've never felt this way about anyone, with the possible exception of you, but I've only just met Wolf."

"Do you think you love him?"

"Is it too soon to know that yet?" Sabrina asked.

"That all depends. There have been many cases of love at first sight, especially in your family. Your mother fell in love with Pike the moment she saw him, and your grandmother married her husband three days after meeting him, and they were very happy together. So, I would say that love at first sight is a very possible thing."

Sabrina didn't want to answer directly, so she evaded the best way she knew how.

"Have you ever been in love Lissa?"

"You know the answer to that Sabrina," Lissa responded trying to brush away the subject.

"No, Lissa," Sabrina responded shaking her head, "I don't. You never want to talk about things like this, and this is the first time that we have held a serious conversation about love. You always just say no and change the subject or ignore it all together. It's almost as if you don't want to admit you have feelings because they cause you problems."

Sabrina had accomplished her goal and had derailed the conversation. Except this time, instead of stopping the conversation and walking away, Lissa continued.

"I don't think I've ever been in love Sabrina," Lissa responded coldly, "so I don't know what it's like. That's what is going to make this even harder for me."

Sabrina looked hard at her friend and then waited, still trying to figure out what her friend was about to say.

"After you and Cairyn went to sleep, Wolf and I went out and had a talk. We talked a little about family and other things, though he still didn't tell me who he was. Then, we ran into a little trouble. Apparently there was a member of the phasia looking for something here in the woods, and she brought along a group of Jeresei as her back-up."

Something inside of Sabrina tensed. They had been preparing to fight the phasia all their lives, and now the waiting was over.

"Which one was it?" Sabrina asked.

"Not one of the ones that Pike told us about. Her name was Rane, and apparently Shau-ling has been busy creating some new phasia. Anyway, Wolf and I fought off some Jeresei, but not before I got cut."

Lissa pulled down the shoulder of her shirt to reveal the wound. Midarin had done a good job of patching it, and Lissa was able to put on a new shirt before anyone had noticed.

"I had to hide this from Cairyn, or there would have been a lot of needless explaining to do. Then this twisted woman calling herself Rane, the daughter of Shau-ling shows up. She is obsessed with blood, and loves the feel of it, so she continually tears at my wound, tasting my blood. Then she threatens to cut Wolf open, and I snap. I hit her in the back with a ball of fire, and she turns and challenges me. With all that I have, I channel some lightning at her which seems to catch her off-guard, but then she uses that black force bubble that Pike told us about and imprisons me in it. I'm lying there thrashing on the ground, trying hard to free myself, but I'm starting to lose consciousness because there is no air to breathe, and it feels like the blackness is burning my lungs, so I have to push all the air out just to take away the pain. Then, just as I am about to black-out, a bolt of lightning hits the bubble and dissipates it. When I finally am coherent enough to see what's going on, there stands Midarin, Gwillim, Nathaniel, Liette, and Aryx."

Sabrina's eyes were wide at the retelling of the confrontation with the phase, but the revelation that Aryx Terian was still alive shocked her even more.

"Was it Nightwing, or was it Aryx?"

Lissa frowned, the corner of her mouth curling into a sneer.

"It was Aryx Terian alright, but whether Nightwing was still present as part of him I can't say. But wait it gets even weirder. Rane made the mistake of making Midarin angry, and got the business end of one of her arrows in response. Then Rane uses a portal and escapes, but she sends her Jeresei to attack us. Aryx was doing his amount of damage, and the rest were starting to get into the fray, but Wolf was isolated by several of the red-skins, and one of them leapt at him from behind. Before I could do anything or anyone else could act, this wave of black energy erupts from Wolf and splits the Jeresei in half. Then he falls to his knees, almost like the Jeresei struck him anyway. He's on the ground trembling, and then there's another explosion of energy. This time, it is enough to shake us all and kill a few more of the Jeresei. When he stands, he looks down at his sword, and it floats up into his hand. By this time, we're all just standing there watching him, and there is something visibly different about him. I could swear that he had gotten larger in just that matter of seconds."

"What do you mean larger?" Sabrina asked.

"I don't mean that he grew taller, or that he was physically bigger like Pike, but it was as if all of his muscles were more defined, and he held himself in a taller stature with his shoulders pulled back. He looked impressive. I could compare him to the way that Pike looks when he is getting ready to ride into battle, or into a kingdom to meet with an opposing king. The way that he held his sword was different too. Before the change, it held it like it was a weapon. It was obvious that he had some training, but it was just a sword. As he stood there then, he held the sword lightly against his body so that it was almost a part of him, and when he moved, it moved with him effortlessly. Then, Wolf called out to the Jeresei in their own language, this primitive growl coming from deep in his chest."

"He spoke to them?" Sabrina asked with a mixture of awe and concern.

"It was an eerie sound," Lissa continued. "The Jeresei were taken off guard by that, but they readied themselves for a strike anyway. They never had the chance though. Between Aryx, Gwillim, Midarin, and myself, the Jeresei were dead before they knew what hit them. There was one Jeresei left though, and Wolf was watching it the whole time that lightning and arrows were leaping past him. He never moved a muscle and just stood there watching. Then Wolf talked to the Jeresei directly, and after a short conversation, Wolf let the Jeresei go."

Sabrina smiled to herself, the telling of the story getting to her emotional attachment of Wolf.

"I'll bet that Aryx was less than pleased with that."

"To put it mildly. He wanted to kill Wolf where he stood, and he just might have tried, but I challenged him."

"You did what?" Sabrina gasped.

"I stepped between Aryx and Wolf and I challenged him. I said that I'd kill him where he stood if he took any action against Wolf."

"Then what happened?"

"He was going to do it until Midarin told him that I was his daughter."

Sabrina sighed and nodded. There was so much information, she was having a hard time processing it all.

"So, Wolf has powers like we do."

"Well," Lissa said after a moment, "not according to Wolf and Nathaniel. Wolf says that the phase Basille gave his string of power to Wolf while he was a baby, because his birthright was taken away from him. He stood there and told us all that he was a member of the Ranthall family and that he had the power of a full member of the phasia. Nathaniel seemed to agree with that when he looked into the strings and looked at Wolf. However, Wolf's powers are not just confined to that of the phasia. He also has the power to draw from the knowledge of the Blaze just like a member of the phasia. He knows almost everything about them, and what he doesn't know, he can learn by concentrating."

"I wonder why I didn't see his powers?" Sabrina asked the air.

"It could be because his powers hadn't fully manifested yet. You know that Nathaniel has always been able to pick those things up faster than any of us."

Sabrina nodded absently, but wasn't finished.

"Or it was because your emotions are clouding your vision. Pike always said that if your emotions are in the way, you are more powerful, but you are less able to see the obvious. After all, all of the powers of the *Erieal* are driven by emotions like anger and hatred, but sometimes they are driven by love and devotion. I'm sure it's true that the powers of the *Coromor* and the

Chosen One are the same way. Either way, you should introduce yourself for who you are and then ask him if you can try to draw on his powers."

"I think I will," Sabrina said.

She sat there for a moment looking at her friend, and then a question came to her mind.

"What else is it Lissa?" Sabrina asked suddenly. "You wouldn't have had me sit down to tell me this. What happened?"

"Well," Lissa replied swallowing hard. This was the hardest thing that she ever had to do, and the fact that it was her best friend made it even harder. "After the battle, Wolf and I came back here to check on you and Cairyn. After we stoked the fire and made sure everything was ok, we headed back to talk to Midarin and the others for a few minutes before calling it a night. Well, I don't know what I was thinking, but I just stopped, turned around and kissed him."

Sabrina just sat there staring at Lissa, the expression on her face unchanged.

"For a second he just stood there, as if he didn't know what to do, but then he took me in his arms and kissed me back, hard."

"How was it?" Sabrina asked flatly.

"It was ok," Lissa mumbled.

"Lissa," Sabrina said as she stood, "I want you to tell me the truth. You can't hurt my feelings worse than they have already been hurt. I just appreciate the fact that you are telling me. Besides, I haven't even talked to him yet without arguing or making a fool out of myself, so why should I mind that he kissed you?"

Lissa exhaled slowly and shrugged her shoulders.

"So?"

"It was wonderful," Lissa admitted both to herself and to her sister. "He doesn't really look it, but his arms are very strong and supporting. I could have kissed him forever if he would have let me."

"So, is that all that happened?"

Lissa stayed silent. Sabrina just stared.

"No."

There was a pressure in Sabrina's chest that she had never felt before. It was like being kicked in the chest by a bucking horse, but worse. For a second she found it hard to breathe, but she tried to cover as best she could. Something was clawing at the back of her mind. Sabrina had always had to contend with the older beautiful woman that she thought of as her sister in her life, but seeing the eyes of men float by her to the red-haired beauty had never bothered Sabrina. There had never been jealousy between them. Now though, something had changed, and the scratching in her mind became louder and more demanding. There was an echo of emotion there, and Sabrina for the first time felt as though the emotion came from somewhere other than her own heart.

"We were just coming back to camp for the night, and I had stopped to look at a path that led to another part of the woods. He must have been paying attention to something else, because he walked right into me. When I turned around he smiled and looked at me with those blue eyes and something in me snapped. I don't know how to explain it, but I just wrapped my arms around him and kissed him again. He seemed almost shocked, but he kept kissing and holding me, and then we somehow found our way onto a patch of grass, and we made love there under the moon and stars."

About this time, Lissa saw a single tear fall from Sabrina's eye. Her breathing was very shallow, and her skin was paler than it should have been. Lissa kept waiting for the rest of the tears to fall, but none did. Finally, Sabrina took a long labored breath and focused her eyes on Lissa again. A cold pall had fallen over Sabrina's emotions, a control that she didn't know she was capable of, but also a barely contained rage that was unfamiliar and frightening.

"So, are you going to continue to be with him, or was this just an accidental thing."

Sabrina's voice was hoarse, and it seemed that choking out every word was a chore.

"I don't know, Sabrina," Lissa answered as honestly as she could. "I didn't intend for anything to happen between us, and I didn't know that you were going to fall in love with him. But I'm not sorry for what I've done, and I'd like to continue to be with him if he wants me to. I'm sorry."

Sabrina looked down at the ground for a moment, and then looked up at her friend and smiled.

"You're right, Lissa," she said as easily as she could, her heart still aching in her chest. "There was no way you could have known how I felt. I didn't even know until a minute ago. Let's just let this go, and act like it never happened. I want you to be happy with Wolf if that is the way the two of you end up. Don't worry about me, I'm ok."

"Are you sure?"

"I'm sure," Sabrina responded.

Lissa took her friend into her arms and held her tight before breaking the embrace and gathering the rest of her things into the saddlebags. In a matter of moments, Lissa was on her horse and looking down at her friend.

"Come on sis," Lissa said as playfully as she could, "we better get going if we are going to make it to Aradon on time."

Sabrina nodded and mounted her horse.

"Lead on sis," Sabrina said smiling.

As Lissa turned her steed and led it down the path toward the clearing where they were to meet Wolf and Cairyn, Sabrina glared at her.

Don't get the idea that I have forgiven you yet, bitch, Sabrina thought to herself the thoughts partially hers and partially a voice she didn't know. *He may want you now, but what happens when he finds out about your little tryst with my brother? What if he finds out about the child you lost? I still have my doubts that it was Duncan at all. I still think that it was Pike in your bed that night, but I can't be sure. One thing is for sure though sister, this is far from over.* Sabrina then dug her heels into the horse's flanks and bolted off after Lissa.

There was motion in the bushes behind where the two girls had been sitting. Finally, one of the branches moves aside, and a flash of green fabric became visible for a moment before it disappeared again. Finally, the bush disappeared, and where it was, stood a woman dressed in a tight and revealing green dress. There was a cruel smile on her face, and a look of victory in her eyes. She had heard the entire conversation between the two girls and she had stoked the fires of jealousy as high as they could go while still being believable, and she was beginning to form a plan to exploit her new discovery. Perhaps it was time to pay her friends in Marcwell and Trelon a visit. With a wave of her hand, a blue portal appeared behind her, and Caris stepped through, laughing to herself the entire time.

* * * * * * * * * * * *

At Midarin's suggestion, Wolf told Cairyn an abbreviated story of what had happened the previous evening while they walked to his encampment. He had left out all of the powers from Lissa and the existence of Aryx, but in essence the story had been a true one. The important part of the story was that they were supposed to meet with Midarin and her family at the clearing. Cairyn seemed rather happy about that, but she also seemed a bit troubled. Wolf noticed this and decided to press the point.

"Is there something about Queen Midarin that bothers you?"

Cairyn seemed a little shocked by the question, but after taking a moment to settle her thoughts, she answered as graciously as she could. The young man was insightful, as she should have expected considering who his mother was, but she was not as practiced as she once was in speaking with someone freely and openly.

"Midarin never had the best reputation while she was growing up, and in most royal circles she was considered an outcast even before she was banished from her kingdom. My mother never spoke highly of her, and most of the gossip that I was told from the visiting princesses of other kingdoms and other dignitaries was that she wasn't to be trusted and that she was a bit of a tramp. In fact, on many occasions, the word whore was used very plainly about her. I took all of these rumors at face value, as one should with court gossip, but then when she was exiled on the charges of treason for seducing one of her fiancé's personal guards, the rumors seemed to be true. However, I soon learned that her circumstances were less than ideal in Brea, and that she had not had the opportunities that I had been given in Trelon. After all, having the name Binosear does carry a lot of advantages with it. Then, after I married Pike, I began to gain respect for her because of her devotion to her dead lover Gwydeon, and to her child Nathaniel. If anything were to happen to that boy, I don't know what she would do. It is likely that she would kill herself out of grief."

"So," Wolf asked trying not to sound impertinent, "what is the problem?"

"Just because I have respect for her, it doesn't mean that I trust her. On the contrary, I trust her about as much as I trust a member of the phasia, or my husband for that matter. Which is the case and point. For about three years now, the rumors have been flying that Pike has been having an affair. Trust me when I say that there are several candidates for this highly desired position, but recently Midarin has been at the top of the list. I would like to give her and Pike the benefit of the doubt, but after a while of hearing the same thing over and over again, whether it is true or not, you just may have to start believing it."

Wolf nodded, and upon seeing that the fire from his camp was still burning, drew his sword and brought the queen's horse to a halt.

"Wait here my queen, there is someone else here."

Wolf moved ahead, using his powers to make him so light that his feet didn't touch the ground, and he walked on air. Upon reaching the clearing that he had chosen for a camp, Wolf waited at the tree line and watched for a sign of the person that had kept the fire going. There by his horse sat an older man, probably in his late thirties, or early forties, smoking a pipe and watching the fire. His clothes were expensive in nature, but they had been heavily worn, and had holes in many places. His hair was well kept, and he appeared to be clean. His clothes, though they were worn were also sparkling clean. On the ground next to him was a scepter, and on his left hip was a scabbard.

"You can come closer," he said after a moment, "I'm not going to hurt you."

Wolf eased himself back onto the ground and then walked forward into the camp.

"I hope you don't mind that I used your camp last night, it is so much easier to stoke someone else's fire than to build your own when you have no flint or steel. Besides, your horse looked lonely, and I decided to keep it company for the night."

"Thank you, sir," Wolf said after a moment.

"Jared."

"Thank you Jared. Now, not to be rude, but I must be off."

"Going to Aradon?" Jared said as he stood.

"As a matter of fact. I have a funeral to attend with some of my friends."

"Do you know of a place there where I can get a hot meal?"

"Of course," Wolf said smiling, "follow me. Least I can do to pay you back for taking care of my horse."

Jared gathered his up his sword, which he had been using to stoke the fire, and his scepter, and followed Wolf through the brush back to where Cairyn was waiting. While he had been standing silent, Wolf had gotten a good look at Jared.

He was about Wolf's height, but he was stockier and had a lot more thickness in his chest and shoulders. His hair was brown, and long, reaching almost to his shoulders. There was something about his face that Wolf found familiar, but with all of the thoughts in his head that had come from the Blaze, there was no way to know for sure. The sword that he used was very familiar though. Wolf had seen one like it every day of his life.

On the mantle back in his house in Aradon lay the sword that had been passed by his grandfather Arin down to his father Logan. The sword was the same one that was given to every member of the Lord Lion, Cedric Binosear's personal guard, the Lion's Mane. The sword consisted of an ornate golden hilt and guard, with a single clear gem embedded in the end of the hilt, just above the guard on both sides of the blade was a gold etching of a springing lion engraved into the blade. There was also an inscription in the Old Tongue that ran down the length of the blade. Wolf had been taken off-guard a bit by the strange discovery, but he felt a little better when he factored in Jared's age. He was about the age that Logan would have been, were he still alive, and he conceivably could have served in the Lion's Mane before Lord Cedric's death. Besides, it could be a situation where it was a sword that was handed down to him just like Arin's sword that was handed down to Logan.

As his mind worked on the puzzle of the sword, Wolf felt a little easier about it. The scepter on the other hand was a pure mystery that no amount of thinking or figuring could uncover. There was no solid handle to the scepter, but instead it was as if a single rod of gold had been twisted into a tight spiral leaving only a fraction of an inch of space between. The center was hollow, about an inch diameter gap. Around the main rod of the scepter was twisted two different smaller rods of metal. The first was a rough gold that shone brighter than the rest of the scepter. The second was a thin strand of silver that added a glow to the overall beauty of the object. At the top of the scepter was the largest ruby that Wolf had ever seen. It had to measure at least three or four inches across, and about four or five inches deep. It was cut like a fine diamond, with a long protruding point which disappeared into the hollow body of the scepter. Whatever the unseen mechanism was that held the ruby in place, it did so without flawing or marking the jewel. When Wolf and Jared finally made it to where the queen waited, Jared immediately knelt and bowed his head.

"Rise good sir, we are not in court."

Jared stood a moment later and smiled.

"And who do we have here Wolf?" Cairyn said smiling down at the younger of the two men.

"This is Jared my queen, he was tending to my fire and keeping an eye on my horse for me."

"A friend of yours then?"

"Not exactly," Jared answered, "I was just tending to the animal because it is the way of Logan's Wood to befriend the animals and to make sure that they are treated well."

"Do you live here in the wood my good man?"

"I do, my queen," Jared answered. "But I would like to accompany you into Aradon if that may be allowed."

Cairyn smiled.

"It is good sir. Can I please have your full name? I find that it is sometimes advantageous to know all about the people you are traveling with."

Cairyn gave a coy look to Wolf and then smiled.

"Jared Vale' my queen."

Something inside Wolf clicked. *That name*, Wolf thought to himself scanning the memories of the Blaze. Finally he found it. *Oh no.*

Death of Pride

Creator's Calendar Year 1205; Dark Mirror

The plains that surrounded Aradon were just beginning to recover from the fires that had burned the town to the ground and eradicated all of the crops in the farmlands. The brown and black stalks of grass had blown away in the stiff wind over time, and there were new spots of green beginning to grow. Within a few years, the place might even have the potential to be as beautiful as it was before the war came, but that was only if the forces of the Light were able to succeed in their task. The sun was just beginning to come up in the sky over Aradon, and its warm golden light glowed through the weave of low hanging clouds, lighting the sky in a faint orange glow in places, and wisps of purple and light blue in others. There was still darkness clinging to the land, but that would only last until the clouds parted and the sun's light could shine through. Not much of Aradon still stood. There were burned out shells of buildings still standing, but nothing that would ever be enough to repair. If there was ever going to be another Aradon, it would have to be completely rebuilt over the broken corpse of the old. However, up on the hill just east of the city stood a single white pedestal with a glass case covering the top of it. The light from the sun glinted off the surface of the case, and it was clear that there was something inside. While there was no church surrounding it anymore, the book that was held sacred by the people of Aradon had survived all the raids and attacks, but that was a mystery to be solved another time.

Gwydeon knew that he was about to be involved in the fight of his life, and he could let nothing else cloud his mind.

As he stepped from the portal and took a good look around, he saw the devastation, and barely conjure the hope that someday it would be a home for his people again. But then his eyes came to rest on the man that had caused all the destruction. Draven stood just a few feet in front of him, his cold eyes glaring back at the portal. The cloak that he wore was flapping in the wind, its pattern no longer control by Draven's theatrical whims. There was no playful confidence in Draven's face or in his eyes. This was not a fight that he was taking lightly, and Gwydeon was sure now that there was no way he could walk away from this battle. The last times he had faced members of the phasia he had been lucky. Rael had only been able to strike the blow to his side, a wound that still ached, but the blade had not cut him as deeply as Rael would have liked. For some reason, Rael's footing had not been as sure as it could have been, and the off balance thrust had only resulted in a flesh wound. It bled, to be sure, but had it been a deeper wound, even by an inch or two, it likely would have been fatal. The battle with Jeroch however had been a much different matter. It was a fight to the death, and Jeroch fully intended to watch Gwydeon die slowly. The combat was long and tedious, neither man truly having an advantage, but finally Gwydeon was able to strike the fatal blow and gain the People of the Dragon access to Shau-ling's throne room. As the memories came flooding back, Gwydeon could feel the power of his old conquests rushing through him, and he began to feel as though he actually had a chance of defeating Draven. Gwydeon may have been older, but the years of fighting against the armies of the Shadow had hardened Gwydeon into a more lethal weapon than he had been during his time with the People of the Dragon.

"Welcome home, old man," Draven taunted in his most serious voice. "I have an offer for you that you may find interesting, if you have the desire to live for a few more moments."

"There is nothing that you could offer that I would want, Draven," Gwydeon retorted.

"Come, come, Gwydeon. I thought that you would be brighter than that. You have to know that all of your skill, even with the Lion Sword in hand is no match for a full member of the phasia, let alone me, wielding the Sword of the Ram. So, humor me for a moment if you will."

Gwydeon nodded. Part of him knew that Draven was right. In Gwydeon's hand the Lion Sword was no different than any other sword. He had no power to channel through it. The Sword of the Ram on the other hand would magnify Draven's power to an unbelievable degree. The foolishness of the challenge that Gwydeon had made had never been more poignant. Even with the comically uneven odds, Gwydeon forced himself to remember the true goal of the challenge. All he had to do was buy time for Logan and Pike. So, the longer Draven wanted to talk, the more time the survivors in Trelon had to get out.

"I like you, Gwydeon," Draven said resting the Sword of the Ram on his shoulder, "I like your family. I have always had the highest regard for you and Midarin, and I admire your abilities. After all, a human should stand no chance against a member of the phasia, but you proved us wrong twice. Most impressive was the way that you handled Jeroch. I must say that he is still rather upset about that."

Draven's smile was wicked and self-indulgent.

"Get on with it Draven."

"I want to offer you a truce."

Gwydeon couldn't believe his ears.

"A truce, between you and I?"

Draven nodded.

"It is not as ridiculous as it sounds. I will ally myself with you to assist you in fighting against Shau-ling. My army will head off any member of the phasia that attacks your kingdom, and I will help you to get the refugees and the stragglers from the other kingdoms into Brea. Also, any captives that I have that are still alive will be returned to you."

"And what do you get out of this agreement?"

"For starters," Draven said switching the sword to his other shoulder, "you will cease all attacks on kingdoms that I control, and you will allow me to control Trelon. Sabrina Binosear will be handed over to me, and you will officially bend your knee to me in front of your people."

Gwydeon chuckled before finally frowning.

"No deal."

Draven held up a hand and smiled wider.

"But you haven't heard what you get out of this."

"Screwed."

Draven laughed at Gwydeon's uncharacteristic reply.

"Wait before you pass such a harsh judgment. I will give you the means to decimate your opponents in battle, and the ability to stand up to the phasia in a fight."

"I have that ability now, Draven," Gwydeon countered, "that is why Brea has not fallen yet, and that is also why you are offering me this deal. You can't win your little civil war without my help. I know all about your War for Power and the Battle for Ascension."

"I'm impressed," Draven retorted, "and you're right, I do confess. You have great power as a warrior, Gwydeon, and your ability in battle cannot be matched. The fact that Emries himself has blessed you is enough to strike fear into any of the phasia, except for me. I am impressed by your Order of the Sword, Gwydeon, but you must realize that if the phasia truly wanted you dead, they could combine their forces as they did in days past and crush you."

Gwydeon nodded to himself, agonizing over the truth of the statement.

"But I want to give you the power to stand up to the phasia even if they all bring their armies to break down the walls of Brea. With the force that I will give you, you could destroy every member of the phasia without a thought."

Gwydeon found himself beginning to be tempted by the thought of crushing the phasia and defeating Shau-ling. But nothing Draven said could possibly be true. Everything with him had strings, and those strings had strings.

"What is this force?"

Draven sheathed the Sword and the Ram and one corner of his mouth cocked into a satisfied smirk.

"I thought you'd never ask."

Suddenly the sunlight that should have filled the sky disappeared as storm clouds began to gather quickly overhead. There were flashes of lightning all around, and the winds in the glade began to blow incredibly fast. Gwydeon had to shield is face from the force of the wind because of the dust and ash being thrown about, but after a moment, the wind died down, and when Gwydeon looked up, Draven was flanked by four unfamiliar creatures, and one frighteningly familiar one.

To Draven's left stood a being of crackling fire. When Gwydeon had seen the Flame before, it had taken on huge stature in order the challenge Logan and Korrd, however, now it seemed content to be just slightly taller than Draven. Relatively little else had changed about the Flame, except now its features were a slightly clearer, and Gwydeon could actually make out and face and eyes in the constantly churning sea of fire.

On Draven's right was a specter of incredible horror and fear. Simply by looking at the creature, one could easily see why Draven would call the thing an ally. The creature's head was merely a human skull. There were no marks or chips in the skull, it was perfect as if it had never been in skin. To further this, the skull was incredibly white, so white that it almost had a glow to it. There were two large curled horns that extended from the creature's head that gave it a demonic appearance, and added to the aura of intimidation. The sockets where the beast's eyes should have been glowed an eerie white-blue light that pulsed occasionally as if punctuated by an emotion or thought. In the advancing wind, the creature's gray white hair, which must have attached at the back of the skull, whipped around it like a collar. But then, when the hair was blown back, it was revealed that the skull itself floated above the rest of the body, seemingly held there by a column of blackness that emanated from somewhere inside the creature's body. It was dressed in flowing red robes that whipped about in the breeze, and on the creature's shoulders were solid silver plates that must have served as some kind of armor. When it saw Gwydeon looking it over, the skull rocked back and an eerie cackling laughter echoed from somewhere inside the creature's chest and reverberated in the wind.

Beside the Flame Gwydeon could barely make out another member of Draven's force. Occasionally, Gwydeon could see the outline of a human-like form, but that was only for an instant. The darkness seemed to close in around the creature. Finally, as if it wanted itself to be seen, the creature appeared. When it stood still, Gwydeon could see distinct features. Unlike the demon-headed thing, this being had a face and eyes very much like a human, except the eyes had no pupils and were totally red. The features of the face were very non-descript, and Gwydeon was reminded of Emries in this regard. With Emries, you could look past him a million times and never pick him out of a crowd, it was like that with this creature. It wore, or at least it looked like clothing, a black tight fitting suit that covered all of the creature from head to toe. Then, suddenly it moved. Gwydeon felt like the creature was moving so quickly that all his mind could interpret were the after images of the movement. A simple move of the hand caused five separate afterimages to appear, each one repeating the movement. When the beast moved its whole body, the afterimages had a truly dizzying and nauseating effect. Finally, the creature almost totally disappeared again, except that Gwydeon could still see its eyes peering out of the darkness.

The woman that stood next to the howling skull demon could be classified beautiful in many respects. Her figure was on that most woman would kill to have, shapely and perfect, with nicely defined, but not over-defined muscles. She had a flat stomach, full bosom, and a slim waist. Her beauty was also erotic in the fact that she wore very little clothing, further displaying her endowments. She wore black leather leggings that covered from her feet to mid-thigh, and long black leather gloves that extended to the middle of her upper arm. Her breeches consisted of only a thin leather piece that covered her crotch and rode high over her hips, and her breasts were covered by a small leather top whose only function seemed to be to cover her nipples and to keep her breasts supported. The function of the top was definitely not to conceal, but to reveal, and Gwydeon could only imagine that the outfit came out of one of Draven's perverse fantasies. Her only other piece of clothing was a black cape that flapped noiselessly in the wind, much like Draven's. Her beauty also took on an exotic twist when factoring in that her skin was white, not pale, but white like the purest snow. Also, her hair was white and stood almost on end, but flowed about like a lion's mane caught in a stiff breeze. Much like the disappearing man in black, the woman's eyes also had no pupils, but her eyes were completely white. In her hand she held a long sword. When Gwydeon took a good look at the blade he realized that it was not made of steel as it should have been. It was truly made of crackling bolts of lightning. Then, when looking back into her eyes, Gwydeon saw that her eyes flickered with sparks of lightning also. Why he had not seen it the first time he did not know, but he was starting to become very uneasy.

The last new arrival stood behind Draven, and it looked to be the most imposing of the group. This had been the creature that Gwydeon saw hovering over the battlefield when Gwillim met his end only a few feet from where Gwydeon now stood. The beast, which is the best word to use to describe it, stood twice as tall as Draven, over twelve feet in height, and had a massive body that Gwydeon could have nearly laid flat across. The monster had huge wings that stretched out behind it, much like the old Shadowwalker wings or that of some ancient bird of prey or dragon. Its body, while human in appearance had several distinct differences. Firstly, instead of feet, the creature stood on massive hooves. They were black and solid, and looked as if a kick from one could kill a man instantly. Its body was covered with thick black fur that stood on end and hardly moved in the breeze. On closer inspection the fur had the consistency of a fine file that would be used to finish wood. On top of the creature's massive neck was its imposing head. The head was that of a bull in essence; huge and fear-inspiring. It glared down at Gwydeon with its red eyes and snorted a thick black smoke from its flared nostrils. The scimitar clutched in the monster's right hand would have dwarfed Gwydeon, and probably stood as tall as he did. Draven looked pleased with himself when he saw the look on Gwydeon's face, and he took a moment to chuckle to himself before he spoke.

"So, Gwydeon, what do you think of my little band of anti-heroes. I call them the People of the Crow. Has a nice ring to it don't you think? It has that insulting to the *Coromor* feel."

"You're truly twisted, Draven," Gwydeon responded trying to hold in his awe.

"No," Draven responded taking a step forward, "not twisted, just evil. Now, I think some introductions are in order. In deference to those who do not share the humor of their true name, they have become known as the Dark Riders to all who are foolish enough to confront them. Their leader you have already met."

"The Flame," Gwydeon responded.

"Very good," Draven mocked, "I see that you remember him. But this is not the Flame that you fought in the Hall of Terrors before you vanquished Shau-ling in the last generation. This is the original Flame. You see, when Shau-ling saw that he was losing the battle against the forces of the Light, he decided that he was going to extinguish the Flame and use his power to create some new phasia. The Flame, being one of Shau-ling's first children, had immense power and was unfettered by the positive and negative power curse that Shau-ling set down upon us to keep us from revolting against him. The Flame, having a sense of self-preservation challenged Shau-ling and probably would have defeated him had it not been for the interference of Jeroch. Shau-ling thought that he had killed the Flame when he was engulfed by the Blaze. However, as that the Flame is a creature of the Blaze, he was only confined to formlessness until someone found a way to release him. Obviously I was the one who discovered the method. He is probably more powerful than ever now, and that is why he is the perfect choice to lead the Dark Riders."

Draven took a few steps forward and stopped in front of the red eyes that belonged to the creature in black.

"This shy fellow is my assassin, Shadow. As you can see, he has the ability to make himself completely invisible and can use that ability to strike anyone and anything he wants. Also, his speed of movement is so fast that he could slit your throat right now while you were looking at him, and by the time you felt the blade, you would only be seeing the first of his afterimages moving. He can fly, portal, swim, run, travel in any way that you can imagine, and he never misses. I would use him to defeat all of my opponents, but that would leave no fun for the rest of us. Besides, Shadow is a perfectionist. He will think of a thousand ways to kill you before he actually does it, and if he doesn't find the perfect way to kill you, then he won't. When he kills, there is no trace of a weapon, poison, or any other outside influence, it just looks like a natural death. I discovered Shadow many years ago, imprisoned in the bowels of Jeroch's Black Tower, another failed experiment that was deemed too dangerous to see the light of day. But Shadow will have his revenge on his captor before too long. Though he and I have had many disagreements on exactly which of us will strike the final blow on Jeroch."

Shadow appeared for a moment and then disappeared again, almost as if it were taking a bow of sorts. Draven smiled to himself and then walked toward the laughing skull.

"This is perhaps my favorite member of the Dark Riders. I call him Holocaust. He is a trained killer in every sense of the word. He doesn't care who he kills or why, he just does it. Mortals are weaklings to him and are not fit to walk on the same earth that the phasia and others touched by the glory of the Blaze do. And he is very inventive in his methods of killing. He prefers to watch his victims die slowly, under painful torture. His blood is the very essence of the Blaze, and he can ignite anything, cleansing it in the Blaze with a thought. Aradon was only one of many towns to be decimated by Holocaust's might, and it will not be the last. He was the one that invented the Blaze whips that you saw in the dungeons of Trelon, and he was also the originator of much of the torturing equipment. Screams of pain are music to him, and I must admit that I am starting to like them too. He is a refugee from the Hall of Terrors, one of the few creatures that escaped the fight with your petty band of heroes in the last generation. He still refuses to tell me who his creator is, but I am sure I will discover that in time."

Draven then turned to the massive beast that stood behind the rest of the Dark Riders.

"Impressive, isn't he?"

Gwydeon nodded.

"Just seeing him on the battlefield is enough to strike terror into the hearts of most mortals. Most of them lose the will to fight all together, and then they flee leaving their countrymen and families to die. It is truly pathetic what fear does to you. But, it is a truly effective weapon to have. That is why Wrath here is one of my most favorite lieutenants. His presence on the battlefield is enough to win most battles, and that is before he even attacks. He, like the Shadowwalkers, can spew a stream of Blaze down upon the battlefield, engulfing everything in fire. There is nothing and no one alive that could withstand that blast, but as with Shadow, that would make life much too easy. That is why Wrath truly prefers the one on one confrontations the best. He likes to stand against an opponent and watch them shiver and doubt their abilities before he strikes them down in a single blow. He is truly an impressive creature. I understand from the memories of the Blaze that Wrath here was the original prototype for the new Shadowwalkers, but Shau-ling felt the creature was too unstable and unpredictable. So he imprisoned Wrath within the Blight. Of course, no one knows the Blight better than Basille did, so it wasn't difficult to find many of Master's secret hiding places there."

He then moved to the woman and stood very close to her. He then began to fondle and stroke her, but she made no move against him. Finally, as if bored, he turned back to Gwydeon.

"Beautiful, isn't she?" he said after a moment. "Another of Shau-ling's experiments trapped in the Blight. But don't let her beauty fool you. This is Vengeance, my personal protector. She has two very profound abilities, the first of which is her ability to redirect the damage done to her or anyone she chooses onto the one who caused the damage. I'll give you an example. Wrath," he said calling out to the huge monster, "cut me."

The beast hesitated for a moment and then obeyed. Wrath raised the huge sword and then slashed downward at Draven. The slash connected, and a huge gaping wound was opened on Draven's chest. Draven winced in pain but did not cry out. Mere seconds later, a bolt of energy leapt from the sword of Vengeance and entered the wound. After a single flash of light, the wound was healed, and Wrath howled in pain as a similar wound appeared on his chest. Wrath then made a sound like rolling thunder, which must have been laughter, and Gwydeon watched as the wound healed itself.

"Impressive isn't it."

Gwydeon nodded.

"I chose Wrath because of his natural healing ability. He has not suffered a single wound from any weapon that did not instantly regenerate. That of course is provided that the weapon penetrated his skin at all. Now," Draven continued looking back at the woman, "Vengeance's other ability is to shape reality in any way that she pleases. I'll give you an example of what I mean. Vengeance."

The woman blinked for a moment and then turned to face the charred remains of the town of Aradon. She then raised her sword and pointed it toward the town. There was a low thunder echoing from the clouds above, and then sparks of electricity shot from the outstretched blade of the sword and leapt skyward. The bolts streaked into the heavens and began jumping from cloud to cloud, seemingly growing with every jump. Finally the two now gigantic bolts plummeted down to earth. Before they hit the ground, they shattered into thousands of pieces, and the shower of sparks rained down on the charred ruins. Suddenly, the city began to slowly rebuild itself. The burned pieces of wood filled out into full form, and then the boards and paint that were once attached to the wooden supports began to reappear. The process was slow at first, and then began to accelerate as more sparks rained down. After a matter of minutes, the Aradon that Gwydeon remembered before the battle with Draven stood again, proud and beautiful as ever.

"That's amazing," Gwydeon said not realizing the emotions that he had let slip.

"That is just the beginning Gwydeon," Draven said quietly approaching him. "Vengeance has the ability to bring people back from the dead, at least that is how it would appear to a mortal."

Gwydeon blinked hard. Coming from the newly rebuilt town of Aradon walked a young man, probably in his twenties. His face was clean shaven, and he wore fine clothes from across the Great Sea. The sword that his mother had given him was strapped to his side, and he had the look of pride in his face that was there even on the day he died. Gwillim was a fine sight, and a welcome one to Gwydeon's heart and mind. But Gwillim stopped in his tracks suddenly and began to fade out of sight, and it was as if he were being slowly erased from reality. Gwydeon felt his stomach tighten and his heart race, but he tried his best to control his emotions.

"That is only a sample Gwydeon. We can make Gwillim's return from the grave reality if we wanted to. But first you have to do something for me."

Gwydeon blinked hard again and then swallowed. There was a bad taste in his mouth, and he knew it was because he was actually considering going along with what Draven was proposing.

"What is it you want?"

Draven smiled again and turned back toward Wrath. The immense beast handed Draven a package of some sort, and Draven quickly opened it and withdrew a piece of black metal that was shaped like a bat.

"My Dark Riders should have six members, which was always the intention. However, thanks to your interfering friend Pike Rhuiden, there are only five. Luckily for me, as powerful as Pike was, he was also inept. While he was able to save himself from the Blaze with his powers, he was only able to kill the body that lay inside Nightwing. Aryx Terian was a thorn in all of our sides, and I am glad to know that he is dead. However, without a body, Nightwing is just a piece of metal."

Draven held up the metallic bat in his hand. Suddenly a streak of understanding hit Gwydeon.

"You want me to become Nightwing and join your Dark Riders."

It was not a question, more like a statement of fact. Gwydeon knew that Draven could be diabolical, but he had never imagined that he would have thought up a scheme like this.

"My plan transcends the mere battle between Light and Shadow, Gwydeon. I have a vision for the future. Shau-ling will surely fall, with or without my help, and I would like to have a hand in his demise, however, I want Jeroch first, and I want the throne of Marcwell. But in order to defeat my brethren and take my quest to the next level, I need a few things. First, I need my Dark Riders to be complete. It would give me an advantage that no phase or even Shau-ling could imagine. Next, I need a creature capable of destroying Shau-ling. Since the *Coromor* of this generation has already been killed, I need Sabrina Binosear, the *Chosen One* to fulfill the prophecies. I have already taken her to my bed once, and hopefully that will produce my heir, the next generation's *Coromor*. If that union does not prove to be fruitful, I will take her again and again until it is. Eventually Shau-ling will be reborn, and my heir can help me to find and eliminate the *Chosen One* and *Erieal* in the next generation. After that is done, I will kill the child and free Shau-ling from the prophecies. Once done, my Dark Riders and I will be free to destroy him without fear of the Light's victory. Once the Shadow rules, it rules eternally, and it does not matter who is in charge, so it might as well be me."

Gwydeon shook his head. For some reason it all made sense. Draven was more intelligent and more evil than Gwydeon have given him credit for initially, and it seemed that Shau-ling finally got his wish for a perfect phase. Unfortunately, in building that perfect phase he had also given Draven the ability to find a sure method to unseat Shau-ling.

"And if I refuse?" Gwydeon asked.

"Then you are a fool," came Draven's plain reply. There was not hatred or venom in his voice, it was just a simple honest answer, strange enough for a member of the phasia, let alone Draven.

"And what if I asked you to hold up your end of the bargain we made in Trelon to duel to the death?"

"Then you would die."

Gwydeon thought quickly for a moment. It was clear the Vengeance was the most important and dangerous member of the Dark Riders, but it seemed that there was no way that Gwydeon could harm her without harming herself. The same was true with Draven. Logan had warned Gwydeon about his power to change the result of an attack against him, but his weakness was that if he were surprised he could not use his power. Gwydeon was in a no win scenario. Shadow could slit his throat at any moment, Holocaust or the Flame could burn him where he stood, Wrath could crush him, Draven could filet him with the Sword of the Ram, or Vengeance could simply erase him from existence.

So many ways to die, Gwydeon thought to himself, *and so little time.*

"I'll fight the duel," Gwydeon said proudly.

"Your pride is getting in the way of your good senses, Gwydeon," Draven said sheathing his sword, "there is no way that you can win a duel with me, and even if you could, the Dark Riders would crush you. I'm sorry to stand here and admit that I would cheat if you were winning, but that would be exactly what would happen. You would die, carrying your pride down to the Great Dark One for no reason."

"Pride is all I have, Draven," Gwydeon said after a moment, "it is what makes me who I am, and it is what helped me to defeat Rael and Jeroch. If I were to surrender that to you now, I would cease to be Gwydeon Sandar."

Draven stood pondering the situation for a moment.

"So, your pride will not allow you to join the Dark Riders and become the second coming of Nightwing."

"That is correct."

"And if you didn't have your pride then you wouldn't be Gwydeon Sandar."

Gwydeon nodded.

"I hate to say this Gwydeon," Draven replied smiling, "but I don't need Gwydeon Sandar to be Nightwing, I need Gwydeon Sandar's skill and tenacity. Even without your pride you still have those. So, what we are going to do is we are going to kill your pride and you are going to beg me to become Nightwing."

Gwydeon laughed and prepared himself for a fight. Suddenly, the Lion Sword was ripped out of his hands, and he was being held by and unseen force. Then, when he saw the ripples of motion from the afterimages he knew it was Shadow who held him. Try as he might, Gwydeon could not escape the hold.

"Vengeance."

At Draven's command, another bolt of energy emerged from her sword and began to take shape in front of Draven. Holocaust quickly moved to the form and took hold of it as soon as it fully emerged from the light. Gwydeon gasped when he saw Midarin standing before him.

"Gwydeon?"

Her tone was fearful, unlike anything that he had ever heard before. She shook as Draven traced her body with the tip of his sword, and Gwydeon looked on in horror as piece by piece he stripped away her clothing with random strokes of his blade. Many times his cuts went too deep, drawing blood which flowed freely down her body. Gwydeon struggled harder, but was still not strong enough to escape Shadow's grasp.

"If you kill her Draven," Gwydeon spat in a mixture of hate and rage, "you'll never get me to join you. I don't know what you think you will accomplish by bringing her here."

"What makes you think that I'm going to kill her?" Draven said coyly. "I am going to take her here in front of you and let you hear her cries of ecstasy in my arms. Then, you will watch as Jeroch takes her, and then Taron, then Rael, Zarsi, Saurn, should I go on?"

The visions running through Gwydeon's mind were too terrible to take. He could only watch as Draven shrugged his shoulders and began to undress. Midarin began kicking as Holocaust forced her to the ground. Vengeance held her legs apart as Draven knelt beside her.

"Stop!" Gwydeon cried out, the suffering in his heart tearing at him.

Draven stood triumphant, and waived his hand toward Vengeance. In a flash of light, Midarin disappeared, and Draven waited. Shadow released his hold of Gwydeon, who fell to his knees at Draven's feet.

"You win, Draven," Gwydeon said in a low tone with his head down. "You win."

CHAPTER 29

Chapter XXX

Funeral

Creator's Calendar Year 1205; Light Reality

There was a new tension that shot through Wolf as he stood looking at the man who called himself Jared Vale'. Maybe it was just a coincidence that he shared his name with one of the most evil and diabolical of the phasia. Anything was possible. However, Wolf could not look past the possibility that Jared could conceivable be the son of the phase Caris, and if that were true, the danger to his life and the lives of his companions had just increased ten-fold. There was something sincere about Jared though. It was not the sickening sweet voice in his memories that constantly came spewing from the mouth of one of the phasia, it was a more honest and trustworthy voice. Despite the possibility that his loyalties could lie elsewhere, Wolf felt compelled to trust Jared. The queen noticed Wolf's tension and quickly tried to afford him some relief.

"My daughters are waiting for us Wolf," Cairyn said after a slight pause. "If you wish to ride with us Jared, you are more than welcome."

"Thank you my queen," Jared said bowing his head again, "however, I have no horse to ride. I have lived here in the forest for many months, and at the time I did not see a reason to keep a steed, so I let mine go."

"You can ride with me," Wolf said almost instantly.

Jared looked up and then smiled. He approached Wolf and waited for him to mount his horse. After Wolf had mounted, he extended his hand to Jared and helped him up.

"Now, let us meet Sabrina and Lissa before they start to worry."

Cairyn led the way back toward the clearing using the paths that Wolf had pointed out to her. Despite the inherent trust that he had for his new companions, Wolf could not help but feel a little nervous about the intentions of the man who sat behind him. In a moment's notice, Wolf could find a dagger lodged in his back, and Jared hovering over his dying body. Shocking himself with vivid images, Wolf shook himself back to reality and tried to keep his mind positive. The trip through the woods took only a few minutes before they had reached the clearing just outside the borders to Logan's wood. However, when they emerged from the woods, they found that Sabrina and Lissa waited for them with another group of riders. Wolf knew that this had been the plan, but he was sure that it was a surprise to Cairyn and hoped it was a surprise to Jared. As soon as Midarin's group was in sight, Wolf made eye contact with Nathaniel. Then, trying hard not to draw attention to himself, he motioned with his eyes back toward Jared. Nathaniel nodded seemingly absently and closed his eyes for a moment. Nathaniel's eyes suddenly jerked open and he nodded back to Wolf very strongly. Wolf's eyes opened wide, and he rode over by Gwillim and Nathaniel. Cairyn was busy chatting with Midarin and the others, and she was introducing Jared around to the others.

"Nathaniel, Gwillim," Wolf said as easily as he could manage, "I hope you slept well during the night. Sometimes Logan's Wood is not too advantageous to sleep."

"It was fine cousin," Gwillim responded rubbing his neck slightly, "but I am looking forward to being back in a bed. I must say that I have gotten a bit spoiled from my time at court, and also that I'm not as young as I used to be."

"How old are you now cousin?" Wolf asked trying to make the conversation as idle as he could.

"I'll be forty-five in the winter. I'm only about a year or so younger than Midarin, and I would be about the same age as my father now, were he still alive."

"The Creator works in mysterious ways," Nathaniel said slowly, "and he saw fit to make sure that we all suffered by having to listen to the grumblings of an old man."

Gwillim laughed. Apparently Nathaniel and Gwillim had a solid relationship as brothers despite the large age difference. Then, the smile dimming from his face, Nathaniel turned to face Jared.

"Welcome friend to our little group. My name is Nathaniel, and this is my brother Gwillim."

"I appreciate your welcome Nathaniel," Jared returned warmly, "my name is Jared."

"He certainly doesn't look dangerous," a familiar voice said from over Wolf's shoulder.

Wolf turned to see that Lissa had moved close to them and was practically right beside him now. Behind Lissa was the princess Sabrina. She had a very odd look on her face. It was as if she were in some kind of discomfort but that she was trying not to let it show. When her gaze met Wolf's she smiled, almost too politely, and then turned her eyes away, looking toward something or someone else. However, when he turned his look back to Lissa, he felt Sabrina's eyes on him again.

"I assure you," Jared said calmly, "I am not dangerous. I am just a simple farm boy."

"Yes," Nathaniel countered, "but we have had experience with simple farm boys who are not always what they seem. Not necessarily is that dangerous, but it often offers an interesting surprise."

"Besides," Gwillim continued, "we are very close to Aradon, and there is no such thing as a simple farm boy in that town."

"Including this one," Lissa said laying her hand on Wolf's shoulder.

Jared was smiling and enjoying watching the others pick on Wolf. The feelings of nervousness were beginning to ease in Wolf, but he still inwardly wondered what Nathaniel had seen while looking at Jared. From the moment that they had exited the forest, Wolf had tried to feel for any powers, but there was nothing that Wolf could find. It was almost like none of the primal strings touched Jared. He would have to wait until he could talk to Nathaniel alone before he could be sure. Cairyn and Midarin had already started the ride toward Aradon, with Aryx and Liette following close behind them. Sabrina had turned her horse away from the rest of the group and rode quickly to catch up with her mother. Gwillim and Nathaniel continued talking as they rode, and Lissa and Wolf followed behind them.

"Is the princess alright?" Wolf asked quietly.

"She'll be fine," Lissa responded. "She's had to adjust to the war we've been preparing for all this time finally being thrust upon us. Now that everything is beginning to move in earnest, I know that she is worried about her father."

Lissa was trying her best to hide the truth from Wolf, without lying to him. She knew in her heart that it would take a long time for Sabrina to be as stable as she presented herself to be a few minutes earlier, and that there would probably be some resentment for a while. But in her mind, Lissa didn't believe that there was any reason to tell Wolf any of that situation. Everyone was going to have to make adjustments to the new normal. Lissa had to adjust to the reemergence of her father, Cairyn would have to adjust to the fact that her daughters were about to be embroiled in the war with the Shadow, and Sabrina would have to adjust to the fact that Lissa had gotten to Wolf before she knew how she felt. They were all in uncertain positions, and these would not be the last shocks they would have to endure in the days to come.

"Where is Pike?" Wolf asked occasionally looking up to check the positions of the rest of the group. "I would have thought that he would be here to say goodbye to my mother."

Again Lissa didn't want to tell Wolf the whole truth. Pike should have been with them, he should have wanted to pay his respects before riding off to war. But that was not the Pike that was now responsible for most prestigious kingdom in the world and who wanted to take the fight to Shau-ling before the people of the world began to suffer as they had in previous generations.

"He received some news from his army in Kandor that required his personal attention. After we are finished here, Sabrina and I intend to join him. You are more than welcome to come with us. I'm sure that my father would gladly accept you into his ranks."

Wolf knew that she was trying to hide many of the facts from Jared, and perhaps many facts from Wolf. Jared was listening intently to the conversation, which Wolf couldn't blame him for. There was still too much to risk by putting full trust in a man they has just met, so Wolf tried hard to curtail his comments.

"I'm not sure that I feel comfortable meeting him yet," Wolf said being as honest as he could. "Mother told me that Pike had become obsessed with the war, and that his life revolved around something that was truly none of his affair. She was worried that once he found out who I was that he would use me for his own gain. That is one of the reasons that I took so long to reveal myself. Mother always said to only trust family."

"With the exception of Gwillim," Lissa said looking down at her horse, "all of your family is gone, isn't it?"

"Yes."

"I know how you feel," Jared chimed in unexpectedly. "I have no family that I am aware of."

"What about your mother and father?" Lissa asked.

"I never knew my father, and my mother abandoned me when I was old enough to take care of myself. As far as I am concerned she may as well be dead too. It is a hard thing to go through life knowing that you had a family but they didn't want you."

Lissa balked at the comment, and Wolf saw that she was desperately trying to restrain herself. There was a fire and an anger inside of her that drove her to be everything that she was, but when her emotions took hold and cut her deeply enough, her fury and rage could not contain the sorrow and despair that was still very much part of her.

"I sympathize," Lissa finally said. "My mother and father both abandoned me. My father walked out on my mother long before I was born, and my mother didn't think she could handle raising me all by herself, so she gave me up. I was just lucky that I was given to Pike and Cairyn. It was nice to have a mother, a father, and a sister to call my own. There were also friends around all the time, and an extended family that included Gwillim, Nathaniel, Midarin and Liette."

"What about your family, Wolf?" Jared asked.

"My father died when I was very young," Wolf responded, "and my mother raised me until she died a few days ago. That's why we are going to Aradon. Her friends wanted to pay their respects at her funeral."

"I'm sorry Wolf," Jared said. "It must be hard for you."

All Wolf could do was nod. For the rest of the morning, there were only patches of conversation among the three of them. Occasionally Gwillim and Nathaniel would drop back and engage in the conversation, but mostly they just rode up ahead, talking amongst themselves. It was just before mid-day when they reached the city of Aradon, and the town had begun the preparations for the funeral of one of its most revered and most beloved heroes.

As was the tradition in Aradon, everyone in town wore black on the day of the funeral. Even if the person was of no relation, or even if you hated the person, you still wore black out of respect for the dead. There was a communal breakfast for everyone in the town, and it was held in the marketplace. There, everyone would tell stories or fond memories about the person who had passed. There was always a place set for the person who had died, complete with a meal that they would have eaten if they would have been there. The cooks were very careful about the meals. If the person who died hated the taste of eggs, then the cooks would not have put eggs on the plate. It was a last tribute to the dead. Next, the members of the town council lead the townspeople up to the old church on the hill to bring the body to its final resting place. All the while, the townspeople sang songs of sorrow and of loss. Finally, the body would be laid in its final resting place, and the last meal is placed at the corpse's feet. Then, the townspeople go back to their homes and sit in prayer for the departed soul and wait for the bells of the church to ring to signal the beginning of the celebration of life. In Aradon it was a custom after a funeral to celebrate living with a wild party that would last until the next morning. It was a way to exorcise the feelings of dread and sorrow. It had been an accepted practice for many lifetimes, and it was probably one of the most important traditions in Aradon, second only to the ancient marriage ceremony that also revolved around the old church on the hill.

As the group of dignitaries from three of the most important kingdoms in the whole of the world entered the town, Wolf saw the line of black coming down the hill toward the middle of the village. Wolf and the others dismounted and waited for the procession to arrive. When they were in sight, Wolf and the others parted into two groups so that the procession could pass through, and Wolf instantly bowed his head. The others followed suit and waited until the last of the procession had passed and then fell in behind them. At the edge of the burial glade, the procession stopped, and the men who carried Elwyne's body: Torris Sandar, Gwydeon's father; Tam Rhuiden, Pike's Father; Joseph Core, Eldar's Step-father; and another man that Wolf did not recognize, took her into the glade and laid her in the grave that had been prepared next to Logan's. As soon as that was done, the procession, with the exception of the priest, departed. As each of the men departed the glade, they stopped to shake hands with Wolf. Torris stopped and hugged Midarin, and then left without a word. Tam gave Cairyn a kiss on the cheek before he left. The last of the four men stayed near the glade and waited before shaking Wolf's hand and nodding to the priest. There was something strangely familiar about the fourth man, but Wolf could not put his finger on it.

"To commend this body to the ground, only family may pass onto the scared soil," the priest said melodically. "Then, once the body has been commended, only the pure blood of the fallen may ring the bells of the church to send the soul to meet its Creator. So says the Book of the Old Church, and so says the Will of the Creator. Amen."

The priest nodded to Wolf and then turned to leave. Taking a deep breath, Wolf stepped forward and knelt at the threshold of the burial glade before entering. He then looked back to Gwillim who repeated the process. The man who had carried Elwyne's body knelt and then entered the glade.

"Who are you?" Wolf asked quietly, trying not to seem too disturbed by the stranger's rash and somewhat forward actions.

"My name is Emries," the man said in an even tone.

A spark of recognition suddenly hit Wolf. Emries was the first being ever created by the Creator. He was the father and brother of all men, and so he had a right to be at Elwyne's funeral. Also, he was regarded as the first *Coromor* even before the prophecies were handed down by Aralias Imstra. It was his mantle that Cedric Binosear inherited, and it was the call of the forces of the Light that had drawn Wolf's grandfather Arin and his grandmother Victoria to join the ranks of the Lion's Mane, beginning the Ranthall family's cycle of service to the *Coromor* and to the prophecies.

"Well," Gwillim said turning to Wolf, "I guess we are the ones to do this."

"There is more family to enter the glade," Emries commented.

"Who?" Wolf asked.

"Two cousins. Granted, one of them is only a cousin by marriage, but that is still family. The other is cousin by blood, though distant. Under the laws of Aradon, they are still considered family."

"Who?" Wolf repeated.

Emries pointed first to Cairyn and then to Sabrina. The queen and princess looked even more shocked than Wolf.

"How are we cousins to Elwyne?"

"As I said, through marriage and through blood. Logan's mother was named Victoria. Her last name, you may be surprised to discover was Rhuiden."

Cairyn's jaw dropped open. There were a striking amount of things that Cairyn did not know about her husband and her acquired family. The people of Aradon were surprisingly tight-lipped about family matters, even to those within their extended families. Perhaps that was why the close-knit community of Aradon had always been so hard to understand and equally hard to penetrate. But they had always managed on their own, and they liked it that way.

"Her brother," Emries continued, "was named Tam Rhuiden, Pike's father. Therefore, Logan and Pike were first cousins. Cairyn, by marrying Pike you became a first cousin to Logan, and Elwyne a first cousin in the same way. It is only logical then to say that your children would be cousins to one another. Gwillim's claim to family is because Elwyne was his aunt by marriage. But perhaps there is another who shares a claim to family."

Wolf looked puzzled.

"Another?"

Emries scanned the remaining faces and then smiled to himself.

"Yes, a distant cousin by marriage."

Wolf shook his head.

"Emries," Wolf said suddenly in a tone that was not his own. "Not that I doubt your abilities or your vision, but that seems rather ridiculous. The only cousin here by marriage according to you is Queen Cairyn and Princess Sabrina. Therefore, you're telling me that a cousin of hers is also here."

"Not just a cousin, but a first cousin," Emries answered.

The look on Cairyn's face was one of dismay and confusion.

"Emries," she said uneasily, "whoever you are. That is just not possible. I'll take your word for the fact that Logan and Pike were first cousins and that Sabrina and I are related to Elwyne in that way. But in order for me to have had a first cousin, that would mean that my Uncle Cedric would have had a child. Everyone knows that he didn't."

"Really?"

Emries by nature and by design did not have a memorable face. There was nothing in any of his features to make him memorable. To say that he was plain would be an understatement. He was not handsome, but he was also not ugly. None of his facial features were either too big or too small. Every part of him was average. That is why he would always be the last person picked out of a crowd. It was not because you didn't see him, it was because there was nothing about him that would cause you to remember seeing him. However, when he made a gesture or changed the arch of his eyebrow or the way he set his eyes on you, it was like his whole face and body came alive with a power that had not been there a few seconds prior. It would be lichened to standing in a room staring at the wall and then a person appearing in front of you. It is a very shocking and effective sight indeed when Emries wanted to make a point.

"What if I told you that Lord Cedric Binosear did indeed have a child? A child out of wedlock, and a child that by all rights should not be alive today."

Cairyn was shocked, as was everyone standing there.

"That's absurd," Cairyn said finally. "If Cedric had a child my mother and I would have known about it."

"You and your mother would only have known about it if Cedric had known about it. However, if it had been kept a secret for many years, no one should know. Well, no one except me perhaps, and of course his mother. Though I am sure Wolf has begun to put the pieces together for himself."

Wolf's eyes immediately locked on Jared. He was the only one in the group who Wolf could not account for. But it was the name. Wolf's mind finally clicked. Caris. Jared saw the look that Wolf gave him and then suddenly reacted.

"It's not me," he said solidly. "It can't be me."

Emries looked at the man and smiled.

"It's me?"

Emries nodded.

"How?"

The question was silent, and was asked while looking around the shocked faces of the group.

"Before I tell this story, let me first preface this by saying that Jared truly had no idea of his parentage until now. Certain members of this group have already questioned his loyalty and his trustworthiness. I am here to say that you need question no longer. Also, I must ask that this information not leave this group. Were anyone else to find out about Jared's parentage, he would be at great risk from both the forces of the Light and of the Shadow. He was drawn here, must as the rest of you have been because the death of Elwyne Tamerlane Ranthall has signaled the beginning of the war that everyone knew was coming. Already creatures lurking in the darkest places of the world have begun to move, and the time for reveling in the peace bought with the blood of the Dragon is at an end."

Everyone nodded, though unseen to Wolf, Aryx's jaw was set firmly and his hand tightened around the hilt of his sword.

"Good. Long before the world realized the threat of the creature called Shau-ling, there were many dangers in the world that no one could explain. There were groups of monsters that somehow just appeared to attack a city, and then quickly disappear. As this began to happen more frequently, some of the larger kingdoms began to form alliances for mutual protection. The kingdoms of Marcwell and Lakestone formed such an alliance. Before long, Lakestone was attacked, and the Lord of Marcwell, a young king named Cedric Binosear was sent on the task to give relief to his allies. During the fated journey in which Cedric would become the great and powerful Lord Lion of the prophecies, he fell in love with a woman by the name of Erika Belnosian. This is the same Erika that is now married to Jerrard Mystic, the king of Scalla."

Midarin nodded and waited for Emries to continue. She had already heard some of this story during her time with the People of the Dragon, but if Emries was retelling it, then there must have been a twist. At the same time, Wolf felt his insides stir at the story. He knew the way the story turned out too, but his memories from the Blaze still had pieces missing, pieces that were tainted with darkness and horror.

"Erika and Cedric were an inseparable pair after a short time, and the talk of marriage ran rampant. Finally, they decided that they would be wed, and on the day of their wedding, Erika was shot through the throat during the ceremony, ending her reign as queen before it ever began. Cedric became crazed and tracked the assassin until he stumbled on the stories of Shau-ling and the phasia. He then took up the symbol of the Lion, and the rest is a legend for telling by better bards than I. But the question you are asking yourselves now is, how could Erika still be alive if she was killed on her wedding day? The answer is that the woman claiming to be Erika Belnosian on that fateful day was not the real Erika Belnosian but a very clever and very powerful impostor."

Emries didn't skip a beat and wove a story that was so entrancing that Wolf almost had to force himself to remember to breathe.

"Erika Belnosian loved riding horses, and it was on a fine spring day that she went riding through the forest outside Marcwell. Something that day spooked her horse and she was thrown to the ground, knocked unconscious by the impact. Then, two people emerged from the forest. The first was Basille Mystic, the last born of the phasia, a soul that has since been redeemed to the side of the Light. The other was the Lady Wolf, Caris Vale'. She immediately used her powers to disguise herself and took the form and identity of Erika. She even went so far as to break her own leg to keep the illusion alive. Basille was supposed to kill the girl and dispose of her body, but he could not bring himself to commit such an act, so he took her back to his kingdom of Scalla and raised her as his own. That is why she is still alive today. However, the real story continues when Caris returned to Marcwell as Erika."

A knife turned in the pit of Wolf's stomach. The veil began to lift from his memory, and one of the most closely guarded of all of Basille's secrets revealed itself. Wolf all at once was hit by the waves of guilt and regret; the years of lies that Basille told to Cedric, a man he counted as his friend. Wolf was not prepared for the knowledge that a member of the phasia could feel remorse for his actions.

"Cedric paid her visits every day," Emries continued, "often bringing her food or drink. During each of these visits, Caris was using her powers to ensnare him in a web of desire. She knew long before anyone else that he was the first *Coromor* of the prophecies, and she thought that by controlling him, she could control the fate of the world. Her plan nearly worked. She was able to tempt him to her bed, and finally became pregnant with his child, you Jared, unbeknownst to everyone but her accomplice Basille. He had been watching her progress and knew what her plans were. However, he then learned that she was going to become Cedric's queen, and that they would rule together over the largest kingdom in the world. Basille knew that she would use this power to gather an army to destroy the rest of the phasia, and then she would use Cedric to kill Shau-ling. At this time, none of the phasia truly knew the consequences of the prophecies, so they acted on pure instinct. It was the instinct of self-preservation that prompted Basille to wait outside the temple in Marcwell for the opportunity to strike. When that time came, he pulled the trigger on his crossbow and set Cedric down the path to destroy all of the phasia and their master."

"If she was killed while pregnant," Jared asked, "how could I be that child?"

"The phasia are truly interesting creatures in that they are reborn in the next generation exactly the way they were previous to their death in the previous generation. So, as that Caris was pregnant before her death, she was still pregnant when she was reborn. Luckily for you Jared, Basille didn't have the presence of mind to aim for her stomach first."

Jared gave a weak smile. Wolf's breath caught in his throat. Emries' assertion had venom that no one else could have detected. There was hatred in his voice. It was disdain, so buried by the flowery and enthralling tone, but clear as a bell to Wolf's ears.

"That is why he has a line of power similar to that of the *Chosen One*," Nathaniel commented. "There must have been a huge infusion of power from Cedric that mixed with the powers of a member of the phasia."

"That is very good Nathaniel," Emries said smiling, "I see that my successor is very intelligent when it comes to the ways of my kind. That will serve you well in the task to come."

"So," Lissa said after a moment, "you must have been the person that Rane and the Jeresei were looking for in Logan's Wood."

"I must be," Jared said finally. "I felt a lot of power in the wood, and I knew that someone or something was using my powers to track me down. I long time ago I learned how to just turn them off, so that's what I did to hide. I had no idea that my powers came from the phasia, and to be honest I'm not sure I really know what the phasia are. But if they are as bad as Emries makes them out to be, then I'm glad I hid."

"Believe me Jared," Midarin said after a moment, "they are much worse than you could ever imagine."

Jared nodded and waited for someone to say something.

"Wolf," Gwillim said after a moment, "I think you should handle the ceremony of saying goodbye. You would know better than any of us what to say, and I think that Logan and Elwyne would have wanted it that way."

Wolf nodded and then turned to face the grave. He had been with his mother up to the very end. There had been nights when he had woken up to the sounds of her crying, and he had held her through the night, trying hard to give her some comfort in a world where she had none. By the next morning the tears would all be gone, but some nights were worse than others. Sometimes she would find one of Logan's old shirts or something that had belonged to him, and she would just sit and stare at it for the longest time, and then the tears would start to fall. Slowly Wolf walked the few steps to the edge of the grave and looked down. Elwyne's body was wrapped in a sheer gauze, but her beauty still shone through. On her brow was a crown that was once a gift from Midarin, and lying beside her was the sword that Logan had once used in his war against Shau-ling. As he stood there, he fought back the tears or sorrow, and pulled an old black shirt out of his pack and laid it over his mother like a blanket. She had once told him that it was Logan's favorite shirt. She had washed it at least once a week, every week after he died. More than once she had to repair a new rip or tear, but the shirt always stayed in the best condition possible. It was her way of keeping the love and the memories alive.

"Mother," Wolf said in a shaky voice, "your friends all came to say goodbye. Midarin and Gwillim, Cairyn and Emries. Pike couldn't make it, and I guess that Jerrard and Erika haven't gotten the news yet. I'm sure they will come to visit you after they find out. I'm glad that your friends loved you so much mother, and I hope that you find peace. You're probably happier now that you are back with father. I wish that he could see me now. I hope he is proud of me. Torris promised that he would tend your grave for me while I was gone. He said it was the least he could do for an old friend. I love you mother. I hope I live up the name that you gave me. Goodbye mother."

Wolf then turned on a heel and walked out of the burial glade. Lissa started to step forward and console him, but Midarin held her back.

"He's not finished with the ceremony yet."

Lissa nodded and watched as Wolf walked the long few yards across the meadow and up the hill to the old church. As he entered, he took a long look at the old book that was encased in glass on top of the white marble pedestal at the front of the church. He inwardly wondered if one day he and Lissa would come back to Aradon to take the vows from the book. But he shook away the thoughts and went back to the task that lay in hand. He walked to the front of the church and then went through a small passageway until he found a set of ropes that dangled from above. He steadied himself and then said goodbye silently as he took hold of the ropes and rung the massive church bells. After five long rings, he release the ropes, and started back toward the village. Just as he was about the leave the church, he heard something that sounded like crying. He looked in the direction that it seemed to be coming from, and saw something in a beam of light that shown through an open window. There was a person lying on the floor, huddled in a corner crying. As Wolf approached the person, he realized that it was a woman, and that she was completely naked. He knelt beside her and put his hand on her side. She shrank back suddenly, shocked by the contact, but she looked back, over her shoulder, her blond hair catching the light. Wolf winced when he looked at her face. There was blood coming from her nose and lip. The area around her right eye had turned black and blue, and there was a small cut above her left eye.

"Help me," she said in a raspy voice.

Wolf took off his shirt and wrapped her in it before running out of the church to get help.

Trauma

Creator's Calendar Year 1205; Dark Mirror

Pike looked on as that portal closed behind Gwydeon and sighed. There was nothing he could do to help his friend now, except do what he had asked. Rachel and the remaining soldiers were looking to Pike for some kind of direction, and all Pike wanted to do was get the hell out of Trelon. Pike put *Fury* back into the loop in his belt and then bent down to pick up Sabrina. She sat on the floor shivering, the voice of the man who had tormented her still echoing in her mind. Whatever she had been like before Draven came to Trelon had been shattered by his unspeakable cruelty. As carefully as he could manage, Pike lifted the scared girl and cradled her close to him. Her shivering seemed to slow and then stop when Pike held her close, and she closed her eyes and snuggled next to him, the tears that had just wetted her cheeks soaking the shirt that covered his armor. She didn't seemed to mind that she was snuggling up to armor, and Pike imagined that even armor had to be a comforting feeling compared to Draven. She wrapped her arms around him and held him as he walked, not moving a muscle as he led his group toward the throne room.

"With any luck, most of the fighting will be over by the time that we get to the throne room," Pike said aside to Rachel who seemed more concerned about Sabrina than Pike did. "Then we can get her and her mother out of here back to safety in Brea."

"I'll take half the men ahead," Rachel responded, "and leave the other half with you to help you guard the princess."

With that she charged ahead followed by a few of the warriors. The remaining soldiers stayed with Pike, flanking him, as he made a slow pace toward where the battle raged ahead. Now that Sabrina had been rescued, all efforts had to be made to make sure she made it back to Brea in one piece. Rachel knew in her heart that the girl was not going to have an easy time recovering from the ordeal that she had been through, but she knew that if there was anyone on the planet that would have the patience to help her through the pain and anguish, it was Pike. Deep down through that rough exterior, he had a good heart, one that understood what it was like to suffer, and Rachel knew that he would not leave that girl until she no longer needed him.

As she and the rest of the warriors strafed though the palace, they saw the remains of the Jeresei and Kalbraks that littered the floor of the halls. There were only one or two humans mixed in with the fallen bodies of the Shadow spawn, so it looked as if Logan's group was faring well in the battle. That appearance changed when they got to the receiving hall outside the throne room. Rachel saw Logan and two of his warriors fighting against three Shadowwalkers. All across the floor were scattered fallen human bodies, many of them burned to a cinder by the flaming breath of the Shadowwalkers. Draven had obviously saved the most deadly and determined defense for the throne room, and once Logan's men had reached the threshold, the innate abilities of the Shadowwalkers had been able to make the most use of the cramped quarters. Between the gouts of fire and the extended reach of the Kalbraks' claws, it would be difficult for any solider to strike a clean blow without putting himself in the line of fire from one of the other beasts. Logan had obviously made liberal use of his own abilities, but by the way he moved, Rachel could tell that he was no longer fighting at peak efficiency.

Rachel's men charged the larger opponents, adding strength to the furious attacks of Logan and his men. Rachel was about to fire her first set of arrows when the first of the monstrous beasts fell. That was followed quickly by the scream of one of the warriors as one of the other Shadowwalkers brought one of its bladed feathers crashing down on the shoulder of the warrior, slicing him in two. Rachel took aim at the monster and fired. The first arrow was blocked as the beast brought its wings up around it like a shield. There was the sound of metal crashing against metal as some of the warriors hacked at the wings of the great beast. One of the blows from a warrior dislodged one of the feathers, and before a new one could reform, Rachel fired again and a scream came from the Shadowwalker, as the arrow raced through the newly created vulnerability. It toppled backward and fell, its wings falling to its sides allowing the warriors to stab it until it no longer moved. Logan was continuing to slash and thrust at the remaining beast, and it was only a matter of time before it fell. The larger creature slashed down at Logan, but he was able to block the strike. The next strike from Logan was accompanied by a battle-cry, and when the Shadowwalker tried to block the strike with the sword like feather, it was shattered by the force of the Dragon Sword whose slash continued until the beast's head was severed from its body. By this time, Pike and the others had arrived to the entryway, and Pike took a long hard look over the carnage in the room. Most of the men that they had saved from the dungeon had already been killed, and it appeared that Logan had been seriously wounded.

There was a large gash in his side that poured blood like a fountain. He had ripped apart what looked like a shirt to use as a bandage, but it had filled up so quickly with blood that it was almost useless. Rachel was tending to him, and it appeared as if she were able to stop the flow of blood again, but if he continued to fight, it wouldn't last long. As soon as Logan saw that Pike was carrying Sabrina in his arms, he pulled away from Rachel's attempts to heal his wound and walked over to Pike. He fell to his knees before Pike and stroked Sabrina's hair lightly. She started trembling again, but when he stopped and stood, she started to relax again.

"What happened to her?" Logan asked quietly.

"Draven had her tied to the bed in her room. She has been roughed up pretty bad, and it looks like he raped her. She hasn't said anything yet, and she only seems to respond to me, but she hasn't moved out of this position since I set her free. It's probably going to take some time before she recovers."

Logan's features contorted. Part of his fears had been realized, and yet at the same time he hated himself for not being able to do more to protect the girl. That hate mingled with the growing hate for Draven, and the intensely burning hatred for the war that had claimed their world and clutched it in shadow. So much of him wanted to take Sabrina into his arms and do his best to comfort her. It had taken the girl some time to accept Logan as a father figure, but once she did, the two had a very close and very difficult to describe relationship. At times it felt like they knew each other were thinking and could have whole intense conversations without saying a word. Perhaps it was because they shared the mantle of the *Chosen One*. Now, kneeling that close to her, he could feel the intense pain rocketing through her body, but more than that was the abject humiliation. That was why she recoiled when Logan touched her. She knew the touch, she knew it was Logan, and she did not want him to see her that way. Again he reached out and laid a hand on her arm and sent as much love and understanding as he could into the bond. Sabrina tensed for a moment and then finally relaxed, but time for healing would have to wait until later. Looking up first into Pike's face and then over to Rachel, Logan then looked down the passageway. When he did not see Gwydeon, he returned his gaze to Pike.

"Where's Gwydeon?"

Pike did his best to hide the grimace that wanted to curl his lips.

"He challenged Draven to a duel in Aradon to buy us some time to get out of here. He said that we should get the queen and the princess out of here as soon as we can manage. Also, he said that the Elder are here in the palace somewhere and that the Dragon Sword can lead you to them. We've got to get them out of here too before Draven returns."

Logan nodded conceding the fact that there was probably a very slim chance that Gwydeon would ever survive a duel with Draven.

"Alright, we get the queen then we find the Elder and get out of here," Logan said firmly. "Let's get on with it."

The remaining men formed up and waited for the signal. Rachel nocked an arrow into her bow, and Logan readied the Dragon Sword to taste blood again. Pike, not really wanting to do it, laid the princess gently on the floor of the entry way and wrapped her in one of the fallen tapestries. Two of the remaining soldiers moved to flank where the princess lay, their swords ready to defend her if any of the beasts from the other parts of the castle had survived the advance to the throne room. She shivered for a moment, but after Pike stroked her hair a few times, she seemed to calm down. He then pulled *Fury* from his belt and readied himself for battle. Upon seeing that everyone was ready, Logan motioned for one of the soldiers to open the door. With a quick hard pull, the door to the throne room swung open, and Logan charged forward followed by the rest of the party.

The throne room looked as if there had been a butcher at work. Blood covered the walls, and bodies littered the floor. Many of the Jeresei and Kalbraks had settled down to feast on the fallen warriors, but they quickly sprang to their feet and launched themselves at the invaders that charged into the room. The remnants of the Army of the Dragon quickly moved to engage the feral beasts, trading slash for slash until one of them made a mistake. Unfortunately, more often than not, it was the human that failed to live through the confrontation. Logan's eyes were set on the open door that led to the queen's chamber, and he slashed wildly at anything that got in his way, most often striking down beast after beast on his bloody trail. Rachel stayed behind Pike, picking off the monstrosities as they finished their individual combats, or when she had a clear shot. Her arrows saved many of the warriors from certain death. Meanwhile, Pike stood firm in front of her burying his axe time and time again into the skulls of beasts that ventured into his range. Blood flowed everywhere in the throne room as more and more bodies began to litter the floor. Twenty Jeresei and ten Kalbraks had fallen already, but so had five of the nine remaining soldiers. Logan was deeply embroiled in combat with as many as three or four Jeresei at a time, but he appeared to be holding his own, and Pike seemed to have things well in hand as he and Rachel moved slowly though the room, killing anything that had red or green skin.

To Pike's right, another warrior fell as a Jeresei slashed him across the throat with its razor-sharp claws. Pike's downward slash cleaved the Jeresei's head in two, and his exposed flank was quickly covered by Rachel who downed a Kalbrak with an arrow to the forehead. Logan was ducking and dodging several strikes from members of the Jeresei, and striking when he could. As he ducked the high slash of one, he buried the Dragon Sword into the gut of another, wheeling the dying Jeresei around to use as a shield. It was then that an arrow slammed into the side of one of the attacking creature's heads sending it to the floor in a heap. One of the other Jeresei was pinned against the dead body shield, and Logan charged forward hard, impaling the second Jeresei on his blade. The beast screamed in agony as it died slowly, and Logan withdrew his sword and waited to face the next challenge. The strike came from above, as one of the surviving Jeresei dove from high above him in an attempt to take him by surprise. Another arrow erupted from Rachel's bow and struck the Jeresei in the throat. The force of the arrow caused it to rip through the front and the back of its throat creating a wide hole for blood to pour through. The creature fell to the ground dead as Logan lunged forward to decapitate the remaining Jeresei threat. Within minutes the battle was over, and all of Draven's beasts lay dead on the floor. Logan took only a second to take a deep breath before charging headlong into the queen's bedroom. Pike and Rachel surveyed the damage. Only four of the soldiers rescued from the dungeon still lived, but one had lost an arm and would probably bleed to death before they got back to Brea. Neither Pike nor Logan had every developed the power necessary for healing, and any attempt they made to save the soldier's life at this point could just as easily kill him. Trying not to dwell on the incredible losses in Trelon, Pike took Rachel by the arm and led her into the queen's bedroom hot on Logan's heels.

Pike was shocked the moment he entered the opulent chambers of the Queen of Trelon. From the look of the room itself, one never would have guessed that the palace had been invaded at all. All of the tapestries and paintings still hung undisturbed on the walls, and there was nothing broken or bleeding on the floor. Logan knelt by the queen's bed, Cairyn's face pressed lovingly to his, nuzzling up against him. She appeared to be unharmed, but if they didn't get out of there soon, there was no way to guarantee her safety. Gwydeon would do his best to delay Draven as long as he could, but Pike had to face facts and expect that it would only be a matter of time before Draven returned. Logan too sensed the urgency of the situation and defected the barrage of questions that Cairyn finally began to lob in his direction. Despite her protestation, Logan helped Cairyn to her feet and led her out through the throne room. Pike and Rachel followed without question, and stopped with Logan and Cairyn in the receiving hall. Cairyn moved as quickly as she could when she saw her daughter on the floor. Cairyn stooped to check on Sabrina, but every attempt to console the young woman was batted away, and Sabrina cried a guttural scream when the queen tried to hold her. Cairyn pulled away as if struck and returned to Logan's side, a look of shock and dismay on her face. Pike quickly crossed to Sabrina and stroked her hair gently. With a quick motion he had unfastened the breastplate of his armor and handed it to Rachel. He then stroked the girl's hair again and took her, blanket and all, into his arms. Again she snuggled up close to him, her head resting on his chest. The tension in her seemed to ease now that she could feel his body rather than his armor, and her shivering stopped completely.

"Alright," Logan said after a moment, "Pike, you and Rachel take the Cairyn, Sabrina, and the survivors back to Brea. After I find the Elder, I'll drop them off and then go for the people in the dungeon. Try to break the news to Midarin gently, there's no telling how she is going to react. Take Sabrina to a healer right away. I want to make sure she isn't permanently injured."

Cairyn tried to question again, but there was no time. Logan opened a swirling blue portal and ushered everyone into it. After everyone was through, Logan closed the portal and drew the Dragon Sword. For a long moment he stood there in the center of the receiving hall with his eyes closed concentrating on the Dragon Sword. Finally, he felt a pull and walked as the sword led him through the palace. The sword led him back the way that he had come on his journey to free the queen. In a matter of matter of moments, the sword had stopped pulling him, and he stood in an empty hallway near the northern armory. The sword then began to shake violently in his hands as if it were possessed. Suddenly a white light flashed from seemingly inside the blade, and when Logan opened his eyes, he found himself staring at the Elder cauldron in a small dimly lit armory.

"Welcome Lord Logan," the cauldron seemingly said, "we are relieved to see that you have come to rescue us. When the monster calling itself Draven began to plunder the palace, we tried everything that we could to keep him from detecting us."

"Why didn't you reveal yourselves to me before he came," Logan asked puzzled.

"It was not the right time."

That was all that was said. Logan remembered the Elder that were in Marcwell all those years ago. They had been mysterious in their methods then too. It was clear that they could see into the future and into the past, but what they were willing to tell was not always clear. Logan knew that he could not press them into telling him when the time would be, so he opened a portal underneath the cauldron and eased it though into Brea as best he could manage. It was not an easy task, as that the cauldron was very heavy, but he eventually set it down in an armory in the castle of Brea. He would go to visit the Elder later to find out what they knew, but at the moment, he had other matters to attend to. When the portal closed, there was a flash of light again from the Dragon Sword, and Logan found himself outside the northern armory again. He quickly entered the armory and used the secret passage to get back down into the dungeon. When he emerged from the passage there were many cheers from the captives. Without a word, Logan opened a portal and started helping some of the more badly wounded men though. It took quite a few minutes to get them all into Brea, but once the last was through, Logan himself stepped through, the rescue complete.

* * * * * * * * * * * *

When Pike arrived back in Brea, Rachel quickly rushed Cairyn off to a private chamber deep in the heart of the palace, one that would be safest from the retaliation that would surely be coming once Draven realized that his prize had been stolen out from under his nose. Pike on the other hand had more immediate concerns to attend to. One of the soldiers was able to quickly direct Pike to one of the healers, who made his residence in a small alcove near the armory. It was little more than a hovel, but as Pike had observed during his limited time in Brea, space was at a premium. After three knocks on the simple wooden door, an older man dressed in egg-shell white robes answered.

"Yes, my son?"

"I need a bed for this young girl. She was injured by a member of the phasia, and I want to know how badly she was hurt."

Pike's voice was filled with more emotion and concern than he had intended. Somewhere deep inside of him it felt as though he were holding Eldar in his arms trying to find someone to help her after Taron had taken her life. He tried hard to shake those thoughts away, but they kept resurfacing. The old man nodded and led Pike down the hall to what must have been a treatment area. There were many cots set up to take wounded, but at the moment and certainly not for long, all of them were empty. Pike found one of the cots and gently laid Sabrina upon it. She remained curled up in a ball, but as Pike stroked her hair, she let him extend her legs and lay her flat. When the healer touched her, she almost jumped into Pike's arms again, and the healer shrank back as if bitten. It took Pike a few minutes to get Sabrina calmed down again, but after some time, she was lying flat again on her back. Pike looked down into Sabrina's eyes and saw the fear. He stroked her hair and smiled, and tried his best to be comforting. After a moment, Pike took the hand of the healer into his own and held it in front of Sabrina's eyes so that she could see.

"He is going to help you Sabrina," Pike said quietly. "He's a friend. He's not going to hurt you. Do you trust me?"

Sabrina nodded.

"Will you let him touch you so he can make sure you are not hurt?"

Sabrina nodded again.

"I'm not going anywhere, darling," Pike said as he stroked her hair again. "I'll be right here."

After a nod from Pike, the healer began to carefully examine Sabrina. His hands moved tenderly over her, finding and cleaning all of the scratches and cuts that were present. She began to wince a little when he started to treat the wounds on her face, but she did not jump once, and just kept her eyes locked on Pike's face. At one point, her hand brushed his, and he held it. That seemed to make her feel better, but she was still uneasy. Finally the healer moved to a position between her legs.

"This will be the most difficult for her I'm afraid, but it is necessary I assure you."

Pike nodded and turned back to face Sabrina.

"It's going to be alright," Pike said in his best comforting voice. "I know Draven hurt you, but we need to know that you aren't in any danger."

Sabrina violently shook her head.

"Sabrina please. Cairyn needs to know you're ok, your mother is going to worry until she knows for sure."

She shook her head again.

"Do you want Logan to worry too?" Pike countered.

The girl appeared conflicted at that question. She had been uncertain when Logan Ranthall had first entered their lives, and she had to admit to herself that she actually resented his intrusion into their lives. She had been cruel in her treatment, announcing to all who would listen that Logan was not and would never be her father. That everyone needed to remember who her real father was at that he too was a hero that died fighting the forces of the Shadow. But Logan was a force that could not be ignored for long. Through his patience and his persistence, he wore the girl down until finally she began to see Logan as a man and not a threat to the memory of her family before the darkness descended upon them all. It was then that she started to feel the connection on another level, a primal level that she could not understand. She always knew when he was close, even when thick walls of stone separated them. She could feel when he was hurt, or worried. She felt his love and concern for her as though the emotions were coming from her own soul. Now, Sabrina could not think of Logan in any other way but as her loving and devoted father. A gentle hand resting on her lower abdomen shocked her away from her thoughts and she refocused wide eyes on Pike. Finally, she knew that she had to relent, and nodded her assent. Wordlessly Pike nodded in the direction of the healer and he went about his work as carefully and calmly as he could manage. After a few minutes, the procedure was finished, and Pike covered Sabrina with a sheet.

"It's clear that she is going to be alright," the healer said returning to her bedside. "There are no internal injuries that I can account for, and the wounds that she has a superficial. As for her mental state, it will take time for her to recover, and it is obvious that at the moment, you are the only one that she trusts. I'll leave the two of you alone so that you can talk, if she's ready of course. I've received word that more wounded have arrived, and I must attend to them. However, I will be back to check on you as I am able. For now this room is not needed, take whatever time you need."

The healer left the room quickly and left Pike alone with the scared little girl. For a moment, Pike just sat there stroking her hair and holding her hand. He wasn't sure what to say, or if he should say anything at all, so he just sat there watching her. It was one of the most uncomfortable situations that he had ever been in, but in a way he felt that he was doing this for Eldar as much as for Sabrina. It had been a long time in the world since Eldar had died, but for Pike, it had only been a few weeks ago. It still pressed hard in on him, and the knot in his chest seemed to worsen every time he stroked the girl's hair. Finally, he sighed deeply and squeezed her hand tight in an effort to let out some of his frustration. She squeezed back and when he looked into her eyes, she smiled weakly at him. It was like a ray of pure sunlight had struck through the gloom. The smile lasted only for a second, but Pike felt it in his soul long after the smile had faded from her face.

"What is your name?"

The voice was cracked and raspy and also very weak. At first it was just a whisper, but after a moment it got stronger and she was able to squeak out the question.

"Pike," he answered after the shock wore off, "my name is Pike."

"Pike," she repeated to herself.

There was nothing else for a few minutes. The advancing morning was beginning to light up the sky, and bring some hope from the gloom of the night. Pike was beginning to wonder why he was gone so long, and if the world was too far under the thumb of Shau-ling to be brought back. He wished that he had been in the war from the beginning. He would have liked to have fought against Draven at Aradon, and he would have liked to have seen his father once more before he died. But those things were long since gone, and there was nothing he could do about it. Suddenly there was a tear that welled up in Pike's eye, and he felt it run down his cheek before he knew he was crying. Sabrina saw the tear and caught it on her finger before it slid off his face.

"Don't cry," she said sweetly.

That simple statement brought a smile back to Pike's face. Despite all that she had been through, there was still a child's innocence there, and it shone through despite the pain that she was feeling.

"Are you hungry, Sabrina?"

She shook her head.

"Tired?"

After a moment she nodded.

"Why don't I find you are room where you can sleep?"

Sabrina nodded and Pike stood and started to leave. Sabrina held tight to his hand and would not let go. Taking the hint, Pike wrapped the girl in the blanket again and carried her back to the main passage. A young soldier waited, obviously unsure what to do with the influx of wounded and the preparations for a possible invasion.

"Can I help you sir?"

"The princess needs a nice bed to sleep in, and I think it would be better for her if she were in a room of her own. Are there any rooms available here in the palace?"

The young soldier thought to himself for a moment, and then smiled.

"There are a few rooms in the east wing. They are safe because they are the farthest from the main wall. Those rooms would be the last disturbed during an attack."

The soldier led them down a corridor and then through a wide hallway past several doors until finally he stopped in front of one. He opened the door quietly and lit the torch that hung just inside the room.

"This is for her," the soldier said motioning toward the room, "she can stay here as long as she likes, Queen Midarin has left orders for no one to disturb her. If you wish you can have the room next door."

Pike nodded and thanked the soldier. After a quick salute, the soldier turned on his heel and headed back the way they had come. Pike eased the door closed and took a quick look around the room. It certainly wasn't going to rival Sabrina's lavish room in the palace of Trelon, but it would do for the time being. He walked over to the bed and gently laid Sabrina down. After getting her under the covers and stroking her hair a few times, he kissed her softly on the forehead and started to leave.

"Where are you going Pike?" Sabrina asked softly.

"I'm going next door to sleep. You need your rest."

"Please don't leave me alone," she said meekly, but with intensity. "Lay with me please."

Pike stood there for a moment and then nodded. He crossed the room quickly and slid in beside the young girl. Instantly, she snuggled up next to him and laid her head on his large chest. For a few minutes he just lay there watching her until finally she fell asleep. Pike sighed to himself and then shut his eyes. All though that morning, a combination of dreams and nightmares of Eldar and Sabrina filled his mind.

Enforcers

Creator's Calendar Year 1205; Light Reality

Since the War of the Dragon, no other kingdom had undergone the amount of change seen inside the borders of the kingdom of Kandor. Almost all of the changes benefited the people of the kingdom, and for a time helped it to become a shining jewel in the center of a world recovering from yet another war. Thanks to the forces of the Light, the oppressive king, and member of the Brotherhood of Phasia, Farax Soar had been banished from his ill-gotten throne, and the banner of the Vulture had been forever removed from the towers of the palace. Farax's banner was quickly replaced with one of the many versions of the Dragon Banner, more out of respect to the title than to the man whom it represented. For many years it flew in fact not to honor Logan Ranthall, but to honor the man who ruled the kingdom, Pike Rhuiden.

After the death of Farax, a young lord named Evan Sinn ascended to the throne and began to rule the people in the way that they had always deserved. He was the son of an aristocratic family who were always outspoken in their condemnation of the appalling practices of the former king. More than one member of Evan's family had been put to death for their heretical beliefs that Farax's rule was flawed. So when the time came to choose a new king, the last of the Sinn family was the nearly unanimous choice. To his credit, Evan rewarded those who had faith in him through his kind heart, open mind, and a firm hand when it came to lawlessness.

He was very popular among the people, and in a short time created a reputation for himself as a very fine and noble king. When Pike Rhuiden came to the city, Evan felt compelled to meet the man that legends had begun to weave themselves around. Pike was gracious and humble in his description of his ordeals, and answered all questions put to him as best he could manage. He, like Evan, was a man of the people, more comfortable holding court in a tavern with a tankard of ale in his hand than in the finery of a royal receiving hall. Upon their first meeting, the two young men spent most of the day together talking, and by the end of the day, the two had walked all through the city and became fast friends.

The next morning, the two men made their pilgrimage to the farthest edge of the Kingdom of Kandor, to the small town of Taren. Throughout the whole of the trip, Pike said not a world, and Evan could tell that the dread of what was to come was beginning to weigh on the man to such a degree that even Evan could begin to feel its weight. But this had been Pike's whole reason for venturing back down the path that eventually led him with the Lord Dragon to the throne room of Shau-ling, to pay his respects to those who had fallen along the way. It was late in the evening when the two came to the field where Eldar and Lane had met their deaths. Pike knelt down beside a small fissure in the soil and stayed silent for a long time. Evan stood by, just watching until Pike rose. The two men then spent the rest of the night in a local tavern, where Pike wove his stories for the people of the city and found some measure of joy in their lauding of him. The second day was spent much as the first, telling stories and bolstering the people who had been effected by the short visit of the war to their doorstep. However, that evening Pike returned to the place where his beloved had fallen. That evening was the beginning of the most powerful verse of the legend of Pike Rhuiden. It was then that he asked permission to build his statue for Eldar. Evan quickly agreed, and with the help of the best stone smiths in the kingdom, the memorial was finished in record time. The statue was beautiful, crafted from the memory of a devoted love with flawless accuracy. When Evan saw the dedication that Pike put into the creation of the memorial, he decided that the whole world should know the greatness of the man who stood before him. His stories of the eventual return of the phasia tumbled through Evan's mind, and he knew that the fight would best be led by a man who knew the phasia better than anyone alive. So, on that field where the memorial to lost love stood, Evan bent his knee and relinquished his kingdom to the man who would soon become the leader of the forces of the light in the third generation of the prophecies.

Evan always looked back on that memory with fondness. Many of the other lords in the world would have called him a fool for just giving away his kingdom, but in his heart Evan knew that he was right to do what he did. Never though did Evan envision the types of changes that would come about after Pike's investiture as king. The army of Kandor, quickly renamed to yet another detachment of the Army of the Dragon, was turned into an elite force of warriors, specifically trained to fight the Jeresei and the Shadowwalkers. Pike taught tactics and methods to ensure victory based on his experience with the foul beasts. He taught that the way to defeating the Jeresei lay in a two stage method. The first stage was to disrupt their continuity in combat. They fought as individuals, but they also had a cohesion that allowed for each of them to know what any other is doing at any time. It was like they were extensions of the same creature. They fought alone, but in a group. The second stage was to work together, using an allies strengths to overshadow and compliment the weaknesses of the individual, in a sense using the Jeresei's own strengths against them. Pairing someone with great hand to hand fighting ability with someone who uses a bow or a crossbow is effective, while pairing two people with large slow axes is not. The Jeresei all had the same strengths and weaknesses, so they were easy to combat. The Shadowwalkers were a much different challenge to approach as far as battle was concerned. Pike's main objective was to not let them get airborne at any cost. Once they were in the air, ground troops were dead, end of story. His training made everyone better, and his generals and commanders were the best of the best. Evan remained in control of the day to day operations of the kingdom for the most part, at least until the money and the soldiers from other kingdoms started to pour in.

Very quickly it became apparent that everyone wanted to support Pike in his endeavor to prepare the world for the third act of the prophecies of the *Coromor*. His reputation and his status had grown immensely over the short time he had held Kandor, and the ranks of his army had grown in almost the same proportions. It was at this point that the truly gifted men and women began to arrive, ready to make a name for themselves fighting for the cause of the Light. It started with the pair of Rachel and Elizabeth, then a short stocky man from the mountains named Valin Kren, then a thief from Trelon named Zak Parthan, then a powerful yet humble swordsman from the kingdom of Scalla named Ren Dalin. They were better than anyone Evan had ever seen. Valin carried an axe into combat, and was like a whirlwind of death on the battlefield. Despite his size he moved with incredible speed and grace. Zak was armed with two longswords that he proudly displayed on each hip. In battle, he was never without both of his weapons, and from time to time he would toy with his opponents by merely dodging and parrying with his superior speed and agility. Ren was very straightforward in his approach to battle. He was humble and reserved, but in combat he lashed out with a quiet power that would easily vanquish his opponents. Rachel was a warrior in every sense of the word, she was intimidating and powerful in appearance, and when she drew her sword, she made a pledge that either she or her opponent would die before the battle would be over. Elizabeth took a different approach to battle. She was not well versed it hand to hand combat, but she could use her staff effectively if need be. She had also been trained in the bow, but it too was only a secondary means of attack. The arcane magic at her command rivaled those at the hands of Pike while he was a member of the Dragon's *Erieal*, and she could use her abilities both to harm and to heal. Evan was grouped with this extraordinary warriors, and they became known as the Enforcers.

Once Evan had been added to the ranks of the Enforcers, it became more and more difficult for him to control the day to day operations of the kingdom, act as General of the Army of Kandor, and keep up with the rigorous training that the Enforcers went through, but he managed. Life for him consisted of early morning training with the Enforcers, followed by overseeing the morning exercises of the army, then tactical sessions with the military advisors, then more training, then matters of the court, then more training, then sleep if there was time. It was rough to get in enough meals to make it through the day, but if there was a way it could be done, Evan always found it. After all, that was why Pike left him in charge. Pike trusted the resourcefulness of his friend and compatriot, and knew that Evan could handle the large task that had been entrusted to him. But then Pike arrived with news that he had become the King of the Marcwell and the husband to Queen Cairyn Binosear of Trelon. With him he brought the new leaders of the Enforcers, Turok Korven and Celina Veshaw. They were both proud and accomplished soldiers from Marcwell, and they had been members of the Lion's Mane and had survived the assault on Marcwell by Jeroch's army. Their experience gave them the qualifications to lead the Enforcers. In a way Evan was relieved, but he was also a little disheartened. But Pike made up for that when Evan was told that he would lead the kingdom while Pike took care of matters in Marcwell. In a way through patience and perseverance, Evan had recovered the kingdom that he had surrendered. Twenty years had passed since preparations began for the continuation of the war against the Shadow, and the Enforcers had been working and training hard, waiting for the return of the children of Shau-ling and their evil followers.

It was early in the day when Evan received word that Pike would be coming and that the Enforcers should prepare for travel. In response to his lord's wishes, Evan hurried through all the training sessions for the day, and made sure that everything was prepared for Pike's arrival. Dinner was held, and the Enforcers waited in the war room, deep inside Kandor's palace for their founder's arrival. Turok paced back and forth across the floor, as was his way, impatiently waiting. He was thick through the shoulders, much like Pike, but not to that extreme. He was taller than Pike, so the muscles in his body did not look as impressive, but he was still very well built. His face was clean shaven and bright, but his eyes had a look to them as though he had seen many trouble in his life. When he walked, there was a slight limp due to an old injury suffered at the hands of a Jeresei during the fall of Marcwell. Evan had seen the brutal scar and was surprised that Turok could still walk at all. Apparently, after Turok had cut down one of the red-skinned monsters, he turned to find another enemy, but neglected to make sure that the Jeresei was truly dead. It reached up with one of its clawed hands and tore at Turok's flesh from the middle of his thigh all the way down to his ankle. Turok turned back to kill the monster, but found himself crippled for most of the battle. Had it not been for his lover Celina, he might not have made it out alive.

Celina Veshaw was a very beautiful woman with raven black hair and dark brown eyes. Her skin was fair and flawless, and her body was one that any man alive would find desirable. As usual, she wore a tight fitting orange bodkin that showed off her breasts, and her arms were folded lightly under them, lifting them further into view. She was very proud of her body, and liked to show it whenever possible, though often her exhibitionism was limited to the meetings with the other members of the Enforcers. On the battlefield as well as on the training grounds, Celina was all business, and considered herself just as fit and capable as any man under her command, if not more so. She reserved her concessions to femininity to times when it would be best appreciated by those she trusted. Celina and Turok were not married in any conventional sense, but they were lovers, and shared the same bed every night. They were happy together as a couple and neither of them looked for another partner on any occasion. They had served in the Lion's mane together for five years under Lord Arathorn Geoffrey, and they were two of his favorite students. They were both very intelligent and tactically inclined. Thought unlike Turok, Celina had a temper, one that had often sent shivers through even the strongest members of the Army of the Dragon. Together on the battlefield they were a formidable pair.

On the other side of the room from where Turok paced stood Ren Dalin. As was typically the case, Ren wore his heavily modified suit of plate armor, his helm sitting on the table beside him. The armor gleamed when light hit it, showing the care that Ren put into his possessions. Whenever there was a dent or a scratch in his armor, he had it repaired. Every night he polished the metal and made sure that it was clean and proper at all times. The soaring raven with its wings spread, the ancient symbol of the kingdom of Scalla, adorned his breastplate, proudly displayed for all to see. Some of the plates in the armor had been sculpted in order to achieve maximum mobility on the battlefield. He wanted to be able to withstand a blow from even the heartiest beasts who served the Shadow, but also wanted to be able to keep up with the most agile. It was a delicate balance to strike, but Ren had continued to perfect the craft. The sword on his hip was also well taken care of, appearing to the untrained eye as though it has never been used in battle. Those who knew Ren however knew that the opposite was true. Ren had seen many battles in Scalla, from the border wars with the armies of the phasia, to the civil war before King Jerrard took the throne. That was the reason that Ren was the captain of the Raven's Wing, Jerrard's personal guard before he became a member of the Enforcers. Ren was a very respectful and quiet man. He only spoke when the situation dictated that he should, and he always observed etiquette and protocol to the best of his ability. His language was flawless, and he very rarely made a mistake in wording or phrasing in a courtly setting. He was gracious and modest, and as Zak was fond of saying, "downright boring." Evan respected Ren for his beliefs, but to Evan, he was just too perfect for his own good.

Most thieves are only comfortable if their back is to the wall and they can see all the exits in their field of view at all times. Zak Parthan was no exception to this. Even with his allies the Enforcers, Zak still stood in a corner with his back pressed firmly against the wall and a window in arms reach. While he was in Trelon, Zak had given up his life of crime, and with the help of one of his associates, he started a business that gave the townspeople some protection from the best thieves in the world. Many people had different locks on their doors and traps on their valuables. The world was not a safe place even when the phasia were not around, so, Zak wagered his reputation as a thief, and his life in many case, on testing these locks and traps for reliability. He was hired by a good many people to test their security measures, and there was never a time that he was not able to subvert either a lock or a trap. This is what brought him to the attention of Pike. His reputation was the best, and he had never once been accused of stealing anything while testing traps or locks. Pike had gotten used to having a thief around while traveling with Gideon, and if his Enforcers were going to emulate the People of the Dragon, Zak would definitely be a part of the equation. Zak was often the breath of fresh air in a group made almost entirely of career military types. There was nothing military about Zak, and he bristled at protocol and broke twice as many rules as he chose to follow. He wore a loose white shirt and black pants, with both swords proudly displayed on his hips. Though he was a little shorter than Pike, and his physical size not as impressive, he was still very well built and his frame spoke of a hidden power.

The power in the man named Valin Kren was far from hidden. While his stature was short, only a little over five feet, the man looked like a pile of walking muscle from head to toe. He had a brown beard that hung down to the middle of his chest, and had thick tree trunks for arms that he kept folded under his barrel chest. Evan almost thought that Valin was as wide in the shoulders as he was tall. He kept his axe clutched in his right hand, and there was a fire in his eyes that held the danger of anyone who crossed him. Valin had a temper that was unmatched by anyone that Evan had ever seen. When wronged or challenged, Valin would not stop until he was avenged or the challenge was won. In those kinds of battles, his ax moved with the speed that blurred everything around the ax so that a person could only see the result of each strike, not the strikes themselves. Plumes of blood were the only evidence that anything had happened. In a tavern once during one of the Enforcers' many travels, a man had challenged Valin because he did not like the way that Valin looked. He said it was undignified for someone to be that short. Valin was a proud man and accepted the challenge, and was well on his way to winning before the man's friends interfered. Valin snapped and began hacking and slashing at everything that was near him. People were dying without even knowing they were struck, and by the time it was all over, Valin was covered with blood and seven people lay dead at his feet. From that day on, everyone was careful not to incite Valin's temper.

Suddenly the door opened behind Evan, and he saw Zak unconsciously tense before Evan spun around. As soon as he saw who was at the door, Evan relaxed and sighed. The woman at the door was a friend to everyone in the room and a fellow member of the Enforcers, a woman by the name of Meredith Heron. Meredith was the newest member of the Enforcers, but it had not taken her long to ingratiate herself into the ranks and earn the trust of each and every member. Of late, she and Evan had been sharing a bed and were fast becoming a very serious pair. Meredith was a skilled archer from the kingdom of Brea, hand-picked by Queen Midarin Sandar to join the Enforcers, and her prowess with both the bow and the sword had been honed during her short three years with the Enforcers. She was a very lovely woman with blue-green eyes and long blond hair that she kept back in a tail most of the time. On this occasion however, she let it hang loose around her neck and shoulders giving her a more sensual and beautiful glow. As with all the other female members of the Enforcers, with the exception of Elizabeth, Meredith was more comfortable in a shirt and pants, often these days Evan's, than she was in a gown or dress. Evan recognized the clothes that Meredith was wearing, and as expected they had come right out of his wardrobe; a black set of pants and a thin black shirt that buttoned up the front. Meredith and Celina had struck up a kind of friendly rivalry, quietly daring each other to racier and more provocative attire during planning meetings. Playfully, Celina had accused Meredith one day of distracting Turok's attention from the planning session to the point that Celina had to elbow him in the side. When the situation permitted, the two women pushed each other to be more and more daring in their attire, and there were times that the two had very nearly crossed the line into poor taste. Like the other members of the Enforcers, Meredith was a complete professional on the battlefield, and used the private sessions with the other members of the Enforces as a way to keep the stress and tension down.

"So nice of you to join us, Meredith," Celina remarked playfully, "I'm sure that Pike would have been disappointed if you weren't in attendance. After all, aren't you the rumored mistress this month?"

Rumors were constantly flying about the man Pike Rhuiden and his tawdry love affairs. Of course, no one knew whether the rumors of his infidelity were true or not, at least not unless they were in his inner circle. Every time that a female member of the Enforcers was seen with him, she was instantly linked to him and placed in his bed. Meredith had become the latest name because she has accompanied Pike on an errand to Falke over a trade matter. The whole city was buzzing the entire time Pike was there over the mysterious woman who was at his side. It was customary for Pike to take at least one member of the Enforcers with him wherever he went, and he was usually flanked by Rachel and Elizabeth. However, there were occasions where the two women were more valuable to him in other capacities, so he would choose another member of the Enforcers to go with him. It seemed though that he almost always chose either Celina or Meredith on those occasions. Evan had once asked Pike why he invited the rumors by the company that he kept. Pike's response was merely that in some situations it was required to give your opponent a distraction or to make them think they have an advantage that is not really there. He then laughed to himself and said that he also liked the attention that the women brought to him.

"I suppose it is my turn, Celina," Meredith responded. "However, my time in the rumor mill should be a limited one. There are too many stories with the names Midarin, Celina, Rachel, and Elizabeth in them."

Rachel and Elizabeth both laughed and tried their best to hide whatever information that they had about the situation. They were not very talkative about much of anything, especially Pike. Evan knew that they were closer to him than anyone else alive, and that they knew things that he could only guess at. If Pike was truly having an affair, they would surely know.

"Well," Zak said laughing to himself, "I won't pay too much mind to those stories until they put all of them in the same bed at the same time. Then I should have both ears open to be sure."

Valin and Turok both joined into his laughter as did Evan and Meredith. Celina scowled at Turok, and Rachel and Elizabeth silently turned their attention to Ren who was shaking his head.

"Why must our conversations always turn to this nonsense," Ren said in a solemn tone. "Rumors are only that, and until they are proven true they should not be given voice, especially when they are pertaining to our lord and master. I'm sure he would not approve of us talking about him like this."

"On the contrary," a familiar voice said from the doorway, "I find it almost as amusing as Zak does. It is ludicrous to think that the infamous Pike Rhuiden would take himself that seriously."

Everyone turned to face the door. Pike was standing there with his hands pressed firmly to the door frame. His shirt was unbuttoned to the waist and he had the smell of drink about him. Whether or not he was drunk was not obvious to any of them, but he had been drinking as was customary during his travels.

"How do you fare, my lord?" Evan asked.

Pike smiled and walked slowly into the room taking a seat by Rachel at the War Room table. His hair was in disarray, and his clothes were covered in dust and soot. The trip had apparently been difficult this time, and Pike also winced a little when he sat down. Clearly that old injury was affecting him more than usual.

"I've been worse, Evan," Pike said, his speech slurring a bit. "I feel like I've been toe to toe with a hundred Jeresei and had to kill every one with my bare hands while being kicked in the side by a Stone. The ale isn't doing much for me anymore, and I can't say that I like the way I feel."

"Perhaps we should forego this meeting until you are more rested, Lord Pike," Ren said gallantly. "I'm sure a good night's sleep would do wonders for you."

Pike dismissed the suggestion with a wave of his hand and took a long look around the room before clearing his throat and speaking again.

"This meeting won't take long Ren," Pike said standing. "The reason that I called you together is because we are riding into Lakestone tomorrow. The rumors of an army of the Shadow massing there are too detailed to be coincidental. Besides, it's obvious that Shau-ling likes to make his emergence from Lakestone. He's done it in each of the last two generations, and I'm willing to bet that he's doing it again this time. Now, we will do this as we have trained to do it. We will split into two teams and canvas the city, looking for something that will give us a clue as to why Shau-ling likes Lakestone so much. He even hit the city when half of it was under water, so there has to be something there that he wants. The first team will consist of Turok, Celina, Evan, Meredith, and Valin. That group will be strong in hand to hand combat with Meredith providing cover with her bow, and Evan using his scouting abilities to keep the group informed of the area and any possible directions that the enemy could come from. The second group will consist of myself, Rachel, Elizabeth, Zak, and Ren. With these groups we spread our experience, our range, and our fighting prowess. Now, are there any questions?"

"Do you have any idea what we are looking for my lord?" Ren asked quickly.

"Shau-ling used to have a palace under Exeter Lake that was supposedly destroyed after Lord Cedric and his people killed Shau-ling. I'm willing to bet that the palace wasn't destroyed and that Shau-ling has some kind of base set up there for his creatures to hide. If that's true, we have to find a way into the palace, and we also have to find a way to destroy it for good this time. Since it's on the bottom of the lake, I can use the little bit of power that I have left to crush the walls and flood the palace. Unfortunately, I'll have to stay down until just about the last second to make sure that it works."

"Are your kids going to be joining us on this mission, Pike?" Zak asked quickly.

Zak was never one to honor ceremony or etiquette like Ren or any of the others, and he always called Pike by his name rather than his title.

"They are on an errand to Aradon. I received word while I was in Trelon that Elwyne Ranthall had died."

There were many solemn faces around the room as Pike paused and caught his breath. Though his mind was spinning from the drink, he could feel the urgency of the words that he had to speak in his mind, and he knew that if he could keep himself clear for a few more minutes, the matter would be clearer for his troops.

"I must now, my dear and beloved friends, make known to you what I have called the Directive of the Dragon. A few days before Logan died, he and I had a talk while I was visiting him and his infant son during one of my long recruiting missions. That was the first and the last time that I ever saw Wolf, and I had stopped by Aradon for the purpose of paying my respects to Elwyne and Logan and to see the boy for myself. Logan pulled me aside at one point during the visit and asked me to walk with him. At that point in his life, Logan was not the same man that I knew. He was happy and content, but there was something that was eating at him, I could tell that in his eyes. We were walked out by the old church up on the hill outside of the city wall and he stood there for a long minute or two looking at the book that sits encased in glass there at the altar. He then turned to me and sighed hard before speaking. He was honestly starting to worry me, but when he spoke, his voice tone, that dark rich troubled voice he spoke in when there was something on his mind, troubled me even more."

* * * * * * * * * * * *

Logan took a long hard sigh after look at the Book of the Creator sitting on the dais of the old church, and then let his gaze move around the room before returning them to his old friend. Of course, his old friend was a king now, the ruler of the Kingdom of Marcwell, the post that Logan had turned down before his self-imposed exile to Aradon. At that time Pike had wanted to know why Logan withdrew, and Logan had brushed away the conversation. However, now was the time for all to be revealed, in the time that he had left.

"The powers that were granted to me by Aerith Seth have been making themselves known again," Logan said. "That can only mean one thing. Shau-ling has been reborn, and the phasia will soon follow. Knowing Shau-ling and the rest of his brood, they will probably lay low for a while until they size up what they have to work against. After the war, it will probably take some time for Shau-ling to get his forces back up to full strength. I know for a fact that we wiped out several clans of Jeresei and more than one Stone throughout the ordeal. You and I both know that the phasia are very sore losers, and they will come after us just as soon as they possible can. However, they won't want to start a war, not yet."

"To tell you the truth, Logan, I don't understand what you're talking about," Pike replied shaking his head, "How do you know any of this, and what are we supposed to do about it?"

Logan sighed deeply again, and led Pike out of the church and back to the crest of the hill. From that vantage point, Logan could see the whole of Aradon, and to the east, the small cottage that had been Logan's home since his birth that was now the home for his son. Elwyne had walked out of the house and locked her eyes on her husband. Even from that distance, Logan could see the discouraged look on her face and the fear in her eyes. Logan had told her what he had seen in that fateful dream a few nights earlier, and it had scared her almost as much as it had scared him.

"I've never told you this my old friend, but before I even met Korrd in battle and before I saw him in the city of the gods during the test that I failed, I knew that he was alive. Aerith Seth visited me in a dream and brought Korrd to me. I had premonitions all throughout the quest and even now, as Shau-ling revives I am having them. The one that I had a few nights ago was the most frightening that I have ever had, and Aerith Seth himself was there to help me to see what I needed to see."

Pike hesitated for a moment before pressing his friend for more information. Pike had never been too comfortable with the type of power that Logan had. Pike's power was simple, he could control water and make it do anything that water was capable of. Logan on the other hand did not have that much definition to his abilities. It was clear that Logan had some control over all of the natural elements, but there was a further level to his powers, and he made that clear when he was able to render Cedric Binosear, the Lion of the prophecies, powerless. That kind of edge made Logan dangerous, and had he been a less stable person, he might have been swayed as Korrd was. Further maddening was the connection to the enigmatic Aerith Seth. So little was known about him, other than the fact that he had worked for both the Light and the Shadow at various points during his life.

"What did you see?" Pike managed.

Logan folded his hands behind his back and looked up at the advancing sunset.

"Some very troubling things Pike, very troubling indeed. You will grow to be a great king, but the hatred and pain in your heart will lead you down a road that offers no redemption if you cannot find love. You and I both know that you and Cairyn will never be in love, though she may love you with all her heart. You have to find someone that you can be with for the rest of your life my friend, and you will find her. She has a broken heart just as you do. Seek her out and make yourself whole."

Pike wanted to say something, but Logan waved him off and continued.

"White Lightning will rise again, and so shall Nightwing. However, they will not be one and the same. There will be new phasia in this generation, that much has been foretold to me, and the fault is not ours. The Creator has decreed that there is an imbalance that must be set right, and that shall favor the Lord of Shadows. How many there will be, I cannot say, just beware. Also, keep your eyes open for the sign of the Raven. It will be your salvation in the war to come."

There was something in Logan's tone that Pike found disheartening. Maybe it was the finality in his voice or the fact that this was being told to him now rather than down the road when Logan could have been more helpful. Unless . . .

"Why are you telling me this, Logan? Won't you be there to help me in the war to come?"

Logan shook his head.

"I have seen my own death, Pike, and it is not too far off. There is a price to be paid for my role in the last war, and I will not be able to prevent my life coming to an end. Here is the cold truth, Pike. Cedric was a pawn after his battle with Shau-ling. He touched the Blaze so he could have enough power to defeat Shau-ling. That pulled him into his slavery. Because I knew this, I would never touch the Blaze, and so Shau-ling has no use for me. I am a liability in what is to come, to both sides. I will be the first to fall. Elwyne will follow me, then Midarin, then Jerrard and Erika, and then finally you. Some of this can be averted, but my death, and Elwyne's are already written."

Again Pike wanted to say something, but Logan continued to speak.

"This has been foretold, and that is how it shall be, Pike. After Elwyne's death, you must launch an offensive against the forces of the Shadow before they have time to strike. The city of Lakestone is where you must launch this attack and I will explain to you why. You must face your demons before you will be of use to the Ram, the third *Coromor*, and to do that you must face Eldar's death, and the creature that caused it. However, you will not be alone. Look to the shadows to find her, and bring her close to you before you fight. Eldar will be with you in part, but you will not recognize her. This is my last command of you my old friend, and this will be the last time that you lay eyes on me. Take heart my friend, there are many dark days ahead, and you will have to face the darkness in your own soul."

Logan started to walk away but turned back suddenly.

"My son is to be kept away from the war, Pike. He has his own destiny to fulfill, and he cannot do so if he is by your side. He must be allowed to follow his fate. You must not approach him, and you must not make him your ally. I know that the name Ranthall at your side would make you more feared, but his path lies with Emries and Aerith Seth, you must not interfere."

Logan then turned away again and walked back toward his house leaving Pike feeling an emptiness inside that he had not felt since he watched Eldar die at the hands of the bastard Taron.

* * * * * * * * * * * *

"Is anyone else lost," Zak said not too long after Pike finished his retelling of his last meeting with Logan, "or is it just me?"

"I'm sure that Lord Pike has an explanation to go along with the Lord Dragon's strange words, Zak, or he would not have told us the story in this way," Ren commented.

"You put far too much faith in me, Ren," Pike said shaking his head. "Logan's words confuse me even more now than they did twenty years ago. However, I hear them ringing in my ears every night before I go to sleep, and it seems that they have become more urgent now that Elwyne has passed. But that does not matter now. You must prepare yourselves my friends. We leave at first light for Lakestone."

One by one each of the Enforcers left without a word. Pike watched each of them go, and he felt a twinge of familiar fear and longing as they left. When he looked at them, he did not see the men and women that he had trained, but the people that he had lived with and shed blood with during that long arduous adventure so many years ago. As Ren turned to leave, he saw the proud stance of Gwydeon Sandar and the pride in the sword that hung on his hip. There was the same grace in his stride and the quiet confidence in his movements. Ren was much more proper than Gwydeon ever was, and there was no trace of that dry sense of humor, but it was still Gwydeon that Pike saw. Then there was Meredith, a proud and fine warrior, very skilled with a bow, but she had a past that she was unwilling to talk about. She had come from a wealthy family, but there was no sign of that wealth around her. Despite the hair color, Pike saw Midarin in her. There was too much alike about them, and they had the same manner and character. There were subtle differences true, but Pike felt the lust for Midarin when he looked at her. There was one night when he was very drunk from traveling that he had called Meredith by Midarin's name and tried to get her into his bed, but she had known enough to knock him unconscious until he could awaken from his drunken stupor.

Zak was Gideon personified, minus the accent of course. There was the same disregard for authority and the quick conscienceless tongue that had gotten them into so much trouble. There was also the arrogance and pride in his abilities that made Zak almost a perfect copy of the sharp-tongued Alimidarian. Turok and Celina were easily copies of Logan and Elwyne, though Celina was more abrupt and coarse than Elwyne ever was, but there was that same stubborn streak. Turok was a fine warrior and a good leader, just like Logan, and his heart and mind was constantly employed by the concerns of his charges, the Enforcers. Evan Sinn had a dark side to him that not too many people had seen. There was a fury in him on the battlefield that Pike had only seen one other place, and that was in Korrd Ranthall. It was clear that Evan was a natural leader and a brilliant tactician, as was Korrd, but Evan seemed to have a darker quality to his genius. Men were men and casualties were dead men, and that was how Evan saw things, but it never bothered him. Death was a fact, not a tragedy. Valin Kren was the easiest to see. Talon Aielin was as brash, confident, powerful, cocky, but had the singing voice of a bard. Valin was invincible in battle, incorrigible around women, but his singing could sour milk.

When Pike looked lastly at Rachel and Elizabeth, he always faltered. Maybe it was because they reminded him of his two fallen friends, Lane and Eldar, that he kept them so close to him. Elizabeth had learned the magical abilities as Lane had, and she was also an expert on many things that dealt with the mysterious. She was quiet and reserved, but she was always thinking of ways to improve a bad situation. Early in her life, according to her own recounting, she had studied under one of the last remaining members of the Moridon and had obviously been an outstanding student. Rachel was the warrior of the pair and a master swordsman. Whether she would have been good enough to defeat either Eldar or Gwydeon in single combat was unclear, but it would have been a contentious battle. But the comparison did not stop there. There was something about Rachel's eyes that reminded Pike of Eldar. Maybe it was the way that she looked at Pike, or the confidence in her eyes when entering a combative situation. While Pike was lost in his thoughts, he didn't notice that Rachel and Elizabeth had returned.

"Pike," Elizabeth said quietly, "we need to talk to you."

Pike shook himself away from his distracted thoughts and focused on the pair.

"What is it?"

"Something that Lord Logan told you," Rachel said in a pointed tone. "He talked about Eldar and we have some additional information that might help you clear up that part of his riddle."

Pike wasn't sure if he was ecstatic or afraid.

"What is this information?" Pike asked in as level voice as he could manage.

Rachel and Elizabeth both looked at one another and then back to Pike. There was something about this that Pike found very disturbing, but he would never be prepared for what came next.

"She was our sister," Elizabeth said flatly.

A Shattered Dream

Creator's Calendar Year 1205; Dark Mirror

When Pike opened his eyes, Sabrina was still curled up next to him, her body pressed tightly to his with her head resting on his large chest. She was still asleep, and appeared to be sleeping peacefully. There was a faint sound in the hallway, and that was what had awakened Pike. Slowly the door to the room opened, and Pike tried not to tense. Brea was supposed to be one of the safest places at the moment, according to Gwydeon, but Pike still had his instincts to contend with. With the world the way it was, Pike knew that death could be walking through even the safest door at any time. However, Pike was relieved to see the eyes of his old friend Midarin peering through the open door. Pike raised his left hand and motioned for Midarin to enter, and then brought his finger to his lips telling her to be as quiet as she could. Midarin smiled down at Pike and Sabrina as she stood at the foot of the bed, and then moved up beside Pike and knelt down so that she could speak without disturbing the girl.

"What are you doing in here Pike?"

Pike smiled and then shook his head.

"She wanted me to stay, so I stayed. I guess I just have that effect on women."

Midarin smiled in spite of herself and put her hand on his shoulder lightly.

"You are a good man Pike Rhuiden, despite what I should think about you. You know she's half your age don't you?"

"I'm half my age, Midarin. Remember, I've been missing for twenty years. Besides, I'm just taking care of her until she is ready to return to her mother. How is Cairyn?"

"She's fine," Midarin answered in the same hushed tones. "It doesn't appear that Draven laid a hand on her at all. She said that he locked her in her bedroom and turned his attentions completely to Sabrina. Of course he made his share of threats, but it wouldn't be Draven if he didn't."

"Midarin . . ."

"I know," she said cutting Pike off. "When Gwydeon didn't come back with you, I knew he had done something stupid. Rachel told me later that he challenged Draven to a duel to buy you all some time to get everyone out alive. Unfortunately, that's the way he is, and if he could give his life by saving his friends, then that's what he would do without question. He may be older, but he's still the same Gwydeon you remember."

"Are you alright?" he questioned, the concern thick in his voice.

"I will be," Midarin responded. "Gwydeon and I both knew the day would come when one of us wouldn't make it through a raid or a battle. We said our good-byes a long time ago. I'm worried about Nathaniel and our baby that's on the way. I haven't told Nathaniel anything yet, but I know that he suspects that his father is gone. Now I have to figure out how I am going to raise this new child and still have it know who its father was."

She was on the brink of tears, and Pike could see them welling up in her eyes, but Pike was shocked to see a small frail hand reach out and touch the older woman's cheek, smoothing away the single tear that had fallen. Midarin looked up, expecting to see Pike's hand, but instead she was shocked to see Sabrina's.

"Don't cry Midarin," the weak voice of the young girl cracked, "Gwydeon is still alive."

Midarin was shocked at the words, and could not stop her tears any longer. As the emotion of the moment overtook her for just those few seconds, she inwardly wondered if it was the possibility that the girl was telling the truth, or the cold hard reality that was hitting her that was causing this breakdown. In essence it really didn't matter. Pike now reached for Midarin and pulled her close to him, her head resting on his other shoulder as he stroked her hair. His old friend hesitated for a moment, and then pulled away from Pike, wiping her eyes and trying to calm herself down. She had to keep calm if she was going to get the answers that she needed from Sabrina.

"How do you know he's still alive Sabrina?" Midarin asked quickly, her voice wavering.

There was a little too much emotion in Midarin's tone for the frightened girl to handle. She clung tightly to Pike again, her face buried into his chest, hiding from the result of her words. Pike held her for a moment until her shivering subsided and at the same time kept Midarin's questions at bay. If there was something that Sabrina knew about Gwydeon's fate, Midarin would do everything in her power to pry it out of the girl, but Pike knew that if she took the time to come back to her senses she would take a kinder and softer approach to her questions. Pike wanted very much to hear the information too, but he was more concerned for the girl in his charge than anything else in the world.

"It's alright Sabrina," Pike said softly stroking her hair. "You can tell us when you're ready."

The girl slowly looked up into his kind eyes, and for the first time, a smile appeared on her face. Maybe it was just the way that Pike held her, but she felt safe around him. The nightmare that had consumed her life since the fiend Draven brought his evil schemes to Trelon did not enter her fragile mind during the past night, and despite the horror that still gripped her mind and soul, she slept peacefully. If not for the traumatized part of her mind that told her that she was soiled and dirty, so much so that she would never be clean again, or the newly burgeoning part of her that would never be comfortable with the tenderness of a man's loving touch, she might have found Pike attractive, or even thrown herself at him in an effort to regain control of her own body. However, the hate for Draven curled inside of her and shut away any possibility of those feelings surfacing. As Midarin stared at her intently, Sabrina pushed those thoughts away and tried her best to talk.

"Ever since Logan came to Trelon and has been with my mother, things have been strange in the palace. Even my father never commanded the kind of respect that Logan does, and when Logan walks down a hallway, the men just sort of snap to attention and try hard not to flinch when he strides past. It's not just the fact that he may one day be king of Trelon and Marcwell, it is because of his powers. The men are afraid of him. I watched Logan and Draven fight after the last siege of Trelon, and when I saw Draven strike at Logan with that last bolt of energy from the sky, I knew that Logan was still alive. I could feel his power inside of me. It was like he and I have a connection that I can't explain. It's been that way between he and I for some time now. When I saw Gwydeon, I felt something like that, but different. Gwydeon has power in him to, but it is different from Logan's. Logan's power comes from somewhere else, somewhere far away. Gwydeon's power comes from inside of him, deep in his heart and in his soul."

Midarin smiled, nodding in inner pleasure. In a matter of a few words, this little girl who had never met her beloved Gwydeon has summed up the very thing that made Midarin love him. Everyone who ever met Gwydeon felt the power and strength that radiated inside of him, but Midarin was sure that this little girl was feeling something different. Emries, the first *Coromor*, had touched Gwydeon in some way, and had dubbed him the Brother to the Angels and the Champion of the Old Gods in the previous generation. It was something that Gwydeon never spoke of, but because of Midarin's closeness to her husband, she could not help but know. Maybe this was the inner power that Sabrina spoke of.

"When Gwydeon went through the portal," Sabrina continued, "to fight Draven, I still felt his power in my mind. If he was dead, I wouldn't feel him in my head anymore, but I still do. There is something different, like a cloud is hanging over it, but it is still there and still strong."

Midarin was elated. She had resigned herself to the fact that she would never see the man she loved ever again, but now she had hope for his return. The information about the change didn't even register with her, but it did with Pike. When Midarin looked to him, there was a pensive and troubled look in his eyes. However, before Midarin could ask him what was wrong, the door burst open, and two guards hurried into the room.

"My queen," they spoke in unison, their voices fumbling the words into a chaotic mess.

"What is it?"

There was a spark of anger at the intrusion in her voice, but she knew it had to be important or they would have never burst in as they did.

"Draven's army is at the walls my queen!" one of the guards blurted out. "The one you told us is called Nightwing is leading the charge!"

Pike shot out of bed the next moment and grabbed his axe off the floor beside the bed. He and Nightwing had a score to settle, and if it was to be done in Brea, so be it.

"Pike," Midarin said grabbing on to his arm as he bolted past, "wait!"

"Midarin," Pike said sounding focused and angry, "take Sabrina to the safest place in the palace and wait there. When it is over I'll come for you. Don't go anywhere until I come for you. Do you understand?"

There was a new power in Pike's voice, one that Midarin had never heard, even back in the days of the People of the Dragon. Pike had always been able to harness his anger in battle so that he raged like a fire that was on the edge of burning out of control, but this was different. There was hatred mixed in with the anger. And it was clear that the hatred was so strong that it almost consumed Pike. Midarin nodded in ascent and watched as Pike ran out of the room quickly followed by the two young and confused guards. As Midarin and Sabrina locked glances, there was a shared emotion of fear and longing, one for companionship that she didn't think she deserved, while the other was for safety that she may never be able to get back.

CHAPTER 30

* * * * * * * * * * * *

The lethal rain of arrows continued to fall from the skies in Brea, just barely keeping the charge of the Jeresei at bay. The young women who were the core of the elite archers in the kingdom fired again and again, ignoring the subtle pain in their fingers and arms. Their nerves were frayed, watching the thing called Nightwing circle above the heads of the mass of Stone and Shadowwalkers. They were being held back for some reason, and only the evil that was Nightwing knew why. Suddenly there was a huge sound like thunder, and one of the Stone came flying through a portal into the western wall of the city. The men arming the twin catapults on the flanking towers were severely shaken, but managed to send a volley off to fell the huge beast. This was a new tactic, one that had never been seen in all the raids against Brea. This brazen change in tactics created a new fear that resounded through the ranks. Their lord had not yet returned, and many of them thought him dead. Without his leadership on the battlefield, there was a better chance that they would be overcome by the forces of the Shadow. Just when the dread and fear was ready to overtake the men and women of the Order of the Sword, the combined blast of thirty horns hit the air, and the gates to the city flew open. The charge of the Order had begun. Out in front of the charge, leading with his axe hefted high in the air was a man of many legends, thought dead for over twenty years. Pike Rhuiden may not have been the tactical genius that Gwydeon Sandar was, but what he lacked in strategy, he made up for in sheer will and fury.

Down on the field Pike ran at his fullest speed, the Order of the Sword pacing behind him. He could see the ranks of Jeresei speedily approaching him, and he said a little prayer to himself before leaping into the seemingly endless waves of enemies. Jeresei rushed past him as he swung his axe from side to side, waiting until he struck flesh. He started to hear the sounds of death behind him, but as he split first one and then another Jeresei in half he could not allow himself to wonder who or what was dying around him. More Jeresei came, their long claws and glistening fangs brought to bear. Two swooped at him simultaneously, but he ducked and parried with the haft of his axe, only then to strike back with a hard downward thrust that split the skull of one of the Jeresei. After a quick backwards jump to avoid the slash of razor sharp claws, Pike let his axe fly free, and it embedded itself in the chest of one of the other Jeresei.

Spotting motion out of the corner of his eye, Pike fell to the ground, just barely avoiding the downward slash of another of the red-skinned monsters. Pike grabbed one of the swords from the body of a fallen member of the Order and struck back at the Jeresei, burying the sword up to the hilt in the beast's gut. Then he saw the focus of his anger and hate. Nightwing had been watching the entire time, probably savoring his chance to kill his longtime adversary. Pike recovered his axe and then walked slowly through the battle, killing whatever got in his way. Nightwing landed on the field in front of Pike and drew one of the bladed feathers from his outstretched wings and then folded them back.

"SURRENDER NOW, PIKE," Nightwing said in a cold metallic voice. "YOU WILL GIVE ME THE PRINCESS SABRINA OR I WILL BE FORCED TO KILL EVERYONE AND EVERYTHING THAT STANDS IN MY WAY."

"So," Pike said spinning the haft of *Fury* in his hands, "Draven's got you doing his dirty work for him? What a pity. I'll make you a counteroffer you oversized tin can. Take your army off the field and we'll fight it out for the Princess."

Nightwing's expressionless face glared.

"THERE CAN BE NO BARGAIN THIS TIME, PIKE."

Suddenly, Nightwing launched himself into the air. Sensing that Nightwing was about to fly away, Pike jumped up and caught the large demon by the foot. Nightwing shot off toward the palace in the next second, and Pike barely had time to get his axe up before he was being buffeted by the torrents of wind that rushed by. For those precious seconds, Pike held on tightly to the metallic beast, but he started to feel his grip give way. So, bracing himself with one hand, he swung hard with *Fury* and buried it deep into Nightwing's back right between its wings. Nightwing howled in pain and began plummeting toward the ground. They had already traversed the distance to the royal palace, and they both came crashing down in a section Pike knew to be abandoned. Stone and dust was everywhere as the two slowly recovered their balance enough to get back on their feet. When Pike looked up, he sighed hard and raised his axe. Unfortunately, out of all the rooms that they could have picked to crash down in, they picked the room where Midarin and Sabrina had chosen to hide. Nightwing seemed to be hesitating, but Pike couldn't be sure if it was a trap or true trepidation.

"ONE LAST CHANCE RHUIDEN," came the metallic voice again, "GIVE ME THE GIRL OR I WILL TAKE HER."

Pike's answer came in the form of a hard downward slash from his axe. Nightwing easily sidestepped the blow and countered with his own sword. The two combatants circled each other, their weapons locked in a deadly embrace. After a back step, Nightwing lunged forward and then spun through an errant slash by Pike. Several more thrusts and parries from Nightwing then resulted in a long broad slash then cut across Pike's chest, sending blood spewing everywhere. It was not a deep wound, but it was enough to get a simple message across. Nightwing had pulled his blow. Pike would have been dead if Nightwing had wanted him to be, but that was not like Nightwing. Midarin sat by watching and saw something very familiar in the swordplay of the monster before them. Then the blow was struck, and Midarin tucked Sabrina back into the corner and drew her sword. Nightwing brought his sword to bear again, looking like he was going to finish what he began and end Pike's life. Midarin didn't hesitate and interjected herself, dashing to a position right between Pike and Nightwing. The metallic beast seemed stunned for a moment, and he took two steps back before resetting himself in a defensive position.

Midarin's plan was simple enough, protect Pike and keep Nightwing busy until Pike could recover. Her first few thrusts were wild, and Nightwing easily parried them away, but he did not try to attack. Each move was parried and countered, but even times where Midarin made a huge mistake or overstepped herself, the larger beast did not move in for the kill. In fact, he did not make a single offensive move against her. Midarin began to feel that Nightwing was toying with her, stalling so that his forces would have more time to get into the palace. Then, suddenly, three Jeresei came sprinting down the hallway. They had their talons extended and ready to strike. As the first leapt into the air, Nightwing turned, opened his mouth and unleashed a stream of death that obliterated the three Jeresei in a matter of seconds. Midarin took a step back at that and held firm beside Pike, who had finally recovered both his axe and his composure.

"I SPARE YOUR LIVES THIS TIME, PEOPLE OF THE DRAGON. MY QUARREL IS NOT WITH YOU. MY ERRAND WAS A SIMPLE ONE, CAPTURE THE GIRL AND TAKE HER BACK TO DRAVEN. HE WANTS HER, AND IF ALL OF YOU HERE IN BREA HAVE TO DIE, THEN YOU LEAVE ME NO CHOICE AND THAT IS THE WAY IT MUST BE. I KNOW YOU ARE MORE INTELLIGENT THAN THAT. I COULD KILL YOU BOTH WITH A THOUGHT. I COULD LEVEL THIS PALACE AND LEAVE NONE ALIVE. GIVE ME THE GIRL AND THE ATTACKS AND THE KILLING STOP. THERE IS NO REASON FOR YOU TO RISK THE LIVES OF YOUR CHILDREN AND THE FATE OF THE WORLD FOR HER."

There was a faint spark of recognition from both Pike and Midarin. For the first time, real fear hit Midarin and she began to tremble.

"I KNOW THAT YOUR CHILD NATHANIEL IS THE *COROMOR* OF THE PROPHECIES, AND I ALSO KNOW THAT SABRINA IS THE *CHOSEN ONE*. DRAVEN WANTS HER FOR HIS OWN SCHEMES, AND THERE IS NOTHING YOU CAN DO TO STOP HIS WILL FROM COMING TO PASS. HEED MY WORDS WELL. IF YOU WISH TO HAVE A CHANCE TO WIN THIS WAR, YOU MUST GIVE BEFORE YOU CAN TAKE. GIVE ME THE GIRL AND PRAY THAT DRAVEN DOES NOT CHANGE HIS MIND AND LOOSE THE REST OF THE DARK RIDERS UPON YOU. HE MAY LEAVE YOU ALONE LONG ENOUGH TO STRIKE AT SHAU-LING, BUYING YOU SOME TIME TO PREPARE FOR THE NEXT GENERATION. DO NOT LET YOUR PRIDE CONDEMN YOU AS IT HAS SO MANY OTHERS. WHAT WILL IT BE?"

Pike stepped forward and put his axe back in the loop of his belt. There was something not right about this entire situation, and he was going to find out what it was. He knew in his heart that he shouldn't have survived his exposure to the Blaze, and he also knew that giving Sabrina to Nightwing was almost as bad as killing her himself.

"Come here Sabrina."

Pike's voice was cold and hard, but the little girl trusted him with all of the strength that remained within her. If he was going to give her to Nightwing, it must have been the only way. She walked quickly over to him and wrapped her arms around his waist, holding him tightly, her face pressed up against his chest.

"Here is the deal, Nightwing," Pike said wrapping his arm around the young girl and holding her close. "Sabrina and I are a package deal. If Draven wants her, he gets me. He can kill me if he wants, but by the Light, I am not giving her up without a fight."

Nightwing stood there and pondered for a moment, and then his metallic eyes glowed red.

"PIKE RHUIDEN YOU ARE PROBABLY THE BRAVEST SOUL THAT I HAVE EVER MET. I ACCEPT YOUR OFFER. THE ATTACKS HAVE BEEN CEASED. EVEN NOW DRAVEN'S ARMY IS LEAVING THE FIELD AND YOUR PEOPLE ARE CHEERING THEIR RETREAT. MANY HAVE DIED, AND MORE WILL BEFORE THE NIGHT IS OVER. IF ANOTHER MEMBER OF THE PHASIA WERE TO STRIKE NOW, BREA WOULD BE LEVELED. MIDARIN SANDAR, TAKE WHAT ARMY YOU CAN MUSTER AND LEAVE THIS PLACE BEHIND. YOUR KINGDOM IS IN RUINS, AND THERE IS NOTHING LEFT FOR YOU. BUT KNOWING YOUR HUSBAND, I'M SURE HE HAD A PLAN PREPARED FOR ALL CONTINGENCIES. IF YOU STAND BY AND WAIT, YOU WILL BE CRUSHED. RAEL AND TRECE HAVE GATHERED AN ARMY AND WILL BE HERE IN TWO DAYS. JEROCH IS ALSO COMING, AND HIS ARMY MAY BE HERE THE SAME TIME. GO NOW, WHILE YOU STILL CAN."

Nightwing's eyes flared again, and a swirling blue portal appeared in the space between Pike and Nightwing. Without a word, Pike and Sabrina stepped through. Nightwing hesitated for a moment and then stepped through the portal as well. Midarin watched as the portal closed behind them and felt an uneasiness in the pit of her stomach. There was something too familiar about Nightwing, and he knew too much to just be one of Draven's lackeys. Just then Logan came rounding the corner followed by Evan Sinn and Nathaniel.

"Midarin," Logan said quickly, "Draven's army is retreating, and when I heard that Pike and Nightwing were both in the palace, I came to find you. Where are they?"

"Gone, Logan," Midarin said, her voice filled with dejection. "Pike made a deal to save us all. I doubt we will ever see Pike or Sabrina ever again."

Logan sighed hard and tried not to let any emotion overtake him. Evan broke the silence first.

"We need to rebuild the defenses around the city my Queen," he said quickly. "Our forces are down twenty-five percent, and with the number who are seriously injured, it could be fifty before the day is over. Whoever that Nightwing is, he knew exactly where we were the weakest and where to center his attacks. In another twenty minutes we would probably all have been dead."

"We are not rebuilding, Evan," Midarin said coldly. "Bandage the wounded as best you can and get them ready to travel. Those who can still fight will need to. Have everyone take what they need to survive, nothing more. The elderly and those too wounded to be of use will have to take refuge in the mountain caverns until our errand is done. Queen Cairyn will have to be left among them. By tomorrow we will have reached Sador, and by tomorrow night we shall have a new home."

Evan was shocked.

"Gwydeon's new plan for the three prong attack should be on the table in the war room," Midarin continued, the commanding tone of the queen of the kingdom coming to her voice. "Logan, I want you to lead the frontal assault on the northern gate. Evan, you will lead the forces into the paths in the wood, and I will take charge of the archers. We shall either take Sador, or we shall die trying."

Evan straightened and gave his best salute.

"Understood my queen," Evan said turning on his heels.

Then, he strode quickly out of the room leaving Logan, Nathaniel, and Midarin standing in silence.

"What's wrong Midarin?" Logan asked softly.

Midarin's mind was churning. All of their responsibilities, all of their plans, and the fate of the war was being distilled down into a hasty retreat followed by perhaps an over-hasty attack.

"There was something not right about Nightwing. He wasn't vicious, he didn't try to kill me, and his mannerisms and tactics seemed too familiar. It was almost like he knew exactly what was going to happen even before it did. He also knows that Nathaniel is the *Coromor* and that in itself is scary. He said he was working for Draven, so if Nightwing knows, we have to assume that Draven knows, and that it's only a matter of time before the rest of the phasia know as well through their connection to the Blaze."

"Things are going to be alright, Midarin," Logan said laying his hand on Midarin's shoulder. "We'll make those bastards pay for what they've done."

Midarin tried her best to smile. As Logan walked away, Nathaniel walked over to his mother and held her tightly. No words needed to be spoken, and the feelings in the room were too powerful to be express. There is a time when hope is no longer just a feeling, when it becomes something you can touch, feel and smell. Gwydeon had become the hope for hundreds of people. They all knew him by name and he knew all their names as well. In battle he was not just sending numbers to die, he was sending people that he knew and loved. Now that Gwydeon was gone, something had descended into Brea that had been gone for many years. Doubt. There was now a doubt in everyone's mind that they would live and succeed. Gwydeon was a terrible loss, not only to his family and the friends that loved him, but also to the people who had devoted their lives to the dream of freedom that he said could be attained. Now the dream was flickering, and it was one failure away from being extinguished forever. Even as Midarin held Nathaniel, she could feel the grief in her heart and the sorrow begin to overtake her. Yet again, she found herself crying tears of true sorrow after the loss of someone she loved.

* * * * * * * * * * * *

As Pike stepped through the portal, he realized that he was alone. Somehow, during the transit, Sabrina had been separated from him. The room that he found himself in was totally black except for the circles of light that surrounded a larger circle in the center of the room. As he counted the circles, he began to feel a chill. There were fifteen of them. There were fifteen phasia now, and this had to be their meeting place. Another portal opened in the room, and Nightwing stepped out. He was followed by another man, a man that Pike recognized as if he had seen him only yesterday. A man with reptilian features and in long black robes. Shau-ling.

"Welcome to the Council chambers of the Brotherhood of Phasia, Pike Rhuiden," Shau-ling hissed. "Nightwing was an unexpected surprise, but now that I know he has been recreated by my pride and joy Draven, I will put him and his brothers to good use."

Pike did not bother drawing the axe from the loop in his belt. He knew it was useless.

"What do you want with me Shau-ling?" Pike asked coldly.

"In a perfect world, I would want you to be a member of my phasia, Pike. Your powers and your ability to handle yourself in battle are very impressive. I was pleased with the way you handled Taron in the last generation, and I am sorry that you lost your bride, Eldar Merin. She was a very strong woman Pike, and it is a shame to see women such as that wasted."

Pike's blood began to boil.

"How can you be sorry for something that you ordered?"

"Come, come, Pike. You know that I have little control over my phasia when it comes to those matters. They have enjoyed centuries of unchecked power, and I am in no position to tell them how to handle themselves. You saw how well I was able to manage Basille, and I always considered him one of my best students."

There was something very wrong about this entire situation. Shau-ling should have killed him by now. Why would Shau-ling want to sit and talk to a man who had dedicated his life to his eradication?

"What do you want?"

The question was not one of anger, but rather one of true curiosity. Despite all his best thoughts and instincts, Pike actually wanted to know why Shau-ling wanted him.

"Your world is sick, Pike," Shau-ling started, "and there is little now that can be done to save it. I remember the world as it was, a beautiful green world with life around every tree and behind every bush. There were animals of such great power and beauty that they would pale the most beautiful rose. But then the Emries made man, and man started to destroy the world. Emries led men to their prosperity, and he became so corrupted by his own power that he forsook his role as guide and took a more active role as god. Trees and animals were killed for food and clothing. Whole forests were burned to make way for cities and roads. Their scourge became the worst plague to ever infest this world. Their evil had to be cleansed from this world."

"You call them evil?" Pike chided.

"Silence!" Shau-ling boomed. "They were destroying a world that I vowed to protect. Your human ears cannot hear the voices of the trees and the animals of the forest. I have heard the shrieks of terror from hundreds of trees as the men with their axes chopped them down one by one. Emries arrogance forced action, and I knew that simply speaking to him and to his followers would not be enough. So for centuries I watched. I took the images from their nightmares and created Shau-ling and his horrible minions of the Shadow. But I alone could not fight the battle against the humans. I had to learn to use their own weaknesses against them. That is why my phasia look and act the way that they do. They are the embodiments of the vice, wickedness, arrogance, and hate that lies in the core of every single human. At the core of this world like every world is a force that sustains it. This world's heart and soul holds a power known as the Blaze. This is the power that my phasia and I draw upon, and this world that the humans have seen fit to reshape to their whim will burn them in fires of their own arrogance."

Pike stayed silent. If this was true . . . no, it couldn't be true.

"Then how did I survive the Blaze when I fell in it?"

"This world chose you, Pike, by the will of the Creator. There is a power inside of you that is beyond what you could ever imagine. You have forsaken the role that Emries wanted you to play, instead you fought for the emotions of your heart and allowed yourself to forget that though you wanted to kill me, there were things more important than his final objective. Win at all costs is not the way you believe. You see the risks and the rewards of your actions, and that is why I am appealing to you Pike."

"This is a trick," Pike said shaking his head. "You are trying to enlist me so that I will do your dirty work and release you from the prophecies. Well, it won't work."

"Prophecies or no," Shau-ling responded, "you will all die. It may not be by my hand if Emries is successful in his plan, but there is more at work here than just a war between the Light and the Shadow as you understand it. I may have made a mistake in making my phasia so much like humans. They began to learn from you human, and now they want to kill me almost as much as you humans do, and a war that should have stayed between Emries and I has now spun to engulf so much more with so much greater stakes. I wish I could say that it was enough now to simply spite the prophecies and end Emries, but now I fear that no amount of action I take will bring a resolution that sees any of us survive."

Pike was staggered by the entire conversation. As much as he didn't want to believe that it could be true, he was starting to be swayed by Shau-ling's very plain talk. He felt something deep inside of him that he could not explain. Maybe it was in a moment of doubt, but he asked a question that would forever be remembered as the turning point in a war that no one would ever remember being fought.

"What do you want from me?"

CHAPTER 30

Chapter XXXI

Lakestone

In a very long and illustrious life, Pike Rhuiden had not been surprised by too many things. In a world where the phasia ran free, and the threat of Shau-ling loomed over everyone, shock became almost passé. But regardless of all that, Pike still felt his jaw drop and his eyes widen in amazement at the revelation given to him by Elizabeth. Eldar Merin had been the love of Pike's life for as long as he could remember. There were even those times before they began their relationship that would lead to marriage, that he silently loved her. She had always in his eyes been unattainable, which of course made him want her all that much more. She was a daughter of nobility, and he was the son of a carpenter. She came from one of the richest kingdoms in the world, and he was from a little farm town that few knew even existed. He wasn't as smart or as handsome or as talented as some of his contemporaries, and for a time Pike thought that Eldar's attention strayed more in Gwydeon's direction. But he did the one thing that no one else could do. He frustrated her. Eldar kept her cool and her ladylike manner in all things, but no one could crack her resolve as Pike did. Whether it was with an ill-timed or off-color joke, or a prank that resulted in embarrassing consequences, Pike could make Eldar laugh, fume, or want to kill him. There was nothing more endearing.

As he looked up at Rachel and Elizabeth, the pangs in his heart began to burn even stronger in his chest. The looks in their eyes that he had always dismissed now seemed to take on an importance that he could not overlook. He scolded himself for trying to see what wasn't there, but he could see the features of Eldar in both Rachel and Elizabeth. The more he looked, the more he found, and the more miserable he became.

"How?"

That was the only question that Pike was able to choke out after those long few moments of silence. His mind was threatening to shut down because of the mass of emotions and memories that were blurring through his mind.

"Not long after Eldar was born," Rachel began to explain, "her mother and father, Alfred and Ariel, decided that their marriage was no longer what they wanted it to be. So they quietly, so as not to create waves inside of Trelon society, divorced in order to search of something better. Though they both recognized that the marriage was over, they had no desire to be acrimonious, and in fact remained close friends long after they parted ways. Ariel took Eldar with her and moved to Aradon to raise her daughter in a quiet community. Ariel had many acquaintances in Aradon through her work with the merchants and traders, and so she knew that there were many children Eldar's age for her to grow up with. Alfred chose to make his new home in Brea, where he could continue his life as a courtier."

"While in Aradon," Elizabeth continued, "Ariel met a man by the name of Joseph Core. He was a young farmer and aspiring member of the Village Council. Both Tam Rhuiden and Arin Ranthall considered Joseph to be one of the brightest men to ever live in Aradon. Ariel instantly fell in love with him, and in a few short months they were married and Ariel was pregnant."

"Much the same was true for Alfred," Rachel commented, taking back over the story. "His money and growing power made him the prize catch of the court. Seeing this, the King of Brea made an alliance with one of his neighbors, the kingdom of Alimidar, and Alfred found himself married to Valarie Conor, and was also soon expecting a child."

"I was born first," Elizabeth said quickly, brushing back her raven black hair, "and was taught in the finest guilds and libraries that Brea had to offer.

The scandal of Princess Midarin Rice had since been passed over, and the coming of the Dragon was just beginning to rise. I was seventeen when Logan Ranthall liberated Brea from the Keepers of the Light, and I knew then that I would have to become part of the war that led our savior to us."

"I was not as lucky," Rachel countered immediately. "My mother eventually grew tired of being a simple farmer's wife, and the two decided to live apart. My mother moved us back to Trelon in an effort to build a new life in the comfort of the family we had left behind. She took over the trading and merchants guild with the support of the farmers of Aradon and the other small farming communities that she had gained ties to. I hardly ever saw her, and was often left to the charge of whichever family member was available. Fortunately, one of my cousins was a member of the Army of the Dragon garrisoned in Trelon. With him, I trained every day as hard as I could when I was strong enough to hold a sword. To afford my equipment, which mother refused to pay for because she didn't want me following in the footsteps of her first daughter, I worked nights as a server in an inn, and sometimes for larger functions I worked at the original royal palace. I actually met Logan Ranthall once, but not directly. I was one of the serving maids at the dinner he and his group had with Queen Anabel Binosear before the palace was burned to the ground by Aldridge. After the loss of the palace, I decided that I would go back to visit my father in Brea, and that was when I stumbled across Elizabeth."

Elizabeth nodded and took up the story.

"It was obvious as soon as we met each other that we were intimately connected. Even though Ariel and Alfred had kept in touch after their separation, we had no knowledge of one another. After we started talking, we were able to piece together much of our pasts, and decided that we would look for our sister. The journey eventually led us to the memorial that you had built for her where she died. We instantly felt indebted to you for preserving the memory of our sister, and so at that moment we devoted our lives to protecting you."

"So," Rachel concluded, "now you know the little secret behind your 'shadows', I hope that it doesn't change anything between us."

"Doesn't change anything?" Pike blurted out as soon as he was able to speak.

His mind was on fire with the different possibilities of what this news could mean. How could he allow these two women to risk their lives to save him now that he knew who they were? Could he even chance taking them with him, for fear that he would have to relive Eldar's death over again.

"Of course it changes things," Pike continued after a moment. "You two are my link to the woman that I loved more than anything else in this world. I don't know that I can allow you to risk your lives for me now that I know the cost I would have to pay in losing one of you."

"Your love for Eldar is a powerful thing, Pike," Rachel commented almost immediately. "However, we are not Eldar. The woman you loved is related to us only by blood, and we never knew her the way you did. In your mind, you now see her in front of you, but we are not Eldar."

"Rachel's right," Elizabeth countered, "and there is something else that you must take into account. We know about your relationship with Midarin Rice. You may not have intended it to go as far as it did, but your devotion to Liette is proof that you were not just trying to drown your sorrows with an old friend. If you could just get past your pride and your pain, Midarin is a good strong woman who can give you back what you have been missing all these years. If you will just let yourself not feel guilty for loving someone other than Eldar, and stop blaming yourself for all the things you can't control."

Pike sat in silence looking up at Rachel and Elizabeth. Their wisdom was powerful enough to keep his tongue in check at that moment, and he knew that there was no rational way that he could argue with them. However, there were times that Pike was better known for being irrational in the face of reason.

"Perhaps we should go now," Rachel said straightening. "As that we are marching at first light, Elizabeth and I need to check in with Evan about the defenses before we sleep."

"Try to sleep, Pike," Elizabeth added warmly. "The night will pass quickly if you let it."

Pike nodded and watched as the two women left. No night had passed quickly for Pike in many years, and this one would be no different. The despair in his heart had soured the sweetness of his soul, and the silver lining of all of the clouds that hung around him was tarnished. He rose slowly from his chair, the pain in his side and his joints assailing him with every slight movement. Beside the war room table there was a small serving dish that had a large bottle of ale sitting on it. Pike sighed to himself and then picked up the bottle. Sorrow and pain had become too familiar fixtures in Pike's life, and as he tipped the bottle up to his lips, he sighed one last time before letting the liquid rush into his mouth and down his throat. Within a few minutes, Pike no longer felt the pain in his heart or in his body, but did feel the old urges returning. A chambermaid would come in an hour to clean up the war room, and he would take her as he had done so many times over the years. And when Pike heard the door creak what seemed to him a few minutes later, he straightened himself up and smiled his widest smile as the young woman walked quietly into the room.

* * * * * * * * * *

Evan laid on his bed staring up at the ceiling. There was always tension in him before the Enforcers rode out, and this night was no different. The silk sheets felt good against his naked skin, and as the cool night air blew in through the open window, Evan caught himself in a long sigh. The royal chambers always seemed lonely during the nights before a battle, and Evan was left with the thoughts of life and death. Suddenly, Evan stiffened. There was someone else in the room, a presence, nothing more. Evan sat up, looking around the room quickly, edging over to the side of the bed where his sword lay. Then, as he looked back toward his sword, he saw the man.

Standing six foot four inches at the least, the man in black was a sight. His hair was short on top, and his face was a memorable sort. His eyes had a fire to them that could not easily be described, and his stature spoke of power. From what Evan could tell, the man was unarmed, but for some reason he seemed more threatening because of it. The man in black looked down and then quickly looked away.

"Would you mind coving up please?"

Evan was puzzled for a moment and then threw the blanket over his lap. As if relieved, the man in black looked back down at Evan and then sat down in a chair opposite him.

"I come here to talk to you and you lay here stark naked. Do I look like Meredith to you? By the Light Evan, I have been dead too long to need to be seeing you in the nude."

"Who are you?" was all that Evan could choke out.

"My name is Aerith. But you already know all about me, don't you? I'm sure your Lord Pike has regaled you with all of the terrible stories about Aerith Seth."

Evan sat back in the bed puzzled for a moment. Everyone in the Enforcers knew the name and significance of anyone in the past who had battled or aided the phasia. Aerith Seth was the first *Chosen One* and had been killed by Shau-ling to start the prophecies. He had been a general both for the forces of the phasia and the Hand of the Light. His mantle was passed down from generation to generation much as Emries' was. Aerith Seth had only been documented as appearing to the *Coromor* and the *Chosen One* in the past, and Evan was puzzled as to why Aerith would appear to him.

"You're probably wondering why I'm here talking to you," Aerith said crossing his arms at his chest.

Evan's shock prevented him from doing anything other than nodding.

"Well," Aerith said pulling a chair to the side of the bed and sitting down, "I have a job that I need done. Now, I know what you're thinking, but you are the right person for the job even if you don't think you are."

While all at once Evan felt insulted and complimented, he remained silent.

"As you might imagine, the war between the Light and the Shadow has continued to be a thorn in my side. Let's not forget the fact that it's what got me killed in the first place. You may not believe this, but I never wanted to be involved in all of this. I wasn't given any choice, Saurn, Bryn, Ellis, Emries, Shau-ling, they all say to it that I would be tied to this until it was all over. But it wasn't enough to kill me. No, the Creator and his cronies had to make sure that others would suffer right along with me. Right now my mantle is with a little girl who is too arrogant and too afraid for her own good. Now, I'm not saying that this is a bad thing, besides, I was not the most humble man in the world. I can't talk to her like I tried to with Logan or Arin, and I can't give her any of my sage-like advice. Now, you, I can work with. You have an edge to you that I like, though you have that damn modest streak that is unbecoming. To be honest you remind me a lot of myself, except for the modesty of course. So you're going to uncover all the strange things going on for me."

The last statement stuck in Evan's mind. Ever since Evan had become involved with the war between the Light and Shadow, the threat of Shau-ling had made everything seem strange. But Aerith had lived through that and probably called it normal. If something registered as strange to Aerith Seth, then it was certainly important enough to take notice of.

"What do you mean by strange?"

Aerith smiled and then leaned forward, speaking in a very hushed voice.

"The past two generations were fought exactly as the prophecies had detailed. Well, there was a little twist last generation I guess. Shau-ling popped up and loosed his phasia and the rest of his nasties on the world and sat back waiting for the *Coromor*. The phasia did their best, manipulating bloodline and families, trying to control the *Chosen One* so that they could eventually overthrow their master. You know of course how this all ends, the *Coromor* kills Shau-ling and those of us who know how this game works waits for Shau-ling to be reborn so that we can do it all over again. Unfortunately, things got a little messed up this time around. You see, Basille Mystic, a member of the phasia, in an effort to repay a debt, made the Creator mad by changing the fabric of time and reality. Now there are two separate realities, one light and one dark, that the battle between the Light and the Shadow is being fought in. This is, of course, the Light reality where the forces of the Light have the advantage and everything is pretty much as it has been the last two times around. In the dark reality Shau-ling and the phasia are this close to ruling it all, and there is only a little bit of resistance left, and that is supposed to be on its last legs."

Evan sat and listened to Aerith's tale with rapt attention and complete astonishment. He was correct with his initial thought that he would have trouble comprehending Aerith's story, but as it began to unfold he could not believe the true depth of the situation.

"Now, being the neutral being that I am, I am caught in the middle in both realities, and I gotta say I'm getting pretty damn tired of knowing there is more going on than we're being allowed to see. Why else would I still be kicking around? I'm not some wannabe god like Emries or Shau-ling, I'm just a man and should be dead and buried and forgotten. The Creator told both Emries and Shau-ling that they can't interfere in the reality where they don't have the advantage, so that pretty much sets them both up to fail. They both have their own secret agendas in this war, and it seems like the Creator does too, and that's what worries me. You see, the Creator said that if there is a draw in this war, each side winning its own reality, then the Creator would sentence us all to fire and start over somewhere else. He doesn't want balance, he wants to know who is better. Well, that really bothers me, because since I am supposed to be the balance, it pretty much means that the Creator couldn't care less about what I do. To everyone on both sides of this war, my mantle and I are just a means to an end. Neither side can really win without me, so they just use me without care. Believe me, I've had a long time to think about all this, and the more I think about it, the angrier I get."

"No offense Aerith," Evan said sighing hard, "but what does this have to do with me?"

Aerith patted Evan's arm and smiled.

"You my dear boy are going to do a little leg work for me. You see, I've been watching Shau-ling and Emries over all of these generations, and the more I watch, the more their behavior leaves me scratching my head. Shau-ling doesn't much care what his phasia do, except when they use the Blaze to do it. His strikes on cities usually don't leave the surrounding landscape damaged, and I haven't heard of any of the members of the phasia going out of their way to unite and destroy the *Coromor*. Oh, they play at teaming up, but they always end up stabbing each other in the back. Shau-ling should be able to do something about it, as they are his children, but he doesn't. Emries on the other hand seems too bent on Shau-ling's destruction, cutting corners and sacrificing anything he needs to in order to win. He is trying to prime every generation's champions, and in some cases invents them so that he can win. I would hate to argue with Emries, but that doesn't sound to me like a position a true champion of the Light would take. Another thing that bothers me is Aryx Terian. There is something not right about that man, and he was too easily drawn to Shau-ling's side. Now he's back fighting for the Light again like nothing ever happened. And every time I start looking into him, it seems like every avenue to discover anything is blocked. I don't like doors being slammed in my face."

Evan seemed a little disturbed by the revelation of Aryx Terian.

"The last thing that bothers me, of the growing stack of problems, is that the prophecies that Emries and the rest of his 'champions of the Light' follow were given out by the phasia themselves. This may seem like a huge error on their part, but I can assure you, it was done with Shau-ling's full knowledge. He may not have agreed with it, but he let them do it. Bryn and Ellis are clever, no doubt about, but are you telling me that they know more than Shau-ling and Emries? Can they see what the gods can't?"

Evan by this time got up and was searching for his pants. Aerith diverted his eyes and groaned loudly until Evan was finished dressing. Evan then sat back down on the bed and fixed his eyes intently on Aerith Seth.

"I still don't know what this has to do with me."

"You see, Evan," Aerith said as he lounged back in the chair again, "I am very curious about what is going on. There are too many unanswered questions about both sides of this dirty little war and I want to know what the answers are. More importantly, I want to know what this all has to do with me. We all have our roles to play to be sure, but this is not what I signed up for. However, everyone knows me. I couldn't find out when and if Jeroch blows his nose without every member of both sides wondering why I wanted to know. But you Evan, you can get this information for me because no one knows who you are. For most of these people you are a former lord of a kingdom you never should have had possession of in the first place, another conquest of the great and powerful Lord Pike Rhuiden. In the other reality, you are just a lackey to Gwydeon Sandar. You are the perfect agent to unravel the mysteries of this war."

Evan stifled a laugh and then locked his eyes back on Aerith.

"Let's say I did want to help you, and that I did want to find out what was going on. How am I going to go in amongst the phasia, Shau-ling, the *Coromor, Erieal,* and *Chosen One* and stand a chance of finding out anything? In case you didn't know it, I don't have any powers of any kind, and I don't know that I would be able to stand up to any of those people in a fight."

Aerith's smile just grew wider.

"I am going to remedy that, Evan. While I may have passed my mantle on to the *Chosen One* of this generation, I do still have my own powers left. Let's just say that Bryn and Ellis were very generous in teaching me how to control the forces of nature. Years after I left them, just before my death, I began to hone my control of over the primal forces and I discovered the true power that lies inside of the world around us. Unfortunately, I didn't live long enough to expand on that power. But, in the years since my death, I have been opened up to all kinds of new areas of knowledge and I have been able to expand my natural powers to their utmost potential and beyond. Now, I am going to give a large portion of my powers to you."

Aerith extended a hand and a green beam of energy emerged and flew the distance between the two men engulfing Evan. Pain racked Evan's body as every cell of his being started to change with the power that was infusing him. The beam of energy changed to red, and Evan felt a new pain began to contort his musculature. His mind and body were both on fire, and he wondered if he would survive whatever transition he was going through. As the beam turned blue, a coolness washed over his pained body. The fire in his stomach and mind had begun to ease, but the pain was still with him, becoming a dull ache that throbbed with his heartbeat. The beam then turned white, and the pain began to ebb. Evan felt different, but he only felt half of what he should be. It was then that Aerith extended his other hand. Lightning, fire, ice, and smoke enveloped Evan and he screamed in agony as the deluge assaulted him. The pain was so intense that Evan thought he was dying. His heart beat hard in his chest, so hard that it threatened to burst right through his ribs. Breathing was a laborious task at best, and Evan had to forcefully drag each and every breath in and out of his tired lungs. Then, just as suddenly as the pain began, it began to ease. When Evan opened his eyes again, he saw the threads of lightning, fire and ice still fluttering around him, lazily entering and then exiting his body. Aerith no longer controlled the torrent of energy, but sat back, looking exhausted, and watched the continuation of the process. Evan felt a new strength begin to permeate his body, and a new window in his consciousness open. He could see the lines of power running through him, and he could also see where the different planes of energy intersected with the plane he called reality. It was like lighting a torch in a dark room to see the walls adorned with the most beautiful paintings in all the world. There was a music in the motion of time, space, and reality. Life as he knew it began to take on a whole new meaning. It was as if in that span of a few moments, Evan had become a god.

"Intense, isn't it?" Aerith said slowly recovering.

Evan finally saw that he has been released from the field of energy that held him. While there were no physical changes to his body, other than a feeling of extreme physical health and superiority. His mind had become a powerful machine, whirling with thoughts that only the Creator should have been allowed to have.

"I feel like I could move a mountain with my bare hands."

Evan made the statement without even thinking. He knew that he had been imbued with an amazing amount of power, but even with his newly expanded consciousness, he did not know how to draw upon the information he need to successfully wield his new found abilities.

"In theory," Aerith replied, "you could."

Evan looked down at Aerith and could not take his eyes off the man. He was completely shocked at the possibilities of what he could do.

"But," Aerith said standing, "that's not why I gave you my powers. If you want to rearrange the skyline, do it on your own time. While you're working for me, try to keep the mountain moving down to a minimum. Now, I don't have to tell you that you just did a major run up the food chain. With your powers, you are a threat to just about everyone on the planet with the exception of the Creator. Don't go thinking that you're a god, because you're not. You're just a little man from Kandor who was given enough power so that you could take care of yourself. Remember that. I won't be able to bail you out, and I don't think you want to go head to head with either Shau-ling or Emries by yourself. Besides, that is not your purpose here. You're not here to win a war, if it can be won at all."

Evan could not help but watch as the images floated by in his head. He saw himself battling Shau-ling to save the world. He saw himself fighting Emries to prove that he was worthy of the task he had accomplished. In his mind he imagined that he could take on all the phasia at once and escape unscathed.

"Now," Aerith said shaking him back to reality, "there are some things you need to know about your powers that are very important. First, you are to never openly engage anyone in combat. That is not your job and it would probably be a bad idea anyway. If you have no other choice but to fight, or another person will die if you do not act, then you are free to use your powers as you see fit. Under no circumstances are you to be the instigator of the attack."

"I don't understand," Evan replied quickly, "why can't I fight?"

Aerith frowned.

"The one thing I've learned in all this time is that I have to keep in the middle of this fight until I know which side is which. What that means is that for every good act that I do, I do an evil act to counter balance it. Just think of what I would have to do if I saved a town from a volcanic eruption."

Evan cringed.

"Not a pretty picture is it. No. Now, most of the time, I don't do anything, so there is no chance that I will have to do something bad. I did my time serving in Bryn's army and having an affair with not only her but Ellis. That was enough of an evil deed for ten people. But then to counterbalance it, I worked for Aralias Imstra and gave my life to start the prophecies. If you're going to use my powers, you have to abide by my rules."

"Understood," Evan said nodding. He may not have liked the condition, but he understood it, and it would probably help him stay alive in the long run.

"Alright," Aerith said pulling Evan toward the window, "point number two. You have the ability to access the powers that the phasia use to create portals, but never do so unless you have no other choice. The phasia can track the power of these portals and find where you are going. That would not be good considering some of the places you will be traveling to. For this reason, I have created the stones."

"The stones?" Evan asked.

"Reach into your pocket and pull out the first thing you come across."

Evan looked at Aerith with a puzzled expression and then dug his hand into his pocket. Suddenly Evan's face contorted into an even more confused look, and when Evan pulled his hand out of his pocket, he was holding a fist sized red stone in his hand.

"How?" was all that Evan could manage to say.

"Your mind has been opened up to the fabric of time and space. Your consciousness can grasp how time, space, and reality flow together in a musical pattern. Because of this, you also understand that it is not a seamless and flawless cohesion. There are what you might call gaps in time, gaps in space, and gaps in reality. This is where you are going to operate most of the time, in the gaps. Because you know where these exist, and because they are the safest places in the world to keep your belongings, when you reach your hand into a pocket, you are actually reaching into one of these gaps."

"I'm beginning to like this more and more," Evan said almost to himself.

"Now, that may look to you like a red rock, but I swear to you that it is much more than that. So much more. Now, take a good hold on both sides of the rock and pull."

Evan stared at Aerith for a moment, and then laughed to himself as he put both hands on the rock. He half-heartedly pulled, and was astonished when the rock stretched in his hands.

"Not quite what you were expecting was it?" Aerith said mocking the wonderment on Evan's face. "Go ahead, open it up and take a look."

Evan smiled and began to stretch the rock in all directions. Finally, it was stretched to make a large circle just a bit larger than Evan. When it was made that size, the center of the rock disappeared, and became a swirling red portal. Evan was amazed and could not take the smile off of his face.

"This portal takes you to one of the planes that intersects this reality and all other realities. It is the plane of Fire. Every one of the basic elements has its own plane of origin, and they all have to connect with every reality, and at times each other. When the planes of the individual elements touch, they form lesser elements such as lightning, ice, steam, and smoke. When all of the elemental planes meet at the same point in a reality, it becomes what it known to us as the Blaze. In that pocket of yours is a stone that will lead you to every one of the elemental and lesser elemental planes. There are also some blank stones in there. With those stones you can make a portal to a specific location. However, try to remember which stone goes where. They can only be linked to one specific location and it is not good when you are running away from a fight to accidentally run into another one."

All Evan could do was nod. He understood exactly what Aerith was telling him, but he did not have the words to combat his wonder and awe.

"Another thing that you will find in that little space is a collection of swords, and a cloak. The cloak is like armor in that it protects you when you are attacked from behind, also though, if you wrap yourself in it, you become invisible to anyone and everyone, even the phasia. It was a gift from Ellis many years ago to encourage me in my liaison with Bryn. There is a brooch that will hold the cloak closed around you so that you could theoretically fight with two weapons and still be invisible. Oh, that reminds me," Aerith commented aside, "you also now have my combat skill mixed with your own. I was always fond of wielding two swords in combat because it always seemed to make my opponent nervous. Well, now you can make everyone nervous without even using any of the power that I gave you. So much is the better. The threat of power is so much more useful than its application."

Evan smiled wider at that.

"Oh," Aerith said remembering something amusing, "one trick that I learned was that while invisible, you can consciously make any part of you visible again without removing the cloak. I used to just make my forearm and my hand visible while I fought to scare away my opponents. If you have ever heard the stories of the great Aerith Seth defeating whole armies by himself, you now know how I did it."

Evan laughed a little to himself and dug back into his pocket. As he was fishing around, examining the stones with his hands, he came across something odd. As he drew it out of his pocket, Evan gasped as the golden blade of the huge sword caught the light. Aerith smiled and nodded as Evan inspected the beautiful blade.

"That is Justice," Aerith said in a proud voice. "That sword was given to me by Aralias Imstra himself when I joined the Hand of the Light. He had never used it in battle, but it had strange properties that he thought fit me better than it fit him. It was created by the most powerful members of the Moridon tribe, and was supposed to be powerful enough to smite any enemy of the Light as well as bring redemption and comfort to those who fought for it."

As Evan held it aloft, it began to hum as he moved it back and forth. For its size it was a very graceful weapon and had a power to it that could easily be seen and felt.

"The whole sword is made of gold," Aerith continued, "but for some reason it has never even so much as been scratched in all the times that I have used it in battle. The weapon in your hand will be able to channel the power of lightning, harnessing the ambient power around you. If there are wounded soldiers in your vicinity, you can also use that power to summon sweet rain that heals any ally that it touches. It is a truly elegant weapon."

Evan marveled at the sword for just a few more moments before putting it away.

"Now, the last bit of information that I have to give you is this. All of the powers that you have are to remain a secret except from certain people. Pick a few that you can trust with your life. You are now a chip that can be used in the war. If you allow yourself to be draw to either side, then you will merely become a pawn, and that is not your purpose. You must keep true to your mission and report to me occasionally at my old stomping grounds outside of Scalla."

Evan nodded. He knew that he had become one of the most powerful men on the planet and with that power came equal if not greater responsibility. The necessity of neutrality was understandable, and it was not a wholly impossible thing to accomplish.

"I understand, Aerith. I will do my best to get the information that you require. Hopefully with what I will be able to find, together we will be able to unravel this mystery we have found ourselves tangled in."

"Good night, Evan Sinn," Aerith said walking toward the window. "Have a good time with Meredith tonight, she's on her way, and she is not thinking about getting a good night sleep."

Evan smiled and looked away. When he looked back, Aerith Seth was gone. Evan knew that this was the beginning of a new chapter in his life. When he heard the knock at the door and watched as a scantily clad Meredith walked in her thought he heard Aerith's voice in the back of his head.

"You did pretty well for yourself, kid. She's no Bryn, but she'll do."

* * * * * * * * * *

It was just after sunup when the Enforcers assembled in the main courtyard of the palace. Evan and Meredith made no effort to stifle their yawns or their growing closeness. Ren looked stoic as usual, and Valin and

Zak seemed a little more anxious than they should have been. Turok and Celina stood idly by discussing something that probably pertained to who was going to get the first kill in the battle to come. Conspicuous by their absence were Rachel and Elizabeth, but when Evan looked up to see Pike approaching with them in tow, he laughed to himself and started to saddle his horse. There were no words exchanged as the members of the Enforcers saddled up and began to ride. On these mornings there were never celebrations and people wishing the Enforcers well and hoping for their safe return. It had become almost routine now that the Enforcers always succeeded in everything that they attempted and never had any of them been seriously wounded in a fight. As Evan rode out of the gates of the palace of Kandor, he inwardly wondered if he would ever see them again.

For the first several hours of the ride, there was very little discussion among the members of the Enforcers. They had gotten so used to each other that there was very little to discuss before a prospective battle. However, things were different this time around. There was an unfamiliar element added to the mix in this escapade, and that element was fear. Training was good for everyone to get a tactical perfection in what they should do against the forces of the Shadow, but none of the Enforcers except for Pike, Celina, and Turok had ever been in combat with a Jeresei or a Shadowwalker. There was now this uncertainty that hung over everyone's heads, and it could be the one factor that would blemish the Enforcers' perfect record.

It was just before nightfall on the third day when Lakestone was in sight. The once proud city looked almost demonic in the advancing sunset, and the fiery backdrop of the red and orange sky began to look more and more like blood as the minutes passed. Evan could see from his vantage point the half sunken city, but his eyes were drawn elsewhere. There was movement just outside the city. There were fifty or sixty creatures moving around in a dead area just outside the city where the frozen pass used to be. The ice had since melted away leaving only desolate land behind. Just at that moment, four of the creatures launched themselves into the air and began circling the city. Pike drew back on the reins and watched the familiar circling forms. Then, there was a crash of thunder, and the Shadowwalkers began to fly faster and faster in the sky. The circle tightened, and began to spark and hiss. It was then that there was an explosion of light, and the large blue portal appeared in the sky. Out from the portal flew several more Shadowwalkers being led by one of the most fearful specters to ever be devised by the twisted mind of Shau-ling. The leader of the Shadowwalkers was none other than Nightwing.

Pike could feel his blood boil as the metal monster landed just outside of town. It folded back its wings and walked to a figure that looked very familiar to Pike. When he finally saw the face of the phase that greeted Nightwing, Pike drew *Fury* from his belt and plunged his heels into his horse's flank. The charge of the Enforcers had begun. Pike was going to kill Taron even if he had to take on an entire army by himself.

Watery Grave

Creator's Calendar Year 1205; Light Reality

Outside the half-desolate town of Lakestone, the thunder of horses' hoofs and monstrous screams of hatred could be heard resounding through the countryside. Pike Rhuiden saw his life flash before his eyes as he dug his heels into the flanks of his horse and started the war that would consume the entire world if he failed in his task. He saw the life he once had in a sleepy little far away town outside the edge of the world's notice. Then the scourge of Shau-ling destroyed his home and sent his life spiraling out of control. One of his friends died in that fateful attack, and the town would never be the same. He saw the quest to defeat Shau-ling and watched in horror as his friends died one by one, the first being his love and his wife, Eldar Merin. His life was out of control, but he knew that if he could get to Taron and make him pay for all the suffering he had brought into Pike's life, then he would have at least some peace of mind.

As Pike charged down the hill at the army of the Shadows, the Enforcers fell into a hard gallop behind him. In a matter of seconds, their weapons were ready, and they had mentally prepared themselves for a fight. On the other side of the fight, the Jeresei had launched themselves into a full sprint when Pike came into full view. With claws extended, the red-skinned beasts were ready to kill and die for their master Shau-ling. Four of the Shadowwalkers had extended their wings and taken to the air, ready to rain death down upon their adversaries. Taron and Nightwing on the other hand were not ready to insert themselves into the battle. As their army advanced, the two children of Shau-ling retreated into the city, their minds set on other dark work. They had known about the attack of the Enforcers long before they appeared, but now they had to ready the trap.

As the throng of Jeresei approached, Pike gritted his teeth and spurred his horse even harder. The pain in his side was beginning to strengthen, but the adrenaline in his system mixed with the hatred of Taron and Nightwing leveled out the pain and made it tolerable. Celina and Turok had caught up to Pike, and they paced beside him with Rachel and Elizabeth close behind. Farther out on the edge of the wedge formation was Evan and Meredith to one side, and Ren, Zak, and Valin to the other. Violently, the sea of red collided with the mounted group. Not content to let their opponents have the height advantage by attacking from their mounts, the first set of attacks from the Jeresei were targeted primarily at the legs of the horses. After the first collision between the two forces, all of the Enforcers' horses had been cut down, sending the men and women tumbling to the ground, praying that they were able to make it to their feet before they were cut down by the superior numbers of the Jeresei.

Pike was the first to scramble to his feet. His mount had been gutted by a single long slash by one of the Jeresei, and as the horse collapsed in a heap beneath him, Pike was able to leap clear and almost land on his feet. The pain in his side was staggering, but he managed to lift his axe and parry most of the blows that came at him. Dozens of claws flew at him in rapid succession, and many of them tore at his flesh because he was not quick enough to avoid them all. However, the momentary pain of the ripping claws was not enough to take down Pike Rhuiden. With all the power that he had in his body, he began to swing *Fury*, impaling Jeresei after Jeresei on his blood soaked blades. The body count around him rose, but he started to feel himself collapse when a strong arm wrapped itself around him, and he saw Valin and Zak out of the corner of his eye. As he turned and focused his attacks on a new set of Jeresei inside the swarm, he saw that Celina, Turok, Meredith, and Evan were grouped together in one cluster a hundred or so yards to the west, while Zak, Valin, Ren, Rachel, and Elizabeth ringed around him. Ren's armor had huge gashes from where the Jeresei claws had raked at him, but there was no bloody wound visible through the cracks in the armor. Zak's clothes were in horrible condition, the victim of many Jeresei claw strikes, and there were puddles of blood soaked into the ripped fabric and flowing freely down to the ground. However, Zak was strong and proud, and he was not about to let some monster overtake him. Valin, Rachel, and Elizabeth seemed to be mostly intact except for a few scratches here and there, but as the ranks of Jeresei continued to swell against the Enforcers, Pike wondered how much longer his people could hold out.

Over in the other defensive circle, things looked much bleaker. The Jeresei just kept coming, no matter how many of them that Celina and Turok cut down. Meredith had long since abandoned using her bow, the numbers and proximity of the enemy made that weapon almost pointless. She stood back to back with Evan, clutching her wounded leg with one hand and parrying with her other. Despite the danger and possible death that surrounded him, Evan felt a twinge of comedy as he looked at the red skinned beasts. He knew in his mind that if he really wanted to, he could destroy each and every member of the Jeresei with a thought, but that was not what he was here to do. He was here to find out information for Aerith Seth, and himself. The catch though was the fact that no one could know about his new powers. Suddenly, it was almost as if time stopped. One of the Jeresei broke into the circle, and with a long slash brought a geyser of blood erupting from Meredith's chest. Evan spun, catching his wounded love in one arm while impaling the vile creature with his sword. Celina and Turok fell back, covering both Meredith and Evan as he laid her to the ground. Her chest had been laid open by the claws of the beast, but the damage had not gone deep enough to be immediately lethal. The creature had not been able to fracture her ribs or puncture her heart. However, if the blood loss were not stopped quickly, she would die. As Evan quickly bandaged her wounds, he exercised a little of his hidden power to bind her wounds, stopping the bleeding. The flow of power was so little that no one would notice, especially with Pike around. Evan then rose to his feet and began to fight harder, letting the knowledge that Aerith Seth gave him about the Jeresei flow into the tactics that Pike had taught the Enforcers. With his fury ignited, the tide of the battle began to change.

Pike could feel the power in him begin to surge. He watched one of his own fall at the hands of one of the Jeresei and the rage in him ignited like it had never been lit before. His saddlebags lay only a few feet from him, and after a long hard slash that leveled one of the Jeresei, Pike ran to the open pouch and recovered the golden gauntlet that was a gift from Lord Cedric Binosear all those years ago. As he slipped the cold metal onto his hand, the gold faded, and the crisp dark blue began to flow into the metal. Though Pike's powers were nowhere near as lethal as they once were, the years of practice had given him more control and a better understanding of what he could do. Several Jeresei rushed him at once. He had moved outside of the circle of protection provided by the other Enforcers, and that made him an easier target. When Pike raised the gauntlet and pointed at the Jeresei, several of them stopped in their tracks. Pike had used his powers to freeze the water that pumped within their blood, killing the Jeresei almost instantly. Two of the Jeresei were unaffected by the attack, as that the numbers were too much for the limited power at Pike's disposal. However, as Pike prepared to fight, the other Jeresei burst into flames right before his eyes. He didn't even have to look back to know that Elizabeth had saved him. Zak danced through the ranks of the Jeresei, leaving his pain and his friends behind. With every quick move, there was a flash of steel and another dead Jeresei. Valin too began to tire of being on the defensive. Hefting his two axes, he began to wade into the enemy, chopping them down in one blow, and blocking any and all attacks with another. Ren and Rachel stayed near to Pike, their functions as guards for their lord not lost in the heat of combat. Ren stayed because it was his duty, but Rachel stayed out of love. While she and Elizabeth had a deep connection to the man they should have called brother, Rachel felt a different beat of her heart when Pike was near, though she would never reveal it to him.

In the other circle, the battle seemed almost over. The Jeresei were coming slower now, their attacks holding less fury and less power. But as Evan looked around, he saw that there were still enough Jeresei that if they all attacked at the same time, they could overtake all of them with sheer numbers and viciousness. Evan scanned the memories that Aerith had given him and came to one conclusion. The Jeresei were waiting for something. Evan had no sooner come to that realization when the Shadowwalkers started their dive from above. Their metallic bodies glowed in the eerie light of dusk, and when their jaws opened wide, the beams of fiery death began to rain down upon them. Evan only had a few seconds to act before the beam hit. Celina and Turok were dodging the first blast, and everyone else seemed distracted by the other blasts that rained down. This was Evan's chance. He knew that he couldn't stay with the Enforcers any longer because of his mission, but he couldn't just walk away. So, here was a golden opportunity to fake his own death. However, because of Meredith's condition, she would be unable to dodge the blast. So, reaching into his pocket, Evan pulled out a white stone and threw it to the ground. The portal opened quickly and Evan dove through, dragging Meredith behind him as the blast of Blaze energy hit the ground mere inches from where the two had been.

Pike looked on in horror as the beam of energy decimated the ground where Evan and Meredith had been. When the smoke and fire cleared, there was nothing left standing, and as Pike looked around, he could not find either Meredith or Evan anywhere. Two of his Enforcers were gone because of the forces of the Shadow, and as the Shadowwalkers wheeled around for another assault, Pike lifted his gauntlet and screamed to the heavens with all the fury and pain inside of him. Suddenly storm clouds began to roll in. The Shadowwalkers seemed to be buffeted by the increasing winds, but they continued to reposition themselves for their next assault. That assault would never come. The dark rain clouds overhead showed the power that Pike had endowed within them in the next few moments when the torrent of rain began to fall. Pike called everyone to him and created a shield of ice over them with Elizabeth's help. Outside the safety of the shield, the storm continued to rage, and as the rain began to fall harder, the screams of pain from the Jeresei began. The needle thin ice rain that fell from the clouds began to rip through every single creature on the plain outside of Lakestone. Many of the Jeresei fell from the accumulation of tiny wounds that bled profusely. Some were lucky enough to avoid prolonged suffering as impossibly sharp needles of ice tore through brains and hearts, stealing life instantly. Even the Shadowwalkers that hovered high above the battlefield suffered major damage from the shards of ice. One by one, each of the Shadowwalkers tumbled to the ground, their lifeless bodies were no more than hunks of hole-ridden scrap metal. When the storm finally ended, the Jeresei and Shadowwalkers were in little more than pieces, the rain a relentless assault on the flesh and bone of the creatures of the Shadow.

Pike felt the drain on the power inside of him begin to slow, and without much effort he released the shield of ice that had protected them from the onslaught. While the Enforcers surveyed the dead, Pike used *Fury* as a crutch for a moment, the drain of his powers taking its toll on him. Suddenly, Rachel ran up to him and put her hand on his side. There was an immense pain that ran through him, and as he looked down, he could see the flow of blood that poured from the old wound. Sometime during the battle, the wound had opened again, and it was only a matter of time before Pike would bleed to death. Quickly Elizabeth rushed to Pike's aid, using her knowledge of healing to both bind his wounds and use her magic to speed along the healing. Pike knew that those wounds would never fully close, but whatever time Elizabeth's healing could buy him was more time he had to hunt down Taron. Without a word he picked up *Fury* and continued on toward Lakestone. Now down two members, the Enforcers seemed less likely to return from this mission, and they knew in their hearts that without Meredith and Evan they were not nearly as strong as they needed to be.

* * * * * * * * * * * *

When Meredith awoke she was greeted by a truly miraculous sight. All around her was the most beautiful clear sky that she had ever seen, with small white fluffy clouds floating through it. When she sat up however, the beauty became even more staggering when she realized that she was not laying on the ground looking up at the sky, but was floating in the sky itself. She began to panic for a moment, but there was no feeling of falling, and as she began to move around, she found that she could control which direction that she floated without much effort. There was an inner feeling of exhilaration in her as she began to fly. Then, just at the edge of her field of vision, she saw a familiar form floating toward her. He had a wide smile on his face and when the two lovers met, Meredith looked at Evan puzzled for a moment and then hugged him tightly. Suddenly she began to remember the battle and the Jeresei that struck her. She looked down quickly, seeing that she was bandaged, and then looked up into Evan's eyes questioningly.

"Relax sweetheart," Evan said trying to console her as he held her in his arms, "you're alright. The Jeresei ripped you up pretty good, but I was able to bandage you up and help heal your wounds. You should be fine in a couple of days, but you're going to have a very interesting scar."

Meredith looked at him again, this time the question more forceful in her eyes. She was still too shocked to find her voice, but she knew that Evan was stalling, and that her look could get him to talk.

"Don't give me that look Meredith," Evan said quickly, "do you know how hard it would be to make love in midair?"

Meredith groaned and against her will let a smile slip through. Even though at times Evan Sinn could be the most infuriating person on the face of the earth, she could not help but love him.

"How are we in midair, Evan?"

Her tone was more of an accusation than a question. Even though they played at arguing, at times there were genuine arguments. She knew that he had the knack for getting into trouble at every turn, but he seemed different now. There was a purpose to his mischief, not just the general wickedness that he usually played at.

"Truth?"

Meredith looked in his eyes for a moment and saw the look that she had expected. Evan was the kind of man that when he spoke his voice was so serious that you never knew if he was joking or not. Then at times he could be so playful that nothing he said could be taken seriously. But the telling factor in all of his moods were his eyes. The look in Evan's eyes said that she would never believe him no matter what he said.

"Truth."

Evan sighed and began to relay the story about Aerith Seth and the meeting in Evan's room the night before. Throughout the entire story, Meredith looked on with an almost amused smirk and when Evan was finished, she waited for several moments before she responded.

"I should have asked for a lie."

Evan smiled and then took her hand, guiding her in their flight together.

"Meredith darling, you are the only one besides myself that knows what powers I have and what my mission in this world is. We had to leave Pike and the others behind because Pike would want to use me to get back at Taron and the rest of the phasia. You see, I understand now that there is more to this war than Pike Rhuiden and the Enforcers, and it took a god to open my eyes, and I am just a bit player in this story. Imagine what it would take to make Pike understand."

Meredith clicked her tongue.

"I think you are underestimating him."

"Do you?" Evan asked with a hint of aggravation in his voice. "And why is that?"

They had come to a stop in their rapid travel, and Evan looked at Meredith with an intensity in his eyes that she had never seen. It wasn't a look of anger, it was closer to conviction.

"Pike fought in the first war with Logan Ranthall and the People of the Dragon. He has seen and done things that we will probably only be able to dream about, and his mind has been opened up to the vast wonder that the prophecies and this war hold. He should be open to anything, especially if it comes from Aerith Seth."

"You forget though," Evan said trying hard not to lecture, "Pike is not the same man that he was during that war. In the beginning his intentions were noble and pure, that much is obvious, but when Eldar was killed, he changed. He became bitter and disappointed and solely bent on vengeance. Plus, he has the distraction of ruling three kingdoms, putting up with three children, one of which hates him. He must deal with the Enforcers and their rather strong personalities, and then he has to deal with his mistresses. He thought for so long that he wanted to be the one leading the way; that he could have filled the role that Logan and Korrd and Gwydeon took, but every man has his limits. Unfortunately, Pike Rhuiden has never been a man to accept limits, and he often strolls right past them without evening noticing, to the detriment of everyone close to him. Perhaps now to the detriment of everyone in this war."

Evan nearly bit his tongue as he scowled from divulging too much information.

"Mistresses? Plural?" Meredith asked shocked barely hearing the end of Evan's statement.

Evan slowly nodded and prepared himself to tell the tale. No one in the Enforcers knew the whole truth about anything, and Evan was no different. However, with access to the knowledge of Aerith Seth, there were a lot of pieces to the puzzle that now fit into place.

"There have been many women to share Pike's bed over the years, and it is no one's fault but his own. Somewhere inside of him he feels that he will never find love again, so he continues to live life from meaningless relationship to meaningless relationship without any end or hope in sight. The real tragedy is the fact that one of the women actually could love him, but he is too blinded by his own melancholy to see it. It started simply enough with one of the chambermaids, then it was the daughter of the lord of Falke, an incident which while still unproved, started a war. Then Pike found his way into Midarin Rice's bed and together they had a child, Liette."

There was a spark of recognition in Meredith's eyes. It was obvious that she has suspected Liette's connection to Pike, but she would never make those thoughts known.

"There have been others, their names will be left untold for now because they are not important. However, there is one mistress that Pike has that I am not allowed to know about at this time. Aerith is blocking that image from me for a reason. Whether or not it will be shown to me later is up to Aerith. I know Meredith that he attempted to seduce you on at least one occasion, and you know how he can be when he is drunk."

Meredith's eyes widened for a moment at the accusation, but then calmed a little. She had not told anyone about the incident with Pike, but she was relieved that Evan did not think that she was this mystery mistress.

"So," Meredith asked after a moment of reflection, "where do we go now?"

Evan smiled in response. He knew it was hard for her to give up the faith that Pike would be able to understand, but faced with the truth, she saw the light and had willingly become Evan's only ally in the arduous task ahead.

"I have to find Wolf Ranthall and uncover his little part in all of this. As the last of the Ranthall line, he is special. What makes him even more special is the fact that he is at the very heart of this war. I don't know why quite yet, but with your help, maybe I can find out."

Meredith smiled brightly, kissed Evan on the cheek and then watched as he pulled a green stone out of his pocket and then opened it creating a portal right in front of them. After a momentary embrace, they stepped out in the sleepy farm town of Aradon.

* * * * * * * * * * * *

The pain in Pike's side was excruciating. Every step was agony, and every breath was torture. Pike had to laugh to himself hearing Eldar's words resounding in his head.

"It's your stubbornness that keeps you alive."

Pike stopped dead in his tracks. The words had been echoing in his head, but someone had actually spoken those words. As he spun around, he saw Elizabeth behind him smiling. She had been the person who spoke. He smiled the best he could and then turned back around, continuing toward the sunken portion of the city. Suddenly, there was a flash of motion out of the corner of Pike's eye. When he spun to his left though, there was nothing there. Over the years he had heard many stories of Lakestone. It was a city imbued with the kind of magic that men fear. That was possibly the reason that Shau-ling had chosen it as the location of his first palace. Pike was so lost in his own thoughts, he almost didn't feel the insistent taps on his shoulder.

"Pike," Zak's voice said quickly. "You have got to see this."

When Pike turned around, he was shocked to see the water level around the city was beginning to rise. The cold water from Exeter Lake was now beginning to flow through the streets like little rivers, but the water level still continued to rise. Distracted by the rising water, Pike didn't hear the scrape of claws behind him. The Kalbrak leapt at him in the next second.

All Pike saw as he turned was a flash of steel as Ren jumped in front of his lord and blocked the blow of the Kalbrak. In a matter of seconds, they were surrounded. Kalbraks were slowly advancing on their position from every alley. While the beasts were not fast, they made up for their lack of speed with fighting prowess and sheer tenacity. Ren pushed the Kalbrak away with his blade and set himself to receive another attack. The Kalbraks though seemed to be waiting for something. A gust of wind kicked up the next second, causing everyone to blink their eyes several times because of the dust that was stirred up. When the dust cleared and everyone's eyes refocused, Pike scowled and tightened his grip on *Fury*. Nightwing hovered there in the advancing darkness, looking more evil than ever. Pike noticed that Nightwing looked different. It was slimmer and less muscular, but it looked quicker and more agile.

"WELCOME TO YOUR DEATH PIKE RHUIDEN AND THE ENFORCERS. WE HAVE BEEN EXPECTING YOU."

The voice was different too. Nightwing's voice had always been commanding and menacing, and not only that, it was definitely male. This voice was different, more feminine and seductive, but still hard and metallic.

"Nightwing," Pike said slowly, "good to see you again. I notice that you are not using Aryx as your host anymore, quite a step up if you ask me."

"ARYX TERIAN SERVED HIS PURPOSE PIKE, A PURPOSE THAT NONE OF YOU COULD EVER HOPE TO UNDERSTAND. THE DARK LORD OF THE SHADOWS PROMISES LIFE ETERNAL FOR ALL OF YOU IF YOU LAY DOWN YOUR ARMS NOW AND JOIN HIM. OTHERWISE YOU WILL NEVER LEAVE THIS CITY, AND YOU WILL SERVE A PURPOSE JUST AS WELL IN A GRAVE."

This was a new wrinkle to the old game. Usually the phasia and Nightwing were tasked with the senseless killing and merciless slaughter of their opponents. The only people they ever tried to recruit were the *Coromor* and the *Chosen One*. What would Shau-ling want with the Enforcers? The defensive formation around Pike tightened, but suddenly there was a cry of pain, and Pike spun around to see Taron pulling

Elizabeth away from the rest of the group, his huge hand wrapped around her neck. Pike's mind suddenly flashed back to that fateful night in Falke. Taron had stood in the same position a few feet away from him with his love, Eldar Merin clutched tightly in his massive hand. In a heartbeat he had ended her life, an act which had tortured Pike for the last twenty-five years. Taron seemed no different in this generation than he had in the last. His seven and a half foot tall frame was laden with muscle from head to toe, and the sheer power of the man was menacing.

"Well, well, well," Taron said in that booming demonic voice, "what have we here? This is a tender little morsel, Pike. It would be a pity if she were to say, break her neck and die."

Pike was stunned. There was nothing he could do in this situation. He knew that in a fraction of a second, Taron could snap Elizabeth's neck just by flinching. Pike lowered his axe and gave the signal for all the other Enforcers to lower their weapons. If it was going to be a fight, he had to ensure Elizabeth's safety first.

"It's so good to see you again Taron," Pike said spitting venom with every word. "I would have thought though that Shau-ling would have sent someone a little more important to face me. After all, I have to be a pretty big thorn in his side by now."

"You should have curled up and died when you had the chance, old man," Taron countered. "The People of the Dragon don't exist anymore, and no matter what you try to do with these would be heroes, they will stay dead. Korrd and your buddy Talon died at the hands of Shau-ling, Arin and Gwydeon died in the Hall of Terrors, Gideon died because he was stupid, Lane and Eldar died because of me. Even your precious Logan Ranthall didn't have the heart left in him to fight a second time around. Then there was poor little Elwyne. That poor lonely little girl, I feel so sorry for her. But, I'm still happy she's dead. All that's left is you, Midarin, and that traitor Jerrard. If you don't surrender, we'll kill you here and now, and then we'll go after that cute little Midarin and her daughter. She was a cute little thing when she was born. I'll take great pleasure in crushing the life out of her while her mother watches."

Pike's blood began to boil, and he tightened his grip even more on the haft of his axe. If he had just a little more strength, he probably would have broken the haft by now, but he had to vent he frustration somewhere, otherwise Elizabeth was dead.

"Now, now Pike," Taron teased, "don't lose your temper. Remember Eldar? Snap. That was all it took. This one will be even easier."

"TARON."

Nightwing sounded annoyed. The whole time the conversation between Pike and Taron raged on, Nightwing had just been floating there watching. Nightwing did not understand the need for Taron to gloat so much and try to goad Pike into attacking. That was not their mission.

"DELIVER THE MESSAGE."

Taron groaned.

"Pike," Taron said half-heartedly, "my master Shau-ling wishes me to deliver a message to you. The Lord of the Shadows requests that you accompany Nightwing to his presence to discuss the terms for a truce between the Kingdoms of Marcwell and Trelon and the countries controlled by all the phasia and by our lord, the mighty Shau-ling. He offers a permanent halt of all aggressions, and will offer you anything that you could desire, even the resurrection of the dead."

Pike was stunned. Never in all the years that he had been preparing for the war to resume had he ever imagined that Shau-ling would do something like this. It was too good to be true, and yet, in the back of Pike's mind the fantasies began to crop up about having Eldar back. But the dreams were not just limited to Eldar. He would have Gwydeon brought back for Midarin, and then Logan and Elwyne could be brought back to be with their son. Then he could bring back Talon, and Lane, and even David. Pike then suddenly ran cold with emotion. His mind was giving him too much to think about all at once, and his heart and body were threatening to give out under the added stress.

"Don't listen to them my lord," Ren interjected. "It is a plot to lure you in so that Shau-ling can finish you off and cripple whatever resistance you have mounted against him. Shau-ling knows it would be a great blow to the forces of the Light if you were to die at his hands."

"I ASSURE YOU, REN DALIN, THAT THIS OFFER IS VERY REAL. THE LORD OF THE SHADOWS TIRES OF THIS WAR. HE WISHES TO END THE HOSTILITIES AGAINST THE PEOPLE OF YOUR WORLD SO LONG AS YOU WILL ACCEPT CERTAIN CONDITIONS THAT HE WILL NAME DURING THE MEETING. I ASSURE YOU THAT THESE CONDITIONS WILL IN NO WAY HINDER THE ADVANCEMENT OF YOUR HUMAN RACE AND WILL PROBABLY AID YOU IN THE LONG RUN. PLEASE MAKE YOUR DECISION QUICKLY FOR TIME IS SHORT."

Nightwing could tell that Pike was hesitant. Shau-ling had told Nightwing that this is exactly what would happen, that is why he insisted on sending Taron. However, not even Taron knew his true purpose for being at this meeting.

"BEFORE YOU RENDER YOUR DECISION, SHAU-LING HAS AUTHORIZED ME TO OFFER YOU A GIFT. THE GREAT AND POWERFUL LORD OF THE SHADOWS KNOWS THE HATRED YOU HAVE IN YOUR HEART FOR THE PHASE TARON. IN AN EFFORT TO SHOW YOU HIS GOOD WILL, SHAU-LING WILL ALLOW YOU TO DO WHAT YOU WILL WITH TARON, BE IT KILLING, TORTURE, OR WHATEVER YOU SEE FIT IN ORDER TO MAKE YOU UNDERSTAND THE SERIOUSNESS OF WHAT HE IS OFFERING YOU, AND ALSO TO EXPRESS HIS SINCERITY."

The looks of shock were almost identical from both Taron and Pike. Neither man could believe the words that had just been uttered by Nightwing, but while Pike began to smile, Taron frowned and drew his sword with his other hand.

"TARON," Nightwing said quickly, "YOU WILL LOWER YOUR WEAPON AND RELEASE THE GIRL. THEN, YOUR WILL FALL TO YOUR KNEES AND SUBMIT TO THE WILL OF YOUR MASTER, SHAU-LING."

Taron stalled. He knew that Shau-ling would punish him if he disobeyed, but he would probably survive the punishment. If he were to surrender himself to Pike, he would most certainly die in the most horrible way that he could imagine. Then Taron smiled. While he never imagined that he would be double-crossed by Shau-ling, he had not put it past Nightwing. He knew the purpose of the mission was to give Pike the request for peace. Taron was never a proponent of peace, so he enlisted another member of the phasia to help him in his little trap.

"TARON," Nightwing said more insistently, "RELEASE THE GIRL NOW, OR I WILL BE FORCED TO TAKE ACTION AGAINST YOU."

"Go home to Shau-ling you overgrown parrot," Taron said in disgust, "I have business to attend to here."

Suddenly a swirling blue portal appeared behind Nightwing, and a stiff gust of wind kicked up and pushed Nightwing quickly into the portal. The large metallic beast was so surprised by the maneuver that it didn't have a chance to react before the portal slammed shut.

"Now," Taron said turning his attention back to Pike, "Shau-ling wanted me to deliver the message, so I delivered it. I wasn't told anything about me being offered up as a prize. So, I'll tell you what I'm going to do. This little girl and I are going to walk out of this town and go back to my kingdom. If you can get me before I leave town, then I'll give her back to you. If not, then I get to do whatever I want with her. Is it a deal?"

"Do I have a choice?" Pike answered.

Taron laughed and began to slowly pull away from the Enforcers. In that split second, the Kalbraks that had gathered around leapt into the fray. Pike and the rest of the Enforcers had been prepared for this tactic, so they were not surprised. As the long green nails came slashing down, Pike spun and buried the blade of *Fury* into one of the huge lizards' chests. Green blood flowed everywhere, and Pike slammed the dying creature to the ground and turned to look for Taron. Pike spotted him ducking into an alley to his east. The rest of the Enforcers tried to fight as well as they could down three members. Valin and Zak fought back to back against the huge lizards, Valin attacking with sheer power in each of his blows, while Zak danced through each of the slashes and thrusts, burying his daggers into vital organs when the opportunity arose. More than one Kalbrak fell to the ground with a shimmering dagger in its forehead. Turok and Celina were a sight in the battle. They moved together as one person, slashing and parrying all of the blows that came close to them. Rachel was wild, the hatred in her heart at the possible loss of her sister was eating at her, and she killed Kalbrak after Kalbrak, ignoring any damage that she took in the process. In just a matter of minutes, all of the beasts were dead, and as the Enforcers surveyed the fallen, Pike sprinted toward the alley that Taron had disappeared into. The Enforcers followed quickly, led by Rachel.

At the end of the alley, Pike caught sight of Taron again and started after him. There were guttural screams all around as Jeresei leapt from the tops of the buildings onto the Enforcers as they emerged from the slim alley. Pike ignored this combat and continued after Taron. Rachel spun as she heard the attackers fall, impaling first one, then another on her blade. Turok and Celina paired off again, fighting very familiar adversaries. Turok would slash, cutting one of the beasts to ribbons, while Celina would block for him, keeping the opportunistic Jeresei from striking him down. But there were too many of them for the defense to stay perfect for long. As Zak and Valin emerged from the alley, one of the Jeresei struck Celina across her back while she defended Turok. She screamed in agony, and fell to the ground, blood flowing freely from the gaping wound. Turok spun and buried his sword to the hilt in the creature's stomach. More Jeresei were coming though, and Turok was not able to recover his sword in time. Luckily, two daggers flew the distance accompanied by one axe, and three of the Jeresei fell. Rachel joined the remaining Enforcers, and together they fought as one, defending their fallen comrade from the onslaught. More and more of the Jeresei fell, but it was not without cost. Zak's leg was deeply cut by the dying slash of one of the monsters. After an errant slash by Valin, a Jeresei ripped through the muscles in his left arm, rendering it useless before Rachel was able to lop its head off. The wound in Turok's leg was reopened by several of the Jeresei, and Rachel had several bloody gashes across her cheek. Finally, after several minutes of intense fighting, the Jeresei stopped coming. Blood flowed as freely as the water through the streets, and the Enforcers collectively caught their breath as Valin and Turok tended to their wounded comrade. She was still breathing, barely, but if they didn't get her to a healer soon, there was a good chance that she would not live. Gently carrying his love in his strong arms, Turok and the other Enforcers moved slowly through the streets of Lakestone looking for the lord who had abandoned them in the middle of a fight.

* * * * * * * * * * * *

Pike did his best to keep the monster Taron in sight, but after a few twists and turns through the flooding streets, he found that he was lost. Inwardly he cursed himself for ever coming to Lakestone, and then cursed himself again for abandoning his Enforcers. They had fought together many times in the past, and never had they been separated during a fight when it wasn't part of the plan. This foray was much different. Evan and Meredith were dead, and Elizabeth was held captive. Suddenly from behind him, Pike heard a noise. He quickly ducked behind a corner and readied *Fury* for action. Maybe he had gotten ahead of Taron, or maybe he was doubling back to get behind Pike. Anything was possible when dealing with a member of the phasia, but as the source of the sound came into view, Pike was horrified to see his bloody comrades, the Enforcers. Slowly, he lowered his axe and walked into the open. Once Turok's eyes caught Pike, the anger crept onto his face, and he moved quickly over to where his lord stood.

"Are you satisfied now, Pike?" his angry voice boomed. "Evan and Meredith are dead, Elizabeth may as well be, and if we don't get to a civilized town soon, Celina will be dead too. Your bloody directive of the Dragon will get us all killed just as surely as it killed your friends in the last war!"

The words stung Pike to the core. Never in all the years that Pike had known Turok had there ever been a cross word put between them. Pike could understand Turok's rage. Looking down at the woman he held in his arms, Pike knew that Turok would kill Pike if he had to in order to save the woman he loved. That was a feeling that Pike understood and could sympathize with. Turok was right. They had to leave Lakestone. The war would wait another few days. This time though, Pike would bring the entire army crashing down on Lakestone, and the forces of the Shadow would rue the day it tangled with the Enforcers.

"You're right, Turok," Pike said after a heavy sigh. "The costs today have been high, and I would like to avoid adding another death to that tally. We're leaving."

As he turned to the east, Rachel ran in front of him, cutting him off. There was a fire and a hatred in her eyes, one that Eldar would have been proud of. The blood on her face was still flowing relatively freely, but she was not in a frame of mind where pain bothered her.

"What about Elizabeth?"

"She's dead Rachel," Pike said half-heartedly, "and even if she is still alive, there is no way that we can save her."

He stepped past her and the rest of the Enforcers began to follow.

"I never thought I would ever have to call you a coward."

Rachel's words struck Pike harder than he had ever been struck before. He turned around again, this time the anger was beginning to well up inside of him.

"There are wounded Rachel," Turok said for Pike, "we need to get Celina to a healer soon or she will die."

"Besides," Zak added, "Taron is just baiting us into another trap. As long as we are fighting on his terms we will surely end up dead."

"Listen to your friends, Rachel," Pike pleaded, "they know what they are saying. Revenge is a powerful motive, but it blinds you to the truth of the situation. I know that I have been blinded by it for a long time, but now is the time that we need to be able to see the truth of our actions."

Before Rachel could retort, another voice did it for her.

"Fitting that the king of double standards would profess to have learned a lesson while at the same time sacrificing lives to save his own pride. I think you're trying to hide the fact that you are the coward that she says you are."

It was an unfamiliar voice. Pike spun around to see a man with pale blue skin seated on top of a horse looking down at him from one of the ruined buildings. In his hand was a sword that looked to be made of pure flame.

"And who are you sir to be questioning my lord's honor and courage?" Ren said stepping forward drawing his blade.

"I am Stryfe, son of Shau-ling and one of the newest additions to the Brotherhood of Phasia. I am also the harbinger of your death!"

Epilogue

Merely a Thief

Creator's Calendar Year 1205; Dark Mirror

Of all the members of the People of the Dragon who had survived the battle with Shau-ling, Gideon Viruci quite possibly had the brightest future on the horizon. With the death of Jerrard Mystic and the banishment of the phase Basille, the kingdom of Scalla would become Gideon's and he would also take the hand of Erika Belnosian Mystic and make her his wife. The kingdom of Scalla became a very powerful icon again under the rule of the crafty Alimidarian, and with his new bride with him, Gideon became a powerful and well-respected ruler. Possibly the happiest day of Gideon's life came when his daughter Taya was born. Gideon had always dreamed of having a daughter, and as he stood by Erika's side and watched her being born, he felt closure in his life for the first time. He had been running away from who he was since he was a child. The more he learned about who he really was, the more he wished it wasn't true. From the phasia tainted blood that flowed through his veins, the identity of his father, the work he did for the phase Basille, and the secrets he was forced to keep, Gideon kept running and finding solace in the identity he created for himself. Merely being a thief was far more palatable than being the son of a member of the phasia and of one of the most notorious warriors in the history of the world. But standing there the first night, watching quietly as his daughter slept, it was as if all the evil he had done in his life melted away, and he had a chance to do something right for once.

Taya quickly became the talk of the court and a fixture at all of the kingdom's functions. Everywhere that Gideon went, Taya was right there with him. Her infancy was spent mostly cradled in her father's loving arms, and as she grew, she was constantly under his supervision and care. Erika too received almost inhuman amounts of attention, and there were times when Gideon would not take time to handle court matters because he was spending time with his family. He was determined to make up not only for the sins of his own past, but for the sins of his parents. Though his heart knew that it truly wasn't their fault who they were and who they would become, Gideon wanted nothing more than to be sure that the burden was not passed to his beautiful little girl, and that nothing would stain this family's legacy. To accommodate this noble goal most of the courtly matters during Taya's formative years fell to Gideon's three trusted lieutenants, Zander Makal, Baron Aeilick, or David Harran.

Zander Makal was a different kind of soldier in the Army of the Raven. His might lay not in his ability with a sword, but rather in his ability to find the weakness in his enemies. His tactics and strategies were some of the best known in the entire world, but no one had a name to go with the demonstrated ability, as he preferred to toil in anonymity and allow others to take credit for his brilliance. Zander had an uncanny knack for finding human weakness. He endlessly studied old written communications of opposing generals, or he would send spies to watch a general at dinner or during a play. Most of the time he went himself to get a feel for the way his would-be opponent thought. Though strangely enough, even given the chance, Zander would never use his spying to enter a war room or a general's quarters because he believed that seeing another general's tactics on a map or drawing would hinder his ability to change his tactics in combat. A battle plan was something that would constantly change, and that was Zander's first law. But, if Zander knew what the general would do before he did it, he would make changes according to whatever he saw. If the general totally changed his plan either before or during a battle, Zander's troops could be in the completely wrong position, and that could be a fatal mistake, to say the least. But Zander did not limit his appraisal of his opponents merely to their eating habits or manners. Zander was also a student of arts and prose. He found that a people's art, music, and writings were a telling sign of the mindset of the people of each kingdom. The mindset told Zander how a general would feel about the people under his command. It would make a huge difference in a battle whether or not a general was so ruthless that he did not care how many of his men fell in battle so long as he was victorious. Or he could be reserved and calm letting the tactics and strategies, rather than numbers of men rule the day. Zander had found in many years as a military leader that the strategies of the man would make no sense if you did not first understand the man behind the strategy. Taking all this into account, it was no wonder that Zander was Gideon's military leader and overall General of the Army of the Raven.

Gideon was not heavy-handed in the matters of the court either, and Baron Aeilick was the man to take over that position in his lord's stead. Unlike Zander, Baron was not the kind of man to sit back and watch things happen. In a political arena, Baron was an animal. He could see through even the most well-constructed deception, and lies did not even come close to making it past him. But while Zander would wait in order to use this knowledge against his opponent, Baron would instantly turn the lie or deception around on his opponent, challenging every statement he knew wasn't true. This would push the opponent off-balance, and force him to reveal his true agenda long before he had intended. This proved to be a two-fold blessing. The first part was the fact that word began to circulate that the kingdom of Scalla was not one to be trifled with, and that to deal with them was one of the best situations because you always knew where you stood. The other side of the blessing was that there were very small chances that Baron would allow the kingdom to enter an alliance where Scalla would be hurt. However, even the best situation is riddled with problems, and the problem with Baron's nearly flawless leadership of the kingdom was the fact that word began to circulate naming Baron as the unofficial king of Scalla. However, this conjecture and speculation about the true ruler of Scalla never did enter Scalla's borders. Baron did not have any desire to rule a kingdom, and he was content to act as an advisor to Gideon. However, the only person he would publicly proclaim this to was Gideon. The reason for this was that if his opponents heard that there was a power-play for control of Scalla, they would come in more confident and with plans to manipulate the situation. However, if there were no situation for them to manipulate, Baron would automatically have the advantage. Gideon grew fond of calling Baron the 'Thief Trapper' for the way that he could sniff out a lie and use the strengths of an opponent against him. The internal joke would also help feed the falsehood of the rift in leadership in Scalla.

The third member of the leadership triumvirate was David Harran. No one outside the royal palace truly realized what it was that David was responsible for, because if they knew, many would begin to fear him. There is a side of every kingdom that no one talks about, and that is the manipulative and diabolical side, which deals with the subjects of assassination, bribery, and spying. This was where David's skills lay. When Zander needed information on one of his prospective opponents or Baron had to know what plots had been launched against either Lord Gideon or one of the visiting dignitaries, they would come to David. David's network of spies, informants, and assassins was unsurpassed in the entire world, and even though Gideon had forbidden it, David still had spies in Brea, Trelon, and Aradon. David was perfect for his position because of his truly cold and emotionless disposition. Death was not a tragedy to him; it was merely a fact of life. To live was to eventually die in his eyes, and that was how he lived every day of his life. When he found out about any plans for assassination, he instantly began to place his agents and spies in positions where Gideon would have some say in whichever way the new regime would go. Gideon didn't know he had this power, but the fact that David was involved was usually enough. However, David soon began to encounter things that he could not explain, and that was the beginning of first act in the new war against the Shadows.

Strangely, David's agents began to disappear one by one, and whenever there was an assassination, David was unable to find out who the culprit was. He began to feel that he was losing his touch with the underworld that he had helped to build, but then one name began to circulate in the web, and that name was Draven Batoe. From what David had been able to ascertain, Draven had quickly become a major player in the matters of several of the larger kingdoms, and Marcwell was one of the kingdoms he had his eye on. Several of Draven's exploits became full-blown wars, and his army had never been defeated. However, there was another kingdom whose name was mentioned in the same breath as Marcwell as far as Draven's desires. That kingdom was Scalla. When this news came to David, he immediately alerted Gideon. Gideon too had heard the rumblings about a man by the name of Draven, but Gideon knew more than anyone that Draven was more dangerous than any warlord that they had ever faced and that the kingdom of Scalla truly had an enemy to fear.

Because Gideon was a child of Aerith Seth and Bryn Aplee of the phasia, he had some special abilities that normal children of the phasia did not. These abilities were honed to a more perfect edge by the teachings of Basille Mystic. Gideon had the ability to see the lines of power exhibited in all members of the forces of the Light and the forces of the Shadow. He knew what they were, possibly before they did. It was an ability that did not truly manifest itself until after his time as a member of the *Erieal* in the People of the Dragon had been served. Suddenly, upon his return from Shau-ling's palace, Gideon could see colored auras around people who had been, or were touched by the Light or the Shadow. Gwydeon Sandar beyond anyone else had a tremendously powerful aura, due to his not at all honorary title of Brother of the Angels, but there were others too who exhibited power. Gideon indeed was shocked when he saw his daughter born with a powerful aura around her. Gideon knew that she would be a force in the next generation, and that her involvement in the next act of the war against the Shadows was already secured. But it was the servants of the Shadow that had the largest and most ominous auras. Many times, Gideon had dismissed pages and members of his own army because their auras showed that they would or had been touched by the hand of Shau-ling or one of his minions. Draven was no different. He had not only been touched by the hand of Shau-ling, but Gideon was shocked to discover that he was a member of the Brotherhood of Phasia. To make matters worse, Draven had been created out of the ashes of Gideon's old teacher, Basille Mystic. When Gideon learned this, the news from David that Draven has his eyes set on the throne of Scalla was not a surprise. Scalla had been Basille's kingdom for many lifetimes, and Gideon was sure that part of Draven yearned to have Basille's kingdom for his own. Unfortunately, there was little time for Gideon to become comfortable in his role as a king before Draven's army came crashing down upon the gates of the kingdom of Scalla.

David received word from his spies only a matter of hours before Draven's army arrived. In that time, Gideon was able to salvage several books out of Basille's private library, and secret himself, Erika, Taya, and his advisors out of the palace. Unfortunately, as they fled, Draven's army struck. Without Zander to lead them, the Army of the Raven fought valiantly, but was quickly decimated by the large and more ferocious army of Jeresei and Kalbraks. With the help of a force of Jeresei, Draven was able to corner Gideon and his companions. Zander and David protected Erika and Taya while Gideon and Baron fought off everything that came their way. When it appeared that the onslaught was too much to defend against, Gideon took his daughter into his arms and with the help of David began to cut a path through the throng of Jeresei. Erika stayed close to Zander and Baron, but she was caught from behind by Draven himself and pulled away. Though he knew his wife would surely be killed, Gideon knew there was nothing he could do to save her, so he continued to flee vowing to take revenge for the loss of his wife. However, for the life of his daughter, he had to let his wife die. It was an impossible choice, the first of many that would come in the years after the fall of Scalla.

By this time Taya was old enough to understand what death was, and that fact that her mother had been killed. For the next six years of Taya's life, she and her father were on the run from the forces of the shadows, and by her thirteenth birthday, she was one of the most fluent people on the face of the earth in how to kill a Jeresei. Then, when she turned fifteen, she and her father had both gotten tired of running. Together they decided that it was time to take the fight to Shau-ling and his perverted children. The phasia had begun their dominance of the globe and ruled every major kingdom with the exceptions of Brea and Trelon. However, even with the help of Logan Ranthall, it would only be a matter of time before Trelon fell. Gideon knew in his heart that it would take the very forces of hell itself to break Gwydeon Sandar, but even he would not be able to stand up to all of the armies of the phasia once the rest of the world had fallen. All the resistance by the forces of the Light would be reduced to pockets of fighting so minor that they would be nothing more than nuisances. So, Gideon and Taya decided that they would begin their strikes against the very heart of Shau-ling's power, the kingdom of Marcwell itself.

Over the years, Gideon and his advisors had been able to gather a few stragglers from some of the armies that fell. Many of them were former members of the Lion's Mane, and the Army of the Raven, but the other faction consisted of members of the long-defunct Army of the Dragon. One of the greatest acquisitions to Gideon's force was a man by the name of Shim Taran. Shim was a member of the Army of the Dragon under the direct command of General Tol, a student of Captain Antrobus and Leane Torne. Shim was a very good student and a very quick learner. While he was masterful with a sword, he was nearly unsurpassed in the bow. While Gideon had seen better skill in Midarin, Shim was nearly her equal. However, Shim was not a tactical genius, he was just a fighter. He went where he was ordered to go and nothing more. But, with the addition of a long distance strike, Gideon's force began to become more than just a momentary distraction. The first strike against Marcwell did not go as well as Gideon would have liked. They managed to sneak their forces into the city, but were quickly discovered by one of the roving patrols of Jeresei. The fight was intense, and many of the patrols met their death at the hands of Gideon's little army before they were able to get out of Marcwell. However, Gideon saw Jeroch standing on one of the towers overlooking Gideon's escape. Jeroch had watched the whole situation with sadistic glee, his smile beaming down at Gideon. Gideon knew that Jeroch had let them all live, his desire to humiliate Gideon rather than to give him the satisfaction of killing him. To kill him would be to acknowledge the fact that Gideon was a threat. However, if Jeroch let Gideon and his pathetic band of warriors live, it would let them know that they were so far beneath Jeroch's notice that they did not even warrant extermination. This fact galled Gideon to the point that he swore he would make Jeroch beg for death before he finally ran him though. However, the assault on Marcwell had not been completely without fruit. The raid was able to gather information from the Black Tower that Jeroch had constructed, and had also been able to recover some of the failed experiments from within the tower. These men and women would eventually become known as the 'sniffers', people who possessed the same ability to see auras that Gideon himself had managed to master. This information as well as the 'sniffers' were sent to the allied kingdoms of the Light, and bolstered the resolve of those who kept fighting despite the nearly impossible odds.

But not all of Gideon's attacks ended in the frustration. Thanks to Zander and David, the pocket of resistance beginning to be known as the Swords of Alimidar was having an impact on the war with the forces of the Shadow. David was able to determine that prisoners taken by the Jeresei were being moved to a base near the old city of Lakestone. From what David was able to find out, none of these slaves ever returned from that horrible place. The base was nothing more than a waystation for prisoners being ferried to Jeroch's Black Tower. If something wasn't done, the forces of the Shadow would receive yet another infusion of monstrous creatures to bolster their ranks. With the help of Zander and Taya, Gideon was able to stage nighttime raids on the camps where prisoners were kept, freeing them and killing their captors. The Swords grew larger with every raid, and Taya was beginning to assert herself as the second in command to her father. On one occasion in fact, the Swords had become so large that Gideon led a raid on one group of captured men, while Taya led another. Both raids were so successful that the forces of the Light lost merely a single life. However, there were more and more bands of prisoners, and there was no way for the Swords to rescue them all.

Then, Gideon would receive the news that he had waited for in dread for so many years. Word came that Trelon had fallen, and Logan Ranthall with it. Gideon would never have believed that Logan Ranthall could die, but when Draven's name was linked to the invasion, Gideon had no choice but to accept the fact. It was then that he made the decision to ally himself with the forces in Brea in order to mount a stronger defense and attempt to convince Gwydeon that it was time to strike back. But, during his travels to Brea, the worst possible news arrived. Gideon and Taya were meeting in Gideon's tent when David and Zander hurriedly entered.

"My lord," David said quickly, "troubling news comes from the front."

"What is it David?" Taya asked. "It must be horrible if you have Zander with you. I would think the world were coming to an end if Baron would have been here as well."

"This is not a time for humor, Princess," Zander replied. "Word is spreading that Brea has fallen and that Nightwing is responsible."

Gideon instantly rose from his seat and grimaced. That was a name that Gideon had never expected to hear again. He remembered watching Pike take that metallic devil down into the depths of the column of Blaze, and he had prayed that if one of the two were going to survive, it would have been Pike.

"But there is more, my lord," Zander continued.

"What's dat?"

"There were two men mingling with the Order of the Sword that should not have been there according to reports that I have been privy to. The first was Logan Ranthall. Several of my spies say that he was in the battle fighting with the men of the Order of the Sword. The second man was actually leading the charge against Nightwing's army. That man has been hesitantly identified as Pike Rhuiden, but from your own recollections of the final battle with Shau-ling in the last generation, Pike Rhuiden as well as Nightwing should be dead."

Gideon was elated. While there was a part of him that mourned over the loss of Brea, the fact that both Logan and Pike were alive meant that the forces of the Light had a fighting chance against the phasia.

"But there are still several things that are puzzling about the battle my lord," David continued. "The first is that Gwydeon Sandar was not seen during the battle. The second was that the Order of the Sword was completely overmatched not only with sheer numbers, which is normal, but also in tactical skill. It was almost as if the army of the Shadow knew exactly where the weak spots in Brea's defense were and how hard to hit them. If I didn't know any better, I would say that Nightwing was able to read Gwydeon's mind to figure out how his defenses were planned."

Gideon suddenly ran cold. He was one of the only remaining people who knew the truth about the creature called Nightwing. It was not a creature that could exist on its own. It had to be carried around by another living person, and in the first generation of his existence, Nightwing had used Aryx Terian as its host. It made Gideon shudder to think that there was even a remote possibility that Gwydeon could be the Nightwing that struck Brea and decimate it.

"What else?" Taya prodded seeing her father's hesitation.

Zander looked to his companion and nodded.

"Nightwing entered the palace, but Pike followed and challenged the creature to a fight. Nightwing easily won, his skill with a sword far outmatching Pike's axe. Nightwing then took both Pike and Princess Sabrina Binosear to Draven. However, not two hours after the assault, the

Order of the Sword mobilized for a strike against an unnamed target. No matter how much my spies pushed, they could not get the name of the target. However, later that night, an army led by the twins Rael and Trece descended on the walls of the Brea and leveled it."

Gideon sat silent for a moment. The loss of Brea was terrible indeed, but the fact that the Order was still together meant that either Logan or Midarin were in charge. However, the loss of Pike to Nightwing, and the possibility that Gwydeon had been corrupted was a point that Gideon could not overlook. There was only one way that Gideon could find out the truth, and it meant doing the one thing he swore he would never do. David saw Gideon's hesitation and then spoke.

"What should we do now, lord?"

Gideon looked up and sighed.

"Prepare da army ta march in da direction de Order of da Sword went. If me guess is right, it'll lead ye ta a kingdom run by a member of da phasia. 'Round here it'll probably be Sador."

"It sounds like you aren't going with us," Zander commented.

Gideon scratched his chin and frowned.

"Ye would be right 'bout dat Zander. Taya and me'll be goin' ta see an old friend. Dat's all ye need know right now. Do ye understand?"

"Yes my lord," Zander and David said in unison.

They both turned on a heel leaving Taya looking at her father with a look of confusion.

"You don't have any old friends, father," Taya countered. "At least none that aren't either dead or well on their way to being."

Gideon scowled at his daughter and shook his head.

"Dat's no way ta talk 'bout me friends, girl."

Taya smiled and then refocused her eyes on her father.

EPILOGUE

"Get yer best dress on lass, 'cause it's 'bout time ye met yer grandmother."

Appendicies

Dramatis Personae

Cedric Binosear
The Lord Lion
First *Coromor* of the Prophecies
Twin Brother of Anabel Binosear
Son of Aerith Seth

Anabel Binosear
Sister of Cedric Binosear
Mother of Cairyn Binosear
Murdered by Aldridge Farran
Daughter of Aerith Seth

Arathorn Geoffry
Earth *Erieal* of the First Generation of
the Prophecies
Brother of Diana Geoffry Terian

Mailock
Member of the Moridon Tribe
Water *Erieal* of the First Generation
of the Prophecies

Aryx Terian
White Lightning
Fire *Erieal* of the First Generation of
the Prophecies
Husband of Diana Geoffry Terian
Former Host of Nightwing

Diana Terian Geoffry
Wind *Erieal* of the First Generation of
the Prophecies
Sister of Arathorn Geoffry
Wife of Aryx Terian
Mother of Lissa Terian

Arin Ranthall
First *Chosen One* of the Prophecies
Husband of Victoria Rhuiden
Father of Logan Ranthall
Father of Korrd Ranthall

Victoria Rhuiden
Sister of Tam Rhuiden
Wife of Arin Ranthall
Mother of Logan Ranthall

Logan Ranthall
The Lord Dragon
Second *Chosen One* of the Prophecies
Brother of Korrd Ranthall
First Cousin of Pike Rhuiden
Husband of Elwyne Tamerlane
Ranthall
Father of Wolf Ranthall

Elwyne Tamerlane Ranthall
Sister of David Tamerlane
Wife of Logan Ranthall
Mother of Wolf Ranthall

Korrd Ranthall
Second *Coromor* of the Prophecies
Brother of Logan Ranthall
Son of Arin Ranthall and Ellis
Chandara
Father of Gwillim Sandar

Pike Rhuiden
Water *Erieal* of the Second
Generation of the Prophecies
Son of Tam Rhuiden
Best Friend of Talon Aielin
First Cousin of Logan Ranthall
Eldar Merin's Former Husband
Lord of Kandor, Marcwell, and
Trelon
Husband of Cairyn Binosear
Father of Duncan Rhuiden and
Sabrina Binosear

Gwydeon Sandar
Son of Torris Sandar
Brother of Bella Sandar
Husband of Midarin Rice Sandar
Father of Nathaniel Sandar
Killed in the Battle of the Hall of
Terrors by Jeroch Yetre

Eldar Merin
Daughter of Alfred and Ariel Merin
Best Friend of Elwyne Tamerlane
Wife of Pike Rhuiden
Killed by Taron Steen at the Battle of
Taren

Emries
The First *Coromor*

Talon Aielin
Wind *Erieal* of the Second
Generation of the Prophecies
Best Friend of Pike Rhuiden
Killed during battle with Shau-ling

Arin Domae
Fire *Erieal* of the Second Generation
of the Prophecies
Former Soldier of the Army of Brea
Killed during Battle of the Hall of
Terrors

David Tamerlane
Brother of Elwyne Tamerlane
Killed in destruction of Aradon

Lane Toridon
Apprentice Magician
Killed by Taron Steen during battle of
Taren

Tam Rhuiden
Aradon City Council Member
Brother of Victoria Rhuiden
Father of Pike Rhuiden

Torris Sandar
Aradon City Council Member
Father of Gwydeon Sandar
Father of Bella Sandar

Gideon Viruci
Earth *Erieal* of the Second Generation
of the Prophecies
Killed in Battle with Shau-ling

Midarin Rice
Queen of the Kingdom of Brea
Wife of Gwydeon Sandar
Mother of Nathaniel Sandar
Mother of Liette Forer

Aerith Seth
General of the Hand of the Light
General of the Army of the Fox
The First *Chosen One*

Cairyn Binosear
Daughter of Anabel Binosear
Niece of Cedric Binosear
Queen of the Kingdoms of Kandor,
Trelon, and Marcwell
Wife of Pike Rhuiden
Mother of Duncan Rhuiden and
Sabrina Binosear

Leane Torne
General in the Army of Rama
Former Member of the Army of Brea

Jerrard Mystic
Lord of the Kingdom of Scalla
Son of Basille Mystic
Husband of Erika Belnosian

Erika Belnosian
Wife of Jerrard Mystic

Sabrina Binosear
Third *Chosen One* of the Prophecies
Sister of Duncan Rhuiden
Daughter of Pike Rhuiden and Cairyn
Binosear

Duncan Rhuiden
Heir to the Kingdom of Marcwell
Brother of Sabrina Binosear
Son of Pike Rhuiden and Cairyn
Binosear

Lissa Terian
Fire *Erieal* of the Third Generation of
the Prophecies
Daughter of Aryx and Diana Terian
Adopted Daughter of Pike Rhuiden
and Cairyn Binosear

Liette Forer
Daughter of Midarin Rice
Sister of Nathaniel Sandar

Nathaniel Sandar
The Lord Ram
Third *Coromor* of the Prophecies
Son of Gwydeon Sandar and Midarin
Rice
Brother of Liette Forer

Gwillim Sandar
Earth *Erieal* of the Third Generation
of the Prophecies
Son of Korrd Ranthall and Gabrielle
Crill
Adopted Son of Midarin Rice

Wolf Ranthall
Son of Logan Ranthall and Elwyne
Tamerlane Ranthall

Shau-ling
Master of the Shadows
Father of the Phasia

Jeroch Yetre
The Lord Shadow
First Born of the Phasia
Father of Hawk Yetre

Bryn Aplee
The Lady Fox
Member of the Brotherhood of Phasia
Former Lover of Aerith Seth
Wife of Grawn Aplee
Mother of Gideon Viruci

Ellis Chandara
The Lady Leopard
Member of the Brotherhood of Phasia
Mother of Korrd Ranthall

Grawn Aplee
The Lord Shark
Member of the Brotherhood of Phasia
Husband of Bryn Aplee

Warron Ysamaran
The Lord Boar
Member of the Brotherhood of Phasia

Basille Mystic
The Lord Raven
Member of the Brotherhood of Phasia
Father of Jerrard Mystic

Farax Soar
The Lord Vulture
Member of the Brotherhood of Phasia

The Flame
Personal Guardian of Shau-ling
Keeper of the Hall of Terrors

Zarsi Aeron
The Lord Cobra
Member of the Brotherhood of Phasia

Aldridge Farran
The Lord Hawk
Member of the Brotherhood of Phasia

Saurn Macco
The Lord Viper
Member of the Brotherhood of Phasia

Caris Vale
The Lady Wolf
Member of the Brotherhood of Phasia

Erdric Yarrow
The Lord Scorpion
Member of the Brotherhood of Phasia

Taron Steen
The Lord Jackal
Member of the Brotherhood of Phasia

About the Author

Brian Kershner is a life-long dreamer, writer, and problem-solver. He grew up absorbing anything and everything he could get his hands on, and as a child of the Star Wars era he constantly wanted to see the worlds beyond the little Indiana town he grew up in. There was no adventure too far, and no problem too big.

Emboldened by parents who always supported his curiosity and his thoughtfulness, Brian found himself bounding from Space Camp to Laser Summer Camp to Athletic Training Camp to Piano Lessons to Football Practice to Basketball Practice to Choir Practice and back again. Despite all of the roaming and traveling, his family remained close-knit and supportive.

Though he flirted with the idea of becoming a doctor, Brian's attentions always fell back to the computer world. He got his first computer when he was six, and not long after found his way into a word processing program and began crafting his own fantastic worlds and even more fantastic characters.

As he has grown and changed and experienced life, so too have his characters. He continues to write, craft, and create; whether it is websites for his customers, or characters and worlds for his audience.

www.ingramcontent.com/pod-product-compliance
Lightning Source LLC
Chambersburg PA
CBHW051319250626
47155CB00007B/2381